Sacrificing Sophie

CW00860302

Catherine MacDonald

ISBN: 978-0-244-82958-2

PublishNation
www.publishnation.co.uk

With thanks to Penny, Richard, David and Henry

Chapter One

'Sophie Elliot! What a coincidence – I was thinking about you only a moment ago. Can you spare the time to come to my rooms for a chat? There's something I want to discuss with you.'

Sophie, a slim, dark-haired third-year student of Modern Languages, halted abruptly in her path across the college quad, sucking in a sharp breath of surprise. She wasn't really meant to be in Cambridge at all, and her first reaction was that this request from her tutor must herald some sort of reprimand, although she couldn't recall any obvious misdeeds. Sophie's last six months of study had been spent on placement at a school in Honfleur as part of her course requirements, but she had returned early for her Easter vacation owing to a sudden illness of her mother. Now her parent was on the mend and she had taken the opportunity to spend time with friends at college for a few days of gossip and catching up.

She followed Jennifer Bradbury up the staircase to the tutor's rooms with her heart thumping in time to the echo of her footsteps on the stone staircase. It wasn't like Sophie to find herself in trouble, because her passage through life was cushioned by a middle-class upbringing and a good education and she was too conventional a personality to fling herself into louche excesses of student behaviour. The placement abroad had encouraged her to ignite a spark of independence, but it was surprising how quickly a juvenile mentality could surface again within the sheltered college walls. Memories of tutorials from her previous terms assailed her as she entered the book-lined study: mostly happy memories, although the recall of embarrassing mistakes could still surface to jab at her with painful intensity.

'Sit down, and I'll get us a glass of sherry.'

Jennifer sounded amicable, but Sophie was skewered to her chair by apprehension. She stared at a fine film of dust on the coffee table before her, wondering irreverently if the dry words of academia uttered in this room dropped from the air to form this soft residue, before her thoughts skittered away again in panic mode.

Why was it so important for Jennifer to speak with her? Sophie believed that she had acquitted herself well in Honfleur, although a budding relationship with an English graduate taking a year out in France before resuming his studies at Harvard had been a recent distraction. She took a large gulp of sherry to fortify herself and it came as a relief to find that Jennifer had something other than a rebuke on her mind, although the relief was tinged with the irritating taint of obligation.

'Liz Lenister was at university with me, and whilst we weren't bosom friends we have always kept in touch. She's been a generous benefactor to the college over the years, and I would like to think we could repay some of her trust in us. She's asked me to recommend a student who might be willing to spend six weeks with her family in France in the long vac, doing a spot of childcare and some basic tuition in French. You are the person who immediately sprang to mind.'

Sophie's shoulders drooped under the heavy implication of responsibility which accompanied these words. Helping with a family in the summer vacation… she wasn't sure about that at all.

'But what exactly does she want? I don't know anything about small children. Aren't there girls who are trained specially for this sort of thing?'

Sophie twisted a lock of shiny hair around her fingers as she spoke, wide-eyed and anxious to wriggle out of this undesired commitment. But she was no match for her tutor. Jennifer simply smiled at her student with lips pursed, recognising the wheedling tone of the undergraduate inventing excuses for missed deadlines or non-attendance in class. She would need to sell this opportunity a little harder because she was convinced it would be profitable for both parties.

'Two of them are teenagers and Poppy and Boo are children, not toddlers. Liz doesn't want a nanny, but she does need someone with a brain; someone who speaks the language, to supervise them on the beach or wherever and give the younger ones some tuition in elementary French. You would live and eat with the family and she's offering an excellent salary.'

She named a figure which caused Sophie's objections to deflate like a shrieking balloon. Pub work, which was her normal summer holiday fate, only paid a fraction in comparison. But the excessive sum

2

was another worry. It made Sophie even less confident that she was a suitable candidate for the job.

'I'm flattered that you thought of me, but aren't there others who might be better qualified? Rhona has brothers and sisters and I'm an only child. I'm afraid I wouldn't know what to do.'

'I expect that the last thing Rhona wants is to get involved with another family – she's probably keen to be off by herself somewhere. And it's also a question of personality. I can't see her in Liz's world, but I do think you could fit in.'

Jennifer's shrewd eyes had been registering a change in her pupil as they talked. Sophie's heart-shaped face and slender frame might give the impression of fragility, but the experience of life abroad had endowed her with a new maturity and confidence which was exactly what Jennifer hoped to see. She knew that Liz would be seeking a poised and socially competent person to take charge of her children. The tutor leaned forward in her eagerness to persuade the reluctant girl, and her cajoling tones were hard to resist. 'Look, Sophie, it's a great opportunity for you. You are a sensible girl; I wouldn't recommend you if I thought you couldn't cope. Consider it as a paid holiday with the opportunity to show off your language skills and eat some fantastic food. I know you will like Liz, and she might even be useful to you in your future career. Think very hard before you say no to this.'

Jennifer continued to smile, but she held Sophie's eyes in a cool stare which read 'please do not disappoint me.' A distant clock struck four with solemn chimes as if to confirm the deal, and Sophie wriggled in dismay as she felt the burden settle inexorably upon her.

'I would need to meet Liz Lenister first,' she said, stalling.

Perhaps she would be deemed unsuitable in the flesh. Perhaps she could derail an interview by employing diversionary tactics with her mobile phone or by wearing skimpy clothing... but even as Sophie tried to conjure up such images, she knew that she would be incapable of behaving in that way. And what was there to be scared about? Think of the money – even if the children were little demons, it would only be for a few weeks. *Poppy and Boo!* She could just imagine their spoiled, rich-kid sense of entitlement. Many of her fellow undergraduates came from moneyed backgrounds which apparently

3

gave them carte-blanche to behave as though Cambridge existed for them alone. It would be satisfying to burst a few bubbles of privilege.

'Yes, of course you must meet one another before anything is decided. I have a contact number for Liz's PA. She will arrange for you to travel to London in the Easter vac and Liz will interview you then. It will be interesting for you to see a big company like Lenister Legrand – I understand their new office has won some prestigious design award recently.'

Liz Lenister was CEO of the Lenister Legrand Group of venture capitalists. Sophie had no idea what that was all about, but it sounded impressive. She had no experience of the world of business. Her parents were doctors and they had a comfortable life, but the recent spell of ill-health meant that her mother was now working part-time, so luxuries were in shorter supply than before. They would be relieved to think that their daughter had obtained a summer job offering both sunshine and money to fund the demands of her social life for her last year at Cambridge. It was impossible to refuse the interview: she had to go for it.

When Sophie left to contemplate her doom, Jennifer Bradbury helped herself to another sherry, then went to her computer and composed a brief e-mail to her old friend.

'I have given some thought to your request and have asked my student Sophie Elliott to contact your PA to arrange a meeting. Sophie is just finishing her third year here and I feel she would fulfil your requirements very well. She is a conscientious worker with a mature head on her shoulders, and someone who can be trusted. But let me know if she doesn't suit and I'll see what else I can do to help.'

The missive whirled away, and Jennifer gazed from her window at the manicured grass of the quad below. The sight always gave her satisfaction. She was a person who appreciated order and regulation, and it would be gratifying if her intervention in the affair bore fruit. 'Sophie will be a fool if she doesn't make this work,' she said to herself. 'But she isn't a fool, and I think that Liz's summer is sorted.'

Sophie sprawled on the bed in a friend's room, googling the Lenister Legrand Group on her laptop and quashing a tendency to panic. She had agreed not to mention the opportunity to anyone else at the college – Jennifer asked her not to make a big thing of it, to avoid accusations of favouritism – and it was frustrating to feel the subject was not up for discussion. The screen grew black and complex with facts and figures and graphs, but the solemnity was leavened by artfully lit pictures of the award-winning building and profiles of the main company personnel.

Liz Lenister was a woman in her forties with a bouffant mane of dark hair and a shrewd, unlined face which might well have received a little help along the way. She enjoyed a stellar career in finance and was on her second husband, which accounted for the gap of years between her eldest and youngest progeny. There were few details about the Lenister children, but Sophie was relieved to read that the youngest was five and presumably house trained.

Sophie rolled on to her back and contemplated the drifting shadows on the ceiling, weighing up the pros and cons. If she and Liz came to an agreement, she would be spending six weeks on the coast of Brittany, well fed and watered, and at the end of it, she would be handsomely paid. That was good. On the downside, sunny weather wasn't guaranteed, and the children might be little brats who would harass and upset her.

'But I could always walk away if I hate them,' she told herself, wondering why she could not muster more enthusiasm for the project. Later that evening she telephoned her father to ask his opinion, and he was reassuringly positive. Somehow, just hearing his familiar voice asking the same questions she had already put to her tutor gave weight and substance to the plan.

'My advice is to follow this up, darling,' he said. 'But you needn't commit yourself until you have met the woman. Why don't you arrange to see her in the first week of the holiday, before we go to the Lake District?'

Liz Lenister's diary seemed to be a matter of national importance according to the inflexible PA who fielded Sophie's enquiries, but eventually an appointment was sandwiched in to suit both parties. When the morning of the interview arrived, Sophie's mother had decided views about what was appropriate for the occasion.

'You're not going dressed like that?'

Mrs Elliot's face puckered in disapproval as she surveyed Sophie in the hallway of their house. Sophie glanced down at herself, prepared to do battle.

'What's wrong with these clothes?'

5

She was wearing a soft leather jerkin over a mini dress, tights and knee length boots, and her abundant hair was coiled into a thick side plait.

'I thought a nice skirt and jacket...'

'You mean like Mary Poppins? I'm not a nanny, Mum, and I don't think I've even got an outfit like that. Liz needs to see me for myself. I feel comfortable like this and that helps me to be confident.'

Sophie knew that she was right. There was no point in assuming a false personality if she was going to spend six weeks in the bosom of the Lenister family. But as she sat in the train from Guildford on the way to the rendezvous, she examined the sober-faced commuters who were her fellow passengers and felt herself assuming a similar mantle of responsibility. Despite her first misgivings, she was flattered that Jennifer Bradbury had recommended her to the financier. She was not merely a student still in the process of growing up, but a capable person who could safely accept the charge of children. The full weight of her twenty-one years was apparent to her in a way that she often forgot in the charmed surroundings of her Cambridge life, and she summoned all her adult self-belief to make a good impression upon her tutor's friend.

The head office of Lenister Legrand was a stunning configuration of glass and steel, and she was thankful that she did not suffer from vertigo as an external lift whooshed her up to the penthouse suite and the city rooftops flashed past her fascinated gaze.

'Liz won't be long. She's just taking a call from Frankfurt.'

The PA fussed with coffee from an espresso machine before handing a cup to Sophie. 'Help yourself to biscuits,' she added, indicating a Harrods box, but Sophie was too nervous to feel hungry. She flicked through the shiny pages of the annual report as she drank her coffee, but the language seemed altogether alien, and the impression she received was that of unlimited money in continual transit between funds and banks like a never-ending merry-go-round.

At last the inner door opened to reveal her potential employer. Liz Lenister was clothed in a dress and jacket which appeared very plain at first glance but was undoubtedly of designer origin – it was the type of garment featured in magazines at a price which causes ordinary women to turn the page with impatient fingers. Her hair was blow-dried into a no-nonsense bob and her lips gleamed vampire-red.

Sophie hesitated for a second; she didn't intend to be devoured by this powerful apparition.

'Sophie? Thank you so much for coming to meet me. I hope you had a pleasant journey.'

The CEO's handshake was decisive, and Sophie marshalled her wits.

'Yes, thank you. You have an amazing office here.'

Did that sound fatuous? Liz Lenister smiled in response, ushering Sophie into her domain which was sparsely furnished, although a jungle of glossy plants writhed towards the ceiling in one corner of the room.

'I am proud of my company's achievements and our new building is a celebration of that,' she informed Sophie, her eyes alight with self-congratulation. 'When I compare this building with the dingy little office where I first started work, it gives me enormous satisfaction. I've never been afraid to pursue what I want, and that's the best lesson to take through life.'

Sophie murmured something in assent, surprised to detect emotion in the career woman's voice. They seated themselves on opposing chairs which owed more to style than comfort and Sophie drew a deep breath as she prepared for her interrogation.

The older woman's questions seemed matter of fact, but Sophie realised that Liz was making a swift assessment of her personality. Sophie took pains to be concise and confident in her answers because she suddenly wanted to impress this woman, who manifested an authority even more pronounced than that of her tutors. She spoke about her family and educational background, and Liz described the house in Brittany, whose garden had steps which led down to a beach and which dated back to the era of elaborate Edwardian architecture.

'I can probably promise you a turret room – they're rather fun.'

Liz smiled and Sophie grinned back at her, intrigued by the description. 'We have agreed a house swap with the owners, who are old friends – their family will take our condo in Florida for the same period. We thought it was time that the children got to know a different environment and took in a spot of culture for a change. Disneyworld is all very well, but it's hardly educational.'

Sophie nodded, concealing her disappointment at the thought of missing out on Florida sunshine and wondering how disgruntled the

Lenister children might be about this change of scene. 'Of course, there will be someone coming in to clean and do the laundry, so you wouldn't have to bother with any of that.'

Liz smoothed her skirt, dismissive of domestic chores. 'Do you drive? Good. Perhaps you would be able to help with shopping then, because even on holiday, I am usually a slave to business in the mornings. I do like to cook in the evening because I don't get much chance to practice my skills here, despite my cordon bleu course, but we usually eat out every other night.'

None of that sounded too appalling. Sophie began to visualise herself taking charge of the household like a domestic goddess in a way she had never contemplated before, and the picture held a certain old-fashioned charm.

'Could you could tell me more about the children and what I would have to do?' she asked, waiting for disillusionment to strike, but Liz became somewhat vague, shrugging her shoulders as if to say: 'you are a person of intelligence; you will figure it out.'

'Poppy and Boo will be your main responsibility. It's a question of supervision – make sure they don't drown or stuff themselves with pizza until they're sick – you know the sort of thing.'

It sounded as though Liz wasn't exactly hands-on with her children and Sophie repressed a smile. 'Of course, I do want you to give them some elementary French tuition, and Jennifer tells me you speak the language well. Abigail is fourteen – a rather lumpy and difficult fourteen, I'm afraid, but you needn't be too concerned with her, except perhaps to take her shopping occasionally. Good luck with getting her to accept anything which fits. But I hope I'm not putting you off! Sean is seventeen, and he will hoe his own row, I expect. Wi-fi on tap, of course… he's a charming boy, and actually very good with the little ones.'

'Forgive my asking, but who looks after the children when you are in London?'

This seemed a reasonable question to Sophie and Liz nodded in response.

'I do have a very capable Australian girl, but she's begged for time off this summer to attend a brace of family weddings back home. *Not* very thoughtful of her, but what can you do?'

Liz examined her well-manicured hands, and a diamond ring so enormous that it only just avoided vulgarity winked in the sunshine as she did so. 'I don't often make mistakes in my judgement of people – it's one of the reasons I've done so well with my company, and I believe I could trust you with my children,' she said. 'My family is even more important to me than Lenister Legrand, and one thing I worry about is maintaining privacy where the kids are concerned, so I'm afraid I would have to ask you to suspend any social media accounts you have during the time you spend with us. Is that a problem?'

Sophie was surprised by the request, but as she thought it over, she could understand Liz's desire for a holiday without uninvited intrusion. A person in Liz's position would have to be careful about publicity for any number of reasons.

'No. I don't think that would be too difficult, because I can warn my friends that I won't be posting over the summer, and I might even enjoy the break. I don't like feeling obliged to share every detail of my life,' she replied, thinking as she spoke that it could be healthy to have temporary freedom from the tyranny of social pressures. Her answer seemed to satisfy Liz, who looked down as if she was making calculations in her head, before looking up again to entice Sophie with a brilliant smile.

'I think we would get on well, Sophie. Will you take the job? Is the salary sufficient for you?'

Sophie was not about to argue on that point. She hesitated for the merest second – whether this was down to the lumpy adolescent, the charming son, or Poppy and Boo she wasn't sure – but it seemed she had already made up her mind.

'I'd love to spend summer in Brittany with your family, Mrs Lenister. And I'll do my best to give satisfaction.'

Why on earth had she said that? She sounded just like a housemaid in a Victorian novel. Colour flooded her face, but Liz Lenister didn't seem to notice the blush or the remark.

'That's *such* a relief. Thank you, Sophie. I'll confirm the dates and travel arrangements in the next month or so. And by the way, I'm not Mrs Lenister – that's my my maiden name but I've always used it for business. I am Mrs Braybrooke at present, but everyone calls me Liz, and so must you.'

She rose to her feet; the interview was clearly at an end. Sophie was struck by the words 'Mrs Braybrooke *at present*,' wondering whether Liz had a third husband lined up somewhere if Mr Braybrooke proved unsatisfactory. And then, just as a sense of achievement was wrapping warm arms around her, there was a scorpion strike. Liz scrutinised Sophie closely, as if searching for an additional reassurance.

'You are rather prettier than I'd hoped,' she said, a tiny line furrowing her forehead, and Sophie gaped, unsure why this was a problem. Did Liz think she would play truant to practice her French on the local youths, or concentrate on acquiring a tan rather than playing with the children? Perhaps Mr Braybrooke had an eye for younger women, despite his dynamic wife – one read about this sort of thing all the time. The next words didn't do much to reassure her. 'Sean's at an impressionable stage, and as I said, he's a handsome boy and very sophisticated for his years. I have no doubt that he'll want to sleep with you.'

Liz was unembarrassed, as though she had said 'I expect he'll need help with his French', but Sophie reddened again in shock and discomfort. 'I'm afraid I think that would be inappropriate and I would have to ask you to leave if it happened. I'm sure you understand.'

Understand! It was on the tip of Sophie's tongue to rescind her acceptance of the job, but Liz noticed her confusion and laid a hand on her arm as if in appeal. 'I'm speaking woman to woman, Sophie, so please don't take offence. Sean can be very persuasive, and seventeen is such a difficult age for a boy. I don't want you to think that your duties include sex education.'

'It never occurred to me for one moment.'

Sophie spoke with definitive chill and Liz pulled a face of mock dismay,

'Oh dear, now I've upset you. Was I wrong to mention it? But Sophie, I can see that you are a sensible girl and I want to be honest with you. Do you have a boyfriend?'

'There's nobody serious in my life at present, but that doesn't mean I would want to pursue a seventeen-year-old.'

Sophie was unable to keep the disappointment from her voice, but her frosty reaction seemed to please her interlocutor and she realised that the issue had perhaps been raised as a kind of test. Obviously, she had passed it, because Liz stopped being placatory and resumed her usual brisk way of speech.

'I see we understand one another. We needn't speak of this again. Sophie, I look forward to having you with us in France, and I'm confident that my husband will like you as much as I do. Make sure that you claim your travel expenses now, because I know that undergraduates aren't flush with cash these days.'

She pressed a button and the PA arrived to usher Sophie away.

'Excellent news, Jean, Sophie is going to help us out in the summer holidays. It will be a comfort to have her there. See you in France, Sophie!'

Another firm handshake concluded the interview and Liz Lenister returned to the mysteries of high finance. Sophie had hardly regained her composure after the embarrassing conversation about Sean and was tempted to make a few probing remarks to the PA about Liz's family, but thought better of it. How could she even begin such a discourse? *'Liz is worried in case I seduce her son...'* No; the whole thing was too preposterous. She waited while her travel costs were reimbursed and then slid down the building to the ground in the company of smartly suited men, who exactly fitted her preconceptions about city gents.

Sophie couldn't bring herself to speak about the final part of her conversation with Liz Lenister, not even with her parents. There was something distasteful to her about the older woman's warning, because she considered herself to be almost old-fashioned where sex was concerned. The hectic meet n'shag generated by Tinder and its equivalents wasn't her style at all – she was not a virgin, but her experiences were tame compared to many of her friends and she intended to keep it that way.

'I expect that Sean will have ample opportunities to pursue the local mademoiselles,' she thought. 'And I don't see how I can be expected to prevent that. Liz will have to watch out for her son herself.'

11

Chapter Two

Sophie was sorry when her placement in Honfleur came to an end in June and she bade farewell to the friends she had made there with genuine regret. She had continued to spend her free time in the company of the Harvard-bound George. It was never a breathless love match, but he was good fun and had a sensitive soul, and Sophie was happy to find herself one half of a pair again. It was her first experience of a partnership where good sex and comfortable everyday relations meshed so seamlessly, and she decided that this was a sign that she was growing up. They were under no illusion that their affair would last, because George would be leaving for America before the end of July.

However, armed with the knowledge that there was a built-in expiry date, so to speak, they appreciated those summer weeks as a romantic idyll devoid of the usual pressures. Sophie hoped that they would remain friends afterwards and trained herself to be content with that. Tears would sometimes prick at her eyes when she contemplated saying goodbye to her boyfriend, and she hoped that her new commitments in Brittany would help her to cope with a difficult parting.

The details of her summer job were now common knowledge, although the only person to whom she talked in depth about her meeting with Liz Lenister was George. He grinned at her account of the swanky office but frowned when she finally summoned the courage to repeat Liz's warning about her teenage son.

'She must be deluded – it's a common failing of mothers where their darling sons are concerned,' he said. 'As if you would have the hots for some spotty adolescent! The woman may be a financial whizz, but she was bang out of order there.'

Sophie laughed, but her skin still prickled with embarrassment when she recalled the scene. She felt that the shock of it was something that would stay with her all her life; something that she would laugh about in years to come, when she was middle-aged and had teenage children of her own.

'And I'm not likely to risk losing that amount of cash by jumping into bed with a boy, no matter how good-looking,' she said stoutly. 'But I've wondered since then if there wasn't a hidden subtext. I've done some research on the family and her current husband is a lot younger than Liz. Maybe she just wanted to warn me off the men in her life.'

'Sophie, the femme fatale... do you know, I rather fancy that idea.'

George stroked her hair, his face creased in a smile which held a hint of sadness. 'I'm relying on you to send me regular updates from the sweaty, lust-filled coast of Brittany. It's got to be more interesting than my Ivy League existence.'

All the same, Sophie felt stretched thin and desolate when she and George parted for good. Although she had no illusions that she wanted a long-term commitment from George, he had provided a stable rock on which to anchor herself for a while and she did not anticipate plunging back into the sea of unsuitable dates with any pleasure. She assumed a forced air of cheerfulness when she returned home and packed her cases for Brittany with gloomy disinterest.

When the time came to depart for France her father drove her to Portsmouth to catch the night ferry, and the sense of an adventure about to happen began to nudge her spirits back to life. The swooping seagulls with their plaintive cries bade her a noisy farewell as the coast of England faded into sea mists behind the wake of the boat. She plucked up the courage to visit the main restaurant for dinner, and the excellence of the food encouraged her to devour a meal very different to anything she was used to. The sea was smooth and glassy which was fortunate for her digestion, and when she was snug in her bunk in the tiny cabin, she fell asleep with diminishing regret for George's absence.

She was less happy when the passengers were roused at an early hour to vacate their cabins as the ship sailed into Saint-Malo, and she trudged up on deck hauling her luggage behind her, feeling sleep-deprived and only partly human. A keen breeze teased her hair and she fumbled for a band to tie it away from her face. But the coastline sparkled in the early morning sunshine and she gazed with fascination at the sweep of sandy beaches laid out before her, each one vying to claim predominance amongst its neighbours.

'Where are you off to dear?' enquired an elderly lady, whose pleasant face she remembered from the restaurant. 'Do you have a long journey ahead of you?'

'No, thank goodness.'

Liz had given her the address of the house and told her to take a taxi from the port, because the small seaside town in which it was situated was some miles down the coast. 'I'm joining a family to spend six weeks teaching French to their children, and the house where they are staying is in Saint-Lunaire, not far away. I'm looking forward to seeing it for the first time.'

'I hope they let you out to play as well. You will love it, I'm sure. Good luck dear and keep smiling.'

It seemed a suitable benediction with which to begin her new responsibilities. Once Sophie had passed through a cursory customs check, she walked to a taxi rank and gave her directions to the driver. His rapid, Breton dialect caused her one or two problems, but when her ear had grown accustomed to the local accent and she had begged him to speak more slowly, communication became easier. He pointed out places of interest as they drove and seemed almost offended that she had never visited the region before.

It wasn't long before they entered the small seaside town where she was to stay, and its faded elegance aroused her curiosity. The houses looked solid and respectable and the streets were quiet apart from a few dog-walkers and busy people returning home from the patisserie, baguettes tucked under an arm. As they approached the end of the main street, her driver swerved down a steep turning towards the sea and stopped his car with a jolt.

'Voici la grande maison, mademoiselle.'

He slammed his door and went to retrieve Sophie's luggage from the boot. She gazed in awe at the crenelated façade of what was very nearly a mansion and was opening her purse to count out a regrettably large sum in Euros when a clear voice cut across her.

'It's okay, Sophie, I'll get this.'

Liz Lenister came hurrying down the path, her bathrobe flapping as she rummaged in a large and fashionable handbag. The driver cast a surreptitious glance at her exposed thighs, but she took no notice, turning her attention to Sophie as she handed over the fare.

'I don't usually get up this early, but as it's your first day…'

She air-kissed Sophie on both cheeks and picked up a case. 'I hope you had a good crossing. Do you like the house? It's a bit Gothic horror for my taste. I keep expecting bats to drop down the chimney, but the views are wonderful.'

Sophie was all eyes as they climbed the front steps and entered a high-ceilinged hall, whose curving staircase reminded her of old country hotels. The grandeur was modified by curtains of moth-eaten antiquity and faded wallpaper long since out of fashion, but there was a salty tang in the air and Sophie felt relieved that this was obviously a holiday home and not a house where things might get spoilt by any children in her charge. She followed Liz up the stairs and along a passage to a room at the far end.

'I'm afraid that Sean and Abbie have bagged the tower bedrooms, but I think you will be comfortable here. You have your own bathroom, at any rate.'

Liz indicated a door with a nod of her head. 'I'll leave you to freshen up while I get dressed and put the coffee on. Come down when you're ready.'

Sophie threw her bag on to the bed and strode to the window, wrestling with the rusty catches to let the curtains billow in the breeze. The room smelled faintly of old people with a stale hangover of crushed mothball, and she didn't think she would care to sleep in such a depressing miasma. But the view over the bay was colour-supplement stunning, and she felt only a fleeting pang of regret for the promised turret room. The bed was clean and comfortable, and she was pleased when she inspected the bathroom to find a modern shower.

She had made a perfunctory toilet on the boat, and now she washed and applied a little eye make-up before picking up a hairbrush to tame her long locks. Glints of auburn gleamed in her dark hair as sunbeams burnished her head, and she smiled at her reflection in the mirror, willing confidence to keep her company.

As she descended the stairs, she hesitated, unsure where to find the kitchen. But the smell of coffee lured her in the right direction, and she opened a door to discover a bright and spacious room with heavy glass doors leading on to a patio. Sunshine dazzled her eyes for a moment, but there were trails of bougainvillea and honeysuckle waving a welcome on the pergola. The kitchen was well equipped in a modern style and Liz noticed her appraising glance around.

'At least everything works in here. The house is in poor condition and I feel a little let down when I think of what we've swapped, but never mind. We've been here for three days and the kids seem to like it. I suppose the novelty hasn't worn off yet.'

Liz addressed her with the clipped, authoritarian tones that Sophie remembered from her interview. She wondered fleetingly what it was like to be the offspring of such a dominant personality, and whether the children were dragooned into obedience or rebellion. It appeared that she was about to find out, as a small girl with tousled fair hair wandered into the room, dragging an old blanket behind her.

'Oh darling, must you take that filthy thing everywhere? I swear I'll chuck it in the bin one of these days.'

Liz grumbled over the coffee mugs, but her youngest daughter took no notice, fixing curious blue eyes on Sophie instead.

'Are you Sophie? You look like Princess Isabelle,' the child remarked, referring to the latest Disney heroine and Sophie laughed, flattered by the comparison.

'Do I really? It's very kind of you to say so. Let me guess – you must be Boo?'

'Yes. Have you come to play with us?'

'I hope so, although we are going to learn to speak some French too. Do you like being in France, Boo?'

Sophie was diffident with children, but there was something appealing about the open, faintly freckled face of her interrogator. The child came to her side and leaned against her, chattering about the beach and and the house without a trace of shyness; very much the child of her confident mother. Liz looked on, smiling and complacent.

'Good. I knew you would get on,' she said, pouring the drinks. 'Sophie, there's a pile of croissants and stuff left over from yesterday which will be fine for breakfast after they've had a quick blast in the microwave. Could you bring them across from the cupboard please?'

Sophie detached herself from Boo's grasp and did as Liz asked. As they ate, they were joined by another, bigger blonde-haired girl – Poppy – but there was no sign of their brother and older sister.

'Sean and Abbie wallow in bed most mornings. It's mandatory for teenagers, I believe,' Liz said as she loaded the dishwasher. 'I have to work now, so I suggest you take the little ones down to the beach and the others can join you later if they want to. We don't need to shop today, apart from getting bread for lunch, and I'll send Sean out for that when he gets up.'

'Isn't Mr Braybrooke here?' Sophie asked, wondering a little at his absence, and Liz shook her head.

'Matthew is busy getting a new start-up company off the ground and he has to be in the UK to finish the negotiations for the first funding round. I'm hoping he will join us next weekend.'

Sophie was carried off by the two little girls to exclaim over the delights of their room and the special toys they had brought from England. She found a holdall in which to pack their beach towels and Poppy and Boo trailed her to her bedroom like two little puppies, eager to get acquainted with this new person in their lives. Then she slipped into the bathroom to don her bikini under a loose caftan and when they had gathered up mats and beach toys, Liz accompanied them through the garden to the steps leading to the sand below.

'We can't get to the beach this way when the tide is high,' Liz explained. 'But it's well on the way out now, so I think it's safe enough. Be careful, because the rocks can be slippery.'

Poppy and Boo led the way and the pathway echoed with their shrieks of excitement. They almost took Sophie's breath away with their torrent of chatter, informing her that the sea was freezing cold compared to Florida, but they loved the surf and the presence of other British families who visited the beach because there were always new playmates to hand.

The day was fair, and Sophie applied sun cream to her small charges, reminding them to keep their sun hats on. The children ran off to search for sea-creatures and shells in the rock pools, and Sophie covered herself with a protective barrier of lotion – she didn't want to burn on her first day. A toe dipped into the waves confirmed her suspicion that it wasn't quite warm enough to bathe, and she uttered a prayer that the girls would not want to swim.

Her head was hazy with all the new impressions she had received but now she could relax, and she was perfectly happy sprawling on her mat and observing the scene. The headlands were rocky and beautiful, and she was relieved that her initial impressions of Liz's girls were so favourable. She had feared having to contend with a pair of privileged

17

brats, but Poppy and Boo seemed biddable, and Sophie felt an increasing confidence that her powers of imagination would enable her to keep their interest. She began to plan how she could introduce an element of language tuition into their day, and some quick questioning when they came to her to display their treasures showed that they possessed only a few basic words of French. So much the better for her, because she would be able to build on this low base with comparative ease to impress their parents.

Poppy caught a hermit crab in her net and screamed with delight when Sophie let it wriggle on her palm. The child was reluctant to touch it herself, and Sophie proposed that they should take it back to its watery home. As they walked to the receding waves, Sophie took the opportunity to enquire whether Sean and Abbie liked coming to the beach. She had visions of them shut away in their rooms, glued to phones and i-pads, and almost hoped this would be the case. It would be much easier to manage two small people rather than a larger group with reluctant teens in tow.

'Sean came with us yesterday – Mummy made him, but Abbie had a headache and stayed in. She doesn't like France,' Poppy said, and Sophie suppressed her surprise. She could still remember the breathless sensation of falling in love with the country during her first visit, but perhaps everything seemed different when you were an only child bathed in your parents' full attention. However, it wouldn't do to pass any judgments on the older Lenister children before meeting them. (Of course, they wouldn't be Lenisters, but she had no idea about the identity of Liz's first husband. There was an awful lot she still had to learn about this family.)

Despite the application of sun cream, Sophie's skin began to tingle as the sun climbed higher and she called Poppy and Boo to finish their play.

'We can come down again this afternoon,' she said firmly, and she disregarded their protests. 'It's lunchtime and we don't want to keep Mummy waiting.'

The mention of their mother stifled further argument, and when they were back at the house, Sophie suggested that the girls display their shells on the table in the shade of the pergola so the rest of the family could admire the collection. This was acclaimed as an excellent idea and Sophie went into the house to wash her hands. She wasn't sure if her help was needed with lunch, but sandy skin wasn't ideal either way.

A teenage girl was slumped on the window seat, tongue extended in concentration as she painted her toenails with a vivid green varnish. She looked up as Sophie entered the room and her eyes narrowed to unfriendly slits.

'Hullo. You must be Abigail.'

Sophie smiled at the girl, who responded by settling the corners of her mouth into a disagreeable pout. She finished coating the last toenail and raised her head.

'Well, full marks there. I suppose you're Sophie.'

Her voice was as sneery as her face. 'I hope you don't think I'm included in this nannying business. I do my own thing.'

Sophie digested the content and tone of this remark. The girl was at an unfortunate stage of adolescence; her skin dappled with eruptions of acne and a figure inclined to puppyish plumpness. 'Lumpy and difficult' ... that was how Liz had described her, and it was evidently an accurate comment. However, it would be preferable to establish mutual tolerance, and Sophie was prepared to be generous in the face of this barely concealed brush-off.

'Well, I hope we can be friends,' she said cautiously. Before Abigail could respond, Liz swept in, bringing her usual no-nonsense energy into the room like a stimulating breeze. She glanced at her daughter and clucked her teeth.

'What a hideous colour. I see you've met Sophie. Please don't make her life too difficult; the little ones like her.'

Abigail did not bother to reply, and Liz turned to Sophie. 'I assume Poppy and Boo gave you no trouble? Good. Sean will be here with the baguettes any moment, so perhaps you could rootle in the fridge for lunch. There are cold cuts, salad and cheese – you know the sort of thing.'

'Yes, of course. I hope the children enjoyed their morning. They are arranging their shells to show you when we've eaten.'

Sophie went to the cloakroom to remove the lingering traces of sand and sea, and when she returned to the kitchen, Liz was barking instructions on her mobile while Abigail glowered into the garden. There was an uncomfortable sense of conflicting personalities in the room, and Sophie suspected that this might be an everyday

19

occurrence; something she would have to get accustomed to. She opened the large American-style fridge freezer and only just restrained a gasp as she viewed the loaded shelves. The fridge was stuffed to bursting with what appeared to be the contents of an entire deli counter: evidence of a family who were used to spending without counting the pennies.

Sophie had no idea of individual preferences where food was concerned, but she already recognised that she would get on better with her employer if she didn't wait for instructions. She selected a variety of cold meats and cheeses and began to prepare a mixed salad with vegetables whose fresh and earthy aroma suggested a local provenance. The morning on the beach had sharpened her appetite, and she was more than ready for her meal. When she had laid everything out, she went in search of Poppy and Boo to clean their hands and faces before they ate. Liz was finishing her call when they reappeared.

'Excellent,' she said, surveying the table. 'All we need now is Sean with the bread.'

'He's probably chatting up those girls at the bar.'

This was Abigail's contribution. But before anyone could reply, the door opened, and Sean walked in with his purchases.

Sophie tried her hardest to appear casual, but she felt the tell-tale warmth of a blush in her cheeks as she recalled Liz's warning at her interview. It would be horribly embarrassing if anyone thought she was likely to fancy a schoolboy, and she felt sure that Liz was scrutinising her reaction as introductions were made. Luckily, Poppy and Boo began to clamour for bread and ham, and Sophie busied herself with filling their plates until her initial discomfort had evaporated. Sean had given her a greeting almost as cursory as that of his sister, and she was unable to devote any time to garnering an impression of the boy until everyone was eating and conversation was sporadic.

When she was able to observe Sean, she began to feel a dawning sympathy for Abigail. It must be infuriating to inhabit a body without allure when your sibling was so well favoured. Sean was tall, slim and unusually graceful for a boy. He had thick hair of a shiny raven black and long-lashed eyes, and as Liz had said, he was scorchingly good-looking, with the high cheekbones and sulky mouth of an Italian film star. Sophie smiled to herself as she recalled Liz's words at her interview – this boy would have no difficulty in finding girls to sleep with him and had probably already done so.

He ignored Abigail, who was picking at the salad as if it was potentially poisonous and concentrated on his small sisters.

'So, you went to the beach with Sophie? Did you swim?' he asked, and Poppy shook her head.

'No, because Sophie said it was too cold. We fished in the rock pools though, and we've put all our lovely shells on the table outside for you to see. Why didn't you come down with us?'

'I'll come with you next time, and we'll build the sandcastle I promised you.'

Sophie had already concluded that the little girls preferred the company of their brother to that of their moody sister. She hoped that the intransigent Abigail wasn't going to infect everyone with her sulking, but it was clear to Sophie that her best policy was to remain aloof from family clashes. Her stay here would be relatively brief and it would be wiser not to get involved.

Sean's eyes slid towards her from time to time, and she had the feeling that he was trying to decide whether she was someone worth getting to know. He had an air of insolent inscrutability which she had never encountered before, and she didn't warm to him.

Chapter Three

Darling George,

It seems such an age since we were together, and I miss you dreadfully. How is life at Harvard? I imagine you surrounded by preppy young people all being very earnest and academic, with the girls wearing knee socks like in American films I've seen which are set in the college. Or am I thinking of Clueless? Have you met any new girlfriends yet? (You needn't answer that unless you want to).

I've been here nearly a week, and it's surprising how settled I feel. The coast is so beautiful, and I'm surrounded by every luxury, although the house has seen better days. Liz gave me a credit card to use for anything I buy here, but I don't think I will ever get used to the feeling that money doesn't matter which comes as second nature to this family. When I came back from the hypermarket yesterday Liz scolded me for my lack of extravagance, but I can't get my head round the waste of food. Anything they don't immediately love or that is within a sniff of it's best-before date goes straight in the bin – that's a habit I mustn't acquire.

Sorry if I'm boring you. It's taken me some time to untangle the family tree. Sean and Abigail are the kids of Liz's first marriage, and their surname is Spenser. Poppy and Boo are Matthew Braybrooke's children, and Boo turns out to be short for Boudicca! Poor child. I thought I would burst trying not to laugh when Sean told me, and he gave me a very dirty look.

You will be pleased to hear that I have managed to restrain myself from seducing Sean, although honesty compels me to relate that Liz wasn't exaggerating and he is wonderfully handsome. It is unfair, because Abigail is quite the opposite, being physically unprepossessing and painfully conscious of her brother's attractions. She dislikes me, and I heard Sean telling her that I was a 'babe', and it wasn't surprising if she was jealous. That wasn't very kind of him. I am still wary of these two and their mother. They have a single mindedness of purpose which is startling, perhaps because they have always had the means to do or buy whatever they want. However, Sean has taken pains to be friendly in the last day or so, and he can be amusing company when he thaws. He's poised on that difficult cusp between teen and adult, and I feel I should encourage him to be more mature about life in general.

But Poppy and Boo and I are great pals. They aren't yet old enough to appreciate their gilded existence and are very happy to muck about on the beach with me. Sometimes our French lessons are conducted with me inscribing words on damp sand with a shell which they find very amusing, but at least it seems to be going into their heads, and Liz is satisfied. I wouldn't like to get on her wrong side.

Mr Braybrooke is expected imminently, and I am eaten up with curiosity to see him. I think it must take a character of iron to cope with the implacable Liz and her expectations. History doesn't relate what happened to Mr Spenser, and I don't feel I can ask Sean or his sister; they never talk about him. I am beginning to realise that I come from a very boring background, and perhaps that's not a bad thing. We have already visited some wonderful restaurants, and I predict I will have gone up at least one dress size, perhaps two, by the time I leave. You won't be able to judge if I'm putting on weight from my pix, because Liz has instructed me not to post anything on social media during my stay with the family, and I feel bound to respect her wishes. For some reason, she's sensitive about exposing them to the public gaze unless she has approved things first – do I detect a mystery here?'

There was a scuffling noise outside, and Sophie hastily closed her laptop. Her email to George would have to wait, but she almost welcomed the interruption. Thinking about George left her unsettled and a little depressed, despite her affluent surroundings. After a soft knock, Poppy peeped round the door.

'Sophie? Are you ready for the beach? Sean says the tide is right out now.'

'Yes Poppy, I'll be down in a tick. Get your things together, there's a good girl.'

The afternoon was warm and bright. So far, they had been lucky with the weather. Sophie knew that her job would be more challenging when cloud and rain curtailed their beach expeditions. Her skin glowed with health as a result of exposure to the Breton sunshine, and as she caught her hair into a ponytail to keep it away from her shoulders, the luminous reflection in her mirror stopped her short. 'You are a babe,' she muttered, retrieving her beach towel from the bedroom chair. 'But you need some discipline when it comes to the cheese and patisserie, otherwise you'll end up as a piglet.'

She would be giving Abbie some competition if she wasn't careful.

To her surprise, she found that both Sean and Abbie were preparing to join the beach party, but Liz had already settled herself in a comfortable chair on the patio.

'What bliss – a chance to catch up on some reading,' she explained, kissing the little girls in an unusual display of affection. 'Don't hurry back. I shall be perfectly happy here.'

The tide was low, and the beach was exposed, golden and enticing, at the end of the private pathway. Sean selected a site sheltered by low rocks where they could spread their mats, and for once, Abbie exerted herself to splash with her sisters in the gentle waves. Sophie reached for the sun spray before rolling on to her stomach to enjoy the warmth and a spot of downtime.

'You've missed a bit.'

Sean's lazy voice caressed her ear. Startled, she began to sit up, but he pushed her down very gently. 'I'll do it for you,' he added, and he massaged her back with a light, sure hand until little tingles shimmered down her spine. 'Mm. You've got lovely skin, Sophie,' he murmured, and Sophie wondered whether the hand was exploring a little too avidly.

'Thanks. That's great.'

She was relieved when he stopped and positioned himself face down on his mat.

'My turn now,' he said, thrusting the bottle towards her. Sophie shrugged, sat up and quickly repeated the process. The boy's body was lean and smooth, like a classical statue come to life, and she tried not to acknowledge the feeling that it was pleasant to touch. 'Nice,' he murmured, and she snapped the bottle shut and lay down again. If she looked to her right, she had a ringside view of a doughy, middle-aged Englishman struggling to change his swimming shorts with the aid of an inadequate towel, and so she hastily turned her head, only to encounter Sean's electric gaze. For a moment, they exchanged a long, searching look.

'You are well buttoned-up, Sophie,' he murmured, wrinkling his brow in his charming, quizzical way. 'Don't you ever relax? Tell me something about yourself. I don't know what makes you tick, and I want to understand you better.'

'What do you want to know? I'm twenty-one, almost twenty-two, and I'm reading Modern Languages at Cambridge. My parents are doctors and I'm an only child. This is a holiday job for me, because your nanny is visiting her family down under. I'm enjoying myself here very much.'

She felt obliged to deflect his curiosity and was unwilling to share anything too personal. Despite the lively sympathy in his face, she understood that it would be unwise to let down her guard with this persuasive young man. Their paths were scheduled to cross for such a short time, and she sensed danger in becoming too friendly with a family whose values and habits were so different to her own.

He considered what she had said, his eyes still locked on hers, as if searching for the solution to a problem.

'But I know all that. I want to discover who you are underneath your Little Miss Reliable act. Like, do you have a boyfriend? I sort of assumed you don't, else you wouldn't be happy to be away from England for so long.'

Sophie had to escape the intensity of his gaze; it was stripping away protective layers and making her uncomfortable. She lay on her back, tilting her straw hat so her face was shielded from sun rays and probing eyes.

'I did have a boyfriend, but he's left to study at Harvard. We don't believe in long-distance relationships, so we've cooled things,' she said, pierced by a sudden pang of regret for the happy, uncomplicated days of her friendship with George. Sean was silent for a while as he considered this revelation.

'Poor Sophie,' he said softly, and she felt him run a finger down her arm with a soft, lingering touch. 'Never mind. You must have to fight men off all the time. Have you had lots of lovers?'

'Don't be a twat, Sean.'

She heard his intake of breath. 'Some things are private,' she added crossly. 'Do you quiz your Australian nanny about her love life like this? No wonder she needs a break from you.'

'No-one would want to shag Ellie unless they were desperate, so it would be useless to ask her anything.'

Sean turned it into a joke, as if he realised that he might have gone too far. 'But seriously, Soph, think what it's like for me. I'm locked up most of the year in a grim dump with hordes of sweaty, hormonal boys who get their rocks off by salivating over third-rate porn. It makes it difficult to understand how to behave with girls in real life. I hoped you might be able to help.'

Sophie knew that Sean boarded at an expensive and exclusive educational establishment.

'I doubt that your headmaster would recognise his school from that description. Anyway, you have a sister; surely you meet her friends from time to time?'

'They are just children.'

This remark prompted Sophie to sit up, feeling it was time she checked on her other charges. The little ones were still frolicking at the sea's frothy margins, but Abigail appeared to be engrossed in chatter with two teenage girls. It gave Sophie a good excuse to close the conversation. An exchange of confidences with Sean might lead to further expressions of intimacy, and she didn't want to risk that.

'Abbie seems to have made some friends. I'd better see if Poppy and Boo have had enough yet.'

She got to her feet, but Sean propped himself on one elbow and caught her hand in his own. The warm press of flesh made her pause for an instant.

'I've never been to bed with a girl. You are so beautiful – I'd give anything to sleep with you,' he said, his eyes wide and apppealing as Bambi, and Sophie decided to be straight with him, although she gave his hand a friendly squeeze before releasing it.

'Look Sean, when I first met your mother, she made it very plain that I should resist any temptation to get jiggy with you; in fact, she said that if I did, she'd sack me on the spot. She's paying me a generous salary, and this is a good gig for me – please understand where I'm coming from. I think you're intelligent enough to realise that not everyone has the advantages enjoyed by your family. I like you very much, but we can only be friends.'

Did he realise how much ground she was ceding here in her efforts to let him down lightly? It would be perfectly reasonable for her to tell him where to get off, and that he had spoken out of turn. But something about the boy got through her defences; some feeling that despite the

26

privileged life and the handsome face, he was achingly vulnerable. She wanted to stroke his head and tell him that everything would be all right, but that wasn't a good idea. He gave a little groan, disappointed by her firm rejection.

'I understand. Not sure where Ma was coming from – she usually bends over backwards to get her kids what they want. But I won't be a brat, Sophie, I promise. Will you forget what I said?

'Yes, of course I will. Subject closed, okay?'

And please don't go complaining to your mother she thought, although it was unlikely that he would do so. The relations between Liz and her older children were still something of a mystery to Sophie. She had observed that there was closeness without affection, whereas with Poppy and Boo, Liz was altogether more physical and relaxed. Perhaps it was because they were so much younger, or maybe it had to do with their father being around. But it was clear that Sean and Abbie had inherited their mother's direct approach to getting what they wanted in life, and she would have to learn to deal with this if she wanted to survive her time here.

She rose and strolled to the water's edge. Boo was getting tired. She stumbled and fell face down in the waves, letting out a roar which could have been heard back at the house. Abbie had lost interest in her siblings as she gossiped with the British teenagers, and it was left to Sophie to scoop Boo out of the water and settle her on one hip.

'It's okay, Boo, no bones broken.'

Poppy rolled over in the surf and landed at Sophie's feet. Both girls were bedraggled and shivering, and Sophie decided it was time for them to dry off. 'Abbie, I'm taking the little ones back to get warm,' she called, but Abbie merely waved an arm and continued her conversation. The three older girls moved slowly away along the waterline, while Sophie, Boo and Poppy returned to their beach mats. Sophie rubbed the children down and wrapped them in fluffy towels until the teeth chattering had stopped.

'I shouldn't have let them get so chilly,' she murmured to Sean, guilt prodding her with uncomfortable fingers, but Sean shook his head.

'Abbie was down there with them; it's not your fault. If you're good, I'll take you for an ice-cream later,' he said to his sisters, and the small faces brightened in their papoose-like bundles.

For the next half-hour Sean soaked up the sun while Sophie superintended the building of sandcastles. The beach was becoming crowded and Abigail had disappeared among a colourful maze of parasols. When Sean finally sat up to make good his promise, Sophie decided it was time to look for the missing member of the party.

'Can you take Poppy and Boo with you, Sean? I feel I should keep an eye out for Abbie. I haven't a clue who she was talking to down there.'

'Really? Who would want to abduct that spotty lard-arse?'

'Don't be like that, Sean. I'd feel happier if I checked things out.'

'Suit yourself. I'll take these two for their ices – do you want one?'

'Thanks, but I'll pass. I'm getting fat with all this wonderful food.'

'I'd say that you are *curvalicious.*'

Sean winked at her, obviously aiming for a renewal of their earlier complicity, but she shook her head at him in reproof as she pulled a shirt over her bikini. He took his small sisters by the hand and Sophie walked with long strides to the water, shading her eyes against the sun as she searched for the errant Abigail. There was no sign of her by the sea and so Sophie weaved her way through the family groups camped on the sand, but without success. She was on the point of turning back when the roar of an engine made her look up, and she spotted her quarry on the concrete sidewalk above the beach, deep in conversation with her new friends and two unknown young men.

Sophie climbed the steps to reach the group. The males were obviously local; mahogany skinned and lavishly tattooed, with the usual rough stubble and messy hair of the professional beach bum. One of them was revving the engine of a rudimentary open-topped jeep, and it appeared from the mixture of broken English and encouraging gestures that they were urging the girls to take a ride. She took a deep breath, fearing that it would not be easy to prise Abbie away from these dubious attractions.

'Abigail!'

Abbie jumped, and turned towards her. Her face grew shuttered and surly.

'What is it? Can't you see I'm doing stuff?'

'What stuff is that? I hope you aren't thinking of getting into that contraption. Your mum would have a fit.'

Her sharp tone caused the others to look her way. Sophie's gaze swept through the inside of the jeep and she shuddered at the oily floor and ragged seating, not to mention the absence of seat belts. One of the men leered at her, addressing some vulgar remark to his companion, and they both sniggered as Sophie faced them down.

'What are you doing? I hope you don't expect these girls to get in that thing. It should be banned from the road.'

Rage inspired Sophie with a colloquial fluency in French which astounded her, and the men hesitated in mid-insult, surprised to be accosted in their own tongue.

'We're not doing anything wrong,' one of them remarked, also in French. 'They asked for a ride, that's all. Are you their nursemaid then? Perhaps you'd like to come instead. You look like you'd be up for a fuck.'

'Oh, piss off, you moron!'

She spun around to confront Abigail and her chums with an angry face. 'You want your brains tested if you're seriously considering going anywhere with these guys. Don't you know they spend their summers picking up girls for a quick shag and an even quicker getaway? Of course, if you want to take home a dose of the clap as a memento of your holiday, then go right ahead. But not you, Abigail. You're coming back to the house with me.'

The men had exchanged muttered words during this tirade, understanding that this furious Englishwoman was putting their game to flight. They swung themselves into the vehicle and accelerated away, gesturing and swearing as quantities of sand swirled in the air behind them. One of the other girls examined Sophie with grudging admiration, hand on hip.

'Ooh, you speak French well! What's your problem? We aren't babies; we can go where we want.'

Sophie fumbled behind her back to locate the low wall. She was shaken enough to need to sit down to recover from the confrontation, feeling that she wanted to slap Abbie, and at the same time, fold protective arms around her. After all, she had been a sassy, giggling fourteen-year-old herself, and she had vivid memories of the struggle for independence against what seemed at the time to be impossibly restrictive standards.

'Look, those guys are trouble,' she said, trying to assume a position of friendly persuasion. 'That jeep is a death trap, and I can't believe that your parents would be happy to see you in their company. And I meant what I said about their behaviour – something like that happened to a friend of mine and she had no end of hassle afterwards.'

The last part of her speech wasn't exactly true, but she knew enough about the habits of young men like these louts to believe her analysis of the situation was correct. The girls stood in a pouting semi-circle, each exasperated face showing unwillingness to accept her criticism. One of them fiddled with her mobile, the other chewed a strand of her long hair, while Abigail's folded arms indicated she wasn't going to accept this interference without kicking up one hell of a fuss.

'My mother hired you to look after my baby sisters, not me. I shall tell her what a snooping cow you are, and you'll be back on the boat home.'

Abbie's defiant glance at her pals seemed to say: *I'll put this one in her place*, but Sophie brushed the challenge away.

'You do that, Abbie. You might find you are the one going home, not me.'

But she didn't want to leave the scene with discord seething around them like a sandstorm. She got to her feet and spoke frankly to the other teens. 'I'm glad that Abbie has found some friends. Perhaps you'd like to come to the house and meet her mum, so everyone knows where they stand, and it will be okay for Abbie to hang out with you. What do you say, Abbie?'

Abigail shrugged, but she seemed to accept that there was sense in this suggestion.

'We'll be on the beach tomorrow after lunch,' the long-haired girl said, glancing at her companion for confirmation. 'Abbie's mum can come and give us the once-over then if she wants.'

As she spoke, a tall Englishman wearing a yachting cap and beach shorts put his head over the wall. He frowned against the sun, shading his face as he observed the tense little group.

'Clare! Alice! Don't go off like that. We didn't know where you'd got to.'

He spoke sharply to Abbie's mates who stared back at him, looking the picture of teenage recalcitrance. However, Sophie was relieved by his attitude, which indicated that the girls came from a respectable background which would be acceptable to her employer. She saw that he was observing her with enquiring and impatient eyes, and she broke in to explain that she had come in search of the girls, but said nothing about the young men, in the hopes of encouraging more friendly feelings from the trio. A short, stilted conversation ensued, from which it transpired that Abbie's friends were staying at the campsite in another part of the town, and a rendez-vous was arranged for the following afternoon. Then the man ushered his teens away and Abbie and Sophie turned to retrace their steps along the beach.

Abbie met Sophie's attempts to engage with her with sulky monosyllables and after a while, Sophie gave up the effort. They found Sean and his sisters, but Abbie flounced away up the cliff path, saying she wanted to speak to her mother.

Sean raised an eyebrow of enquiry at Sophie. The little ones were fishing in a rock pool some distance away, and Sophie briefly outlined what had occurred. She was annoyed when he burst into raucous laughter.

'Why didn't you let the silly cow get herself into trouble? She'd have been home with her tail between her legs soon enough.'

'You don't really mean that, Sean. If you had seen the jeep... there was no way I could have let her go off with those men. And she shouldn't have walked away from us like that in the first place.'

'She'll be spilling some very selective beans to Ma, I expect. Poor old Soph. I'll stick up for you.'

Although Sophie knew she had acted for the best, she entered the house with her stomach entertaining a swarm of butterflies. There was no sign of Abbie. Liz was fidgeting around in the kitchen, but she assumed her best brooking-no-nonsense air as she instructed Sean to take the little girls upstairs to shower the salt away. Then she turned to Sophie wearing a guarded, speculative face.

'Abbie has been bending my ear. Suppose you give me your version of events,' she said coolly, taking a sip from a large glass of wine. Sophie looked at the glass with a sigh, feeling she was the one who could do with a drink. She recounted the bald facts, taking care not to dramatise the situation and Liz listened, her head on one side. There was a long, pregnant silence, while Sophie tried to ignore a little voice teasing her that she had miscalculated. She wasn't ready to go home; she hoped that Liz understood that her daughter had placed herself in an untenable position.

'I suppose it might have been more innocent than it appeared. Abbie says that the boys were known to her friends,' Liz suggested, and Sophie sent her a long, hard look.

'Trust me, they were not boys, and they are not innocent. Look Liz, you are paying me to use my judgement where your children are concerned, and that's what I did. Abbie may not like it, but I know I was right.'

Sophie waited, watching a mosquito waver menacingly through the air before Liz reached for another glass, poured some wine, and pushed it across the table like a peace offering.

'Fine. I'm happy with your explanation. I'll make sure I meet these children so I can decide how much further Abbie takes things, but for now, let's say no more about it.'

Sophie felt that she had gained brownie points by defending herself, and her standing with Liz was now higher than before. The upshot was that Clare and Alice and their parents met with the family the next day, and approval to continue the friendship was given from both sides. Sophie knew that Abbie was hoping for the freedom to pursue more beachside Romeos, but as soon as her new friends clapped eyes on Sean, their attitudes reversed in dramatic fashion. They took every opportunity to hang around with Abbie's family, making sheep's eyes at and giggling over her handsome sibling. It was impossible to say whether Sean or Abbie was more irritated by this turn of events.

Chapter Four

When Sophie yawned her way into the kitchen for breakfast on Saturday morning, she found a fair-haired man sitting at the table, with Poppy and Boo hanging around his neck. He stood up when she entered and greeted her with a confident smile, although Sophie was surprised by the undisguised appraisal sparkling in his eyes as his glance swept over her.

'You must be Sophie. I'm very pleased to meet you. My daughters can't stop singing your praises.'

'Sophie looks like Princess Isabelle, doesn't she, Daddy?'

A momentary blankness in the man's face indicated that he had no idea who Boo was referring to, but he was not about to dampen his daughter's enthusiasm.

'Yes darling, she does. How lucky you are to have a princess to play games with you.'

He gave Sophie a complicit wink as she shook his hand. Sophie went to make fresh coffee, keeping a curious eye on the newcomer as she pottered around the room. Matthew Braybrooke was tall and gym-honed, with the kind of rugged, mature looks of a male model sporting outdoor gear in the back pages of the *Telegraph*. There was an open candour about his clean-shaven features which suggested either extreme good temper – or the mesmerising countenance of a successful conman. Sophie was shocked as this thought rushed through her head, because she had no reason to question the man's integrity. She had developed an unfortunate habit of trying to second-guess the older members of Liz's family as a form of self-defence, and it would have to stop before she committed a real *faux pas*.

However, a morning passed in Matthew Braybrooke's company inclined her to a favourable view of his person. He was attentive to his wife, playful with his daughters, patient with Abigail and man-to-man with Sean, and he welcomed Sophie as though she was now part of the family. Poppy and Boo evidently adored him, and even the steely Liz softened under the warmth of his smile.

'What you must remember about Matt is that he knows which side his bread is buttered.'

33

This was said to her by Sean later that day, when they were alone together in the kitchen. Sophie had remarked in passing that his stepfather was a pleasant man, which caused the boy to drum his fingers on the table and regard her with his head on one side. 'He wasn't particularly successful in business until he met Mum and he's still reliant on her for contacts. I don't give a shit about his work, but I think this new venture of his shows that he feels the need to prove himself. He can always run home to mummy if it doesn't work out.'

Sophie paused as she rinsed the seawater from her bikini.

'What a cynic you are, Sean. I can't believe your mother would have married someone she didn't respect. I thought you had a good relationship with your stepfather – are you telling me you don't like him?'

'Matt's okay. He doesn't interfere with me and I don't get in his way. Mum's happy with him, that's the main thing.'

Sophie was unsure where Sean wanted the conversation to go. He stared at her with the abstracted air of someone both fascinated and repelled by the topic. 'Anyway, what do you think, now you've met Matt?' the boy asked. 'I accept that he's quite a looker, if the type floats your boat. He's younger than Mum, and I sometimes worry that might become a problem down the line.'

'Well, I've only exchanged a sentence or two with him, but he seems very – affable, I would say. I don't want to pry, Sean, but it helps me to understand your family.'

Sean did not respond, but his mouth turned down and his face invited sympathy, which led Sophie into a blunder.

'Would you like to tell me something about your father? I worry that I might put my foot in it, because no-one's told me anything about him,' she said softly, thinking that this was the ideal time to raise the subject. Sean expelled a sigh and she was shocked to see the harsh expresson of pain stamped on his brow.

'We hardly ever see him now; he's not part of our lives.'

He screwed up a piece of paper with twitchy fingers and flung the ball away into a corner of the room. 'Look, the guy's into Eastern European women and he lives in Estonia. Mum paid him to go away. The only influence he's had on my life has been a rubbish one, so forgive me if I don't want to talk about it. At least Pops and Boo have a father they can trust.'

34

'Oh Sean, I am so sorry. I didn't mean to upset you.'

Sophie left the sink and walked across the room to put a hand on his shoulder by way of apology, but he grabbed her and buried his dark head against her chest. She hesitated, but her arms stole around him of their own accord – it seemed the only possible thing to do. Sean sighed again, squeezing her in a python-like embrace and pressing his face into her breasts until she was worried that he wouldn't be able to breathe. He let out a smothered sound, but she couldn't tell if it was pain or pleasure.

Hot, intimate, embarrassing seconds passed. Then a squeaky floorboard in the hall alerted them to the presence of a third party, and by the time the kitchen door opened to admit his mother, Sophie was back at the sink and Sean was perusing his mobile with sullen immobility. Sophie was conscious that the air seemed to vibrate with guilt, but Liz didn't appear to notice anything out of the ordinary.

'Will you go and help Matt put the girls' tent up in the garden, darling? I've just seen them from my bedroom window, and he seems to be making heavy weather of it,' she said to Sean, her voice light and amused. He nodded, obviously glad of an excuse to slide from the room. Liz replaced a bottle in the refrigerator and slammed the door shut. 'I thought we'd go out for dinner as it's Matthew's first day here,' she said to Sophie. 'You are very welcome to join us.'

She was smiling, but Sophie intuited a lack of enthusiasm in the invitation and hurried to make her excuses. It would be therapeutic to have time to herself after her recent busy days.

'Thank you, Liz, but would you mind if I said no? I think it ought to be a family occasion, and I have lots of things to catch up with here.'

She hoped that Liz wouldn't ask her what those were, but Liz merely nodded, and followed her son to the garden. Sophie pegged her bikini on the line outside and when she returned to the kitchen, she discovered that Abigail was sprawled at the table.

Relations between them had been frosty since the beach affair, but Sophie refused to enter a sulking match. She thought it was time that they moved on – after all, Abbie was seeing her pals almost every day and Sophie's efforts had helped to bring that about.

'Are you meeting Clare and Alice tomorrow?' she asked in a friendly way, and Abbie shook her head.

'No. I'm a bit fed up with them drooling over Sean because it's no fun for me. It's bad luck, having a fit older brother,' she added, her face assuming its usual discontented droop. This was more than she had said to Sophie for some days and Sophie felt encouraged to prolong the conversation.

'It was funny when they tried to get him to go in the sea with them yesterday,' she observed, remembering Sean's desperate attempts to shake the pair off, and Abigail suddenly dropped the frown and smiled too.

'Yes, it was. Even Boo was laughing at him, and he's usually such a favourite with her. It's good for him to be made fun of for a change.'

Her eyes dwelt on Sophie, who was casual in shorts and T-shirt, with her hair scrunched in a knot. 'Aren't you coming out with us this evening?'

'No. I thought you guys should have some family time tonight, and there's plenty for me to eat here.'

She was still attempting to control the over-stocking of the refrigerator, with little success. Abbie hesitated for a second or two.

'Are you sure? We won't mind if you come.'

This was an unprecedented mark of favour, but Sophie was not to be persuaded.

'Thanks, but I've already told your mother I'm staying in.'

'Sean will be gutted.'

Sophie felt that she had taken some giant strides with Abigail in the last minutes, but she wasn't going to push her luck. She didn't react to the comment, which she suspected was dangled as a piece of bait and was relieved when Poppy burst in from the garden to invite her to view the tent. Afterwards, she helped bathe the little girls and fussed over their posh frocks with them. Hair was brushed until the tangles resulting from wind and sea water were smoothed away, faces washed, and noses wiped, and at length Sophie was satisfied with her work.

'Go and show yourself to Daddy, Boo. He will be delighted with how pretty you look,' she said. The family were assembling in the hall, and there was a pleasant bustle of laughter and anticipation as the little ones scampered down the stairs to display their finery.

Sophie had not been alone with Sean since the incident in the kitchen. He merely gave her one of his dissecting, enigmatic looks when he realised that she was not included in the party, but Matthew Braybrooke expressed polite disappointment.

'Please don't feel you have to stay at home, Sophie. We'd love to have you come with us,' he assured her, and she noticed Liz give him a quick, interrogatory glance.

'Sophie has things she wants to do here, Matthew. Don't make her feel awkward,' she said in a brittle way, thereby ensuring that everyone felt faintly ill at ease. As the family trooped away, Sophie closed the door on them with a sense of reprieve. She had grown fond of three of them and respected the others, but it would be good to feel she was at nobody's beck and call for a few hours.

The first thing she did was to pour herself a large glass of wine and sit in the garden to wallow in the sunset. The sun dipped low, making a fiery crescent against the sea and the far headlands loomed black and hazy on the horizon. It was a view that Sophie never tired of, and she was delighted to be able to appreciate the evening without interruptions. When the freshening night breezes began to nag around her seat, she went back to the house and pulled on a sweatshirt. She made a lazy, leisurely meal from rich pickings in the kitchen and gorged on Abbie's discarded copy of a gossip magazine, enjoying the switched-off sensation of being alone. It wouldn't be for long, because the little ones would need to be back for bed soon.

It was just after nine-thirty when the front door banged. She paused, alert to the incomer, and Sean tumbled into the room. He looked bright-eyed and his face was glowing. Sophie's immediate thought was that he was tipsy.

'Sophie! The front door wasn't locked. You are a careless girl. Any old burglar or rapist could have got in, and then what would you have done?'

He stood over her, swaying gently, his eyes unnaturally wide and accusing.

'Been burgled or raped, I suppose. Are you okay, Sean? You look as though you have enjoyed yourself.'

Sean sank on to a neighbouring chair and smothered a hiccup.

'I'll say this for my stepfather, he doesn't mind splashing out on the wine. Shame you weren't there, Soph, you would have enjoyed it too.'

He scanned the shorts and the sweatshirt and the smooth expanse of her tanned legs, and his face tightened in an expression of longing.

'Soph… can I go to bed with you? Please say yes.'

'Whenever you call me Soph, I know you want something. And we've already had this conversation, so you know the answer.'

'Shame. But I enjoyed our hug this afternoon. Suffocating in your lovely tits… what a way to go!'

Sophie smothered a giggle. Sean was outrageous, but there was something endearing about his audacity, especially when his dark hair was tousled, and he looked like a young Don Juan. At times like these, she felt she could almost be tempted to grant his wish… then she pictured Liz's frowning face, and the temptation melted away like snow in sunshine.

She could hear the rest of the party discarding their jackets in the hall. Sean cast a last, sultry look in her direction, then flung himself on to a sofa and buried himself in the gossip mag. Poppy and Boo pattered in to demand bedtime kisses and chatter about the meal, and Liz surprised everyone by announcing that she would put them to bed herself. Was this to please her husband? She never did it on a normal day. Sophie reminded herself not to question her employer's motivation; she was growing cynical and she didn't like it.

Matthew enclosed his daughters in a goodnight hug. He was in jovial spirits, looking sleekly satisfied with his evening, and he turned to Sophie as little footsteps clomped their way up the stairs.

'We missed you, Sophie. Will you join me for a nightcap? I thought I saw a bottle of Calvados in the cupboard.'

He didn't wait for an answer but strode off to get the bottle and some glasses. Sophie had never tasted Calvados before. It smelled delicious as she swirled the liquid around her glass, like a very spicy apple pie, but she took too large a mouthful to begin with and almost choked on the fiery liquid. Matt patted her on the back, trying not to laugh.

'Oh dear… I should have warned you. Small sips are best. But this is a good, smooth example compared to some of the rough stuff in the supermarkets. What do you make of it, Sean?'

Sean had tossed his glass back like a seasoned drinker, but Sophie could see he was struggling not to splutter.

'I prefer the wine we had at dinner,' he said thickly. 'This has too much bite to it, it's like an alligator slithering down your throat, all spiky and sharp.'

Sophie didn't want to finish hers, but was reluctant to offend Matt. She got up, cradling the glass in both hands.

'I think I'll take mine up to bed with me. Goodnight, all.'

Sean and Matt rose politely to their feet as she left the kitchen. She heard them laughing together as she climbed the stairs and was pleased to think that Sean was so comfortable with his stepfather after his upsetting revelations about his own parent.

One benefit of Matt's presence was the temporary lessening of Sophie's responsibilities. He was keen to spend time with his daughters, and so the next day, Sophie and Abbie took themselves off to do some girly shopping at the local mall. French clothes were pricey compared to those back home, but this was not a problem for Abigail. Liz had told Sophie to use the credit card to pay for Abbie's purchases, and Sophie contented herself with biting her lip when the girl selected a new swimsuit costing almost as much as Sophie's entire holiday wardrobe. At least she had managed to guide Abbie into choosing a design which had a conventional cut instead of the skimpy, thong type which was apparently in fashion – Sophie didn't think that Liz would approve such a purchase, and she could imagine the sneer of derision on the face of Sean only too vividly.

One of the smaller boutiques was advertising a sale. Abbie went to find a loo, and while she was gone, Sophie strolled into the shop to cast a casual eye over the clothes on offer. Liz had paid her first week's wages into her bank account, and she was feeling almost flush.

At the end of a rail, she found a delectable little sundress which was cut away to leave one shoulder bare. It was made from a soft, floaty cotton, with a floral pattern in sweeping blues and greens. After a rapid internal battle with her meaner self, Sophie decided she was meant to buy it. The dress was smart enough to be worn in the evening, and Sophie looked forward to occasions where she could use it to display her deepening tan to good effect.

She completed the purchase rapidly before she could change her mind. Abbie glanced at the bag when they met up again.

'What have you bought?'

'Just a dress. It was in the sale, so I thought I could afford it.'

39

'Why didn't you put it on Mum's card? She'd never know.'
'I couldn't do that!'

Sophie stopped short in shock, almost colliding with a plump French woman who was scolding a whiny toddler. 'That card is to pay for things for your family. It would be taking advantage to use it for myself.'

'I don't suppose Mum would care. I won't tell on you if you want to do it. We're loaded, we won't miss the money.'

Sophie didn't reply to this. She felt that Abigail's view was misguided, also, that her comments demonstrated that she didn't know her mother very well. In Sophie's judgement, Liz was not stingy or mean, but she was a woman of principle and a breach of trust would be noted in case it could provide ammunition in the future. Did Abbie really think that she would casually commit what amounted to theft?

Sophie was still pondering on this as they went for a coffee, but Abbie chattered on about her new swimsuit without appearing to comprehend Sophie's scruples. There was a simple explanation, Sophie thought, staring into the creamy swirls of her cappucino. Abbie had never known what it was to lack money, and she only could only see things from her own fortunate viewpoint. However, when they rose to leave, Abigail surprised her by suggesting a return visit to the sale boutique.

'You might find something else you fancy, and I'll use the card for you; it'll be fine.'

Abigail's demure face rang immediate alarm bells in Sophie's head. Here was a trap waiting, baited, for her to tumble into. She had underestimated the girl: it was apparent that Abbie was all too aware of her mother's character. Sophie could almost hear the crafty complaint to Liz when they returned – *'Sophie bought herself something with our money, Mum, I couldn't stop her...'*

She thanked the girl politely, but declined the offer, leaving Abigail thwarted and inclined to sulk again. When they returned to the house, Sophie spirited her purchase away in case it prompted Sean into suggestive comments. She realised that after the episode in the mall she could never become close to Abigail, but her attitude towards the boy was shifting to an unexpected, deepening friendship. They shared the same sense of humour and cynical attitude to life, and whilst Sophie was very fond of Poppy and Boo, they could not offer her the

40

same companionship as Sean. He was important to her sense of place in the family, and she hoped that his occasional indiscretions wouldn't spoil that.

Chapter Five

The weather changed. Huge clouds billowed up over the sea, threatening and stormy. Torrents of rain punished the windows and the house groaned and shuddered in the wind. Chilly draughts whistled in uncomfortable places, and the distressed fabric of the mansion was apparent in a way that had been concealed under the calm of former sunny days.

The bad weather brought a similar dampening of spirits in the household. It was suddenly imperative for Matthew and Liz to commandeer the kitchen with their laptops, and Sophie was banished to the gloomy shadows and musty furniture of the drawing room where she strove to amuse the little ones. The older children kept to their rooms, permanently plugged into electronic gadgets and phones and lamenting the lost joys of Florida.

It was hard going. On the third wet day, Sophie organised a trip to the aquarium and that got them through a morning, but a splashy walk on the headland in the afternoon resulted in muddy feet and mutinous faces.

But next day the skies were calmer. Sophie inserted the children into trainers and sweaters and took them to gorge on artisan ice cream in Saint-Malo, and when she returned, she found her employer busy making plans.

'It's going to be 25 degrees again tomorrow,' Liz exulted, scrolling down the weather forecast on her laptop. 'I've arranged to meet up with some friends and their kids to spend the day at Mont St Michel. I think you deserve a rest after all your efforts this week Sophie, so you can have a day off.'

Sophie would have liked to see Mont St Michel for herself, but she felt unable to press for her inclusion in the invitation. It was obvious from two unenthusiastic faces that Sean and Abbie were not excited at the prospect of the trip, but they made only a cursory protest. Everyone knew that Liz dictated the terms which ruled the household.

'I expect you to tell me all about it when you get back,' Sophie said to Poppy as she helped her on with her sandals the next morning. The day had dawned so soft and warm and beautiful that it was hard to believe that only a short time before they had been cowering from the tempest. 'And I want you to do me a big drawing of the abbey afterwards, so make sure you pay attention. Sometimes the waves go right round the mount and make it into a tiny island – that would be exciting to see.'

Sean was leaning against the newel, painting a study in gloom as he pulled a sloppy top over his jeans. It was one of those days when he reverted to being an adolescent and not a young man. His dark hair was squashed under an unflattering baseball cap, and a spot was painfully prominent on his chin.

'You can count yourself lucky you aren't coming today,' he informed Sophie. 'Mum loves the Randalls for some reason, but their kids are superbrats. I only said I'd go because otherwise, Poppy and Boo get trampled on – last time we met them, I had to peel Charlie, the youngest boy, off Boo because he was trying to beat her up. He'd better not try that today.'

Liz overheard him as she came into the hall and she uttered a little snort of disapproval.

'Don't exaggerate, Sean. Peggy wants you to spend time with Roderick, because they are thinking of trying to get him into your school. His last report was very poor, and they feel a different educational approach would be good for him.'

'That's all I need. I must make sure I put him off. I can't face having Rod Randall hanging round my neck.'

Before Liz could reply, her husband opened the door from the kitchen, his face bereft of its usual genial smile. He ran a hand through his hair and an untidy strand fell over his forehead.

'Liz, I'm sorry to ask this, but could you manage without me today? I've just had an email that concerns me, and I need to address the problem before the bank gets wind of what's going on. It's a bitch, but I can't see a way round it.'

There was an anguished outcry from Poppy and Boo.

'Oh, Daddy! We want you to come with us.'

Boo clung to one of his legs like a determined limpet, and he frowned down at her.

'Sorry, darling. I promise to spend all day with you tomorrow, and we'll do whatever you want. But I have no choice just now. It's hard

43

to explain it to you, but there's too much at stake for me to ignore the matter.'

Sophie noticed the pursed, narrow profile of Liz's mouth as she packed bottles of water into a backpack and considered her husband's words.

'It's not at all convenient, Matthew, but I suppose I can hardly object. Are you sure it won't wait until tomorrow?'

'Quite sure.'

His tone barely concealed a note of tetchiness.

'You will probably do better with my input, in which case you should leave your response until later,' she continued, and this time, it was Matt's face which registered impatience.

'I think I can handle this, thank you. Have a good day and give my apologies to Chris and Peggy. Sean – I trust you to look after my girls.'

He turned abruptly and went back to the kitchen, slamming the door behind him. Sophie had been an unwilling observer of this little scene, caught in the chilly crossfire between the pair. She busied herself with Poppy and Boo, making sure that they had cardigans and that Boo's blanket was stashed away safely in a bag, because it was the first time she had sensed discord between her hosts, and it wasn't a comfortable experience. Liz turned towards her as the family made their way to the people carrier.

'Could you rustle up something for Matt's lunch, do you think? I'm sorry he's being such a bore. Don't let him start moaning to you about his problems. He's inclined to be an old woman at times, and we mustn't encourage him.'

Liz made it sound as though her husband was a pouting child and Sophie's sympathies veered towards Matt, but she nodded acquiescence and waved them off as the car pulled out of the drive. She decided that the kitchen was best avoided if Matt was having a bad day, so she slipped down to the beach through a side door to take a quick stroll among the rocks. The storm had strewn large mounds of seaweed everywhere, and a small tractor hummed over the sands to scoop the fly-ridden heaps away.

Sophie wedged herself in a crevice, watching the surf crash and sigh beneath her. She knew that if she paddled at the shallow tideline, she would be amused by whole colonies of hermit crabs rolling about in their daily quest for food, but she was content to stay put and enjoy the sun warming her skin after the previous dull days. The scene in the hallway was still on her mind, and she was surprised by the undercurrents of marital discord which had suddenly appeared. Had Matt invented an excuse to stay behind or was there real trouble brewing with his embryo business? His manner had revealed a coldness at odds with his usual jovial façade, and Liz, who was normally the most unflappable of women, had made her irritation obvious.

Sophie sat and pondered, and after a while, the sun grew toasty on her arms and legs. It was mid morning, and soon she would need to prepare something for Matt to have for lunch. He was talking on his phone when she entered the house and she skipped upstairs, thinking that she would try on her new dress now that the weather was sunny again.

She slipped it over her her head and paraded before the mirror, pleased with her purchase, and thinking with complacency that it would stun her fellow students at Cambridge if a British summer ever allowed her to wear it. She entertained a happy vision of herself sprawled in a punt on the Cam, attracting envious glances from the other boating undergraduates, but a yell from downstairs interrupted her in mid-pirouette.

'Sophie! Can you come down here, please?'

Should she remove the dress before descending? She lingered before her reflection, and then decided to go downstairs as she was. No-one else had seen the garment and maybe Matt would confirm that she'd made a good choice. As she entered the kitchen, he looked across at her and his eyes grew wide and hungry.

'Wow, Sophie, you look amazing. Did you put that on especially for me?'

He was teasing, but the suggestion pleased her in a way she didn't want to examine too closely.

'I was just trying it on. I bought it when I was out with Abbie the other day. Do you think it's okay?'

'It's more than okay. It's a dress which is asking to be taken out for lunch. I've held my partner's hand and things have calmed down on the work front, and I wondered whether you'd like to join me in Dinan for a bite to eat as it's such a nice day.'

The warmth of his approbation washed over her in a pleasant tide, but Sophie hesitated, mindful of a previous request and unsure whether this invitation would meet with Liz's blessing.

'Liz asked me to fix you something here,' she began, and Matt's face crinkled at the prospect.

'I don't think Liz will mind, and I don't see why we shouldn't go out and enjoy ourselves, which is what everyone else is doing. Can you call a cab? Your French is so much better than mine.'

'Give me five minutes to get ready first.'

'You look fantastic as you are. Mind you keep that dress on. I want to see the good citizens of Dinan swooning in the streets.'

Sophie giggled as she ran upstairs to fix her hair and face. She hadn't indulged in this kind of banter since George had left for America – she didn't count the conversations with Sean; he was still a kid really – and Matt's teasing made her feel grown-up and sophisticated after her recent nursery duties. She brushed her hair, leaving it to fall around her shoulders in a dark cloud, applied a freshening of perfume, and went back downstairs to ring the local taxi firm.

Matt was waiting for her at the foot of the staircase wearing a white shirt and dark jacket, which lent an attractive gravitas to his person.

He's not quite old enough to be a silver fox, but Liz is a lucky woman, Sophie decided, feeling almost aggrieved that Liz had snagged such a good-looking husband. And a new thought popped into her head; one which was accompanied by a tiny red flag of warning. It wasn't a good idea to indulge in a fancy for her employer's husband.

'This is my treat, naturally,' Matt said, with another smiling glance at her figure. 'I've been looking at the Michelin and we'll find somewhere really special.'

Dinan was thronged with tourists of all nationalities who were enjoying the quaint medieval streets and colourful gardens. Sophie chatted to the taxi driver during the journey, pleased with the chance to show off her facility with the language, and when he understood the purpose of their visit, he took them to a restaurant in a hilly and cobbled side street which was tucked away from the visiting hordes. He assured her that this was the place to eat if one was serious about food.

46

The entrance was dim and unremarkable, but it opened out to a surprisingly spacious room where businessmen were already frowning over menus and making their solemn selection of wine. Sophie and Matt were in luck. A cancellation meant that a table was available, otherwise... Madame shrugged her shoulders as if to say: who knows where you would be eating? She led them to a table in the centre of the restaurant with a ceremonial flourish; her heels clicking decisively on the wooden floor.

Sophie couldn't help but see that the room turned its collective eyes upon her as she sank into her seat. The few women present in the restaurant were elderly or dressed in dark business suits and were no competition for a girl in a pretty frock. Matt held her chair for her, and she noticed him glance around at the other diners, straightening his shoulders and standing tall. *See what I can pull* was his covert message to the less fortunate men in the room, and Sophie was tickled by amusement as she interpreted his stance. It was flattering to be the subject of such open admiration, although she was still sensible of the fluttering red flag. She decided to do a little teasing of her own, leaning across the table and opening her eyes very wide.

'They probably think that I'm your daughter,' she whispered in seductive tones, and Matt gave a very good imitation of a man with a punctured ego.

'What? Well, I suppose you could be; just about,' he said grudgingly, and she grinned.

'And now you look like someone on *Antiques Roadshow* who has just received a much lower valuation than they were expecting,' she continued, and this time he brought down his menu on the table with an exasperated thump.

'I can't think why I have brought you out to insult me,' he exclaimed, but Sophie felt no twinge of compassion. She suspected that Matthew Braybrooke wasn't used to outsiders undermining his excellent opinion of himself, and it wouldn't hurt him to realise that she could see through the handsome smokescreen.

They turned their attention to the menu. It was short, offering a surprisingly limited choice of dishes.

'That usually means the food will be very good,' Matt mused. 'They have some first-rate wines on their list as well. I'd like to ask the sommelier's advice when you've decided what you want to eat, but you will have to help me out.'

The sommelier approached them with a face of frozen condescension, which rapidly thawed when he realised that the attractive girl with Monsieur spoke his language so well. There was an animated bi-lingual discussion and Matt selected a bottle whose cost almost silenced his companion.

'Well, I'm glad that lunch is on you,' Sophie observed, when the wine had been poured, tasted and approved. Matt was gazing around the room as if he owned it.

'I've only seen this wine on a menu in England once, and that was at *Le Petit Prince* in Cambridge,' he informed her. 'It's even more expensive there. Cambridge is your stamping ground isn't it? Have you ever eaten at the *Prince*?'

'I'm a student, Matt. I can't afford to go somewhere like that.'

The thought amused her – had he forgotten the realities of life for young people at college?

'You need to find a rich boyfriend. The reason I know it is because my new venture is based at the Science Park and I find I'm spending a fair bit of time in Cambridge. If you are very nice to me, perhaps I'll take you to eat there when you are back at college in the autumn.'

'That would be lovely.'

Sophie spoke politely, but she thought a more likely scenario was that Matt would dismiss her from his mind as soon as she was back in England. However, it behoved her to be gracious now he was giving her this unexpected treat, and it really was a special treat, with food which was exquisitely cooked to accompany the excellent wine. Sophie tried to calculate how much each mouthful was costing but mental arithmetic had never been her strong point; besides, it seemed a shame to reduce the occasion to a question of economics.

It was a long, leisurely meal, during which Matt and Sophie were lulled into a pleasant state of candour. They were sharing a guilty sensation of taking time out from the demands of the household, almost as though they were playing truant, although this was never put into words. Sophie realised that Matt could become a different person once he was away from his masterful wife, and she appreciated the company of this relaxed and amusing version of the family man. He gave her a sketchy outline of his business plans, and she retaliated with tales of her college life and what she hoped to do after finishing at university. Then the topic switched to France and she realised that Matt was fishing for her opinion on life in Saint-Lunaire.

'Have you enjoyed your time with us so far, Sophie?' he asked, swirling the remnants of his wine around his glass. It was evident that he was revelling in his role of benefactor; primed by the envious glances towards his attractive companion. Sophie felt serene and replete, looking around her with a small, contented sigh. Matt's interest warmed and flattered her, and she didn't realise that this might lead her into indiscretion.

'Yes; it's been very good really. I adore Poppy and Boo, and they aren't anything like the spoilt little brats I anticipated. Abbie is beginning to thaw towards me, thank goodness, and I've always got on well with Sean. And of course, Liz is very... supportive.'

She had been going to say 'kind', but she suspected that Liz regarded her merely as an employee, without any emotional investment in her as a person. Matt regarded her across the table, his face taut with amusement.

'You and Sean... I have to say that I'm amazed he hasn't been making any moves on you. At his age, I couldn't have resisted a gorgeous girl like you, Sophie. And of course, anyone can see that he is going to be a heartbreaker when he's older, the lucky sod. Aren't you tempted to indulge in a little flirtation?'

'No. Flirting with Sean is not in my contract of employment,' she replied, hoping that her frown would close this line of conversation. 'Come on, Matt – he's still at school! I know there are only a few years between us, but that's a huge gulf at this stage of our lives.'

What was wrong with this family? They delighted in twisting things and speculating about events in a way which got beneath her skin. Matt probably thought he was being funny, but this was a joke which was beginning to wear very thin. He sensed her drawing back from him and looked contrite.

'I apologise, Sophie, that was a crude question. Of course, Sean is exceptionally mature for his age, and it's all too easy to forget he's still a schoolboy. I know that he can't wait to leave and get on with his life.'

Sophie shrugged her shoulders. Some impulse within prompted her to be honest.

'I have grown fond of him,' she admitted, brushing away a few crumbs with one fingertip. 'I think I feel protective towards him, without really knowing why. Sometimes I see a nervous little boy underneath the swagger, but perhaps it's silly of me to think that.'

'How much has Sean told you about his father?'

'Almost nothing, and I haven't wanted to force information out of him. It isn't any of my business.'

'It might be useful for you to know the basic facts. Sean was relatively young when Robert Spenser scarpered with an exotic mistress, and I'm afraid that he was damaged by the breakdown of his mother's relationship and the loss of his father. He is skilled at hiding his emotions, but I think he battles with an inner instability that he can't cope with, because despite his grown-up exterior, he can suddenly lash out in a way that's very unsettling. He's had years of counselling, but I'm not sure how much it has helped. He's also inherited his mother's need to control everything around her, although I don't think he understands that yet.'

There was silence for a while; a poignant and reflective interlude while Sophie considered everything that Matt had told her. She was struck by his final sentence and wondered if she was brave enough to pursue this interesting line of thought. How did Matt deal with the dominating tendencies of his wife? Matt had pushed her towards some personal truths, and she could not resist the urge to do the same for him, because she suspected that there was a person of sensitivity underneath his smooth exterior; one which wasn't often allowed to surface, and one she would like to get to know. She was unaccustomed to drinking at lunchtime and the wine warmed her sympathies, urging her towards intimacy and fuelling a growing appreciation of Matt's easy charm.

'And what about you, Matt? How do you manage Liz's need for control? I can see that it might make life difficult in certain circumstances.'

She was thinking about the cold words in the hall that morning. Matt sat very still, looking away into the distance as though revisiting an unpleasant memory. They were among the last of the diners, and waiters were beginning to clear around them in an ostentatious manner, wanting them to settle the bill and leave.

'Oh, Liz and I understand one another very well, so you don't have to worry about me. When we met, I was a junior at Lenister Legrand, and she was a rising star. We worked together on a couple of projects, and it became obvious that marriage would suit us. Liz needed a husband who would stay put and not embarrass her, and she wanted more children. I was happy to provide those things, because she could propel me out of the lower tiers of the firm to make some real money. And before you mention it, yes, there is an age difference, but it isn't a problem. Does that answer your question?'

Sophie had a sudden memory of Sean at the kitchen table – *Matt knows which side his bread is buttered.* Matt had transferred his gaze to her face, and she was conscious of his eyes; blue, steady, smiling. She had once read that a person wishing to deceive will look at you in such a way, and she recalled her reaction to him at their first meeting. Was Matt really this genial dad and husband, or was there some part of himself he kept concealed? It was impossible to interpret his real thoughts. She jolted herself into the present because he was waiting for an answer.

'And do your current projects involve Lenister Legrand?' she faltered, wanting to return to safer ground. He responded with a funny, lopsided grin.

'No. I wanted to get involved with something outside the group, to see whether I can make things happen, so I'm not on the Lenister Legrand payroll anymore. Luckily, my wife is a tycoon – so I can pay for your lunch,' he added, as a waiter despaired of their tardiness and thrust the bill under his nose.

As they made their way out to the street Madame detained Sophie for a moment, asking her whether they had enjoyed themselves. Sophie replied in French, congratulating her on the meal they had eaten, and Madame bridled like a blushing girl, pressing them to return in the evening when they served a more extensive menu. Matt looked quizzically at Sophie as they strolled away in the sunshine.

'She was asking if my father appreciated the food,' Sophie explained in a honeyed tone and Matt seized her upper arm in a grip which made her wince.

'I hope you said that your father was a very generous man to take you there,' he hissed, and she let her laughter bubble up at the sight of his irritation.

'Ouch, that hurts. Thank you, Daddy, I had a wonderful time.'

He released her arm and they began to walk down the street towards the walls of the old chateau. Sophie was wearing light, strappy sandals, and the combination of wine and the steep gradient of the street caused her to stumble and almost fall. Matt caught her by the hand.

'Whoa there! I don't think your shoes can cope with cobblestones, Sophie. You had better hold on to me.'

He grasped her hand more firmly, but Sophie hesitated, torn between the enjoyable warmth of his skin and the potential for embarrassment.

'Matt, I can't walk about with you hand in hand! You are Liz's husband – it feels all wrong. Please let me go,' she pleaded, and he raised an eyebrow, evidently surprised by this sudden access of prudishness on her part.

'Who do you think is going to see us? Would you prefer to get your knees skinned? Don't be so prissy, Sophie my dear.'

Prissy! Sophie flushed, feeling that she was receiving a scolding. She considered wresting back control of her hand but was fearful of making a scene in a public place. Before she could decide what to do, he laced his fingers through hers and strode off, tugging her in his wake. She felt like a child atoning for some unspecified sin. His wedding ring chafed against her skin and it served as a painful and timely reminder that this charismatic man belonged to someone else.

Chapter Six

They reached the bottom of the street in silence. Matt still held her firmly by the hand, and Sophie's attempts to release herself from his grasp were met by increased, almost painful pressure, so that she abandoned her attempts to escape. It began to feel degrading, as though she was being towed in his wake like an animal, and she returned the creaky smile of a passing crone who obviously thought they were a romantic couple with an agonised grimace.

'Matt, can we sit down? And I'd like my hand back, please.'

Before them was a bench shaded by an ancient, spreading chestnut tree. Matt hesitated, then pulled her down next to him on the seat. The wood felt rough beneath her thighs and she stifled a little cry of distress. He raised her hand, regarded it as if it were something alien and distasteful – for a moment, she almost feared he was going to bite it – and dropped it on to her lap. Sophie massaged her fingers, relieved to be free, although she was reluctant to meet his eyes. His usual friendly smile had been replaced by a face of stone which defied interpretation. 'Thanks,' she murmured, and he gave an impatient shrug.

'There's no need to behave as though I am abducting you, Sophie. I am very sorry if my concern for your welfare has offended you. I will let you manage on your own from now on.'

His voice was glacially polite, and Sophie felt as though ice had been dropped down her back. The world grew blurry before her eyes. Their lunch had been a delightful, intimate occasion, and now she had spoiled things.

'I just thought...'

She could hardly get the words out.

'You thought I was being a bit too friendly?'

His eyes were disappointed, and she was mortified by the looming cloud on his brow. 'Well, you are a delightful companion, and I have enjoyed spending time with you, but I am not the sort of man to paw at you as if you were some little pick-up. Give me some credit, won't you?'

The remaining weeks of her stay with the family stretched ahead with a miserably altered dynamic. It would be hellish if she and Matt got across one another as a result of an awkward misunderstanding. How could she explain a public coolness between them without invoking her own guilt? She wiped a tear away with the back of her hand; her self-esteem lay shattered in the dust at their feet. Matt noticed the tear and groaned.

'Oh, Sophie – please don't weep on me.'

He sighed and put his arm around her, and she tried to quell the desire to lean into his body. At that moment, he reminded her fatally of George, because there was something very reassuring about his broad shoulders. She needed the solace of an embrace very badly.

'I shouldn't have drunk so much wine…'

It was a pathetic attempt to justify herself and her voice squeaked, but at least it lightened the atmosphere and drew a reluctant laugh from her companion.

'Well, please don't accuse me of trying to get you tipsy,' he said, stretching his long legs and stifling a little yawn. 'Look, Sophie, let's forget about this silly misunderstanding, shall we? I was only looking out for you. Wear more sensible shoes in future. Friends?'

Matt tilted her chin towards him, and she was consoled by the renewed warmth of his gaze.

'Friends,' she murmured, summoning a wavering smile. He hesitated, then imprinted a gentle kiss on her cheek. It was the kind of kiss a father gives a doubting child, and she felt a tiny flutter of disappointment.

'Good. Let's look for a taxi now we've cleared the air,' Matt said, rising to his feet. 'I need to chase up some stuff from this morning. But we will remember this place for the future. I know Liz would like it.'

Things always came back to Liz, but Sophie accepted this humbly, conscious of her lowly position in the pecking order. In the taxi, she concentrated on gazing at the not very interesting countryside, only speaking when Matt ventured a remark. The driver wasn't inclined to conversation, and most of the ride was passed in a silence which couldn't quite conceal faint vestiges of embarrassment.

When they reached the house, Sophie was glad of the quiet and stillness which meant that the other family members had not returned from their trip. She began to climb the stairs, suddenly desperate to shed her seductive dress in favour of her usual casual attire but stopped abruptly when a thought struck her. Matt looked up from the hall and his eyes narrowed.

'Now what?'

This time, she was aware of vexation grating in his voice.

'Will you tell Liz that we went out for lunch?'

'Yes. Why wouldn't I? Try to be an adult, Sophie; your aggrieved little girl act is becoming tedious.'

He stalked off to the kitchen and Sophie hurried to her room. She slipped off the dress, letting it lie in a heap on the floor as though it had contributed to her disgrace, and flung herself on the bed. Seagulls screamed in sympathy outside the window, sounding as if they were mourning a loss. But what had she lost? Trust in her own judgement had been shattered for a start, and she was afraid that Matt might now temper any friendly feelings he had harboured towards her.

Sophie heartily regretted the outing. She reached for her laptop because it was becoming a habit to fire off emails to George whenever she experienced situations where she wasn't comfortable, but this time, she didn't get further than typing in his name. He had been slow to respond to her recent communications, and his replies were more perfunctory and less analytical. His new life had taken him away from her and there was nothing she could do about it. And if she so much as hinted to her parents that she was having problems, they would urge a prompt return home. She wasn't ready to give up on her job here, despite the morning's misunderstandings.

Sophie stretched on her bed. The scudding patterns of light from the windows lulled her into a fitful doze before she awoke to the beep which signalled an incoming text. She scrabbled sleepily to find her phone. The message was from Sean, who had demanded to be given her number 'in case of emergencies'.

'On way home TG. Had a good day, dorbs? CU soon. XX.'

She had to look up the abbreviation 'dorbs' – apparently it meant adorable – but she was pleased Sean had alerted her to their imminent return. She doused her face with cold water in the bathroom and felt better for doing so. Then she went downstairs prepared to meet Matt with renewed courage, and if necessary, another attempt at an apology.

But he wasn't in the kitchen. Perhaps he was also sleeping off the effects of the eventful lunch.

Sophie made herself a cup of tea and began to think about supper for the family. Liz would be tired, and the little ones would not want the bother of eating out for a second time in the day. She set to work, and the task of making a bolognese sauce turned out to be an ideal way to allay her sense of mortification, so that her thoughts settled and became bearable. However, the bread left over from breakfast had hardened into a rock-like lump, so she decided to make a visit to the patisserie. She almost bumped into Matt as she was leaving the kitchen and was chastened all over again to see the rueful wariness in his face.

'I'm off to buy bread.'

Sophie sounded breathless with nerves as she reached for her bag. 'Do you want anything else while I'm out?'

'A big tarte aux pommes would be nice. I'm very partial to the ones at the bakery. Is there anything I can help with here?'

Matt spoke mildly as if making an extra effort to be conciliatory, and she responded in kind, feeling generous with relief.

'I don't think so, but thanks for the offer. Sean says they are on the way home, and that they've had a good time,' she said.

'Mm. I'm pleased you are cooking tonight, because the tinies will be tired, I expect. Off you go then, and don't forget the tarte.'

It was pleasant to stroll to the patisserie under the gentle warmth of the declining sun and with the feeling that perhaps things weren't as bad as she had feared. Sophie made her purchases and was setting off home when a familiar people carrier came to a sudden halt in the street and a lithe figure jumped out to accost her.

'Soph! I'll walk back with you. I need some human company.'

Sean's face split in a delighted grin as he relieved her of the baguettes, and Sophie felt unexpectedly glad to see him, as if he was an old and trusted friend.

'How was your day?' she enquired. His grin was smothered by a dismal grimace.

'I did my duty. The Randall kids are appalling, but at least Charlie didn't try to strangle Boo this time. It's a bloody long walk up to the abbey at Mont St Michel with the gawping crowds. You didn't miss much.'

Sophie remembered his text and decided that a little rap on the knuckles was required.

'*Dorbs*?' she queried, trying to sound disapproving, but he sent her a sweet, sideways glance and they both laughed.

'Well, you are. You should see the Randall's nanny: she slays at twenty paces. I showed Roddy a picture of you and he was well jeal.'

'A picture? Since when have had you a picture of me?'

Sean assumed a blank expression which didn't fool her for an instant.

'Er – I've taken the odd shot on the beach. Nothing revealing, you needn't worry. But I must have something to remind me of you when I'm stuck in school again.'

'Oh, *Sean...*'

But in a way, she was flattered by this admission. Despite his youthful follies and his habit of surprising her like a bouncing puppy, they had reached an affectionate truce and his company was increasingly important to her. It was the yeast which leavened the bread of life with the Spenser-Braybrooke clan and all its complexities. They walked on and he suggested a detour.

'Let's go back via the seafront and watch the tide coming in.'

Sophie accompanied him down the alley to the esplanade, their footsteps ringing on the old stones. He pounced on a vacant seat and they sat for a while to watch the waves devouring the warm sand. 'What did you and Matt get up to while we were gone?' he asked.

'Matt worked this morning and I went for a walk. We had lunch in Dinan later,' she replied, making it sound nothing special, but Sean pricked up his ears.

'Did you now? Was it somewhere nice?'

'Yes. Very nice.'

She stared at the breaking surf, keeping her voice flat in the hopes that he wouldn't ask too many questions. Sean's hand stole out to grasp her fingers, and she wondered why he was so keen to pursue the subject.

'Don't get a thing about Matt, will you Soph? I know he's an attractive bastard, but you'd be wasting your time. Also, I don't want my family falling apart again: once was quite enough. Mum's happy with him and I don't want that to change.'

'Sean, I don't have a thing for Matt, as you put it. And he certainly isn't interested in me.'

There was no way she could reveal the events of the day to the boy. 'I think he regards me as a kind of grown-up daughter, and I hope your mother feels the same way,' she said, with an attempt at heartiness.

Sean's hand was nothing like the muscular one belonging to his stepfather. It was slim and cool, and he frowned as he sat there, separating her fingers and stroking them with a gentle, tickling touch. Sophie knew he was deriving comfort from the contact and so she allowed him to continue for a minute longer before she withdrew her hand. He patted her on the knee.

'But you aren't part of my family. Just as well – isn't incest a crime?'

Sean sniggered with adolescent irreverence, and Sophie jumped to her feet.

'Can we talk about something more interesting? Anyway, we should be getting back now, because I'm sure Poppy and Boo want their supper.'

'Me too. If I see another plate of moules frites, I am going to throw up. I hope you have planned something nice and ordinary. Bacon and eggs would go down a treat... can you get brown sauce in France, d'you think?'

Poppy and Boo were so pleased to see her that she almost forgot about the disturbing exchange with their father. There was something soothing about their childish prattle, and even Abigail was in a good mood because Roderick Randall had sat next to her at lunch and chatted her up. ('No, he didn't; he was stuck in a corner and couldn't move,' her brother argued, but his mother shushed him into silence.) Sophie found that she was able to sit at the dinner table as though nothing untoward had occurred, and at last, she allowed herself to relax. There was only one tense moment, when Liz asked her husband how he had passed the time while she was away.

'Did it take you all day to get your ducks in a row?' she asked, displaying the smallest hint of contempt in her tone, and Matt responded with a face of smooth restraint.

'No. I had everything clear by lunchtime, so Sophie and I took ourselves into Dinan for a meal,' he said. 'Our taxi driver found us a

58

great place away from the tourist traps – I will take you there one night, darling, if Sophie will book us a table.'

'It was a real find,' Sophie broke in, before Liz could reply. 'But they serve a very limited menu at lunchtimes. I think you'd find the evening menu would be amazing. Madame said they pride themselves on being the best restaurant in the town.'

She realised that she was gabbling: would this alert Liz to the fact that the lunch might not have been as innocent as it appeared? Boo distracted her mother by knocking over a glass of water, and Sophie was relieved to jump to her feet in search of a cloth. She thought that a sceptical light had gleamed in Liz's eye as she listened to the details of their outing, although she couldn't be sure.

'Well, I am glad that you didn't have to spend the whole day slaving inside, Matthew. How fortunate that you found yourself so well catered for – I'm afraid the rest of us had to be content with more basic cuisine.'

Liz was goading now, but Matt wisely chose to ignore the challenge. He turned to his daughters and asked whether they wanted to play in their tent before bedtime, and Sophie began to clear the plates. Liz mused over her wine glass, and Sean and Abigail lightened the atmosphere with an exchange of lively views regarding the shortcomings of the Randall children. It was unusual to find them in harmony, and Sophie smiled as she listened to their unsparing adolescent criticisms. She ran hot water to wash the saucepans and was astounded when Abbie came to dry them. It quickly became apparent that she had an ulterior motive.

'Sophie, will you take me to the mall tomorrow?' she asked. 'I'd like to get my hair cut and I need you to translate for me. Matt can take care of the teenies, seeing as how he got out of coming today.'

Liz looked up as her daughter spoke but didn't intervene, although her face showed a wry sympathy with the sentiment.

'Yes, provided that's okay with everyone else.'

Sophie peeled off her rubber gloves and checked that the bin didn't need to be emptied. A young Romanian woman came to the house on alternate days to clean and do the laundry, but Sophie accepted that many of the basic household tasks always fell to her. She didn't really mind, because she was being paid to help, and she could often use the opportunity to retreat into her own thoughts. She was amused that despite Liz's vaunted cordon bleu qualifications, her employer showed a marked reluctance to take control in the kitchen and appeared to be satisfied with Sophie's very basic cooking skills.

Everyone went to bed early that night. Sophie listened to the waves slapping against the rocks below the house as she lay in bed with her Kindle, finding that she was reading and re-reading the same sentence as memories of the day intruded into her consciousness. It seemed that her hand still burned from the intensity of Matt's grip and Sean's gentler caresses had done little to relieve the sensation of injury. She felt as though she had exposed herself to ridicule by her behaviour in Dinan. Thank God she was going out with Abbie the next day, so she could begin the process of putting distance between herself and the embarrassing episode.

Chapter Seven

Sophie tried in vain to convince Abigail that it was pointless to set off for the mall until mid-morning, because she knew the hair salons would not open at an early hour. However, Abbie fussed and complained until Sophie was forced to give in to her whining. Of course, they arrived to find only the hypermarket and some smaller stores ready for business. Abbie lamented loudly – 'honestly; how do they expect to make a living if they won't open proper hours?' – and they retreated to a nearby café to wait until there was a sign of activity in the salon that Abbie wished to patronise.

'Mum was cross with Matt yesterday, although she didn't say much.'

Abigail leant across the table, her face aglow with indiscretion, and Sophie forced a brief smile in response.

'Well, he was definitely working all morning. I believe he managed to sort things out more quickly than he expected,' she replied, wondering why she felt obliged to come to Matt's defence. Abbie dipped a sugar lump in her coffee and sucked it.

'Good for you for making him take you out to lunch. Do you think he fancies you? Sean says he probably does,' she said, looking as though she hoped to harvest some incendiary details.

'Sean spouts a lot of nonsense. Matt seems perfectly happy with your mother, not to mention Boo and Poppy, so I think that theory won't stand up,' Sophie replied, wanting to shut the girl down.

'Sean says that he liked the look of one of our nannies a few years back, and that's why our Aussie girl Ellie is such a dog. Mum feels safer if Matt's not surrounded by attractive women.'

'I can't comment on that, Abbie, but I think you are being unfair to everyone, not least poor Ellie.'

Some memories of her interview with Liz floated back to Sophie as she drank her coffee with studied unconcern, but she finally detected movement in the hair salon which came as a relief. A stylist was available and after some discussion as to what was required, Abbie was gowned and led off to a back basin.

'Don't leave me, Sophie,' was the wavering cry, and Sophie laughed. It would serve the girl right if she abandoned her to the hairdresser, but she couldn't quite bring herself to do that. She settled down with *Paris Match* until Abbie had been shampooed and her translation skills were required again.

Abbie had very long, slightly raggy locks like almost all girls of her age, and the stylist suggested that taking six or eight inches off would improve the condition of the hair and enable her to wear it as a long bob; a style which was newly in fashion. At first, Abbie was adamant that she only wanted a trim, but when a junior with a similar haircut was produced as an example, she capitulated, although her face was aghast as she watched the chunks of hair falling around her. Sophie was limp with relief to see Abbie's smile grow from a twitch of the lips to a full-on beam as the blow drying progressed. She didn't want to be accused of forcing the new style upon Abbie, and she knew the girl well enough to understand that the blame would be laid at her door if it wasn't successful.

'It looks like someone else's hair,' Abbie whispered, reaching up to run a strand through her fingers. 'This guy is amazing, Sophie. Why don't you get your hair cut too?'

'Another day, perhaps.'

Sophie had seen the prices; besides, she had been for a trim before she left for France and was fortunate in possessing thick, glossy hair which only required the minimum of help to look good. The stylist added some finishing touches with a hot brush and a very different Abbie arose from the chair, flicking her hair around like a happy animal.

'I can't wait to show Mum! Sophie, can we go and buy a hot brush now, because I will need one to do this myself at home. Will you tell the man that it's really great and I love it?'

Sophie produced the magic credit card and tipped the stylist well. Then they visited the hypermarket to buy the hot brush and some groceries, and Abbie almost bounced around the aisles, feeling confident and happy with her new look. And when they reached the house, Abbie dashed up the steps with the light bounds of a gazelle, eager to show the family the result of her morning's expedition.

Sophie quietly stowed away the shopping as everyone gathered to pronounce their verdicts on Abbie's haircut. Liz exclaimed in delight to see a happy daughter for a change, and even Sean made the grudging admission that his sister looked less of a mess than usual. Matt and the little girls clapped their hands in noisy approval, and Sophie found it hard to persuade them that the stylist was the person who deserved credit, and not herself.

'Are you tempted to have the chop as well, Sophie?' Liz enquired, stroking Abbie's hair as if to persuade herself that it wasn't a wig. She seemed to be almost emotional about her daughter's transformation – it was the first time that Sophie had seen any real demonstration of intimacy between the two, and she found that sad. But before Sophie could answer, Matt butted in.

'No, we don't want to lose our Princess Isabelle and her lovely locks, do we, girls? We like Sophie just the way she is.'

The little girls yelped in agreement and Matt employed his most guileless countenance as he nodded towards the Princess, but Sophie saw the pursed lips which indicated his wife didn't appreciate this statement of allegiance. Liz switched her attention from Abigail and began to chide her younger daughters for some misdemeanour, and Sophie felt she was included in an implied rebuke. But she had learned by now to ignore Liz's mood swings because anyone attempting a counter argument risked being flattened by the heavy weight of Liz's opinion; the conversation squashed as if by a steamroller. Sophie wisely concentrated on her kitchen duties and by the time she had cooked the pizza for lunch, Matt's unwary comment was forgotten, and the atmosphere was amicable once again.

Sophie was taken aback by unexpected overtures of friendship from Abigail following the success of the haircutting expedition. She shadowed Sophie faithfully over the following week when Sophie was busy with the little girls; pressing Sophie for advice on anything from boyfriends to periods, with the result that Sean often found himself relegated to the position of looker-on. Sophie was amused to see his handsome face grow sour with frustration when he came across the two girls indulging in what he referred to in disparaging tones as 'chick chat'.

'Why didn't you come to the café with me and Abbie this morning? You told me you wanted to understand how girls operate – now's your chance,' Sophie teased him, entertained by the scowl of revulsion which her words aroused. They were standing ankle deep in the surf while the younger girls played in the waves with a large inflatable duck. He chucked a pebble out to sea, looking as though he wished it were something heavier.

'I don't count Abbie as a girl, although she is more human with that haircut. You're always too busy to talk now, Soph, it's not fair. Come for a walk along the beach with me.'

'I'm watching Boo and Poppy, Sean. I can't leave them in the water unsupervised.'

A shadow fell across them as Matthew Braybrooke appeared at the water's edge. He had stripped down to his swimming shorts, and stood there, flexing his muscles and exhibiting a torso which admittedly was very fit. Sophie suspected that Matt managed to spend a fair proportion of his time in the gym when he was at home, and he liked to display the results. She hadn't seen much of him recently, because he and Liz had taken themselves off to do some touristy things without the children in tow.

'Aren't you swimming, Sophie?' he enquired.

Matt's eyes cruised slowly over her body. She felt he was challenging her to find fault with his behaviour and she sensed Sean's disapproval of this overt examination. The boy moved closer to her, as if shielding her from his stepfather's familiarity, and Sophie shook her head.

'It's a bit cold for me, Matt. I'd go in after the girls if they needed me, but I'm happy to stay dry.'

Poppy caught sight of her father and shrieked a welcome. Matt laughed and plunged to join his daughters in the rolling waves, tossing them in the air and pretending to duck them when a big breaker caught them unprepared. Sophie couldn't help smiling at this exhibition of family fun, but Sean didn't seem to be impressed.

'Old Matt pervs after you, Soph. I don't suppose he'd do anything – he's far too scared of Mum, but I wish he wouldn't look at you like that. You don't encourage him, do you?'

'What do you think? Don't you look at me in a pervy way at times as well? Men do it without thinking, and girls get used to it.'

Sophie spoke with a smile, although she knew that Sean was right. Matt hadn't initiated any close conversation or contact with her since their momentous lunch, but she was often conscious of the weight of his gaze and a sense of unfinished business in his demeanour towards her. It was a little unnerving, but her response was to behave with a collected calm and concentrate on his daughters. She wouldn't allow herself to entertain the suspicion that Matt might like her more than he should, because she was afraid of admitting that she felt attracted to him in return.

'That's not fair, Sophie. I'm available, and it's okay for me to lust after you. You're a hard-hearted hussy not to take pity on me.'

He broke off abruptly as his mother approached. Liz made very infrequent visits to the beach and Sophie wondered at her presence, although it might be that she simply wanted to watch her husband and children at play for a change. Sean surveyed his mother with open mouth, evidently sharing Sophie's surprise at seeing her.

'Are you going in too, Mum?' he asked, although Liz wasn't dressed for swimming, and she gave a decisive shake of her head. Her eyes were sparkling, and she seemed even more animated than usual.

'I've had some exciting news,' she announced. 'Anna de Vos wants to interview me for a feature in the *Sunday Times* and she and a photographer are coming here in a few days to shoot the pictures and speak to us. It's great timing, because we have a new initiative about to take off at the office and to get any publicity in the silly season is good. I'll have to make sure that Matt's start-up has a mention, too.'

'What? You have to be joking!'

Sophie jumped as Sean snarled at his mother, turning from a cool adolescent to a freaked-out child before her eyes. Liz tensed in alarm, evidently at a loss to understand this violent reaction, and she reached out a hand to her son, which he rejected with a furious gesture of annoyance.

'What do you mean, Sean? There's nothing to be concerned about. The article will feature my business, and I will make sure that nothing personal appears about our family. Anna is someone who owes me a few favours, and this is an opportunity for her to pay me back.'

'I can't believe you'd do this. You know how I feel about journalists.'

'Don't be so melodramatic, Sean. Matt will tell you it's a good move.'

Liz shaded her eyes, beckoning to her husband and daughters, who waved back and continued with their play. She tutted impatiently, wanting Matt to know about this latest development, but he showed no sign of leaving the water and Liz's patience evaporated like so much sea spray.

'Sophie, will you go in and tell Matt that I have to speak to him now, please? He doesn't seem to understand that I want him to come out,' she said.

Sophie gulped as she looked at the breaking waves. The tide was turning, and the surf had suddenly grown heavier, leaving the sea churning in a mass of unfriendly white foam. Sean noticed her hesitation.

'I'll go, Mum. It's getting rough anyway, and I think the girls ought to come back to the shallows.'

Even as he spoke, a large wave crashed around the bathers and Matt floundered as a screaming Boo was swept from his grasp. Sean and Sophie fought their way through the surf, reaching the tumbling body at the same time, while Matt carried Poppy back to the safety of the beach. Boo coughed up a mouthful of sea water and began to bawl and Sophie was knocked under by the next breaker as she tried to help the child. Her bikini top, never very robust, was loosened by the force of the waves, and Sean was confronted by an unexpected revelation of her breasts as he turned to pull her up. An embarrassed Sophie surfaced, clutching at her chest, until they saw the funny side and began to laugh. By now, Matt had waded back in to take Boo from her brother and he couldn't help observing that a wardrobe malfunction had occurred.

'You make a fantastic mermaid, Sophie,' he told her, his eyes crinkling in an appreciative laugh. 'How fortunate that Sean was here to help you.'

'I went right under the water, and Sophie's top came off!'

This was the triumphant verdict of Boo now she was safely back on dry land. It was impossible to fasten the bikini top without risking further exposure, so Sophie clamped her arms around her chest and hurried up the beach to bury her shame in her towel, leaving the rest of the party in her wake. Abbie had slept peacefully in the sun throughout the whole adventure. As Sophie swished her wet hair around, drops of water fell on the somnolent girl and she sat up, giving a little scream.

'Ugh, Sophie, what are you doing? I was having a lovely dream…'

'Sorry, Abbie. The sea's very rough, and I got caught out by a wave. What a bore. I'll have to wash my hair again now.'

Sophie secured the towel under her armpits, feeling that everyone had seen enough of her body for the afternoon. She was expecting a barbed reprimand from her employer, but the incident was immediately forgotten in the whirlwind of planning for the journalist's arrival. Sophie was summoned to arrange appointments at the hair salon for Liz and Abbie and there was animated discussion amongst the females of the family as to whether they should dress smartly or be relaxed in holiday gear for the photographs. Sean was the only one who showed a marked disapproval for the event.

'Thank God I won't be back at school when the piece gets published,' he growled to Sophie, treating her to a thunderous scowl. 'I get a whole load of stick when there's stuff about Mum in the media. She doesn't realise what it's like for me and Ab.'

'Do you mean that other boys tease you because your mother is so successful?'

Sophie was interested in this aspect, which would never have occurred to her. Sean nodded slowly, flinching at what seemed to be a painful memory.

'Something like that. It's a lot to live up to. And when my father left, some bitch of a journo wrote a catty article about the split which totally assassinated Mum and dumped the blame on her. I found it online when I was about thirteen, and I've had it in for the press ever since. I'll be in the family photo if I have to, but only if it's what Mum wants.'

'I suppose that your mother thinks that this is important publicity for Lenister Legrand.'

'I can't think why else she'd go for it. She's twitchy about exposing anything personal to the press now, and I can't blame her. That's why Ab and I have been told we can't have social media accounts until we're eighteen; Mum doesn't trust the way these things work.'

Sophie didn't know how to console Sean. Her own experience of the media was negligible, although she knew that Anna de Vos was an investigative journalist who usually went after big fish. Maybe Sean was right to be concerned. She wished that she felt able to ask Matt for his views, but she didn't feel comfortable enough around him now to initiate such a direct conversation.

The journalist and her photographer arrived after lunch on the appointed day, arriving with an air of royalty in a flashy convertible car laden with equipment. Sophie was introduced almost as an afterthought, but she didn't care. It was interesting for her to observe the proceedings, but she had no wish to be involved, thinking that she might be better employed keeping Sean occupied to help him deal with his unhappiness about the situation.

'My God, Liz, this house is a joke! I didn't expect to find you, of all people, spending your precious holiday in the House of Usher. Do you have a resident ghost?'

The journalist's voice was loud and sarky, and Sophie saw Sean send a vitriolic glance in her direction before Liz intervened with a laughing account of how the family came to be in residence. A cork popped in the kitchen as Matt opened champagne and a breeze of anticipation swirled through the shabby rooms along with the bubbles as Liz and Matt welcomed these important visitors.

Sophie was tempted to hang around the edges of the interview because she had never been in a situation like this before. Anna de Vos was forty-ish; determinedly blonde and buxom but possessing the sharp eyes of a hawk selecting its prey. She was attractive until she opened her mouth. This seemed to contain too many teeth, or perhaps the teeth were too large, and her lips took on a hamsterish pout in repose. Sophie was surprised by Anna's appearance, but Sean pointed out that the glamorous photos which accompanied her by-line in the press had been carefully photoshopped to give the most flattering image.

Anna exclaimed in a friendly way when introduced to the children, but Sophie was given instructions to make sure that they stayed well away from the drawing room, where the formal part of the interview was underway. This only involved Anna, Liz and Matt – even the photographer, Paul, was sent packing at this point. He was a thin man with a nervous, seamed face, and Sean's truculence dissipated as he asked to examine his cameras and heard something of Paul's experiences when covering the stars at the summer music festivals.

'Glasto was a right mess this year. Can't get enough commercial material when the weather's bad, because everyone looks the same when they're covered with mud,' Paul informed the boy, who was listening with interest to his tales of backstage life. 'Give me a nice catwalk any day. This job ain't so bad, and at least it's not pissing down. Think I might pose you in the garden, because the sea makes a nice backdrop and the light's okay at the far end away from the trees.'

He peered closely at Sean, observing his elegant features and eloquent eyes. 'You've got fantastic bone structure. Ever done any modelling?'

Sean flushed, shaking his head in emphatic rejection of the suggestion.

'Shit, no way would I want to do that. It's bad enough having Mum in the limelight, and I keep well out of it.'

'Shame.'

The man continued to stare at Sean, with the professional, calculating gaze of someone used to seeing beneath the skin of his subjects, but he didn't pursue the suggestion. Sophie's attention was claimed by the girls, who were getting tired of waiting around in their party dresses, and she was hard put to keep them amused in the garden. Abbie had withdrawn into her old uncommunicative self for some reason and had retired to her room to take a nap.

At last, the kitchen doors opened, and Sophie concluded that the formal part of the interview was at an end. Liz sent to her to wake Abbie, and the photographer began to position the family group for the required shots. Sophie had to shake Abbie before she came to and it was evident from her wild hair that the girl had been rolling around as she slept.

'Oh dear, Abbie. Quick, let me plug in your hot brush, and we'll sort your hair out again.'

Sophie switched to practical mode while Abbie swung her legs over the side of the bed. She looked mardy and hostile, as if she actively resented Sophie's efforts to help.

'What's up?' Sophie enquired, wielding the brush and frowning as she tried to coax the hair into place again. Abbie shrugged; the difficult teen was back.

'It does my head in when we're all photographed together. Everyone always says, 'oh, isn't your brother hot', and I feel like an elephant. I hate Sean. It's not fair.'

Sophie swirled Abbie's hair round the brush, wondering what to say to her. It wasn't fair, but very few people were fortunate enough to possess Sean's unusual good looks. She didn't want to spout clichés about inner beauty, because frankly, Abbie didn't show any signs of having a wonderful nature, and she was sufficiently intelligent to recognise when she was being indulged. Sophie brushed the last locks and stood back to survey her work.

'There – you'll do nicely. Abbie, all I can say is that in a few years, you'll be living away from home and Sean's looks won't matter to you. Go downstairs now and give them a big smile. You've got fantastic teeth.'

This was true – Abbie's mouth had benefited from years of expensive dental attention. Abbie looked up at Sophie, but not with any hint of a smile or a thank you.

'Oh, it's all very well for you. You swish about the house with your sexy body and great hair... don't think I haven't noticed Sean drooling in buckets. Matt can't keep his eyes off you, either. How can you have any idea what it's like to be me?'

Her voice went up in a petulant whine, and Sophie had to restrain the urge to shake her.

'What do you think it's like being me, Abbie? I am having to spend my summer holiday working, because my family aren't rich, and I need money to see me through my life at college. I dare say this is a cushy job compared to what many of my friends are doing, but it's still a job. I think you need to count your blessings. Things will improve as you get older, and you could help yourself by adopting a more positive attitude, you know.'

Abbie looked as though she had bitten into something sour. She flounced from the room, leaving Sophie to wonder whether their recent friendship was now on the rocks. Sophie couldn't blame herself if that was the case, but she wished that the journalist had chosen some other occasion to disrupt the fragile family harmony.

Chapter Eight

Anna and Paul left for their hotel at six, leaving an unsettled household in their wake. Liz and Matt decided to accept their invitation to dinner in Saint-Malo to tie up some loose ends after the afternoon's interview, and Sophie obtained permission to take the children to McDonalds for their supper. This was considered a great treat and a real indulgence because Liz frowned upon fast food, and Sophie could only suppose that the interview had pleased her enough to put her in a generous mood. The Braybrookes stepped into their taxi looking the epitome of a power couple, but Sophie and the others enjoyed their laid-back meal, especially the younger girls, who approached their burger and fries with the reverence that gourmets show towards a special banquet.

'You'll never get Boo into bed after all that sugar,' observed Sean, watching as the child greedily slurped on a chocolate milkshake. Her hands and face were sticky with ketchup, and she wore a grin as wide as a clown after the unexpected outing to a destination which was usually out of bounds.

'I don't mind if she's late tonight. It's been a funny sort of day,' replied Sophie, smiling at the happy little girl.

Abbie looked up from her mobile as Sophie spoke. She had skirted round Sophie with a truculent face after her earlier outburst and offered no apology, but her bad mood was less pronounced now the photos were out of the way.

'I've been texting with Ellie,' she informed her brother. She'll be waiting for us in England when we get home. It'll be great to have her back again.'

She darted a snarky glance at Sophie, but her brother's shoulders sagged, and he shook his head.

'Not sure I'm with you there, Ab. How much longer will you be staying with us, Sophie?'

'Another two weeks, I think. Your mother mentioned a six-week stay, but I haven't booked my return ferry yet.'

'I'll be glad to leave France, but I wish you could be with us in England.'

Sean whispered this into Sophie's ear as Abbie went to the counter to fetch more napkins. His breath felt hot against her skin, and she resisted the impulse to pat his hand,

'You will forget about me soon enough when you are back home,' she said, almost feeling sorry at the prospect. 'And you only have one more year to go, then you will be off to uni, taking your pick of the babes. I hope they teach you about safe sex and consent at your school – you'd be surprised how many girls I know have had a bad time.'

She stopped abruptly as Poppy pricked up little ears.

'What do you mean by a bad time, Sophie?' she asked, her eyes huge over the top of her drink, and Sophie was obliged to invent a fabrication to distract her from the dangerous turn of the conversation. She shepherded her charges home shortly afterwards, because the little ones were drooping, despite the sugar rush. Boo and Poppy flopped into bed and were instantly asleep after their fragmented day, and Abbie secluded herself in her room at the same time. Sophie and Sean sat in the dusky garden in the soft evening light and fought a losing battle with the ever-hungry mosquitos. The air was scented, and the receding sea was still and calm, singing a lullaby instead of its habitual robust concerto. She was conscious of Sean's eyes glowing in the twilight with a feverish brightness.

'We could go to your room and do it now and no-one would ever know…'

'You don't give up, do you, Sean?'

'No. I want you so badly, Soph.'

'Don't, Sean. You know the rules by now.'

'Is it because I'm too young? Would you do it if Matt asked you?'

'I don't spend all my time wondering who I would *do it* with. I'm enjoying just being here, and you would feel better if you tried to think about something else.'

'I can't. Haven't you ever seen French or Italian films about teenagers in love? I'm burning up and if you knew how uncomfortable I was, you'd want to help me.'

'I call that blackmail.'

'Oh, *Sophie!*'

They lapsed into affectionate silence. Now that her return to England was growing closer, Sophie realised with something akin to shock that she would miss the children, even Abbie with her moods

72

and sulks. She would not be sorry to escape the clinical, dissecting gaze of her employer, but Matt had been a pleasant and supportive companion, despite their misunderstanding in Dinan. She accepted that she had come to find his presence unsettling. He bore no physical resemblance to his stepson, but both possessed a magnetism which left her intrigued. If Sean had been older, she knew that she would have found it almost impossible to resist his request, and if Matt wasn't married... she chided herself that it was time to return to her usual haunts, away from this fascinating pair.

'Will you come and see us when we're back home, Sophie?' Sean asked, and his voice held a forlorn appeal.

'If I'm asked by your mother, I will,' she said. 'I don't know where you live in London, and you'll be at school again in September so you might not see me even if I did come.'

'I'm sure you can find your way to Hampstead. You'd like our house; it's been in lots of property features. Mum's got a good eye for up-and-coming artists, and part of downstairs is like a mini gallery.'

'Is there anything your mother can't do?'

'I'm not sure she always gets what she really wants.'

This remark came out in a whisper. Sophie glanced at Sean, but his face was shrouded in shadow and she wasn't certain that she wanted to prolong the discussion. They sat in silence for some minutes as the sky darkened around them. Sophie was tired, and she didn't want the weight of other people's problems oppressing her – it would soon be time for her to detach herself and leave the Spenser-Braybrookes to get on with their normal existence. In some ways, she couldn't wait to go, but she was also conscious that there would be a gap in her own life for a while.

'I think I'll turn in now.'

She yawned, getting up, and a light shone out from the kitchen behind. 'Looks like your mother's back. It's just as well we're not *doing it* upstairs.'

The only answer was a frustrated groan. Someone peered out, and Matt sauntered slowly down the path towards them. 'I was just going up to bed,' Sophie informed him, and he inclined his head in a courteous gesture.

'Did my girls enjoy their trip to the forbidden territory of McDonalds?' he enquired, smiling, and Sophie assured him that a very good time was had by all.

'Where did you dine in Saint-Malo?' she asked, thinking that it was polite to show interest in his evening.

'Somewhere Anna was raving about, although it wasn't a patch on the restaurant in Dinan. Anna de Vos is a gigantic pain,' he added with feeling, and his stepson laughed.

'Well, she had better be a gigantic pain who is going to be good for Mum's business. I hope they are going back to the UK tomorrow. Please don't tell me that we have to put up with them for another day.'

Sean's voice tailed off on a plaintive note. The three remained, wrapped in a dreamy kind of inertia in the night garden until Sophie roused herself and bade the two men goodnight. Matt settled himself in the chair she had vacated, and she hoped he would be able to provide Sean with the reassurance that the family would be spared intrusive publicity after the interview. It was a huge point in Matt's favour that he treated his stepchildren with kindness and appeared to be as caring with them as he was with his own girls.

Sophie found herself running errands on her own the next morning. Sean and Abbie were sleeping in as befitted their teenage years and the little girls clamoured to play mini golf with their parents at the other end of the beach. It was rare for Sophie to be given time to herself, and she drove to the big hypermarket feeling pleasantly vague and relaxed, and looking forward to choosing the food she liked to eat for a change.

As she was loading the people carrier with her shopping afterwards, a voice hailed her, and she turned in surprise. Anna de Vos and Paul the photographer were stashing booze into the spare crevices of their car boot, and the woman had evidently recognised her from the day before.

'Hi there – what was your name again? Oh yes, Sophie. You are working for Liz and Matt, aren't you?'

Anna was dressed down in jeans and a tight top, but Sophie remembered the alligator intensity of her stare very well. She stood transfixed as Anna sauntered across to her over the tarmac. 'This is a piece of luck. Will you come for a drink with Paul and me? I never got a chance to speak to you yesterday.'

74

She noticed Sophie's hesitation, and turned on the charm. 'Look, it's nothing sinister, but I like to make sure I cover all the angles. I just want to understand what it's like to come into such a dynamic family.'

'I'm not part of the family.'

Sophie didn't want to go. She distrusted the journalist and was fearful of saying something which might land her in trouble, but Anna continued to press her, and in the end, it seemed simpler and less suspicious to agree to her invitation. Sophie followed their car to a small bar down by the estuary and they sat round a table in the shade of a willow tree. She refused alcohol, although her companions fulfilled her expectations of journalistic life by ordering pastis, despite the relatively early hour.

Anna de Vos was sweet and friendly, playing down the hint of menace that Sophie had sensed before.

'How did you come to get the job?' she asked. 'I understand that Liz's regular help is away.'

Sophie was able to give a truthful account of the circumstances leading up to her employment with the family, but Anna seemed disappointed to hear that it was so uncomplicated. She leaned forward, and cunning crept into her eyes again. 'How have you found them? It can't always be easy working for such a human dynamo. And Matthew Braybrooke ... might he be the teeniest bit handsy? There has been talk...'

Sophie almost expected to see saliva dripping from the crimson lips, such was Anna's hunger for salacious tit bits. She shuddered slightly and gave a vehement shake of her head.

'I thought that you owed Liz a few favours,' she muttered, and the journalist brayed with laughter.

'Oh, my dear! It's dog eat dog in our world, you know. That's the trouble with students; you have no idea about life outside academic circles. Don't ever believe that Liz Lenister would fight for your corner, because she's got where she is through sheer bloody single mindedness, and everyone else can go hang. I admire the woman, but I'd hate to work for her.'

She paused to light a cigarette. 'We owe it to our readers to give them as balanced a picture as we can, so if you did think of anything...' Anna delved into her handbag and produced a business card. 'This profile won't come out for a week or two, and you can ring me directly if you want. We have been known to pay for information if it's good enough.'

The hint hung heavily in the air between them. Paul, the photographer, gave Sophie an encouraging smile across the table.

'Tell us something about Sean. He's got exceptional looks, and I've told Anna she'd do well to run a feature about him aimed at our younger readers. Son of well-known entrepreneur, enigmatic teen idol… is he already on social media, do you know?' he asked, barely disguising the voracious curiosity in his voice.

'I don't think so. He dislikes the idea of personal publicity, and I'm quite sure that he would never agree to anything you could suggest.'

Sophie was relieved to be able to deflect his interest. She felt that Paul and Anna were like two sharks circling around weaker prey and she wanted to divert their attention away from her family favourite. 'What did you mean about talk regarding Matt?' she asked Anna, then wondered whether she should have let that subject alone.

'Oh, the usual stuff. Liz seems to go for the pretty boys, but I understand there were difficulties with the first husband, and of course, Matt Braybrooke is a lot younger than she is. It wouldn't be the first time a pairing like theirs ran into trouble.'

She sounded confident, but Sophie suspected that Anna lacked hard facts, and was fishing. Sophie opened her eyes wide and assumed a face of cheerful innocence.

'All I can say is that I've found him very helpful and charming and I'm not aware of anything like you are suggesting. I hope you aren't chasing after hares, Anna, because I'm sure you wouldn't want to be sued for defamation.'

Anna smoked in silence, apparently considering this remark. At length, she said,

'Of course, it's a classic sub-plot: the husband unzipping for the nanny. Look how many times celebrity women discover that there's been hanky-panky at home when they are out shooting films or running Footsie companies. And you are such a pretty girl, Sophie. I'm very surprised that Matt and Sean aren't battling it out for your favours.'

'That's ridiculous! And what makes you think I'd go along with that kind of behaviour in any case? I have a good working relationship with all the family. I'm afraid I don't have anything sensational to tell you.'

Sophie spoke boldly, hoping there was no incriminating colour in her face as she remembered Sean's constant pleas. It was so innocent really, but she could imagine how a writer without principles could twist and distort simple facts into lurid allegations. She was seized by a pressing desire to escape from this cesspit of journalistic conjecture and finished her coffee with a hasty gulp, burning her mouth in the process. 'It's been lovely to talk to you, Anna, and I can't wait to read your piece when it's published,' she said, with cool finality. 'Will you please excuse me? I need to get back to prepare lunch for the family. I hope you've enjoyed your trip.'

She was uncomfortably aware of Anna's sceptical gaze boring into her back as she hurried back to her car. Hopefully, she had acquitted herself well without giving anything about her hosts away, but the incident left an unpleasantly sour taste. She drove back to the house thinking hard, wondering what, if anything, she should say to Liz and Matt about the accidental encounter. Handsy indeed! If only they knew...

There was no one around when she entered the kitchen which was a disappointment, because she was burning to off-load her awkwardness about her predicament. At length, Matt and Liz appeared with the little girls, and in the excitement of hearing about the mini-golf and Poppy's unlikely hole-in-one, she was forced to put her own emotions on hold. But Poppy and Boo soon ran off to their tent outside leaving her alone with her employers, and her tongue was loosened in a dramatic waterfall of distress.

'Liz, I had an unfortunate experience this morning. Anna de Vos was in the car park at Super U and she insisted on taking me for a coffee. She was asking all sorts of horrible questions, and I think you ought to know.'

She paused, breathless, and watched with agitation as Liz's brow contracted and her tight mouth formed a thin line of vexation across her face.

'What sort of questions?' Liz demanded. It felt as though a blast of Arctic air invaded the room.

''Oh, whether I found it hard to work for you, and were there any personal problems in the family. She was obviously wanting to dig up something unsavoury, although I can't think why. I thought the two of you were friends.'

Sophie didn't find it easy to put her distress into words. She caught Matt's eye and was aware that his body stiffened and became very still. Matt had an inkling of the paths that the journalist wanted to explore, that was evident, and Liz's sharp eyes weren't about to allow her any wriggle room.

'Well, you must have given her some reason to question you! I don't suppose that Anna would waste her time on you otherwise. You were talking to the photographer all yesterday afternoon. Did you drop any hints then that you were privy to gossip?'

Liz's face was taut with accusation, and Sophie felt annoyance rising inside herself like bubbling magma.

'No, of course not! I don't know any gossip, as you put it, and even if I did, I wouldn't talk to someone in Anna's position. I know that you don't want the kids in the limelight, and don't you think I would always put the interests of your family first?'

'No, I don't know that you would. If Anna was offering cash for inside information, you might well be tempted to hint at some irregularities. Why should I believe you?'

'What I don't understand is why you agreed to let them take a photo with your children if keeping the family private is so important to you!'

Sophie was stung by the accusation that she might be up for trading secrets, and she couldn't prevent herself from striking back. She and Liz locked eyes, each furious, each shocked by the confrontation, and an uncomfortable, poisoned silence was relieved only by the entrance of Abbie, sluggish and yawning after her morning in bed. Liz indicated that she did not want to pursue the conversation in front of her daughter, but Sophie felt sure that Liz would want to quiz her again to make sure that she had refrained from giving the journalist what she wanted. It would be too much to hope for an apology for the unfounded accusations. Sophie was thoroughly unsettled, only managing to pick at her lunch, and it didn't help to have Sean absorbing the tension and staring at her with concern shadowed in his face as he ate.

When lunch was finished, Sean cornered her in the garden, demanding to know what had happened to cause the hostile

78

atmosphere in the kitchen. She gave him a faltering account which omitted the contentious details, but she couldn't conceal her agitation over Liz's reaction to the accidental meeting with Anna.

'It is a bit much, Sean. Your mother must have a low opinion of me if she believes I'd be prepared to barter tittle-tattle. Sometimes I think she sees everything in terms of a battle. She doesn't seem to trust anyone, and I don't think that's natural. On second thoughts, it's rather sad,' she said.

Sean glanced around to make they sure that they were unobserved and put both his arms around her. It was a sweet, tender gesture.

'Darling Soph, please don't beat yourself up. You didn't do anything wrong. If I know Mum, she'll come to realise that she over-reacted, and I expect that Matt is already telling her to calm down.'

He rubbed his cheek against hers, and she let him hold her close because she needed comfort. His heart was beating so hard that it seemed to be in rhythm with her own, and she felt relieved and thankful that she had one friend amongst the adults in the household. When he began to kiss her hair, she drew away from him, but very gently, not wanting him to feel that she was rejecting his affection.

'Oh, Sean… I mustn't get you involved in this mess. My skin isn't as thick as a Lenister one, that's the trouble. But I'm glad you can see my point of view, because it makes me feel better. As it is, I'm almost tempted to pack my bags and leave today.'

'Don't do that, or Mum will think that she's right. I'm here for you, Sophie.'

They drew apart as voices rang down the path. Matt and his daughters were en route for the beach, and Matt observed his stepson and Sophie with a keen eye, as though he suspected some private dealings between the pair. Sophie returned his stare with unusual defiance, because Matt hadn't come to her defence during the heated words before lunch and she wasn't inclined to forgive that lapse on his part. He paused, although the little girls trotted on towards the beach clutching their kites and intent on their pleasure.

'So, this is where you've got to… Sean, could you go on down to keep an eye on Poppy and Boo for a few minutes, please?' he asked. 'I think that Sophie deserves an apology and I'd like to talk to her about what happened this morning.'

It was obvious that Sean would rather stay and hear what his stepfather had to say, but after a swift glance at Sophie to check that she was happy for him to leave, Sean reluctantly disappeared down the path after his sisters. Matt waited until he was sure they were out of earshot before addressing himself to Sophie. He was smiling his mega-watt, confidence-boosting smile, although she knew that it didn't always mean what it seemed to indicate.

'I know that you are annoyed with Liz, Sophie, but I don't think you understand why she reacted so strongly this morning,' Matt began, speaking calmly, in the way one might address a fractious infant. This caused Sophie's hackles to bristle all over again, and Matt held up both hands, palms outwards, as he scanned her flushed face. 'Let me finish. I know that you wouldn't let us down,' he continued, and Sophie turned her head away, her tummy feeling as though someone was mixing cement inside. Matt's voice dropped to a persuasive murmur until she could barely hear him above the sound of the surf. 'You need to realise that Liz is very touchy about her life and the reputation of the company – after all, it's her baby that she's built up by years of hard work. It's okay for her to deal with people like Anna because she knows what she is up against, but she worries that others may not be equally canny.'

'Does Liz have something going on which she wouldn't want Anna to know about?' Sophie faltered, and Matt shook his head, although a shadow of hesitation was apparent in his eyes.

'There's nothing of that kind, but she hasn't always been treated fairly by the media and she's been badly hurt in the past. It comes with the territory I'm afraid, but even Liz has her weak spots.'

'I find that hard to believe.'

'Oh, it's true enough. Not that she would ever admit to it.'

Sophie suddenly felt exhausted by the whole silly business.

'I just feel that there's been a nuclear explosion over nothing,' she protested. She lowered her head, unable to quell her sense of grievance, and Matt took a step closer.

'I hope you realise that I'm on your side,' he said, smiling again, and she stifled a shocking impulse to fold herself into his arms – what did she think that would achieve? – but when he emulated Sean and drew her into a gentle hug, she allowed herself to remain in his embrace rather than pushing him away.

'Oh, Matt. It's important that you believe me.'

She felt none of the angst that had assailed her during the hand-holding episode, because she needed his understanding. As Matt tightened his hold on her, she raised her eyes to his and read something more than understanding in his gaze. His lips caressed her neck and moved upwards until they fastened themselves upon her mouth with the soft, lingering touch of a butterfly alighting on skin, and she didn't try to stop him because she was aching to return the kiss. It was wonderful, but it didn't last long enough, because both knew the risks they were running.

'Now look what you've made me do.'

Matt pushed her away, leaving her with a pleasing sense of disquiet and excitement tracing a path along her spine. He swore under his breath. 'You look like an angel, but I swear you are a siren in disguise. I shouldn't have kissed you, and I can only say I'm sorry.'

'Don't be sorry.'

She wasn't sure if he heard her whisper. He composed himself and patted her on the shoulder, although his touch was tentative now, as if he feared she was something wild which might bite when startled.

'Please don't worry, Sophie. We'll have forgotten about this by tomorrow,' he said quietly, and Sophie nodded, unable to find any sort of voice to answer him. 'And now I had better go and see if there is enough wind to fly the kites today. Chin up. I know you won't let this get you down.'

He dropped a wholly paternal kiss upon her head before taking the path to the beach, and Sophie stared after him, trying to decide whether she felt better or worse for his intervention. He looked back at her and waved, but his face showed a lingering and stunned surprise, as if the kiss had affected him more than he expected.

Neither had noticed the presence of Abigail, lurking like a dark wraith in the shadow of the old pine tree.

Chapter Nine

Sophie tottered across to a seat which had a view over the beach below, and sat there for some minutes, still tasting the delicious sensation of Matthew's mouth upon hers. A smile blossomed over her face. She was shocked and elated because Matt had kissed her and she had wanted him to, but perhaps it wouldn't do to find herself alone with Matt in future. It would be impossible to explain herself to Liz if there was a repeat performance, although in fairness to Matt, she felt that it hadn't been planned. Sophie shivered at the memory, ashamed because she was drawn to another woman's husband; something she would have condemned as a matter of course in the past. Nice girls didn't get themselves embroiled in other people's marriages, but circumstances in France were leading her to revise some of her previous beliefs. The inescapable truth was that she fancied Matt more with every day, and now she would need to make a conscious effort to subdue her feelings. She wondered what would await her as she wandered back to the house, where a note was displayed on the kitchen table.

'Sophie – would you please take the car and get yourself to Saint-Malo to buy some of that anchovy butter we like from the special butter shop? About a quarter kilo should do. Thanks, L.'

Sophie swore. It would be hellish trying to park at the walled city at this time of day, but she couldn't think of an excuse not to go. She trudged upstairs for her handbag and a sweater and set off for the town, and when she returned two hours later, sweaty and frazzled, the house was still unnaturally quiet.

Abigail was reading one of her gossip magazines at the kitchen table, and she looked up as Sophie walked in clutching the butter. The girl's face was a curious mix of apprehension and self-satisfaction and Sophie wondered what Abbie had been up to whilst she had been running errands in Saint-Malo.

'Where is everyone?' she asked.

Abbie shrugged, turning back to her mag.

'They've been in and out and now they are down at the harbour. Mum and Matt are taking me and Sean for a meal tonight, so you'll have to stay with the little ones. I expect you'll manage to cope, won't you?'

Sophie didn't bother to answer her. She chucked the pack of butter into the fridge and stalked to her room, throwing herself on her bed in frustration. She suspected that the butter purchase had been a ploy to remove her from the house for a while, but she couldn't see where this was headed. Perhaps it was just as well that she had only a fortnight left before her time working with the family would be over.

After a time of angry reflection, the squeals of the younger children roused her, and she clomped downstairs to resume her duties. She found everyone in the kitchen, and Liz was the first to acknowledge her.

'Oh, Sophie… did you get the butter? Good. It will be just you and Poppy and Boo tonight. Matt and I are taking our big kids out for a treat.'

'Fine.'

Sophie wasn't feeling conversational. She realised that she would have to wait for a long time, if not for ever, for Liz to admit that she had been wrong about Anna, and so she busied herself with the little girls, asking about their afternoon and trying not to engage with anyone else. Matt and Sean were intent on a game on Sean's laptop. Liz frowned over huge spectacles at what Sophie assumed to be company business on her own machine, and Abbie smirked as she daubed a sickly scented cream over her bare, fleshy legs. Sophie glanced at Sean, hoping for a sign of solidarity, but he was unusually quiet and didn't acknowledge her presence after giving one brief nod in her direction. She opened the fridge to survey the choice of food for supper.

'Boo – do you fancy pasta or some chicken and salad?' Sophie asked, and the child screwed up her face in dissent.

'Can't we go to McDonalds again? Mummy and Daddy and Sean and Abbie are going out,' Boo said, pouting, and Liz looked up at once.

'I knew it was a mistake to take them there,' she exclaimed, and Boo pulled another discontented face. 'Boudicca, if I see you scowl like that once more, you will go to bed without having anything at all to eat. She will have chicken and salad, Sophie, and no ice-cream tonight.'

Boo crumpled as though her mother had hit her and Matt frowned at the sharp reprimand, but he didn't contradict his wife. Sean slammed his laptop shut and stood up.

'I'm going to take a shower,' he announced darkly, and almost ran out of the room, as if he wanted to escape the charged atmosphere. Abigail trailed after him and Matt walked across to console his younger daughter, picking her up and wiping away the tears caused by her mother's rebuke. He carried her off to a small sofa and picked up a storybook, and the little girl sucked a thumb and stroked his chin as he read to her.

Sophie kept her head down and began to prepare the children's meal, thinking that she was unable to make up her mind about Matthew Braybrooke. Sometimes she thought he was a chancer, a chauvinist male of the worst kind, but then he would do something which made her believe he was a genuine and nice person. He had been sweet to her today, even if she would have appreciated a more public defence of her position during the morning spat with Liz. She told herself that what had happened in the garden was a little lapse of no great significance, but she couldn't repress an inner, juvenile satisfaction that she had taken a small revenge on Liz by kissing her husband.

Liz was observing her husband and daughter with an abstracted look in her eyes, and Sophie wondered whether she was jealous of his close connection with the little girl.

'I'm going up to change now,' she said to Matt, but he merely nodded and kept on reading.

He didn't speak to Sophie, though, but finished the book and left the room without any further acknowledgement of her presence. Sophie was chilled by this rebuttal. She had no wish to intrude on the family, but she hated being made to feel that they could pick her up and put her down as if she was a person without consequence; almost as though she was some lower form of life. At that moment she almost hated Jennifer Bradbury and her stupid sense of obligation to the college which had brought her into contact with these impossible people.

Abbie put her head round the door later, to say that the four adults were leaving for Dinan.

'Enjoy yourselves.'

It was hard for Sophie to summon enthusiasm, and Abbie retaliated with her own brand of provocation.

'Thanks. We are going to the place you went to with Matt, so I expect it will be amazing. Sorry you won't be with us, but I'll tell you *all about it* when we get back.'

Sophie decided that she would assert herself by disregarding Liz's instructions, and so ice cream and chocolate featured prominently on the children's evening menu. She played games with them, and at bedtime, Boo demanded a chapter or two from her favourite Princess Isabelle book. Sophie complied with the request, thinking that her life was beginning to mirror that of the put-upon heroine, although she was plagued by demons in human form rather than wicked fairies.

She turned in early, having remembered to secure the front door, and some instinct made her fasten her bedroom door, which she didn't usually bother to do. Towards midnight she stirred in her sleep, thinking that she could hear a faint knocking on the wooden panels, but she wasn't tempted to open the door in case further trouble waited there.

It was late when she opened her eyes the next morning. A car revved its engine in the drive, and she was struck by the unpleasant notion that Anna de Vos had returned to stir up more problems for her. But when she entered the kitchen, nerving herself for another scene, only Liz and the younger girls were sitting at the table, eating croissants and jam.

'I thought I heard a car,' Sophie murmured, and Liz nodded, her face tight with satisfaction.

'Yes. Matthew has had to return to England, and he's flying back from Dinard airport this morning. The taxi has just left,' she said. 'He asked me to say goodbye to you, as you won't be seeing him again.'

The words dropped into Sophie's ears with the resonance of stones down a well as she took in the full meaning of Liz's statement.

'Do you mean he isn't coming back to France?'

She concentrated on keeping her voice unconcerned, conscious that Liz was poised to analyse her reaction.

'Yes, that's right. Actually, Sophie, we have agreed a major change of plan. The weather is set to deteriorate here, and a friend with a villa has invited us to join them at Lake Como. It's too tempting a prospect to turn down, because we have all missed the Florida sun – Brittany has been something of a disappointment in that respect. I'm afraid there isn't room for you at the villa, and so I have booked for you to go back to England on the Saturday morning ferry. I will pay you for the six weeks as we agreed in London, so you won't be out of pocket.'

Sophie tried not to reveal her astonishment. Her first thought was one of relief, because the last day or two had been anything but pleasant for her, but this was superseded by a gnawing resentment that she could be wiped so speedily from the annals of Spenser/Braybrooke history by this unexpected move. Liz wanted her out; that was the bottom line, but inside she felt hollowed by a fierce regret that she wouldn't see Matthew again.

Maybe it was for the best. She had to acknowledge that she had taken unacceptable risks during the last day or so, and a flirtatious friendship with a married man wasn't something that she ought to contemplate, even as a holiday distraction.

'I see.'

Sophie was determined not to give her true feelings away. Poppy and Boo were voicing their distress that she would not be accompanying them to Italy, and their mother told them not to fuss.

'There will be plenty for you to do in Como, and two other little girls to play with. I expect that Sophie will be glad to get back to England to see her own friends and have a rest.'

She emphasised the word 'friends' as if to suggest that Sophie didn't have any among the household in France, and Sophie gave herself a mental shake. *Look on the bright side. You won't have to put up with this poisonous atmosphere much longer, and she's paying you the full salary*, she told herself. But she couldn't avoid the feeling that she had been snubbed, put down, call it what you will, and it was all a fuss over nothing. Anna de Vos had stirred up a hornet's nest, but the only person who had been stung was Sophie.

She decided to deal with her dismissal by adopting an attitude of freezing courtesy to the family. It was even difficult to act naturally with Poppy and Boo who were blameless in the affair, but when she was alone with them and they expressed their sorrow that she would be leaving with little hugs and kisses, their affection melted her defences and she found some solace in their childish disappointment.

The day was cloudless – despite Liz's weather forecasting, it appeared that they were in for a settled hot spell – and Sophie and the little girls set off for the beach as usual when they had breakfasted, because Sophie wanted to avoid spending time with her hostess as much as possible. They had to walk round by the road because the tide was high, and they hadn't long been settled on the sand when a black-clad figure came scrambling down the rocks to join them.

Sophie knew that Sean would be tactful in front of his sisters as he sat down beside them, and they kept their conversation to pleasantries after the first brief acknowledgement. But when Poppy and Boo took their buckets down to the water's edge, the boy sat upright, and began to address her in low, urgent tones.

'Soph, I don't know what's got into Mum. She's gone off the deep end about this Anna de Vos stuff. It's so unfair, and I'm fucking furious;' he said. 'And there's something else that I can't get my head round. Matt's buggered off to England this morning. Is something going on that I don't know about?'

'You are asking a lot of questions, and I don't have an answer for any of them.'

Sophie bent her head, hoping that Sean wouldn't sense her discomfort because there was no way she could admit she had accepted a kiss from his stepfather. She was still trying to persuade herself that it hadn't been wrong, but it was puzzling how everything seemed to have accelerated after that brief action. Sean's questioning gaze burned into her and her guilt made her feel spiky and uncomfortable.

'And Ab is going around with a grin like the Cheshire Cat. Have you fallen out with her too?' he demanded, and she frowned, trying to recollect what might have happened to bug the adolescent girl.

'I did tell her to stop being so negative about herself on the day Anna was here and she was kicking off about the photos,' she admitted. 'But I can't think of anything else I've done to upset her. Anyway, didn't you discuss this over dinner last night? Surely Matt told you he was going back to England then?'

'No. I knew nothing about it until I came down this morning, although I guess he had to make the arrangements late yesterday. It wasn't a fun evening in that restaurant, although I can see the food is great. I suppose that Mum and Matt had already decided things, but I have no idea why they didn't tell us. God knows, I don't want to go to

Como, and it sucks to think you have to leave us at the weekend,' he said, his voice trailing off miserably.

'The way things have turned out, I shall be glad to go.'

Sophie was even finding it hard to cut Sean some slack. She resented being cast as the whipping boy for whatever deficiencies plagued the family and was still feeling wounded after Liz's accusations. Sean gazed at her with anxiety clouding his eyes, pushing back dark locks from a forehead crumpled in dismay.

'I'm really sorry, Sophie. You mustn't think we're horrible people. Pops and Boo adore you, and so do I. I wish that bloody Anna had kept well away, and none of this would have happened.'

'It's too late now. And something tells me that Abbie has been stirring. She's much more devious than I thought; you might want to bear that in mind for the future.'

They sat in silence for a while, watching the little girls playing at the water's edge. Sophie squinted against the sun, trying to imprint the scene on her mind, because she had loved it here and would not be around to view it for much longer. The time had gone quickly, and it seemed now as though the first weeks had been a paradise from which she was being painfully ejected. Sean's head was down, and she was touched by his obvious unhappiness. 'Forget about Abbie, Sean. We won't let the others get to us, and I want to leave Poppy and Boo with happy memories.'

'I'm with you there. You know, your trouble is that you are too soft, Soph. Ellie stands up to Mum like you wouldn't believe, and Mum appreciates that. Perhaps I should have given you a few more hints at the beginning of the holiday.'

Their conversation was cut short by the girls returning with full buckets of water to aid the making of sand pies, and Sophie joined in to help. She was careful not to let them hear her speak a word of criticism about their mother and older sister and hushed their brother when he began to blame his parent for spoiling their summer plans.

It was noticeable that Abbie avoided her company when they were back at the house, and Sophie conjectured that the girl was somehow at the centre of the recent unpleasant developments. Liz watched them beadily, but Sophie did not allow her dislike of mother and daughter to reveal itself. If they were disappointed by her icy calm and acceptance of the situation, so much the better, but Sophie found it hard to persuade Sean not to take sides in the dispute. She wanted the remaining days to be peaceful and untainted by argument, because then she could return to England in a positive frame of mind and with the satisfaction of having acquitted herself with dignity.

Chapter Ten

Sophie was astounded when Liz plotted a punishing schedule of visits to places of interest to be crammed into the remaining days of the holiday. She tried to jolly the kids along, but it wasn't a relaxing or agreeable time because they would have preferred to make the most of the great weather on the seashore. The children dragged themselves around historic churches and ancient streets and markets with exceedingly grouchy faces; the cobbled pavements echoing with their discontent. None of it had any effect on their mother, who seemed even more determined to force antiquity and culture down their unwilling throats if they dared to voice a complaint.

Sophie went to bed early on the third day, exhausted by the demands made upon her as a tour manager and babysitter in one. She sat cross-legged on her bed, writing to George as she struggled to get recent developments into perspective.

'Darling George,

Thanks for your email, even if it was rather a brief one! I'm glad that you are making new friends and enjoying yourself, but I'm so jealous. I can't wait to get back to Cambridge and my real mates, because I feel out of my depth here and could use some support.

Liz has handed me my notice a week early, the excuse being that they want to visit friends in Italy and there isn't room for everyone to go. I'm almost sure she has cooked this up as an excuse to get rid of me. I think that my crimes are speaking to a journalist without her agreement – although I didn't say anything remotely contentious – and getting too friendly with Sean and her husband Matt.

Honestly, I didn't set out to flirt with either of them. Sean and I are good mates, but I have taken pains to keep my distance because he's just a boy, and because of what Liz said at the beginning of all this. I admit that Matt kissed me the other day when he was consoling me for being on the receiving end of Liz's fury, but it was a spur of the moment gesture and not a passionate snog, and TBH, I went along with it because at that moment, I needed comforting and he reminded me of you. Big mistake, obvs. I get that it's easier to dispose of nannies rather than sons or husbands, but I don't think that Liz has much of a case against me.

Do you think I should have been more assertive? None of this is a total disaster, but I feel like an outsider who has been manipulated without regard to my feelings and I really resent that. I hope that Liz doesn't complain to my tutor, but if she does, I won't hold back from giving my version of events.

I shall be sorry to leave Boo and Poppy, who are darlings. Sean, too. He is such a funny mix of sensitivity and cynicism, and his company has been a great comfort to me. The lessons I am taking away from this experience are that money means power, and that it's permissible to pursue one's own agenda while disregarding anything or everyone else – hardly revolutionary thoughts, but ones that I never gave much credence to before my time here in company with the lady tycoon.'

Sophie stared out of her window at the sunset, her heart sore and sad. Could she expect George to be interested in her problems now that there was an ocean between them? Even if he didn't take them on board, she wanted his reassurance that she had not acted stupidly and that she was not a bad person, despite her burgeoning crush on Matt. She wondered what Matt was thinking now. Had he been banished back to England, or was his absence due to another business crisis which needed his attention? If it was the former, she couldn't believe that he would accept Liz's diktats without any sort of struggle to assert his own wishes. The sun slipped down beneath the waves, and she shivered as the air began to cool with the approach of night.

Her door was opened abruptly after the curtest of knocks, and she had just time to close her laptop before Abigail sauntered in. This was a surprise, because the girl had shunned her company in a pointed fashion during the last days and had been very sullen towards her when they were forced to share the same space. Even Liz had turned away with a studied and blank face when confronted by Abigail's rude behaviour, and Sophie wondered how far the girl would have to go before her mother felt that she had finally overstepped the boundaries of civility. Abbie was holding out her hot brush with disdainful fingers, as if it were a dead rat.

'You'll have to take this back, Sophie. It doesn't work,' she stated, throwing the item on the bed with a thump. Sophie retrieved it with care, turning it over and checking the controls.

'Are you sure? It was fine the other day,' she said, and Abbie gave an impatient shrug.

'Well, of course I am. I should never have let you buy it; it's obviously a crap model,' she said, and Sophie gave her a derisory glance. She had no hand in the purchase as far as she could remember and had certainly not tried to force Abigail to favour one brand over another. She walked across to the power point on the wall and plugged it in. The red light came on at once, and the brush began to heat up without delay.

'It's fine. Perhaps you didn't have it plugged in properly,' Sophie said, switching the brush off again. Abbie looked disconcerted for a moment but hastened to find another reason for the malfunction.

'It's more likely that the sockets in this dump don't work right. I shan't be sorry to go,' she stated, and Sophie murmured something non-committal. She didn't want to begin a discussion with Abigail about life in Brittany, or anything at all, when she came to think about it. But Abbie showed no inclination to leave the room. She wandered across to the window and stared at the horizon where lights were winking across the bay.

'Are you pleased to be going home at the weekend?' she asked, and Sophie considered how much truth to convey in her reply.

'It will be good to see my parents,' she said, employing caution. 'I have enjoyed myself here, but it's time for me to move on. It's time for everyone to move on, because I don't think that being here has really suited your family.'

And that's a shame for you all, she thought to herself. It was clear to her that the Spenser/Braybrookes had no clue how to divine the soul of a country. The delicious immersion in a different way of life and appreciation of being elsewhere was not something they could understand – their instincts were materialistic and unemotional. They wanted the certainty of good weather, subservient foreigners, the best food and drink and accommodation which befitted their status. She knew with inner irony that the forays into 'culture' this week had been undertaken with a grim determination that Liz could boast later of having 'done' this part of France.

Abigail fiddled with the window catch and Sophie sighed, feeling sure that she was trying to work up to another controversial exchange of views. The girl flicked her hair about and huffed out a sigh before getting to the point.

'Are you having an affair with my stepfather?' she demanded, and the abrupt change of subject and blunt attack caused Sophie to laugh out loud.

'What on earth makes you think that?' she replied, and Abbie's face flushed with self-righteous irritation.

'I saw you kissing him in the garden. You didn't see me, though,' the girl retorted, and a number of things clicked into place in Sophie's head. She stuck on a smile, sensing that her calm reaction wasn't what Abbie had been hoping for.

'Oh, that didn't mean anything – it was a friendly kiss. Matt was just telling me not to be upset after the furore about Anna. It wasn't exactly a moment of passion, Abbie, but perhaps you aren't experienced enough to know that.'

And perhaps that remark was below the belt, but she felt that Abbie deserved it. Abbie scowled as she registered the implied insult.

'Well, Mum doesn't think much of you. Do you think it's cool to jump on someone else's husband? You might look ever so demure and innocent, but you are just a slut really. Look at how you flirt with Sean and lead him on. We'll be well rid of you.'

'Stop for a moment and listen to yourself, Abigail.'

Sophie's tone was light, although she knew she had to tread carefully now. 'Where is the evidence that I have jumped on Matt?' she asked. 'There isn't any, because it hasn't happened. If you go through life making unpleasant allegations about people without any proof, you'll end up in trouble, big time. And I can tell you that you're backing the wrong horse here. As for Sean, he and I are good friends, and it wouldn't surprise me if you're jealous about that.'

Sophie's response resulted in a puzzled frown from her accuser. Abbie had probably hoped for a blushing and embarrassed denial, but the fact that Sophie hadn't even bothered to conceal the fatal kiss was obviously unexpected. 'I suppose you went and blabbed to your mother,' Sophie continued, sounding as though she was coolly unpicking a bothersome knot. 'And poor old Matt got it in the neck. Did Liz send him back to England with a flea in his ear? I hope…'

She had been going to say, 'I hope her money makes it worth his while,' but discretion prevailed. Abbie already looked as though she had swallowed a frog, and Sophie allowed herself a moment of satisfaction before distaste overwhelmed her. 'If you don't mind – I'm busy,' she said, opening her laptop, and Abbie took the hint. She picked up the hot brush and stalked from the room without another word, but Sophie didn't immediately return to her email. She was shaken to think that her suspicions had been correct, because the silly business showed her hosts had a singular approach to life. If what Abigail had said was true, then neither Liz nor Matt came out of this well – Liz, for over-reacting, and Matt for accepting his removal from the scene of crime like a whipped schoolboy. What really went on between them? She suspected that their relationship was like a glass vessel with cracks under the surface which would probably shatter completely one day.

Sophie ended her missive to George on a lighter note and began to contemplate the remaining weeks of her university vacation. Her parents had been pleased when she texted to say that she was returning early from France and suggested she might like to accompany them on a visit to relatives in Scotland. She was tempted to agree, because it would be soothing to return to a dependent status for a while after shouldering so many burdens in France. Sophie knew that she would need time to process the conflicting experiences of her weeks in Brittany. Would she ever see any members of this family again? It was doubtful. She wished none of them ill – even Abbie, because she was generous enough to comprehend the reasons behind her sullen personality – but she understood the wisdom of returning to her usual world and reclaiming her own individuality. Her first task would be to consign her relationships with Sean and Matt to history before she did or said anything she might regret.

Sophie's last full day with the family dawned bright and sun kissed. Liz relented sufficiently to agree that it could be a beach day, although she declined to join her children on the sands. Her excuse was that someone had to wait in to receive a delivery of new clothes which she had ordered especially for the Italian visit, and Sophie was relieved to have escaped that tedious chore. Abigail decided to keep her mother company, but it was a sober little party who set up camp by the clear waters of the bay. Poppy and Boo were growing excited about the trip

94

to Italy but lamented that Sophie would not accompany them, and Sean's distress grew more apparent by the hour.

'Can I come to see you in England, Sophie?' he asked when his sisters were occupied with their play, and Sophie looked at him with a sorrowful face.

'I don't know, Sean. I'm not sure whether your mother would be happy about that. Besides...'

Her voice trailed off as she struggled to find the right words.

'Besides what? I hate it when people say that; it never means anything good.'

Sean trickled sand through his fingers, looking tense and almost feverish. Sophie reached across and stroked the back of his hand.

'Look, Sean, we are returning to different worlds. When I'm at Cambridge, I will be working all hours if I'm to get a good degree. You'll soon be back at your school – prison, then,' she added as he mouthed the word at her. 'I'm sure that your mother has plans for you in London when you get home after Italy, so it would be difficult to get away. I'm happy to keep up with you by text and email, but there is no way we can have any sort of relationship – except as friends. It's not that I don't care for you – I do; I'm very fond of you – but let's be realistic.'

The boy was silent, searching her face for signs of hope.

'But I don't want to lose you,' he murmured, and a seagull crying overhead seemed to echo his distress.

'You ought to know that holiday romances never last, and we haven't even had that.'

Sophie wasn't sure how to make things better for him. Her own heart was sore because she really was fond of Sean, and because she had been denied the opportunity to say a proper goodbye to his stepfather. She would have liked to look Matt in the eyes one last time; to receive an acknowledgement that he had admired her. The prospect of parting with her little friends Poppy and Boo loomed over her like a raincloud. She thought back to her meeting in the quad with Jennifer Bradbury – that seemed an age ago now – and wished that she had never agreed to take the job. The payment wasn't enough to compensate for the difficulties she had been forced to confront, nor the emotional turmoil of the last few days.

Sean's mouth turned down in a mutinous scowl.

'We could have been closer if you hadn't got hung-up about what Mum told you,' he complained, but Sophie shook her head.

'No, Sean, that was never going to work. Pretty soon you will meet a girl of your own age who you fancy like crazy and things will fall into place. You don't need me to tell you how fit you are. Remember Claire and Alice? That was just a foretaste.'

She smiled at the memory of the giggling girls, but Sean's face of disgust caused her to drop the subject. Poppy ran up to show them an unusual shell that she had found and asked Sophie if they could swim, and Sophie welcomed the opportunity to return to simpler matters.

'Yes. Just give me a minute, and I'll come in with you.'

She rose to her feet and stretched. 'Coming for a swim, Sean?'

'Not sure. Maybe.'

Sophie wasn't going to press him. She followed Poppy down to the water, and soon they were laughing and splashing in the surf. The sea temperature had warmed in recent days, and they were all delighted when Sean finally waded in to join them. He let the little girls ride on his shoulders and splashed Sophie, and then they stretched in the shallows to recover their breath. Sophie was pleased to see that Sean looked happier now and he grinned wickedly at her as she lay on her back and allowed the wavelets to break over her body.

'Don't suppose there's any chance of you losing your top today, Soph?' he asked, and she shook her head.

'Water isn't rough enough, I'm afraid. But I've seen one or two girls further along the beach who don't have my inhibitions. You could go and check out what's on offer.'

'Not tempted, thanks.'

'What about Italy? You might find some hottie waiting for you there.'

'I doubt it. And you, Sophie? Do you have plans to hook up with anyone back home?'

'There's no-one who comes to mind. Anyway, I have a tough year ahead of me. I think I ought to avoid getting into anything heavy until I've left Cambridge.'

Boo dropped a handful of seaweed on Sophie's stomach, and she screeched. In the rough and tumble which followed, she nearly did reveal more than she meant to, and they were still laughing when they walked up the beach to dry off. Sean volunteered for ice cream duty, which made Sophie recall the first day spent in his company. A little shudder half sympathy, half regret, shook her as she watched Sean walk away holding the hands of the little girls. She had always wished for brothers or sisters, and the caring relationship between Sean and his two half-siblings was something she would remember with pleasure.

When the party returned to the house for a late lunch, they found Liz and Abbie swathed in tissue paper as they unpacked their new clothes. Sophie was interested, despite her vow to remain aloof from the pair and Liz was keen to display the smart garments, as if to demonstrate that she had impeccable taste as well as a bulging purse. Although it was high summer, Liz's choice was dominated by tailored garments in bright, blocked colours, with an emphasis which was almost masculine. Sophie recalled Matt's face when he saw her wearing her flowered sundress for the first time and wondered how Liz would react if she asserted that Matt liked women to look feminine. That was one moment which she could cherish for herself alone.

'I have paid your final salary into your account, Sophie,' Liz said unexpectedly, as they lunched off galettes saucisses from the van which stopped at the end of the street. Sophie nodded her thanks, pleased to be returning home with money even if not with goodwill, and she noticed Sean look up with an approving glance at his parent. He was always on her side, and she breathed a little, loving wish that life would bring him what he wanted.

Liz had softened enough to insist that they had dinner at a local restaurant to say goodbye to Sophie. She was almost ebullient in her efforts to end things on a cheerful note, and Sophie wondered whether her last night's conversation with Abbie had been reported back and altered Liz's opinions; maybe even caused her to feel a smidgeon of guilt. Would Liz ever admit that she was in the wrong? It was doubtful. In any case, it was too late now to change their plans, and Sophie packed her cases before bed with a feeling of relief that she would no longer be subject to the moods and whims of the family. She remembered at the last minute to return the credit card to Liz, who accepted it without comment.

Chapter Eleven

Sophie had switched off her bedside light and was on the verge of falling asleep when she heard the light creak of wooden floorboards. She sat up at the same time as her door opened and Sean crept, stealthy as a mouse, to the side of her bed.

'Sean! What are you doing here?' she hissed, although she realised that she knew the answer before the words were out. He was barefoot, wearing an old T-shirt and boxer shorts and his lean body shivered in the cool night air.

'Budge up, Soph. I want to get in with you; I'm freezing to death.'

He nudged his way under the duvet and imprisoned her in his arms, exhaling loudly with a mixture of cold and pleasure. 'Mum's paid you all the money, hasn't she? That means we can have sex and you won't lose out. Oh, Sophie… I've been waiting all the fucking holiday for this.'

'Ssh! Do you want to wake everyone? And no, we can't have sex!'

Sophie was electrified with alarm. She was conscious of Sean fumbling under her nightdress to stroke her breasts, and the weight of his body hampered her attempts to push him away. 'Sean, stop that! Sod the money; this just doesn't feel right. How many times have I told you that I'm not up for any sort of romantic or sexual relationship? Sean, this is not going to happen.'

He bent his dark head and his lips silenced her mouth. His kisses were urgent and loving and his body gave off an adolescent aroma of sweat and longing which was neither unfamiliar nor unpleasant. Panicked, Sophie decided her best course was to allow Sean to kiss her before she put an embargo on more intimate caresses. She could feel his erection pressing hard against her thighs, and for the first time since she had come to France, she was uncomfortably aware of him as someone with sexual potency.

'I heard you telling Ab that you're on the pill. That's a result for me.'

Sean stopped his onslaught to whisper in her ear, and Sophie made another attempt to roll his body away. But he fell to kissing her again as if she was a delicious plate of food which had to be devoured at a single sitting, and she struggled without success to break free.

Her thoughts were a blur of conflict. It would be very wrong to allow her employer's teenage son to have sex with her, although she felt no loyalty to the woman who had accused her of flirting with the press. At the same time, a wave of feminine emotion left her floundering. If she was Liz, wouldn't she prefer Sean to sleep for the first time with someone who was fond of him and who would treat him tenderly rather than a pick-up from a club or dating site? Wouldn't it be a nice thing for her to do for this boy, who she had grown close to during the last weeks? Sophie wavered, although she had the sensation of tumbling into a pit, frantically reaching out as she tried to grasp at something, anything, to arrest her fall. Sean began to explore between her thighs, and she made a last appeal.

'I could scream for your mother,' she gasped, and he curled his other hand around her throat.

'No, you won't. Come on, Soph, you want this as much as I do.'

She didn't want it, but it seemed impossible to get off the roller-coaster without ending up in another explosive scene, and she tried to convince herself that she owed Sean; that she had depended on his support during some difficult times in France. It wasn't the best sex that Sophie had ever experienced. Sean was passionate and eager, stopping only to enquire with a kind of embarrassed desperation whether he was 'doing it right'.

'Just do what your body tells you,' she murmured in response, and he resumed his enthusiastic thrusts, but it was over long before Sophie could reach a state of satisfaction. She didn't care. It had been about what Sean needed, and she was almost relieved that she had not found a responsive passion within herself. His eyes were wet and his breath uneven as he returned to himself from the depths of physical love and emotion.

'I'll always remember tonight.'

Sean gulped, sounding as though he was struggling with tears and Sophie grimaced, thinking that the scene might have been written in the pages of a teen romance. Her own deflowering had been a more matter-of-fact affair with an older student who approached the situation with enthusiasm, but also as if he was following an instruction manual and the earth had not moved for her in any way.

'Sex by numbers' she complained when describing the occasion to her best friend afterwards, and the experience left her sceptical about the whole business for a long time. It was only with George that she had begun to appreciate that the right time and the right person could combine so that sex was something of real delight.

'Please go back to your room now,' she urged hopefully, as the spectre of a furious Liz fulminating in her nightdress loomed in her imagination, but Sean was reluctant to move.

'Let me stay for a bit. You're going away tomorrow. I just want to hold you,' he murmured, sounding again like the boy she had grown fond of, and although she longed for solitude, she had not the heart to kick him out of the bed. The last thing she remembered was the silky sensation of his hair on her cheek as they fell asleep.

Sophie and Sean slept peacefully until she awoke at about five in the morning with a sense that something was wrong. The sight of another face on the pillowcase brought everything flooding back. She wriggled out of Sean's grasp to go to the bathroom, and when she returned, she shook him gently to rouse him from deep slumber. It took a little while before he came to, and he clung to her with renewed intent.

'Just once more,' he pleaded, his eyes burning bright like an animal, and Sophie tried to disentangle herself from his determined caresses.

'No. I don't think...' she began, but she had not allowed for the resilience and tenacity and the brute strength of a teenage male. He pulled her back into the bed, and this time, he knew what he was doing. There was no way that Sophie could stop him or call for assistance without alerting the rest of the household, and the horrible thought that this second action was akin to rape shocked her into submission. She had to press a hand against his mouth to smother the noise as he groaned to a climax, and now she was frightened by the genie she had let out of the bottle.

They lay, sticky and panting, and he moved his lips against her ear.

'That was awesome. God, I wish I was your first lover, Soph. I can't stand to think of you being with someone else.'

'Don't get sentimental.'

Her tone was snappy, and he propped himself on an elbow to gaze at her with puzzled eyes.

'Why are you being so cold? We are a proper couple now. I shan't let Mum stop me seeing you when we get back, and she'll have to accept that we need to be together.'

Sophie made no reply to this statement, which struck her as unlikely in the extreme. She prayed that Sean would come down to earth after her departure when he had time to process the encounter and realise what his mother's reaction might be to that plan. The memory of Matt and the gentle kiss he had bestowed upon her was painful to recall now. That seemed so innocent compared to her night with his stepson, and she wished that she was able to ask his advice on what to do about the tangled situation she had fallen into.

Her phone beeped to signify an incoming message, and she was glad of the excuse to pick it up.

'You must go now, Sean. It's almost five thirty. For God's sake, don't make a noise or let anyone see you. And don't make eyes at me over breakfast. This has to stay secret – got it?'

'Okay, okay. Anyone would think I was underage. I'm going to be hyper in Italy when I think about tonight, and I can't wait until we do it again. Promise me you won't sleep with anyone else, Sophie. You can't even look at another man. I think I'd kill anyone who laid a finger on you now.'

This was not a comfortable thought for Sophie as Sean slipped from her room like a grey shadow. She had told him emphatically that a relationship between them was going nowhere, but memories from her lunch with Matt in Dinan suddenly surfaced with technicolour radiance. What was it that Matt had said to her?

'He can lash out... he's inherited his mother's need to control everything around her...'

Sophie sat on the end of her bed and stared at the wall. Please God, let that be an exaggeration on Matt's part. The last thing she needed was an adolescent boy round her neck, making demands which she had no desire to comply with. Her feelings towards Sean had undergone a rapid change during the night, and now she wasn't sure whether she felt the same affection towards him as before. He was much more like his mother in temperament than she'd realised. How lucky it was that she was about to go home; how likely was it that Sean would cause problems for her when she got there?

101

There was no point in trying to go back to sleep. She lathered herself fiercely in the shower, wishing she could wash away the memories of the night with equal ease, and then she stripped the bed, placing the sheets on a chair beneath her towels for Yulia, the Romanian help, to launder. The house was quiet as she tiptoed downstairs and she let herself into the garden without making a sound. The morning was fresh and sweet, but she trod the path to the beach feeling almost overwhelmed with anxiety as she recalled the events of the night. If only she had locked her door... if only she had not succumbed to Sean's pleading... it was too late to change things now. She halted briefly at the spot where Matt had kissed her, wondering what he would say if he knew about his stepson and the guilty night they had shared. He would probably condemn her, and she felt that he would be right to do so.

Sophie was alone on the shore, and the waves washed her feet with reproach as she walked along the tideline. The beauty of the day was lost on her as she replayed the last hours in her mind, her thoughts growing increasingly panicky as she began to picture possible repercussions. At length, she gathered herself together and returned to the house with dragging steps. Her taxi was booked for nine o'clock, and Liz and the little girls would be waiting to bid her goodbye. It was probable that Abbie wouldn't bother to come down, and she hoped that Sean would be sleeping off his energetic night. She wasn't sure she wanted to see him again, even if Liz might think it strange that her son chose to absent himself from the farewells.

She cast a last yearning look at the coast before retracing her path to the house. Then she brought her bags down to the hall, leaving two little parcels on her bed containing presents for Poppy and Boo, and met Liz coming down the stairs. Liz was wearing the same bathrobe as on her first morning in France, and Sophie swallowed hard as a sense of déjà vu swept through her, leaving a poignant taste of regret.

'Oh, Sophie... have you been up long?'

Sophie detected an unusual tone of self-consciousness in her employer's voice as Liz opened the kitchen door for her.

'Yes. I wanted to say goodbye to the beach.'

Liz raised her eyebrows to express surprise at this eccentricity, but she didn't pass any comment. Sophie brewed coffee, and they were soon joined by the little girls. Their solemn faces encouraged Sophie to quell her own woes, and she devoted herself to enthusiastic exclamations about their trip to Italy and the fun they would have there.

'And Daddy will be back this afternoon to play with you,' Liz interjected. Sophie tried not to smile. How convenient had it been for Liz to arrange matters so her path and Matthew's didn't cross again? It was pathetic, and she began to long for her departure as the clock ticked towards nine.

Liz had the fidgets. 'Would you be dreadfully upset if Abbie doesn't come down to say goodbye to you? She's suffering with period pain this morning,' she said to Sophie, and Sophie assured her quite truthfully that she didn't mind at all. Nothing was said concerning Sean, but Sophie sensed that Liz was puzzled by his absence, although she made no attempt to rouse her son to say goodbye. Then a horn beeping in the drive alerted them to the arrival of the taxi and they stood up in an awkward, chair-scraping way.

'Is Sophie going now?' whispered Boo, and her mother nodded.

'Goodbyes are so difficult. Thank you for all that you have done, Sophie, and I hope you have a pleasant trip home. Do give my regards to Jennifer when you are back in Cambridge.'

Liz spoke in clipped tones of cool relief and Sophie took her cue.

'Thank you, Liz. I have enjoyed my time here with the children.'

Not with you was the unspoken message. 'Say hi to the others for me, and Poppy – if you and Boo run up to my room when I've left, there is a little surprise waiting for you there.'

She kissed the little girls, her eyes brimming. 'Be good in Italy and let me know how you get on. Don't eat too much ice cream, Boo darling.'

Now she just wanted to get away. They accompanied her to the front door, and as she picked up her cases, a whirlwind with black hair flew down the stairs.

'Soph! How could you run out on me like this without saying goodbye?'

She was seized and hugged by the apparition, and Sean placed his mouth against her ear. 'I love you forever,' he breathed, and Sophie watched over his shoulder as Liz's face curdled, although there was no way she could have heard what her son was saying. But Sophie merely returned the hug and muttered a farewell. 'We'll be watching

103

for the ferry going out to sea mid-morning, although I don't know if you'll be able to see us waving,' Sean added. Boo's little face was screwed up with sadness, and Sean hoisted his sister on to his shoulder to comfort her as Sophie climbed into the taxi. As she turned to wave goodbye, an unexpected tear blurred their figures and she had to dig around to find a tissue in her bag, but whether the tears were of sadness or relief was impossible to tell.

When Sophie boarded the ferry, she made her way to the outer deck, watching the busy bustle of loading and the departure of small yachts from the marina; their sails billowy and pregnant with wind as they headed out to sea. She wished she could recapture the sense of adventure she had felt upon leaving England, but the last weeks in France had left her feeling that a monster was on her tail. She scanned the headlands, wondering if Sean and Boo and Poppy were waving there, or whether she was already consigned to a footnote in their history.

'And now I have to forget about them,' she told herself, returning to her cabin to rest before lunch. Her phone beeped – reception was patchy as they sailed further from the coast – and she opened it to find a rambling message from Sean, professing undying love and swearing that they would be together again before too long. She thrust the phone into a pocket without bothering to reply, telling herself, like a more famous heroine, that she would deal with the issue later.

Sophie ate, slept, and awoke to find the chalky cliffs of the Isle of Wight signalling that she was almost home. Her father would be waiting for her at the docks, and she began to rehearse a favourable account of her life in France, not wanting to hint that her stay there had been anything other than a success. There was no way she could mention the indiscretions of last night. She was upset and annoyed with Sean and even crosser with herself, and as for Matt... all would be whitewashed until it was suitable for a parent's ears.

Her body was surprisingly sore, and a few bruises had blossomed in purply colours as the day wore on. She had left her phone on silent during the time she slept, and she picked it up to find... a screenful of messages and five missed calls from Sean.

Sophie swore. It was apparent that she would have at least a short-term problem with the boy, but the most urgent response was to make him understand that he had to take every precaution to avoid his family knowing about their continued contact. The thought of Abbie getting hold of his phone or laptop was worrying, even if Liz could no longer wreak revenge of a monetary nature. On second thoughts, Liz could cause Sophie lasting embarrassment if she complained to Jennifer Bradbury that the girl she had recommended had turned out to be a corrupting influence on her son! Liz would always ensure that her family was absolved of any blame. Sophie's heart hammered as she pictured her stumbling attempts to explain her actions and the icy distaste of Jennifer's condemnation.

Her hand trembled as she picked up her phone. She sent a brief message to her tormentor, explaining that reception was patchy on board and that she would email him once she arrived home.

'Don't keep texting; someone will get suspicious,' she pleaded, but a reply pinged back almost instantly, repudiating that idea.

'In my room. Tell me that you love me.'

She switched the phone off. Once they were in sight of Portsmouth, reception would be fully restored, and she could not risk a call from Sean coming in when her father was present. Embarrassment would be heaped on embarrassment if she had to field public declarations of passion and commitment from a seventeen-year-old boy. If only she could turn the clock back!

Chapter Twelve

'You are very quiet, darling.'

Sophie's father Eric surveyed his daughter as she slumped in the passenger seat of the car and his brow was puzzled. She stretched her limbs and gave a yawn of theatrical proportions.

'I'm just knackered, Dad,' she said. 'The last few days have been hectic. Liz suddenly decided she wanted to visit every place of interest for miles around, and don't forget that I've been on call for the last five weeks. I can't wait to have some downtime when I get home.'

'We were surprised when your employer cut the holiday short.'

'Well, I think she was disappointed in the house and the climate, and the prospect of some Italian sunshine was too tempting. She's paid me for the whole six weeks, so I'm not going to complain.'

Sophie turned her head to watch the green downs of Hampshire fading into a sapphire twilight. It seemed strange to be driving on the left again, and even stranger to think that she would wake tomorrow morning in her bedroom at home without the savour of the sea and the harsh shout of gulls. She ought to be relieved she was home, but her focus was still on the family and the house she had left behind.

'Mum will be pleased to have you back,' her father said. 'She is getting stronger every day, although I have to watch that she doesn't overdo things and get tired.'

'Now I'm home, I can help out in the house. Is the Scottish trip still on?'

'Definitely. Everyone is looking forward to seeing 'little Sophie', and I've had a hard time convincing the great-aunts that you are not a wee lassie now.'

Certainly not a wee lassie after France, she thought, feeling a spasm of guilt nip at her tummy. They drove in silence for a while, and she allowed herself to put the tumult caused by Sean to one side as she absorbed the comfort of her father's presence. Perhaps things wouldn't be so bad once there was distance between herself and the boy and he came to understand the impossibility of maintaining a one-sided affair.

Sophie's mother was overjoyed to welcome her daughter home. Despite the busy finale to her stay in France, Sophie had found time to purchase gifts for her parents and the evening ended in cognac, artisan chocolates and affection with the promise of a full account of her French adventures to come the next day. But it was a sad Sophie who entered her old bedroom because she was a different person to the carefree girl who'd set out on the night ferry all those weeks ago, and she didn't much like herself at present.

Sophie knew there was one task she couldn't escape before she could lose herself in sleep. The screen of her laptop flickered in the darkness as she began her tentative reply to Sean's continued protestations of love.

'Sean,

This is hard for me. Please don't think I'm a bitch if I start by reminding you that I never promised to love you or that we could hook up again after France. Last night was difficult; you were so full-on, and I thought that maybe I was doing something good for you, but now I see it was a huge mistake.

Your company was important to me in France. You helped me to cope with life when your mother and sister made it difficult and I'll always be grateful for that, but I wish things hadn't gone so far.'

Sophie paused, aware that she was being generous by shouldering the larger proportion of blame. A scratch on one breast was a painful reminder that Sean hadn't been entirely tender and loving when achieving his objective, and he'd disregarded her pleas to stop without compunction.

'You must be super-careful that your family don't twig that you are messaging me so much. Your mother could make life difficult for me in Cambridge if she knew about what happened. I don't think you want that – I hope you don't. It's okay if you email or text me sometimes, but there's no future for us as a couple. One day you'll know I was right.

Forget me now and enjoy Italy. I'll always keep a corner of my heart for you.'

She clicked send and closed the machine. The bed was familiar and comfortable, and she fell asleep almost at once, although her dreams were haunted by a dark, scowling presence. Next morning, it took some moments of blinking and staring at the ceiling before she remembered that she was home again. She reached for her phone out of habit and was jolted to consciousness by the evidence of yet more missed calls and messages from her persistent teenage lover. Then the door opened to admit her mother bearing a cup of tea, and she hastily concealed the phone under the bedclothes, relieved to have an excuse to put off reading Sean's anguished responses to her last communication.

'Oh, thanks Mum. I was shattered after the journey.'

Sophie's mum placed the cup on the bedside table, her face smiling and full of mystery.

'There's a lovely surprise downstairs,' she said. 'Someone has sent you the most enormous bouquet of flowers that I've ever seen. Of course, I haven't opened the little envelope which came with it.'

But you are longing to know who sent it, Sophie thought to herself. She felt that it could only have come from one person, unless Matt…no, he wouldn't know where she lived. *How did Sean know, come to that?* She levered herself upright and a silly, bleating laugh bubbled out, taking her by surprise.

'I'll just nip to the loo before I come down.'

She seized her dressing gown and was soon downstairs, where an ostentatious collection of blooms elevated her feelings of guilt sky-high. It was an ordeal to have to open the envelope before her parents' curious gaze, and she was immediately forced into a falsehood. The card read '*To darling Sophie with all my love. Can't wait until we are together again. Your Sean.*' This she translated aloud as '*With many thanks for all your help in France, from Liz and family*', before thrusting the card deep into a pocket.

'Oh, I call that a really nice gesture. Don't you think so, Eric? And these blooms must have cost a fortune.'

Mrs Elliot stroked the petals of a spectacular carnation and Sophie summoned a weak smile.

'Well, there isn't exactly a shortage of money in that household, but it is very kind of them. I will write to thank Liz later.'

'Yes, make sure you do that. They're a family who might be useful to you in the future, so you should try to keep in touch with them. I'll have to see if I can put my hands on enough vases for all these wonderful flowers.'

Her mother hummed happily towards the kitchen and Sophie clenched her hand around the incriminating card. She had told Sean that she lived in Guildford, but she could not recall telling him more than that. If he knew where she lived, there was nothing to stop him turning up on her doorstep when his family returned from Italy.

'When are we going to Scotland, Dad?' she enquired, crossing her fingers that the visit would coincide with Sean's return to England.

'Well, we thought you'd like some time to yourself here first, so we won't be off until next weekend. Does that suit you?'

'Yes, that sounds perfect.'

She was absent minded at breakfast, but no-one noticed amongst the bustle of flower arranging. Her father joked that the excess was worthy of a tart's boudoir, but Sophie found it a struggle to join in the mirth occasioned by this remark.

'I suppose there was no expense spared in the housekeeping over there,' commented her mother, and Sophie seized upon the excuse to change the subject.

'Liz gave me a special credit card to use, and no-one ever set a limit on expenditure. It doesn't give a good example for the children really, but they are remarkably normal, considering everything.'

'I think you said the teenage girl was difficult, but her brother was much nicer?'

'Yes. He and I became quite friendly.'

And that was the understatement of the year. For a fleeting moment, Sophie was tempted to burst into howls and confess her guilt to her parents, but she couldn't bring herself to incur their disapproval so soon after her return as the prodigal daughter.

'How did you get on with Liz and her husband?' asked Mrs Elliot, 'Is she as formidable as everyone seems to think?'

Why did her mother have to put her through this catechism? Sophie sighed, trying to dredge up enthusiasm for difficult memories.

'She's a hard person and someone I could never get close to, but Matthew was a very pleasant man. And their two little girls were darlings; I loved being with them.'

'What a terrible name the youngest one has. I wonder how parents can do that to their babies.'

Sophie made no reply– she found it impossible to think of Boo with any other name, and anyway, it suited the little girl. Boudicca

Braybrooke was a mouthful, but it had the merit of being unforgettable. Her mother rambled on. 'And when do you think you will see them again?'

'Oh, I don't know. Never, probably. This was a one-off job, and they live in north London, so our paths aren't likely to cross.'

'It seems a shame when they liked you so much.'

Sophie escaped as soon as she could. When she was back in her bedroom, she scanned through all the messages from Sean before reading the response to her late-night email. Her plea for sanity had not been well received, and she found it impossible to comprehend the gulf between fact and fiction in Sean's understanding. What had triggered this disconnect between fantasy and reality in his mind? She didn't recognise the boy she thought she knew.

Darling, darling Soph,

WTF? I love you babe and to hell with what anyone else thinks. What we have is special, and you know it. Are you kicking off because you are worried about Mum and what she'll say? I couldn't give a fuck for that. As soon as I get back home, I'll find you and this time, I won't let her send you away. I know we can't live together until I leave school, but I am going to marry you, so you'd better get used to the idea of being Mrs Spenser.'

There was another page of rambling declarations which she could hardly bear to read. Sophie deleted everything, and slumped on the bed, lost in anxious speculation. Although she dreaded the thought of speaking directly to Sean, it seemed the best way to bring him back to his senses because she could express herself more forcibly in person. Eventually she texted him, not referring to his recent communications, but saying she would ring him at noon the following day, when he'd settled in at the villa in Como. In the meantime, she'd have to put up with the corrosive stream of messages; fending off his ardour with the occasional brief response. How could she bring him back to his senses? What planet was he on? And as for being Mrs Spenser... the mere thought made her feel shaky and nauseous.

Next day, her parents were both at work and Sophie had the house to herself. Even so, she felt the desire for absolute privacy, and she walked down to the end of the garden as she called Sean's number. The call was answered as though he had been waiting with his finger on the screen.

'Sophie! Oh God, I miss you babe… I don't know whether to walk around grinning like an idiot when I think of our amazing night or kill myself because you're so far away. Say you're missing me.'

Sophie lowered herself on to an old wooden bench under a maple tree and concentrated on the sunlight dappling the leaves.

'Sean… thank you for the flowers, they are beautiful. How did you know where to send them?'

'Mum's PA. I emailed her because I knew she'd have the address from your interview, and she gave me the account number for the florist Mum uses at work. I told her that Mum wanted to say thanks.'

'Oh, of course.'

No mystery then; it had been a simple transaction, although she would have preferred to keep her privacy. 'Listen, Sean, you are making me antsy,' she said. 'Please get one thing into your head. We are not in a relationship. Why can't you accept that? You know I'm fond of you, and I don't want to bum you off, but the way you are carrying on is not cool.'

The silence at the other end was so prolonged that Sophie began to think Sean had ended the call. 'Sean? You still there? Do you understand what I'm saying?'

'Yes, I'm here. Not sure I understand. Don't you feel different now we've slept together?'

'Sex doesn't always mean commitment. You must know that, Sean; you belong to the Tinder generation. It's very sweet of you to be so… so romantic, and that's a good attitude to keep hold of for the future, but we're not in that place. Please don't get daft ideas about marriage. You have a whole lot of growing up to do before you settle for anyone.'

'Don't tell me what I want.'

The boy's tone was waspish. 'I can't believe you would just walk away from me, Soph. Why are you being so cruel? Are you afraid of Mum? You don't know this, but I have a trust fund set up for when I come of age, so we wouldn't ever have to think about money. I don't believe you understand how much I can offer you.'

Sophie studied a patch of daisies at her feet, resisting the urge to stamp on their bright faces. It wasn't their fault she had become embroiled in this nightmare. She tried again.

'You aren't hearing me, Sean. Can you – is there any way you could talk to Matt about things? I'd rather you didn't tell him we've had sex, but you could say that you are pissed off because I was sent away. He might be able to help you get your head round this.'

'Are you crazy? Matt always plays Mum's game. I wish you were here, Soph, it isn't the same without you.'

His voice cracked, and Sophie felt a pang in her heart. It was much more difficult for her to be severe with Sean when he reverted to a suffering boy rather than a macho would-be sweetheart, but she had to persevere.

'Forget Matt, then. Promise me something, Sean,' she said, trying to sound friendly and reasonable. 'You mustn't message or call me for at least three days while you take a reality check. Go out and see who you can pick up in a local bar: you might get lucky. I know it's hard saying goodbye to someone you are fond of, but it gets easier over time. How are Boo and Poppy doing?'

'Don't change the subject. Why are you torturing me like this?'

Sophie ran out of steam. She was being pushed to a point where she wanted to scream at him down the phone and tell him to butt out of her life, and it was difficult to remember that only a few days ago they had been exchanging friendly confidences on the beach. Ominous headlines about stalking loomed at the back of her mind, and she wondered whether she would need to take a harder line to keep Sean in check. Sophie had planned to reactivate her social media accounts now she was back in the UK, but that might have to wait until she had the Sean situation under control. It was simple with her mobile and email: she had the option of blocking the boy or changing her number and address. She hoped that would be a last resort.

'Sophie?'

'Sean. I don't know what else to say. Maybe I should just 'fess up to your mother and ask for her help in bringing you back to earth.'

That was calculated to make him think, and it did so. She was aware of his hesitation at the other end of the line and wondered whether he was pushing the black hair away from his forehead with the gesture he often employed when he was lost in thought.

'No, that's a crap idea. I thought you loved me, Soph.'

'I'm fond of you, Sean, but I'm not in love with you. Can we get back to real life? Tell me about Como and what's going on.'

She did eventually succeed in making him talk more rationally about his surroundings, which sounded luxurious and decadent. He conceded that the amenities of the villa were a welcome change from France and that Poppy and Boo were water babies in the swimming pool, whilst Abbie had developed a heavy crush on a local youth and was making all the family suffer as a result. 'And how are your mother and Matt?' Sophie asked, unable to restrain a note of scorn in the question. She hadn't forgiven Liz for her suspicions or Matt for his obedience to marital behests.

'They are okay, I guess. Mum kicked off a bit about you and Anna de Vos again, but Matt told her not to be paranoid. Anyway, the article will be out soon, so you can see what you make of it. I'm coming to you as soon as we get back.'

'I won't be in Guildford, Sean. I'm going away with my parents, so you would have a wasted journey.'

'You're avoiding me?' he asked, hurt and anger spilling from his voice.

'No. It's a holiday that has been planned for a while. But Sean, please don't come to my house. Maybe we can meet up in London sometime, but only if you promise not to put pressure on me. I can't deal with this otherwise.'

She was conscious of background noise at his end of the line and he swore under his breath.

'I have to go. When can we talk again?'

'Not for a few days – remember what I said?'

'I love you.'

The line went dead. Sophie stretched and exhaled, looking up through the leaves at a beautiful summer sky. She hoped it was a good omen; that Sean would come to see sense and that his desperate longing for her would fade away like scudding clouds over the horizon. Sophie was learning a salutary lesson. She knew now that the reactions of other people couldn't always be predicted and that acts of intimacy shouldn't be undertaken lightly. She hoped that the lesson might not have come too late for the pair of them.

Chapter Thirteen

Sean did as she had asked, and Sophie allowed herself to enjoy a momentary sense of relaxation when a day passed without her receiving any calls or texts from him. She stopped hiding her phone and flinching if she received a message, and she cautiously updated her Instagram account with one or two pictures of herself in France, which received a satisfactory number of likes and comments from friends who had wondered at her lengthy absence. An email arrived from George but much of it was incomprehensible, with references to people and places and events which meant nothing to Sophie, and she accepted that a door was gently closing on that relationship. However, she was energised by constant peeks at her bank balance, which was larger than she had ever known it. She visualised the money as warm and glowing, like an egg whose shell could crack to give birth to any number of possibilities, and she was in no rush to diminish its glory.

But on the morning of the fourth day she awoke to a novel's worth of missed calls and messages, and her inbox was loaded with communications from Sean. Nothing had changed. It seemed that he had saved up his emotions during the three days of forbidden contact and now they had flooded forth like a river in spate after rain. They had to be dealt with, and she excused herself from a shopping trip with her mother to attempt the task, grimly determined to undertake a damage limitation exercise. She took a huge risk and called Sean's mobile, but it went through to voicemail and she left a message.

'Sean. This must stop now. You can call me this morning, because I need to make you see sense.'

But what could more could she do? She considered speaking directly to Liz, but instantly dismissed that plan, knowing that Liz could exact a horrible retaliation involving Jennifer Bradbury. She didn't have Matt's mobile number, and in any case, something held her back from confessing the truth to him – she was reluctant to lose his good opinion, and she could visualise disbelief and then disappointment clouding his blue eyes when he learned that she had succumbed to his stepson's embraces. She was still trying to unearth new options when Sean called her back.

114

'Soph! I can't believe I missed you. We've been visiting some crap villa and our phones had to be switched off in the house, but I can talk now I'm out in the garden. I'm standing in front of a statue of a water nymph and she's got fantastic breasts like you; I feel horny just looking at her.'

'Stop it, Sean.'

Sophie clenched her fist around the phone, wishing she could take him by the shoulders and shake him into reason. 'Please use your head. You are being a bore. I'm not going to rehash everything I said the other day, but if you go on with this bullshit, I shall have to block you. I don't want to do that. I'd like us still to be friends.'

She could hear Italian birds carolling through his silence, and a spluttering Vespa roared away in the background while she waited for him to reply.

'If you block me, I won't be responsible for my actions.'

'Don't be a dickhead. Honestly, Sean, you make me wish I'd never come to France in the first place. I thought I was doing you a favour, and now you are making me pay for it. I'm not taking any more crap from you, so tough luck.'

Wham! Unexpectedly, he ended the call, leaving her nervously uncertain as to whether this was due to temper or expedience. She almost dropped her own phone, feeling as though it possessed an electric energy; as if the charge of Sean's emotion could be felt physically from hundreds of miles away. Did he understand now that she was serious, and they had no future? She prayed that he would write her off as a bad experience; something he could recount to drinking mates in future on occasions when his guard was down. *That bitch I slept with who pied me off afterwards...*

Sophie couldn't face a repetition of these frustrating, dead-end conversations. Her fingers trembled as she followed the instructions to enable her to block Sean's number, and then she trailed back inside to set up a similar action for his email address. She was counting the days now until the holiday in Scotland, hoping it would offer her an escape from the harsh consequences of her last night in France. Sean would soon be back in Britain, but she was confident there was no way he could discover her whereabouts once they had left Guildford, and the distance between Scotland and London seemed mercifully large and impenetrable.

There were no further calls or messages from the boy from other sources, nor were there any deliveries of mail or flowers to her home address. However, in the days before they left, Sophie felt as though she was continually holding her breath as she carried out the chores and routines of a dutiful daughter, and she was so keyed up to get away that she slumped into a grateful, soothing sleep as soon as her father's car was heading north on the busy lanes of the M40. She didn't wake until they stopped at a service station in the bleaker surroundings of the Lake District, where she sat clutching her coffee cup as though it contained a life-giving elixir.

'Are you quite well, Sophie?'

It was obvious from the disapproving lines of her mother's face that she was wondering where her usually serene daughter had vanished to during the time she had been back from France. Sophie knew she had been jumpy and distracted, pushing her plate away with meals half-eaten, and demonstrating a fiddly preoccupation with her phone. Mrs Elliot had even hinted at a belief that Sophie was enamoured of a young Frenchman and was pining for his company.

Sophie murmured something appeasing, but her mother was off on a maternal inquisition. 'You've been very distant since you came home from France. Aren't we good enough for you after Liz Lenister and her family? I'm beginning to think you wish you were back with them,' Mrs Elliot said, and her voice was petulant

'God, no, Mum. I'm sorry if I've been moody. I think I'm just tired and missing the sun and sea. Scotland will soon put me right.'

'Well, I'd like to see you looking happier. It's not as though we've forced you to come with us.'

Mrs Elliot sounded querulous and her mouth turned down. Sophie's phone rang before she could pacify her mother and she tried not to snatch at it to check the caller's identity. It was a number that she didn't recognise and so she let it ring until voicemail kicked in, conscious of her mother's impatient and puzzled face.

'Someone from uni I'd rather not speak to. She's always trying to borrow money off me,' Sophie lied glibly, knowing that her parent would disapprove of such behaviour. The inquisition ceased and they drank their coffee in restored harmony as Mrs Elliot veered off-course, happily recounting examples of people who had tried to take advantage of her own good nature over the years. Once she was safe

116

in the loos, Sophie listened fearfully to the message from the unknown number. As she had suspected, it was from Sean.

'Sophie... it's killing me not being able to talk to you. Please call; I need to hear your voice. I promise I won't be an asshole. We're all back home and this is Ellie's phone. She doesn't know about us, but I've told her my mobile's acting up which is why I'm using hers. Please, Sophie. I love you.'

Sophie hung her head, grieved to hear the desolation in Sean's voice, but she didn't hesitate to block this new number, knowing she had no choice but to stick to her decision to cut all contact with the boy. Then she reassembled a bright holiday face and slunk back to the car.

It was some years since Sophie had visited her relatives in the Highlands. The sight of once-familiar lochs and stony grey villages revived her interest and her spirits, and by the time they drew up outside the Victorian house belonging to her great-aunts she was invaded by an unexpected happiness. Memories of childhood holidays spent walking and fishing revived, and she sucked in great breaths of crisp, pine-scented air like a tonic. Her great-aunts, Mhairi and Ishbel, seemed unchanged at first glance – halos of fluffy grey hair, sensible woollies and shrewd, piercing eyes – but they voiced a babble of surprise at finding such a bonny young woman standing before them. It was comforting to allow herself to be shepherded into the sitting room where a fire blazed despite the summer afternoon, and Sophie fell upon home-baked scones and honey as if she hadn't eaten for days. Her bedroom was furnished simply with a small single bed, wall press and basin whose porcelain was stained from long years of peaty water, but the view over the still waters of the loch and mountains shrouded in purple cloud made up for any deficiencies in her accommodation. She stood at the window drinking it in, repressing the recollections of sea and sand which still threatened to spoil her return to tranquillity.

'Have ye no young men in tow, Sophie?'

Sophie smiled to herself as Ishbel got straight to the point; subjecting her great-niece to a thorough cross-examination about her life over the washing up after dinner. She was feeling dozy after the long journey and a hearty meal of home-made soup and loch trout, but she roused herself to deflect the old lady's interest.

117

'There's no-one special, Aunt Ishbel. I did have a boyfriend earlier this year, but he's gone to America to finish his studies,' she said.

'Well now! That isn't the way at all. But you are a pretty creature, my dearie, and you won't lack for a sweetheart. Get ye back to Cambridge and find yourself a lovely man.'

'That's just what I intend to do.'

Sophie slept peacefully in her narrow bed for the first time since she had returned to her home country. She spent the days walking with her father or braving the cold loch waters afloat in a rocky little boat as they tried to lure fish to their lines, and the load on her heart was lessened because she felt she had taken back control of her life. There was only one bad moment. She was buying bread in the village when she caught sight of a slim, dark young man across the street. Panic invaded her and she almost dropped the bag of baps, slinking from the shop and averting her head before she finally dared to peer over parked cars to where the boy was standing. Of course, it wasn't Sean. Relief coursed through her leaving her limp and saggy, but the incident preyed upon her for the remainder of the day.

They stayed for almost a fortnight before bidding an affectionate farewell to the old ladies and heading south to spend a night or two in Edinburgh. Sophie was pleased by the sight of schoolchildren in uniform during the journey. It meant that Sean would either be back at his school or be about to return there, and she had convinced herself that his opportunities to harass her would be severely curtailed once he was back at his studies.

'I am glad you enjoyed yourself with us, Sophie. We were worried you might find the holiday somewhat dull after your foreign adventures,' her father remarked as they turned for home again. Sophie sighed as they crossed the border and wondered why a tingle of trepidation had chosen that moment to trace its way down her backbone. She glanced at the back seat, where her mother was peacefully asleep.

'I have had the best time, Dad,' she said. 'It was amazing to see the aunts again, and I feel all that exercise has done me good, despite those huge, starchy meals they dish up. Not sure I really like haggis, though. I hope my reluctance wasn't apparent at the table.'

'You disguised it admirably.'

Mr Elliot hooted crossly at a lane-hogging lorry driver. 'It's wonderful to see you looking more relaxed, darling. Your mother and I have been a little worried. We felt that something had occurred in France to upset you, but it isn't our business to pry.'

That meant, of course, that he wanted her to disclose her secrets. Unfortunately, that wasn't going to be possible.

'I did have words with Liz before I left.'

Sophie thought that she could safely tell him about the row over Anna. She recounted the bare details of the conversation, and he nodded in sympathy with her predicament.

'That must have been frustrating for you, but I can't see that you were in the wrong in any way. You should put it out of your head now. When is the article due to be published?' he asked.

'Oh God – I'd completely forgotten. I think it was in last weekend's paper, and of course, the aunts only take the Scottish ones. I wonder if I can find it online?'

She was intrigued at the prospect of reading Anna's take on Liz and her affairs. Despite the frigid parting and the hassle with Sean she still felt a strong link to the family, and such was her loathing for Anna and her methods, she was even conscious of a desire for Liz to acquit herself well in print. Now she grew impatient to be back home, where she would have the opportunity to search for the article on her laptop.

Two weeks free from Sean's attentions had induced a lack of wariness in Sophie. When the Elliots arrived home, she was first to the front door and found to her surprise that it was reluctant to open. After a few hard shoves, she understood why. Her parents had forgotten to cancel the papers and she also had to wade through a heap of mail, which included six handwritten letters addressed to her bearing a London postmark. It was lucky that a neighbour had detained her parents outside to welcome them back from their holiday, giving her time to scoop up the correspondence and stuff it in her bag.

Sophie helped with the remaining luggage and escaped to her room as quickly as she could. She sat on the bed and examined her mail, frightened in case she was handling something explosive. The writing was strangely immature and lacking in grace, a feature she had noticed before in young men who had grown up using keyboards. The first letter was dated from the day she had left for Scotland; the last had

119

been posted yesterday, and she had no doubt about the identity of the author.

Sophie was tempted to destroy them all unopened, but caution stayed her hand.

'If I was really brave, I'd flush the lot down the loo,' she thought, miserably conscious of her indecision, but she finally decided to open the most recent letter. She tore the envelope and drew out a sheet of paper covered in tightly packed scrawl before peeping at the ending; her face a study in apprehension. A quick scan of the contents showed that nothing had changed, although Sean seemed to have toned down his desperation and was making elaborate plans for a future where he assumed that Sophie would have had a change of heart.

'Sophie!'

A plaintive call from her mother forced her back downstairs. Sophie entered the kitchen to find both parents with their heads in the Sunday paper, and she realised that they had found Anna's feature on Liz and her company. 'I'm so glad they've published a photo. Now I can visualise everyone when you are talking about the family,' exclaimed her mother, who hadn't yet taken on board the fact that Sophie tried very hard never to discuss her companions in Brittany. Sophie's father was frowning as he read through the copy.

'Anna de Vos doesn't pull her punches, does she? She starts by saying 'A dilapidated cliff-top house on the cool northern coast of France is the last place you would expect to find Liz Lenister, CEO of financial high-fliers Lenister Legrand, spending her summer holiday.' Was it really that bad, Sophie?'

'Mm. It was a bit run down, but the location was amazing. Can I see, please?'

She tried not to snatch the paper from her father's hands. Mrs Elliot peered over her shoulder as Sophie greedily absorbed the contents of the article.

'The boy is very nice looking, isn't he? And which one is Boo?' she asked.

Sophie pointed a finger at the little girl, who was sitting on her father's lap and squinting slightly in the sun. Poppy leaned against her mother, and Abbie had turned her head away, so only part of her face was visible. Liz challenged the camera with her usual professional, hard stare, but the shot had caught Matt at an angle which made his handsome face appear even more rugged than usual. 'Ooh, the husband is a bit of all right. He looks a lot younger than Liz, though.'

Mrs Elliot's avid curiosity was something Sophie could do without.

'Yes, he is. I'm sorry that it isn't possible to see more of the background, because the view from that part of the garden was so beautiful,' she said.

Sophie stifled a disturbing memory as she gazed at the photo. She didn't want to forget the heart-thumping pleasure of Matt's embrace in that very spot, although she was endeavouring to expunge everything that had happened during her night with Sean from memory. But there were no contentious revelations in the article and Sophie didn't know whether to be pleased or sorry about this. The focus was on City business and Liz's latest deal, and Matt's start-up was merely mentioned in a paragraph or two right at the end, like a bone thrown to a dog. Sophie wondered how happy Matt would be about that. There was the briefest comment about the children, and she assumed they were included simply to soften the profile of a tough and thick-skinned entrepreneur.

Perhaps that's why Anna was so anxious for me to give her some bitchy feedback, she reflected. It appeared that Liz had controlled the interview proceedings in her usual dominant way and the journalist hadn't been given much to work with. The published result made the row with Liz seem even more unnecessary, but Sophie was pleased to feel that she had been exonerated by the lack of controversy.

'Liz is evidently Wonder Woman,' her father said, although his face showed a healthy scepticism. Mrs Elliot was still devouring the article, enjoying a spot of fame-by-association.

'It says here that Matthew Braeburn's business is based in Cambridge. You should look him up when you are back there, darling,' she said, and Sophie tried to tell herself that would be a terrible idea.

'It's Braybrooke, not Braeburn. And I'm not likely to be visiting the Science Park, am I?' she said with ill-concealed impatience, wondering why her mother was so keen for her to keep in contact with her ex-employers.

'Oh yes, Braybrooke. I thought he might like to see you and find out how you are getting on.'

Sophie left her mother to her innocent conjectures and returned to her room to read Sean's letter more carefully. He was back in confinement at his public school and she assumed that she was safe from the prospect of an impromptu visit, but the snowshower of correspondence would have to stop before her parents began to ask difficult questions. She debated the problem without finding an answer as she ate her supper, but later that evening her college friend Hannah called, giving her an unexpected reprieve.

Hannah had spent the previous month inter-railing around Europe, but she was now home with a plan for the last weeks of the vacation.

'I met this guy who's got a flat in Castle Street,' she told Sophie. 'He won't be back in Cambridge until term starts, and he's looking to sublet two rooms until then. Do you fancy going up early, before we can get into our rooms in college? He's not asking much, and we could do some fun stuff we don't usually have time for before the weather gets bad again.'

The Cambridge academic term was due to begin in the first week of October. Hannah's suggestion meant that the girls could return for a two-week period before that date, and Sophie leapt upon this idea. She had enjoyed reverting to childhood for the duration of her time in Scotland, but the prospect of renewed independence was tempting. She authorised her friend to make the arrangements and broke the news of her imminent departure to her astonished parents, trying to sugar the pill with excuses about advance preparation for a term of intensive academic study.

Next morning, Sophie borrowed paper and envelope from her father's bureau and composed a brief missive to send to Sean at his school address.

'I'm not going to comment on what you've written, but you should know that I am going away again. Please don't send letters to my home, because I will tell my father to destroy them unopened. I hope you soon settle back into school life and forget about me.'

Mrs Elliot was upset at the prospect of losing her daughter, but Sophie's father soothed her with the promise of a visit to Cambridge when Sophie had moved back into college.

'I can hardly believe it's your last year – it seems only yesterday that we were driving you up the M11 for your first term,' he mused. 'Have you begun to think what you might do when you graduate?'

'Perhaps Liz Lenister could find you a job,' Mrs Elliot suggested, and Sophie winced at the thought of approaching Liz with that request.

'I'll bear that in mind, Mum. Please don't be miffed that I'm going back to Cambridge – after all, I haven't seen any of my friends for months, and I want to catch up with everyone again.'

'Of course, you were away in France all last year,' agreed Mrs Elliot, talking herself into acceptance of her daughter's early departure. 'I expect you can't wait to tell them all about your time in Brittany. How jealous everyone will be.'

'Mm.'

Sophie doubted that, but she was invigorated by the prospect of a new beginning. The spectre of Sean; sad-faced and pining, which had haunted her thoughts since her return from France was beginning to fade into history, and not before time.

Chapter Fourteen

Cambridge was still in summer mode when Sophie returned, although the emerald shades of trees and lawns were beginning to merge into a palette of earthy autumn colours. But the sun shone brightly on the grey stones of the city, and she rejoiced to be back in the company of her old friend and the familiar streets. The rooms Hannah had found turned out to be less than luxurious but were bearable for a short period, although the mouldy grouting in the bathroom induced shudders. The girls escaped to go walking and punting on the Cam, but it wasn't warm enough for Sophie to show off her French sundress.

One fine afternoon, they idled away some hours floating along the Backs in company with Joe and Daniel, two friends Hannah had made during the previous year. Daniel was reading economics, and he was all gaping attention when he heard how Sophie had spent her summer.

'You mean you were on holiday with the woman who runs Lenister Legrand? My God, what an opportunity for you to get your legs under that table! I don't suppose you could get me an introduction, could you?'

He almost dropped the punt pole in his enthusiasm, and rivulets of water dripped down his thigh. Sophie shut him down at once.

'No. Liz is a very private person, and I don't think she works like that.'

Hannah groaned and glowered at her from under fierce eyebrows.

'I can't get Soph to tell me anything about her time in France,' she told Daniel, looking to soften her friend's curt response. 'I know that Liz Lenister stopped her from posting stuff, and I'm beginning to think Soph's still under a gagging order, because she won't let on about them at all. Isn't that true, Sophie?'

'Don't hassle me. There's nothing to tell. It was a seaside holiday with some great meals thrown in, and I don't think you'd be interested in my beach adventures with two little girls.'

Sophie stared at her friend; her face smooth with defiance. She had been tempted to confess to the extent of her activities with Sean more than once, but something held her back. It was more than a sense of shame; it was the feeling that she had allowed herself to be used by members of the family, and she didn't want to appear pathetic in the eyes of her contemporaries. 'She did pay me well, but I earned the money,' she said. 'The family were pretty much a nightmare, apart from the younger children.'

'I read about Liz recently,' Joe remarked. 'She sounds like a tough cookie. Did she splash the cash when you were with them?'

'It wasn't an environment where big spending was an option, but it's obvious the kids are used to getting what they want – the teens, that is.'

'Did they ever make you feel awkward?'

'Not about money, no.'

'Why, what else did they do?'

Why wouldn't Joe drop the subject? At that moment, another punt crashed into them and Sophie was glad that Liz and co were forgotten in the ensuing chaos. Since her run-in with Anna, she appreciated the wisdom of reticence regarding her experiences with the family and was already rehearsing an expurgated version to give to Jennifer Bradbury.

Joe's continued attentions made it plain that he liked Sophie's company. He asked her out to see the latest Bond film and when they ended up in a pub, he reached for her hand in a tentative, endearing way, while she wondered whether he might be someone she could grow close to. He had an open, self-deprecating personality which was attractive, but his blunt face and stubbly chin could not compete with the image of blue eyes, confident smile and clean-cut features which had lodged stubbornly in her mind as the epitome of a desirable man. Sophie's fantasies had veered in a new direction – she found herself casting an approving eye over smart men in suits, and knew that this was because of the attraction she had felt for Matt. She had to tell Joe that she wasn't up for anything physical or romantic, leaving him disappointed.

'You've changed, Sophie,' Hannah scolded her as they shared a takeaway pizza on the sofa before the tv. The state of the kitchen discouraged them from all but the most basic cooking, and their diet was unhealthily restricted as a result. Hannah's tone was accusing, and Sophie stiffened in self-defence as she looked at her friend.

'What do you mean, changed?' she asked.

'I dunno – you seem closed off; a bit harder than you were before. I blame your rich friends. Did anything happen in France to upset you, or have you adopted their habit of bulldozing through life? Poor Joe's in bits, but you don't seem to care.'

'I don't fancy him. That's not my fault. He's a lovely guy, but…'

'I see you're going to be even more fussy than you were before. When are you ever going to have sex?'

'Can we talk about something else? You can't make generalisations about stuff like this.'

All the same, Sophie had a feeling that Hannah was right. Her experiences with Sean and his stepfather had left her with an unsettling sense of confusion. She no longer trusted her own responses to the opposite sex and felt that it was preferable to stay on the sidelines of romance and relationships until her confidence had returned.

The girls moved back to college with unconstrained relief. Their rooms, although simply furnished, seemed luxurious after the experience of the flat. But when Sophie investigated the pigeonhole she had been allocated, a familiar sense of frustration descended upon her. Two letters in Sean's writing nestled there. She flung them into her bag and disposed of them unread, but they left her with a renewed sense of dread. When would the boy accept that she wanted nothing more to do with him? Sophie felt as though his desire for her permeated everything she did; it left a sensation like wading through treacle. His grip was tenacious, and sometimes she feared he would never be persuaded to let go.

Sophie knew she would not relax until she could get her interview with Jennifer Bradbury over, and so she called on her tutor as term got underway, feeling as though she was reliving her experiences in March as she clattered up the steps to Jennifer's rooms. Her tutor was in residence and was delighted to see her.

'Sophie – how nice to have you back with us. You are looking very well. I hope your time in France was successful. How did you find the family?' she asked.

Sophie recited a bland account of the holiday, knowing that Jennifer's concern would be limited to her dealings with Liz. She had to inject a more realistic note about this part of her narrative.

'Liz isn't the easiest person to live with, but I think I did what she wanted,' she said glibly. 'It was a beautiful place, and she was

126

complimentary about my French. The little girls were sweeties, and we had a good time together.'

'I'm so glad. I was sure you and Liz would get on. She has promised to endow a scholarship for a student to read economics, and I think we can thank you for helping there. I'm very glad that everything worked out so well.'

Sophie galloped down the stairs, feeling a weight shifting from her as she realised that her holiday secrets remained undiscovered. It was good to be free of one worry, even if it was too early to tell if Sean would finally accept the status quo.

The friends soon slipped back into routine, although it took time to adjust to the renewed emphasis on formal work as they began to consolidate the skills acquired during their overseas placements. October brought gales from the east, and the students hurried along cobbled streets, muffled and shivering as autumn set in with chilly certainty and falling leaves thickened the air. On the second Saturday of term, Sophie breakfasted in hall and returned to her room, contemplating a walk into the town centre to spend some of her nest egg on a new winter coat. There was a rap at her door.

'Come in.'

She was expecting to see a friend, but the door opened – and her gaze grew glassy as it fell upon the figure of Sean. A tremulous smile lit up his beautiful face. He looked alarmed and yet delighted, like someone who has unexpectedly been granted a long-held, keenly anticipated wish.

Sophie stood as though sewn to the carpet in amazement.

'Oh, *Soph*!'

He slammed the door behind him, took two swift paces and seized her in his arms. 'Sophie, why the fuck have you been so cruel to me? Don't you know you have almost broken my heart?'

Sean was kissing her now, his lips devouring her hair, her ears, her face, and she struggled to escape his feverish grasp. She was helpless; winded by a curious sensation of both pain and pleasure at his unexpected appearance. Sean's hair had been cropped to a schoolboy brusqueness which made him appear younger than before, and Sophie wasn't used to him in trousers and a conventional shirt and sweater. The combination made her remember the boy she had been fond of rather than the monster of recent weeks.

At last, he ran out of breath and pulled back, gazing thirstily into her eyes. 'I've waited for you so fucking long, and I love you so much, my darling Sophie.'

He motioned towards the bed. 'Can we have sex again? Please; I've tortured myself thinking about your body.'

This was not an option. He reached for her breast and Sophie's mind moved rapidly, selecting a reason which he couldn't argue with.

'I've got my period,' she lied, calculating upon the standard squeamish reaction of young men to this feminine mystery, and the lie worked. He released his grip on her and his shoulders slumped in disappointment. 'And anyway, sex is out of the question. Didn't you understand *anything* I've been trying to say to you since I got back to England? I've had it with all this crap from you, Sean, and I don't know what you think you're doing here.'

The light died from his face and he burst into shattering, shoulder-heaving sobs which tore at her defences. He was just a boy, albeit a misguided, fixated boy, and she couldn't bear to see this misery. 'Oh, Sean! Don't, just don't…'

She put her arms around him and pulled him down to sit on the bed next to her. This time, she couldn't give in to him – it would only prolong the impossible situation, but she had to offer him some comfort, for her sake as much as his. She held him, murmuring nursery words of consolation until he regained some self-control and straightened up, scrubbing at his face with one sleeve.

Sophie handed him a box of tissues and he made a sketchy attempt to wipe away the tears. 'Please don't cry, Sean; it hurts me to see you like this. I'm so sorry I can't give you what you want, and I wish I knew how to make things better,' she said.

'You could make things better by saying we can be together,' he mumbled, sounding like an aggrieved infant. She stroked damp strands of hair away from his forehead with a maternal touch.

'But that's not possible. How did you even get here, Sean? Aren't you supposed to be at school?'

'I'm on an Upper Sixth visit here to help us decide about final UCAS choices. There's a group of us staying in a poxy hostel, and later, they've arranged talks and a dinner I can't get out of. But we had a couple of hours free before lunch to look round for ourselves, so I took a chance…'

128

His shoulders shook in a shuddery sigh, and he stroked her fingers in a way that made her recall a less momentous conversation in France. 'I'm sorry if I've bugged you, Soph, but you are so important to me. You don't seem to understand that.'

'And you to me, but not in the way you seem to want.'

As Sean grew calmer, Sophie repeated all the arguments she had used before and he listened without interrupting, although he clutched her hands in his own like someone trying to escape from drowning. Sorrow was etched in dark circles around his blue eyes, but Sophie steeled herself to resist their appeal. When she had finished speaking, they sat for some minutes in silence, and she wondered whether this time she had managed to get her message across.

'You've been stalking me, Sean,' she said, recalling her sense of entrapment. 'Would you want your mother to know that? It's been hard not to tell my parents what was going on. There were so many times when I was tempted to ask for their help.'

'I'm not ashamed of anything I've done, and I don't give a toss if Mum gets to know about us.'

That stung. Sophie removed her hands from his grasp.

'I don't want her involved. Can't you see how it will look if Liz realises that I've done the one thing she asked me not to do? You were the instigator, Sean, but how can I prove that? I wish now that I'd screamed blue murder when you came into my room. At least I'd only have had a few hours of embarrassment, rather than weeks of harassment.'

Sean scowled. He looked nothing like his mother, but her indomitable strength of will was suddenly apparent in his hard mouth and lowered brow and Sophie recoiled from this unfamiliar person. He spat words towards her.

'I thought we were in love. Were you playing me along all those weeks in France? You encouraged me, you let me hold your hand and I don't remember you objecting when I shagged you. You are a total bitch.'

'None of that is true; not one little bit! We were good friends and nothing more, and I told you it was a big mistake to have sex. If that's the way you feel, why don't you fuck off now? Good luck with the rest of your life.'

129

They stared at one another, breathless; furious. Sophie was alarmed by Sean's change of mood, wondering whether his sudden aggression was prompted by embarrassment because he had shown weakness by breaking down before her. A clanking noise in the corridor recalled her to reality, and she jumped at a reprieve.

'Look, I'm going to have to let the cleaner in to do my room. I don't want to leave things like this, Sean. Let's go somewhere for a coffee and try to apply some common sense.'

Sean rose slowly to his feet as if on autopilot. He peered at the mirror on the opposite wall, running a hand through his hair and examining his face for signs of weeping.

'I look like shit. I hope you're satisfied, Sophie. Sometimes I wish you'd never come to France,' he said.

'So do I.'

Sophie was bitter, but she reminded herself that she was the adult in the room. 'You look okay,' she reassured him. 'Let's try to be civilised, shall we?'

She hunted for her phone and straightened the bedcover. Sean stood there in a zombie trance, but he allowed Sophie to retrieve his jacket from the floor and drape it around his shoulders. The polished corridors were mercifully empty as she led him back down towards the porters' lodge, and she searched for anything which might relieve the tension between them. 'Would you like to see round the college now you're here?' she asked, and he shook his head.

'I'll never get the grades for this place, and it's too much like school anyway. I want to stay in London. You won't be here after next summer, will you?'

'I don't know where I'll be or what I'll be doing.'

This wasn't a brush-off, but a simple statement of fact. Sean opened his mouth as though to challenge her, but a sudden press of young people made him circumspect, and they passed out into the road in silence.

There was a Saturday morning cheerfulness in the streets, which were busy with shoppers. The fight had gone out of Sean. He stumbled along next to Sophie, hands in pockets and with his face set in moody disappointment. Sophie took him to a café not far from the river where she knew there were suitable nooks for private conversation, and she would be safe from the inquisitive gaze of people she knew. She asked

130

for coffee for herself, but Sean ordered tea. His face was ashy, and she added a request for teacakes, thinking that he might need a sugar boost.

'I bet you haven't eaten much this morning. I don't want you passing out on me,' she said, trying to make a joke out of the situation, but he didn't respond. However, he devoured a teacake when it arrived, and faint colour began to glaze his cheeks as they sat there. The young waitress who brought their order was gazing at him as if he was the latest Instagram idol, and Sophie nudged him with one foot. 'See that? You could pull her without trying. I wish you'd get out there and date a few hot chicks – you'd soon forget all about me.'

Sean's eyes grew fiery with displeasure.

'Don't patronise me. How do you know what I want? We've slept together, Sophie; you are my first love. That's an unbreakable bond – why can't you feel it too?' He leaned across the table and his breathing quickened. 'Please tell me you haven't been with anyone else since you got home. That would finish me.'

Sophie bit her lip. Would it be a good idea to fabricate a new boyfriend? That might result in Sean becoming even more unreasonable, besides, it would be a lie. She felt that the truth was the best thing to cling on to in this choppy tide of feelings.

'Well, I haven't been seeing anyone, although that's got nothing to do with our situation,' she said. 'Please be reasonable, Sean. We don't have a future – at least, not at present.'

She added this proviso because she was disturbed by the fanatical light in his eyes, and she didn't intend to be a sacrificial lamb. 'Who knows, maybe we'll meet up again one day, and things might work out for us then. We both have a lot of growing up to do first. But it isn't going to work now.'

The atmosphere felt sticky with awkwardness. Sophie gazed at people strolling past the window, envying their uncomplicated lives and desperate for escape. Sean glanced at his watch and expelled a breath of frustration.

'Fuck. I'll have to go any minute. Listen, Soph, there's one thing you need to understand. I can make big trouble for you. Aren't you ashamed of grooming and seducing a schoolboy? People do time for that sort of thing. Your parents would be shocked to think their darling daughter behaved like that, not to mention this Jennifer woman who seems so important to you. I don't think Mum has coughed up for the scholarship for your college yet – yes, I know all about that – and she might think again when she finds out what you did with me. *I could easily give a very different account of what happened in France.'*

Menace edged his voice as he spoke the last sentence. He rose to his feet, leaving her turned to stone. 'You'd better think this over and we'll talk again tomorrow morning – I can bunk off for half an hour at eleven before we head back to school. I'll see you outside this place. At the end of the month it's half term, and I've told Mum I'm going to a friend to stay over. But I intend to spend the time in Cambridge so we can pick up where we left off in France. You can choose the hotel.'

He smirked, then bent and clamped his mouth upon hers. There was no affection in the action, only possession; it felt to Sophie like a Judas kiss. 'I know you'll come to see things my way.'

Chapter Fifteen

Sophie barely registered the flutter amongst the waitresses as Sean brushed past them on his way out of the cafe. Her head was dizzy as she tried to make sense of his threats. Her actions didn't constitute a hanging offence, but she understood that he could make allegations which would embarrass and upset her parents and damage her reputation within the college beyond hope of repair. She didn't want to give in to blackmail, and the thought of being intimate with him again made her spine shiver, and not with desire.

The charming boy who had gained her friendship in France had vanished. Perhaps Sean had learned from his mother that it was permissible to seize what he wanted, using any means that came to hand. His threats today demonstrated that he lacked a moral compass, and that was an omission Sophie laid at his mother's door.

'You want anything else?'

The waitress interrupted her reverie, surveying her with ill-concealed envy. 'Your fella's well fit,' the girl added, and Sophie shuddered.

'Nothing else, thanks.'

Sophie fumbled for a credit card and went to the till. There was no way she could contemplate shopping after this unexpected drama, and she had no idea how to extricate herself from the dilemma. She considered going to Jennifer Bradbury and confessing her secret, but then she pictured the ensuing weeks of tutorials where she would sit crushed beneath the weight of her tutor's disappointment, and that was insupportable. If she told her parents, there would be a restraint on relations which might take years to dissipate. Hannah was away for the weekend, and there was no-one else she could trust to keep a secret of such magnitude.

The miserable day ebbed away while she lurked in her room, mulling over a suitable course of action. She couldn't risk shirking the meeting with Sean tomorrow. There had been too much of his mother in his face as he uttered his ultimatum for her to doubt the seriousness of his intentions, but she was unable to find a response which might counter his threats.

She was trying – and failing – to finish an essay before dinner when she was disturbed for a second time by a sharp rap at her door. Sophie froze at the keyboard. Had Sean managed to escape from his fellow pupils again? She stared at the wooden panels, unwilling to contemplate whatever lurked outside.

The knock was repeated. Sophie knew that her light was visible through a glass transom above the door, so it was useless to pretend that she wasn't there. She gathered her courage and croaked an invitation to enter, and discovered Matthew Braybrooke looming in her doorway. The shock of his appearance on the heels of her morning visitor hit her like a brick.

'Sophie! Surprise! I hope I'm not interrupting anything.'

'Matt... come in. I wasn't expecting to see *you*.'

Sophie was shaking now; a mixture of relief and astonishment almost depriving her of speech. The dramatic events of the day bore down on her with the force of a tidal wave, and it was her turn to collapse in a fit of racking sobs.

'My God... I don't usually have this effect on women.'

Matt slammed the door behind him and stood scratching his head. 'Am I that unwelcome?' he asked. 'Do you want me to leave?'

'N-n-no.'

It was an effort for Sophie to get the words out. 'It isn't *you*. I just thought...'

How could she admit that she had been dreading the sight of his stepson? Matt put his arms around her, and he uttered warm, soothing murmurs in her ear. He was wearing a navy coat of soft wool; a grown-up garment which gave off a pleasing aroma of rainwashed pavements and autumn evenings as she buried her face in his shoulder. She thought that his lips moved on her hair, but the soft caress was nothing like the rough kisses of the morning.

'What did you think? Poor Sophie, something has happened to upset you, that's obvious.'

She pulled back, searching his face to see whether she could trust him.

'I've made your coat all wet,' she said, idiotically, and he laughed.

'It was pretty damp to begin with. Do you mind if I take it off now? I'd like to get to the bottom of this.'

He released her and hung his coat across the back of a chair before drawing her down next to him to sit on the bed. She was sensible of an uncanny symmetry with the events of the morning and quailed at the thought of what was to come. 'Why don't you tell Uncle Matt all about it?' he said, with persuasive gentleness. 'You know what they say about sharing troubles.'

Sophie hiccupped. Matt was the last person she wanted to tell about her predicament, but he was also ideally placed to understand both parties. She stalled for a second or two, giving herself time to decide.

'What are you doing in Cambridge on a weekend, Matt?'

'I had a meeting scheduled with someone flying in from Stockholm, but the plane's delayed until tomorrow because of bad weather. I remembered you saying what college you belonged to, so I thought I'd see if you were free for dinner. Can't promise you the *Petit Prince*, but I'm sure we can find somewhere nice, if you don't already have plans.'

Sophie felt that he might not want to take her to dinner when he learned about her and Sean. That would be a pity, but it was more important to ask for his assistance in dealing with her immediate issues with the boy. Matt kept her hand in a loose, friendly grasp as she began to stutter out a halting account of her relationship with Sean, beginning with Liz's instructions at her interview. She told him honestly why she had grown fond of Sean, despite his frequently expressed wishes to get her into bed. When it came to her last night in France, the words tumbled out of her and she was brave enough to recount events without false embarrassment.

'I didn't know what to do for the best, Matt,' she said. 'If I'd gone on resisting him, there would have been a terrible scene in the house. My God – I even decided I was doing something good for Sean, because I felt it was nicer for him to lose his virginity with me and not with a girl he barely knew that he'd met in a club, or something. And I didn't realise how determined he was. Later… well, it felt a bit like rape, because he was so forceful that I couldn't stop him. But I wish so much that I'd locked my door that night.'

Sophie was conscious of rising tension in Matt's body as he listened to her tale. She felt that he must be condemning her, but when she raised her eyes to his, she was heartened to read only sympathy there. He gave a jerky shake of his head.

'My stepchildren never fail to amaze me,' he commented, and his tone was grim. 'What happened next?'

'I made it plain that we were weren't in a relationship, but he wouldn't stop calling and messaging me and, in the end, I had to block him. Then he sent letters – lots of letters. Flowers, too; it was like a rainstorm that wouldn't blow over. And this morning, he turned up here, escaping from a school trip. Now he's threatening that if I don't sleep with him again, he'll tell everyone about what happened in France, saying that I groomed him and forced him into having sex with me. By everyone, I mean not just Liz, but my parents and my tutor here. I know I haven't done anything illegal, but I can't bear to think that people I respect might believe I abused someone like that. I don't know if I'd ever be able to deal with the shame. Sean won't listen to reason.'

Sophie hated the long silence which followed her admission. She felt that Matt must regard her as tainted by the episode, and she waited for the withdrawal of his hand and the excuse to abandon his invitation to dinner. However, he merely clasped her fingers more firmly between his own and regarded her with the candid blue scrutiny which had made her heart beat faster in France.

'Sophie, I don't know what to say. I'm so sorry that a member of my family has put you through this.'

'Well, Sean isn't your child…'

'I regard him as one of my own, but I think that his genetic background has a lot to do with this appalling behaviour. Liz indulges and reprimands him by turn, and she doesn't always set the best example for him to follow. He's used to getting his own way. And Robert Spenser isn't a father to be proud of.'

There was silence, while Sophie tried to find it in herself to feel sorry for Sean. She felt sorrier for having to confess all this to Matt.

'Do you think I'm a terrible person?' she asked. 'I apologise for dumping this on you Matt, but you did ask me what was wrong.'

'I don't think you are a terrible person, and you were right to tell me. Listen; here's what we'll do. I will keep your rendezvous with Sean tomorrow, and I'm pretty sure I can get him to back off. I know where some bodies are buried.'

He saw her astonished face and guffawed. 'I don't mean literally, you goose. But I understand how I can exert some leverage upon him. Just don't ask me for the details.'

'Oh Matt! If you could only get him to see sense...'

'Sean owes me a favour or two. And whatever he's been saying to you, he wouldn't want Liz to know about the way he's carried on since France. I can see it's been a distressing time for you, Sophie, but I think I can help.'

'I've felt desperate. It's such a relief to talk about it at last. And I'm so ashamed of myself, although I can't see that I'm really to blame.'

'You shouldn't feel ashamed, Sophie.'

Matt squeezed her hand and replaced it on her lap.

'We obviously need to talk further, but I suggest that you go and freshen up and we'll take ourselves off for the evening. I could do with a drink after all this, and I'm sure you could too.'

She was reassured by the calm tones in which he spoke. 'That is, unless you have a hot date with some hulking great rugby blue,' he added, and she laughed at that, shaking her head. 'Good. Can I wait here, or would you rather I skedaddle down to where the porters hang out?'

'No; do wait here, Matt. I'll take what I need to the bathroom.'

A wave of self-consciousness swept over Sophie as she jumped up to hunt for her toiletries and a change of clothes. Matt's presence, and especially his promise to deal with Sean, had energised her, so that she already felt more hopeful about the future, although it had been painful to admit to her part in the saga. It didn't take long for her to get dressed and renew her make-up, but she regretted that she hadn't washed her hair that morning. She drew the dark strands away from her face and secured them with a band, aware that she wasn't looking at her best. Matt looked up from his phone when she reappeared and grinned.

'You look gorgeous,' he commented, just a fraction too heartily. She knew she didn't look gorgeous tonight, what with the hair and the crying. 'I suppose it isn't the right weather for that little dress you wore in France,' he continued, as if anxious to smooth away a difficulty, and Sophie was touched that he had not forgotten a significant moment. When they were outside, he offered her his arm in a grave, fatherly way, and now she had no qualms in taking it. She enjoyed walking in step with him through the damp streets, conscious that this was an occasion when his assistance was essential.

Matt took her to an Italian bistro for dinner, remarking that it was a place where he wouldn't feel inferior by not speaking the language, although she understood this was meant as a tease. Sophie gradually allowed herself to relax in the candlelight, feeling stress melt away with the restorative powers of good food and wine. She clung to the assurance that Matt would find a solution to her problems. He still had the remnants of a summer tan and looked suave and handsome, and Sophie noticed the women at an adjoining table send chippy smiles and glances in his direction, in contrast to the glacial looks she received. Sophie accepted that she was out of the running, telling herself not to entertain any silly ideas. She'd almost come a cropper in her dealings with Sean, and his stepfather was certainly out of bounds.

'Tell me about Poppy and Boo. I really missed them when I came back home,' she said, and Matt smiled; looking pleased to hear this.

'They missed you, too. I think that Ellie's nose was out of joint for a while when we returned from Italy, because they would keep talking about you. They are both well, and looking forward to Halloween, because they are going to a party dressed as hobgoblins, naughty little things. Boo says that fairies are *so* out of fashion.'

'I'd love to see a picture of that.'

He nodded, but didn't pursue the subject, and she wondered whether he felt it necessary to keep her at a distance from the rest of his family. Even if he wasn't apportioning blame for the events in France, he probably thought less well of her than before. However, it seemed rude not to enquire about Liz and Abbie, and she framed a tentative question about their well-being. His eyes narrowed, and he took his time to reply.

'I'm relieved to say that I hardly ever see Abigail when she is at boarding school. Liz is hot-foot after a new merger, and I'm keeping well clear.'

His tone did not encourage further probing.

'And I hope your business is thriving,' Sophie murmured, and at last, his eyes came to life.

'Things are beginning to take off, thank God. We've identified a spin-off market, and the future looks a lot more positive. I had a few doubts as to whether we'd make it during the summer, but we've come through without incurring any casualties.'

'I'm so pleased.'

'Yes. We're more than busy, and as a result, I'm having to spend several days in Cambridge every week. I can't stand hotel life, and today I've found myself a quaint little bolt-hole – the smallest pad you can imagine – so in future, I can come and go as I like. Liz thinks I'm crazy. But I don't get the chance to be independent at home, and I'm very comfortable with a beer, a carry-out curry and the prospect of a good football match on the box. It takes me back to my bachelor days.'

Sophie finished her pasta, thinking about the implications of this remark. She was curious to know where he would be living but didn't like to press him for further details in case it looked as though she was invading his privacy.

'When do you move in?' she asked.

'It's vacant now, so I'll settle myself in next week.'

His glance fell upon her empty plate. 'I'm pleased to see that this upset with Sean hasn't affected your appetite. Do you remember the restaurant in Dinan? That seems a very long time ago.'

'Yes, it does.'

Sophie decided it was wise not to revisit that occasion. She recognised that sharing memories prompted waves of nostalgia which were both pleasant and painful, and she hardly knew which to wish for. 'Tell me about your time at Como. I expect you were pleased to find yourselves living in luxury again,' she said.

Matt smiled, as though remembering a sentimental moment.

'Funnily enough, I think we all missed the old house in Saint-Lunaire,' he replied. 'It may have been shabby, but it had character, and it was wonderfully situated on that headland. Did you see how Anna de Vos described it in her piece? What a cow that woman is.'

'I suppose that's a requirement for a successful columnist.'

Anna's name brought a frisson between them, causing both to hesitate as they recalled the aftermath of the journalist's visit. Sophie didn't want to embarrass Matt – after all, she was relying on him to help her deal with Sean – but the circumstances of his abrupt departure were a mystery which had preyed on her mind, and this seemed a good opportunity to discover the truth. 'I was surprised when you left France so suddenly,' she continued, trusting that the eggshells on which she was treading would bear her weight. 'I hope it wasn't a result of anything I did.'

Matt took a long swig of wine. His face was carefully non-committal, but he moved in his chair with a shrug of unease.

'You know that Abigail saw us together in the garden?' he said. 'I couldn't get Liz to understand that the kiss meant nothing, and it became obvious to me that she might kick up such a fuss that you would pack your bags there and then. I didn't want you to lose out financially, so it was easier for me to remove myself from the scene. I believe that Liz accepted she was wrong in the end, but by then, she was focussed on going to Italy. Anyway, that's water under the bridge now.'

The kiss meant nothing. Sophie withdrew into herself, mortification creeping across her like a slow paralysis. It had meant something to her, and she believed at the time that it was important to Matt as well. *Back in your box* she chided herself, and she wasn't aware that her face reflected internal disappointment. Matt looked at her and frowned.

'What's the matter? Don't beat yourself up thinking about the past; it's never worth it. Learn a lesson and move on, that's my philosophy. But you look shattered, Sophie – I expect this trouble with Sean has knocked the stuffing out of you. Shall I ask for the bill?'

She nodded, incapable of speech. Somehow, she'd expected more from the evening; had perhaps been hoping for a renewal of Matt's interest in her. That wasn't going to happen, and she gave herself a mental shake. Once Matt had settled the bill, she steered the conversation back to practical matters.

'Should I give you my mobile number, Matt? I'd be so grateful if you could give me a quick update when you've spoken with Sean tomorrow.'

'Yes, of course.'

He handed his phone over for her to enter the number and placed his hand over hers when she returned it. 'Trust me, Sophie. I'll do my best to get Sean to back off. And if he doesn't, we'll have to find another way to deal with him.'

Their footsteps made solemn echoes in the empty streets as Matt escorted her back to college, and Sophie was reluctant to bid him goodbye. She wanted to cling to him and to feel the reassurance that he was still her friend. But he stopped outside the lodge and planted a chaste kiss upon her cheek. 'Mm, your face is frozen, Sophie. Your jacket isn't thick enough to keep out these icy east winds. You'd better get to bed with a hot water bottle.'

'I would, if I had one. Thank you, Matt, for the meal and for saying that you'll help. You are a nice man.'

She added this almost under her breath, and Matt gave her a quick nod of farewell, as though pleased by her commendation. Sophie watched him stride down the street, feeling choky with desolation. He was a reminder of happier days and she fought down an urge to run after him and insinuate herself into his arms one last time. As it was, she returned to her room, and waited for sleep to bring an end to what had seemed a terribly long day.

Her dreams that night were disturbed by a progression of nightmares. Sean's face loomed over her and his hands were busy with her body. Liz's mouth twisted into a silent scream as she flung open a door to reveal the guilty pair, and Abigail crouched in the corner, her face a cat-like mask of satisfaction as she observed the wreck of lives unfolding before her. Next day, Sophie crept down to breakfast, deflecting kind enquiries from friends who were concerned by her weary eyes and the pallor of her skin. Afterwards, she tried to apply herself to her essay, but as the clock ticked on towards eleven, she felt herself shrivelling up with anxiety. It wasn't that she didn't trust Matt, but she was afraid that Sean was no longer a person who could be reasoned with.

The minutes crawled by. Sophie stared at her phone, willing a message to appear, but the screen remained obstinately blank. Midday came and went, and there was still no word from Matt. Perhaps he was finding Sean more difficult to subdue than he had anticipated, and as this thought took root, she stared, unseeing, into the distance as a familiar feeling of depression began to cloak itself around her shoulders.

Chapter Sixteen

Sophie had arranged to meet a friend at lunchtime and so she roused herself to drag a brush through her hair and pull on a clean sweatshirt before wandering down to the college dining hall. The students were lining up to take their places in a queue and she leaned against the wall, pleased to be anonymous in the crowd. She caught sight of her friend Sarah weaving her way down the corridor, and at the same moment, her phone pinged with an incoming message.

She snapped open the screen with shaking fingers.

'Sorry, can't talk. Mission accomplished; stop worrying now, M.'

Oh, blessed, wonderful, amazing Matt! The world burst into light and life around her, and she greeted Sarah with a seraphic smile which caused her friend's mouth to drop open in surprise.

'Christ, you're buzzing! What's up – have you met a new man or something?'

'No. Got shot of an old one, I hope.'

'I never know with you, Sophie. You keep your love life under wraps these days.'

The queue moved forward, and a savoury aroma of roast beef began to drift in tantalising waves through the open doorway. Sophie's stomach uttered a loud complaint and she suddenly realised that she was ravenous.

'I haven't got a love life to speak of. Hold on, I must reply to this text.'

Her thumbs flew over the screen as she composed her answer. Her first instinct was to reel off exclamations of gratitude, but as she re-read the message, she decided it was way over the top. She deleted it and answered briefly, thanking Matt for his help. *'I won't press for details, but you've saved my life. Sx.'*

Sophie realised that she was unlikely to know the steps Matt had taken, and it was better for her to remain in ignorance. That didn't stop her feeling liberated by a delightful sense of reprieve as she linked arms with her friend. Lunch was a self-service meal, and as they seated themselves with heaped plates at one end of a long refectory table her phone beeped once more.

'I'll update you when the dust has settled. Mx'

That was even better – it meant that she might get to see Matt again, although Sophie knew that she could only regard him as a friend. She deflected curious comments from Sarah regarding her sudden burst of high spirits and managed to switch the subject to whether they should take themselves off to the cinema when they had eaten.

'There's that new film about a stalker at the *Odeon*,' Sarah said. 'I've been told it's a good watch, although the end is a gore-fest. The heroine does in the bloke who's been hounding her with some sort of ceremonial sword. Serves him right, I say.'

That didn't appeal to Sophie in the slightest.

'I think I'd rather go for a walk – I've been slogging in my room all weekend,' she countered. 'Shall we stroll by the river and watch the fools who like to go boating in this cold weather?'

The girls wrapped up warmly to make the most of the watery rays of October sunshine on the banks of the Cam, and Sophie sent her worries fluttering away with the wind as she walked. Now she would be able to concentrate on her work, and maybe find herself a new love. The stress of the past weeks had left her emotionally wrung out and listless. She missed the sense of being close to someone that she had enjoyed with George and was more than ready to fall in love again in order to banish the unattainable fantasy of an older man. On the way back to college, Sarah hesitated before the coffee shop Sophie had visited with Sean the day before.

'I'm gasping for a cuppa and this place is decent enough. Come on Sophie; I'll treat you.'

Sophie couldn't get out of the invitation, but her steps dragged as she accompanied her friend inside the café. By an unfortunate quirk of fate, the nook where she had argued with Sean was vacant among the occupied tables, and Sarah advanced towards these seats with satisfaction. 'I'm starving again now,' she said. 'What shall we have? I think crumpets are called for.'

The little waitress from the previous day hovered by the table, wrinkling her forehead as she stared at Sophie.

'Ooh, you were in here before! Where's the boyfriend today?' she demanded with offensive curiosity, and Sarah looked up from the menu with a pleased smirk on her face.

'I knew you were hiding someone. What's he like?' she asked the waitress, and the girl assumed a silly, swoony expression.

'He was dark and dreamy; a total hottie. Maybe a bit young for her, though,' she remarked with a shameless, juvenile lack of tact, and Sophie only just restrained herself from chucking the menu at her.

'He wasn't my boyfriend. He's the son of someone I know.'

She was damned if she was going to satisfy the curiosity of her questioners. Sarah exchanged a sly look with the waitress, and an angry flush rose to Sophie's cheeks. 'Honestly, he's just a kid – he's still in sixth form!' she exclaimed.

'Okay, Sophie. We get the picture – he wasn't a hook-up. We'll have tea for two, with crumpets, please.'

Sophie clenched her hands under the table. Why couldn't people mind their own business? The last thing she wanted was to have to explain Sean's presence, but it seemed that Sarah couldn't let the matter rest. 'It's about time you got yourself into a proper relationship again,' Sarah continued, probing like a nagging mother, and Sophie glared at her.

'I'm fine, thanks very much. It's not as if you are seeing anyone special, so I can't think why you feel you have to pair me off.'

'Will you let me set you up with a mate of mine from King's who's seen you at lectures and been sighing from afar?'

Sarah's face was a study in innocence as she tried to engineer a date for her friend. 'I could arrange for us to go for a curry on Wednesday after Italian,' she said brightly.

'I'll think about it. Can I eat my crumpet in peace now?'

But Sophie couldn't remain in a grump for long. She began to imagine what she would say to Matt when – if – they met again. She wouldn't press him for difficult details, but she would like some indication of the methods he'd employed to convince Sean to back out of her life. Perhaps she could offer to take Matt for a meal to express her thanks, and she would have the bittersweet satisfaction of admiring his mesmerising features across the table before bidding him a final goodbye...

Sophie was aware of a gradual deflation in her mood during the next day or so. She heard nothing more from Matt and she didn't like to call him. It was even possible that he might decide to avoid seeing or speaking to her again, because she believed that his priority would be Sean rather than someone outside his family. Matt deserved her gratitude for what he'd done, but she had no further claims upon his time or attention.

She checked her pigeonhole for mail, wanted and unwanted, but it remained empty.

Sarah arranged a group curry on Wednesday night, and Sophie felt obliged to go along with the plan. The young man who had been fancying her across the lecture room was tall and bespectacled with unruly hair. Sarah had puffed him in advance as *not unattractive if you like the nerdy type* – Sophie wasn't convinced that she did, but she agreed to meet him again on the following Saturday evening, to please Sarah as much as herself.

'Where would you like to go?' he asked, delighted by her acceptance of his invitation. 'French, Chinese, Italian? You choose, Sophie.'

The student was named Charles, and he hovered over Sophie with the breathless excitement of a dog about to receive an unwarranted treat. She thought quickly before responding.

'Not Italian. How about that pub down past the weir?'

She was reluctant to spoil hallowed memories of her last evening with Matt and the boisterous atmosphere of a pub would discourage romantic approaches if she decided Charles wasn't the answer to a maiden's prayer.

'Are you sure about that?' he said, sounding surprised. 'I don't think I've ever been there. But if that's what you want – I'll book us a table for eight o'clock, and I'll come to collect you first.'

Sarah squeezed her arm as they walked back to college.

'I'm glad you're seeing Charles,' she said. 'I've always thought he was a sweetie, and he's been longing to ask you out. Be nice to him, won't you?'

'I hope I'm always nice to guys if they're not total jerks.'

Sophie tried to inject enthusiasm into her attitude towards the date. She was frustrated to think that the men who wanted her didn't arouse her interest, while the ones – the *one* she wanted, wasn't available. There was a lesson in there somewhere, but she was in no mind to learn it.

When Saturday evening came, Charles arrived at Sophie's door clutching a bunch of roses. It was a nice gesture, although she immediately clocked their supermarket origin, and then felt bad for doing so. She fussed about, borrowing a vase from a friend, and so they were late setting off for the pub. Charles reached for her hand as though it was made of something breakable, and his tentative touch was irritating. Sophie couldn't help recalling the satisfying pressure of more confident hands, and she wasn't in the mood to tolerate a simpering and love-struck companion.

Don't be a bitch, she cautioned herself, remembering Sarah's instructions. She exerted herself to smile upon the young man, and he responded with a display of effusive and delighted self-promotion, presumably designed to boost his appeal in her eyes. But Sophie couldn't relate to his aristocratic forebears and the 'country place in Somerset' which he talked about with careless complacency. It dawned on her that the time spent with Liz and Matt had fostered an appreciation of achievement resulting from hard graft and the self-confidence which comes from individual effort. Charles would have to do more than reel off a list of family fortunes to gain her interest.

'Tell me about your background, Sophie,' he invited, when he had come to the end of his enthusiasms, and she quashed the urge to suggest that she'd barely scrambled out of a gutter somewhere.

'Oh, I'm very dull. My parents are medics, and we live in suburban Guildford.'

She paused over her shepherd's pie and laid her fork down on the plate. 'I suppose you know exactly what you are going to do when you leave Cambridge, Charles. It sounds as though your life is mapped out for you.'

There was a barb in this statement, but Charles didn't seem to feel it.

'Well, not quite. My pa thinks I should go into the City for a few years, but eventually, I'll be running the estate. Which reminds me; Sarah tells me you spent your summer rubbing shoulders with some very wealthy types. I read the article about the Lenister woman a few weeks back. I imagine they were a vulgar crew – it must've been pretty tedious for you.'

'Not at all. They were a charming family, and I developed a real regard for them.'

She stabbed at a carrot, wishing she could puncture Charles' self-esteem in a similar fashion. 'I admire people who have made their own way in the world,' she added in a tone of icy reproval and waited for this to sink into his head. Sophie was amazed to find herself defending the family after all that had passed, but she couldn't allow this callow undergraduate to get away with slurs which were the result of ignorance. His mouth fell open and he looked stunned by her robust attitude, but he recovered enough to quiz her on less contentious topics and the evening passed away without further discord. However, Sophie wasn't anxious for a repeat performance. She ignored his attempts to invite himself back to her room and turned her head when she bade him goodbye, so his diffident goodnight kiss was fielded by her cheek and not her mouth.

'Thanks so much, Charles. I had a good time.'

Sophie hoped that her effort at a smile concealed her true feelings. 'See you at Italian on Wednesday.'

She almost galloped into the college buildings in her eagerness to escape him. Sarah was disappointed to hear that her attempt at matchmaking had been unsuccessful.

'I like Charlie! And it's not his fault if his folk own half Somerset. If he isn't an eligible catch, I don't know who is,' she said, eyeing her friend with disfavour.

'I suppose it depends on what you want. Thanks for trying, though. I'll repay the compliment one day.'

Sophie amused herself by picturing the unsuitable man she might find for Sarah; it was a kind of retaliation for the tedious evening she had spent with Charles. However, Tuesday brought a new pressure. A bouquet of autumn flowers – florist flowers this time – was awaiting her at the college lodge when she returned from a lecture. She was frightened to think that they might come from Sean and it was almost a relief to discover a note from Charles tucked inside.

'I realise I was unforgivably rude about your friends on Saturday. Please come for another curry on Wednesday, so I can attempt to redeem myself.'

'Oh, bugger it!'

Sophie didn't voice these words, but this sentiment was uppermost in her mind as she collected the floral tribute from an admiring porter. She would appear to be the rude one if she refused the invitation, and so she texted a glum acceptance of the olive branch, determined to make sure that Sarah would also be joining the party.

She woke on Wednesday with a sour sensation of obligation hanging over her. Perhaps she'd been too ready to accept this second invitation – it wasn't as though she found Charles attractive, and his unacceptable attitudes had provided a good excuse for walking away. However, she felt committed to the date... until she received a text at lunchtime which dispelled her bad mood as if a rocket had been lit underneath it.

'Sorry for long silence. Meet tonight at entrance to John Lewis in St Andrew's Street? 6 pm? Mx.'

Sophie's fingers felt possessed by magic as she sent a rapid, affirmative reply. The curry assignation was relegated to where it belonged, and she hastily sent brusque apologies to Charles and Sarah. She felt no compunction in doing this, and she also decided the Italian class would have to take place without her, because she had work to do.

This wasn't academic work: Sophie spent the afternoon grooming herself with breathless care. She wanted to go to Matt presenting a harder, polished exterior, unlike the tearful and slightly scruffy girl who had accompanied him to the Italian restaurant. Her wardrobe was ransacked for suitable clothes, and she didn't question her motives for selecting her prettiest underwear. She scolded herself that she wasn't expecting anything physical to happen between them – but it was important for her to feel feminine and alluring down to the last detail.

Sophie was late for their rendezvous, owing to a last-minute decision to change her outfit. She regretted that her outer layer didn't do justice to the slim-fitting jumpsuit she wore, but she hadn't got around to purchasing a new coat. The department store was busy with late-night shoppers, but Matt's tall figure and well-remembered profile made him easy to spot in the crowd. She halted before him, smiling more broadly than she wanted, because she was unbelievably pleased to see him.

'Matt! Have I kept you waiting?'

'No; I was early. How are you, Sophie?'

She reached up to kiss his cheek, and he returned the embrace, looking delighted in his turn.

'I'm fine. Matt, you have no idea how grateful I am...'

148

'Mm. We'll go into that later. Where's the women's clothing in this place?'

Sophie was puzzled by the question.

'Uh – I think it's on the next floor.'

'Come on, then.'

He took her hand and led her into the store; the intimate contact prompting happy little flutters in her tummy. When they reached the women's department, he tugged her across to the racks of winter coats on display. 'Take off that terrible jacket, and let's find you something suitable for a Cambridge winter. Does it have to be black?' he asked. 'I'd like to see you in a warmer colour; something that shows off your beautiful hair.'

Sophie opened her mouth to protest and shut it again as an assistant pounced; the woman's sharp glance detecting an unconventional relationship and scenting a sale. Matt treated the saleslady to his most charming smile.

'Perhaps you could help us, please? We're looking for a winter coat; something stylish, but warm. What's in fashion now?'

The two took charge of the quest. Sophie found herself trying on a range of garments and began to enjoy herself. She hoped that Matt wouldn't urge her towards one of the pricier coats because her nest egg might crack under the strain, but after solemn deliberation, they agreed on a long, slightly flared coat in dark red wool. It wasn't cutting edge but it suited Sophie, and she was aware that she made an unusually elegant figure as she turned to admire herself before the looking glass.

'I feel like a princess,' she exclaimed, laughing to cover up her embarrassment, and Matt reached out to rearrange a stray lock of hair which fell across her cheek.

'Princess Isabelle,' he murmured, and their eyes met in a perfect moment of understanding before he turned back to the saleswoman. 'She'll wear it now, so you can wrap up the old one,' he declared.

There was a scuffle at the till when Matt brushed aside her attempts to pay.

'I can afford it, Matt, I haven't spent much of my holiday money,' Sophie protested as he proffered his credit card.

'I think you ought to accept this as an apology for the … let's say, the inconvenience you've suffered at the hands of my family. It'll make me feel better if you do, so please don't argue.'

The assistant packed her old jacket away, and Sophie sneaked a final glance at her reflection. She felt buoyed up to see the chic, self-assured person smiling there, and Matt's wide grin showed that he was delighted by her reaction. 'That's better. Now I don't have to worry about you traipsing the streets and catching your death of cold,' he said. 'Shall we find somewhere to celebrate?'

'Yes – I'd love that.'

It seemed natural now to walk to their destination with her arm linked through Matt's. Sophie was burning with questions about how he had dealt with Sean, but she decided not to be the first to raise the subject. Matt was bound to give her an account of how he'd worked his magic, even if the precise details were omitted. He took her to a small pub in a part of the town which she wasn't very familiar with, and she was careful to hang the coat where she could keep a possessive eye upon it.

Matt went to the bar and returned with a pint and a gin and tonic.

'Are you hungry?' he asked. 'They do a good steak here.'

As far as Sophie was concerned, they could serve her a bad one – it was enough for her to be in company with Matt again. She accepted his recommendation, and sat back in her seat, waiting for him to begin his story. But he showed no sign of wanting to discuss Sean. He talked instead about his business plans, in much greater detail than he'd ever done before, and Sophie tried to understand the significance of what he was telling her. The steaks arrived, savoury and sizzling, and still she was in ignorance of what had happened. She'd sworn to leave the subject to him, but maybe she would have to drag it out into the open after all.

Chapter Seventeen

'…and I'm really pleased with the way things are shaping up.'

Matt smiled at Sophie across the table as he finished his steak, and she nodded in approval, chewing hard and unable to respond. Apprehension had taken the edge off her appetite, but she forced herself to eat her meat because she was doubly indebted to him after his dealings with Sean and the gift of the coat and she didn't want him to think she was ungrateful. At last, the final piece of steak went down, and she found her voice again.

'I'm delighted to hear that, Matt. And you were right about the steak. It was lovely, but I think I'm full up now,' she said, putting down her cutlery. Matt glanced at her plate and reached across to snaffle a rejected chip.

'I hope you aren't watching your weight – you really don't need to,' he commented, and Sophie hesitated. The elephant in the room was growing more intrusive by the minute, and she decided to risk a direct approach.

'Matt – I have to ask you. What happened with Sean? Is he okay?'

Sean's name dropped between them with an awkward thud. Sophie stared at Matt, hoping she hadn't offended him, and trying to detect the truth in his gaze. She thought that his face changed and became guarded and sad.

'He isn't in the best place, shall we say.'

Matt's voice cracked a little, and he cleared his throat. 'Poor chap; he's finding it hard to accept that you have such different views about what happened in France. But he's seeing his therapist again and I suppose things will work out eventually.'

'Oh no…'

Tears pricked at Sophie's eyes, and she dabbed at them with a tissue before her eye make-up had a chance to run. 'That makes me feel terrible,' she said. 'I hoped that talking it over with you might have got him to understand my take on the situation, and he'd begin to accept he made a mistake.'

'It did, after a fashion, but not entirely. Sophie, I don't think you need to know exactly what happened, but I've had to get Sean out of a couple of tricky situations in the past: things which even his mother doesn't know about. I'm one of the few people that he trusts.'

Matt's face showed signs of tension, as if what he had to say was painful for him. 'When I showed up outside that café, he realised that he'd gone too far. I spoke to the staff member in charge of the trip and invented a family reason to whisk Sean back to London with me, telling Liz that he'd been suffering from stress and needed a few days out of school. She isn't aware of your problem in France, by the way – at least we've been able to keep that from her.

'We managed to get him in to see his old therapist, plus I made damn sure he understood what a dangerous game he'd been playing. His head's in a different place now and I don't think you'll have any further trouble.'

Sophie stared at the table, wondering how it was that a summer friendship had ended in such a messy and conflicted way. She was unwilling to meet Matt's eyes now; fearing what she might read there.

'I wish that I could turn the clock back,' she said, for want of anything more positive.

'I daresay you do, but you can't. Look, Sophie, what happened was unfortunate, but no-one's going to die from the fallout. My concern now is making sure that Sean gets over this upset as quickly as possible, and I'm planning a family trip to the States over Christmas. It's partly business, but we'll take in a week's skiing in Aspen, and he's looking forward to that. He needs something positive in his life to hang on to now.'

His words struck Sophie with the force of a blow, because she realised for the first time that despite his protestations to the contrary, Matt held her equally responsible for the sorry situation. The bright room grew dark and pulsating. It didn't seem fair. The sense of being judged and rejected left her in panic, and she could see only one thing to do. She fumbled inside the bag to grab her old jacket and wobbled to her feet.

'I am very sorry to have caused so much trouble for you all,' she said, her voice sounding ominously calm before the advent of the storm. 'In the circumstances, I don't think I can accept the coat – you'd better return it. Goodbye, Matt.'

'Sophie – for fuck's sake!'

She didn't look at him as she struggled to shrug her old garment over her shoulders. She was aware that he strode to the bar and pulled notes from his wallet, then he grabbed the red coat from its peg and followed her as she weaved an unsteady path to the street. By now, she was crying so hard that she could hardly see where she was going, and Matt caught her by the arm. 'Sophie, stop a moment. What's got into you? Why this dramatic dash into the night?' he demanded.

He pulled her into the shadow of a wall. A group of students walked past and burst into jeering catcalls, but one young man hung back and confronted the pair.

'Are you all right?'

His query was addressed to Sophie: she was conscious of the man glaring at Matt with suspicion shrouding his face.

'Yes. Thanks. Everything's f-fine.'

The words stumbled out between sobs, and the group moved away. Matt put his mouth against her ear.

'Please tell me what's upset you,' he pleaded, and she shuddered as he held her.

'You do think it's my fault. I wish I'd never gone to France. You have no idea how much your family have abused me.'

He made no reply to this accusation but allowed her to weep until she had cried herself out of tears. His proximity was torture now, and she summoned the energy to extricate herself from his arms. 'I'll be all right. Goodbye, Matt.'

'I'm not letting you go back to college in that state. My flat's only a few streets away. You'd better come back with me until you've calmed down,' he said, with quiet authority.

Sophie's limbs seemed to have no volition of their own. She allowed Matt to guide her along pavements slippery with drizzle; wondering how badly her hair and face were disfigured by the ravages of hysteria. Then Matt stopped, searched for a key and propelled her up a steep, narrow flight of stairs. He unlocked another door and pushed her inside, and she winced as he flooded the room with light.

'Where's the bathroom?' she muttered, anxious to soothe her swollen face.

'Through the bedroom on the left there. I'm going to make you some tea.'

It was indeed a tiny flat. Sophie noticed a small kitchen and table at one end of the room, and a sitting area at the other. One wall was dominated by an enormous television screen. The bedroom managed to squeeze in a double bed and a small wardrobe, but the bathroom leading from it was surprisingly spacious. She slammed the door shut and perched on the loo until she could summon the courage to look in the mirror.

When she felt more human, she dampened a wad of tissues with cold water and applied it to her swollen eyes. So much for her elaborate preparations during the afternoon, when her thoughts had been busy with a very different situation. Sophie had allowed herself to construct a fantasy where Matt invited her to his flat (it had been much more glamorous and like a love-nest in her imagination) and delicious intimacies developed, but that dream had come crashing to pieces. Nothing in her dealings with the family ever seemed to go the way she wanted.

The mirror wasn't encouraging, but Sophie knew that youthful skin bounces back quickly from trauma. She found a small brush in her bag and forced it through her hair, and by the time she'd finished, she was looking more like herself again. She let herself out and returned to the main room, to find Matt hovering anxiously over mugs and glasses.

'I'd like to give you a whisky to perk you up. It's a good malt, and I've put a little water in it.'

He pushed a glass towards her, and she shook her head. 'Please, just have a sip. I think you need it,' he insisted.

It wasn't such a shock to the system as the calvados had been, but the unaccustomed taste made her gasp as the drink went down. Matt smiled, and the strain around his eyes lessened and went away. 'I think you are the only woman I've met who can cry like that and still be beautiful,' he said softly, and Sophie responded with a very sceptical look.

'Have you made many women cry, Matt?'

'I seem to have made you cry twice in succession. I'd like to think I can do better in future.'

He led her across to the sofa and placed the whisky and a mug of tea on a small table. Sophie sank into the cushions, feeling like a rag doll with inadequate stuffing. She drank her tea, and forced down a little whisky, and wondered what would happen next. She'd need to call a cab to take her back to college, because it was too far for her to walk in her current state of exhaustion, and the hour was growing late.

Matt eased himself down beside her.

'Look, Sophie, I didn't say that you are to blame for what happened. I've never said that. Maybe it would have been better if you'd screamed for Liz at the time, but I understand that you were in an impossible situation. I'm trying not to take sides.'

He emphasised these words, and she thought that she believed him. 'Sean shouldn't have behaved in the way he did, but he's devastated because he feels that once again, someone he loved has rejected him,' Matt said. 'You can't object if I want to do the best for him as well as helping you.'

It didn't make Sophie feel any better to think that Sean's behaviour might owe something to past tragedy in his life. She sat in silence, pondering what Matt had told her, and remorse began to prevail in her thoughts. He stroked her hand, and she took a long, shuddery breath.

'I don't hate Sean, although he has made life very difficult for me. It would be nice to think that one day we could meet and put this behind us, but I guess that won't be possible for a long time, if ever,' she said. 'What kills me is that If I hadn't come back to Cambridge last spring, none of this would have happened.'

'Well, you did, and it has, but we all need to move on. Please don't make me take the coat back. You look so very beautiful in it.'

The warmth in his voice almost brought more tears. Matt put his arm around her shoulders, and she leaned against him. They sat there without speaking, and Sophie's unhappiness eased a little. It seemed to her that the silence was filled with thoughts which neither were capable of voicing, but after a while, he leaned over and bestowed another butterfly kiss upon her lips.

It wasn't satisfactory, and she wanted more. Perhaps she needed to make that clear to him. Sophie put her arms around his neck and kissed Matt properly; a long, imperious, demanding kiss. She stopped to draw breath, then kissed him again. She was aware of his halting astonishment, and then he succumbed to temptation and kissed her back. When he finally drew away from her his forehead was creased, as though he was anticipating trouble.

'Jeez, Sophie… what the hell are you doing? What do you want from me?'

155

He traced a finger down her cheek, and she thought hard. Things couldn't get much worse, and she had nothing to lose by telling the truth.

'I want you to make love to me,' she said, and she felt shock pulse through his body.

'You're not serious! I can't do that.'

'Why not?'

She placed her hand on his chest and inserted her forefinger through the gap between two shirt buttons, stroking his skin, and he groaned.

'What do you think that would do to Sean? Anyway, you know very well that I'm married.'

'Sean doesn't have to know. And I am aware that you have a wife.'

Sophie's voice thickened with irritation. 'Something tells me that you've been up for the odd extra-marital adventure in the past. What's different now? Do you not fancy me after all?'

She could hardly believe her own effrontery, and Matt dissolved in reluctant laughter.

'Well of course I fancy you – I'm a hot-blooded male. And you're gorgeous; you know you are.'

But his eyes were troubled, and he tugged her hand away from his body. 'I'm not sure you understand, Sophie. I'm not going to leave Liz, and I can't think you would be happy to have an affair. You've never struck me as that sort of girl.'

'I don't expect you to abandon your marriage,' Sophie said, suddenly sounding rather prim. She had seized the moment, and it was too late to retreat. 'That doesn't stop me from wanting you, especially now you're living on my doorstep. I've had a crush on you ever since France, and I think you'd be a wonderful lover. Sorry if that shocks you, but I can't help the way I feel.'

Matt appeared to be deprived of speech, but Sophie was strangely pleased to find that he exhibited some moral scruples. She continued to address him with uncharacteristic recklessness.

'Anyway, I know from experience that you guys always go for what you want; it's like a philosophy of life for you. Why can't I do that too? Are you surprised that I want to go to bed with you?'

Matt pulled out his phone and began to tap at it. 'What are you doing?' she enquired, annoyed because he hadn't answered her question.

'Calling an Uber. Sophie, you've been thoroughly upset tonight, and I don't want to take advantage of you.'

'So, this is goodbye?'

She drew back from him, summoning a wavering dignity, and he caught her hand and squeezed it hard between his own.

'Don't be a drama queen,' he said, but his voice held affection and warmth. 'No, of course it's not goodbye, but we need a breathing space to think about this.'

He smoothed back his hair, looking as if he'd been dumped in a difficult situation and was buying time to process matters. 'Why don't you come here for supper tomorrow night and we can talk again when we've both had a chance to cool down.'

'I think I'm perfectly rational now.'

'I'm not so sure about that.'

Matt got to his feet and looked around for the red coat. 'Come on; the cab will be here any minute. Put this on. I'm taking your old one to work with me to dispose of, so there's no argument.'

Sophie was aware of exhaustion creeping through her body with paralysing effect. She allowed Matt to pull her to her feet and insert her into the coat, and then she stumbled after him down the stairs to the waiting Uber. He opened the door for her and deposited a formal kiss on her cheek. 'I'll see you here at seven tomorrow,' he said. 'Get some sleep; you look all in. Goodnight, Sophie – my dear.'

Next morning, Sophie felt that she hadn't merely slept like a log, but like an entire forest of trees weighed down by a winter snowfall. The combination of emotion and fatigue conspired to stun her with lethargy, and she would have missed breakfast if Hannah hadn't barged in to wake her at eight-thirty. As it was, she couldn't face anything apart from a piece of toast and a banana. Her stomach felt wrung out and jittery, and she went straight back to bed instead of working in the library as she had planned.

She managed to rouse herself in the afternoon and took a lengthy, refreshing bath. Sophie lay in the tub, up to her neck in foam, wondering how she had found the nerve to be so upfront about her desires. Was it through fear that she would never get another opportunity to let Matt know her feelings? She didn't know whether to be pleased or mortified when she considered her blatant invitation to him.

She suspected that Matt would let her down gently when they met. It was probable that he hadn't forgiven her for causing his stepson so much anguish – and she didn't like to think what Sean might be going through; it was too much like probing a nagging tooth. However, she was certain of one thing – she would never accept the greater share of responsibility for the fatal night in France.

Hannah and Sarah knocked on her door as she was getting ready to leave for the flat.

'Are you coming down for dinner, Sophie? Ooh, I see you have other plans – when did you buy that coat? You look amazing.'

Hannah reached out and caressed the thick wool as Sophie finished doing up the last buttons.

'I got it yesterday. And I won't be eating in hall; I have a date,' Sophie replied. Her friends exchanged glances and smirked.

'Dare we ask who the lucky man is?' asked Sarah. 'I can't see you going to all this trouble for Charles, poor darling.'

Sophie hesitated for a moment. There was no reason for her to be untruthful at present, and she could make her assignation sound routine.

'I'm meeting Liz Lenister's husband. He works in Cambridge some of the time, and he's invited me for dinner so I can catch up with what the family have been doing recently.'

She gazed at her friends with wide, innocent eyes, daring them to challenge this statement. But either they didn't know that Matt was a hunk, or they assumed that he was merely a dull businessman, because neither girl appeared to find this out of the ordinary.

'Hope it's not too boring for you, then. I expect he'll take you somewhere nice. We'll see you later – unless you're going to take him clubbing afterwards.'

This snide suggestion produced hoots of laughter which echoed down the corridor as they walked away. Sophie smiled to herself. Matt wouldn't be out of place in a club scene, in fact he would fit in with no problem, but she didn't intend to let him out in public this evening.

Chapter Eighteen

There were two bells at the side of the doorway to the street outside Matt's apartment. One was marked '*Braybrooke*'; the other name wasn't fully legible, as if the rain had seeped in on some past occasion. Sophie pressed '*Braybrooke*' and was admitted to the foot of the narrow staircase.

Matt put his head out of the door on the landing. He looked pleased to see her, albeit it appeared as the guilty, almost doubting pleasure of a man about to burn some bridges.

'You remembered where it was, then,' he said. 'I wasn't sure if you were properly compos mentis last night.'

Sophie didn't answer him. She would never forget anything which concerned Matt, but he didn't need to know that. He gave her a brief embrace when she reached the top of the stairs, and stood back to let her in. There was no sign of food in preparation, and she stared at the barren kitchen worktops in some astonishment.

'Hope you don't mind, but I've ordered a Chinese for half time,'

Matt looked leery, like a guilty schoolboy. 'The boys in blue are on the box tonight, and I'd like to keep an eye on the action. It needn't stop us talking.'

'You want us to watch football?'

Her question ended on a high squeak of disbelief.

'Well, yes. Chelsea are my team, and I don't often get the chance to see them play. Liz hates soccer. I promise it won't interfere with anything,' he said, and she frowned.

'I can always go away again, if you'd prefer to be alone.'

Sophie was annoyed and disappointed at the prospect of competition for Matt's attention, but he helped her off with her coat and put his hands on her waist.

'God, no, I need to see you, Sophie. You've been on my mind all day, and there are things we must discuss.'

That was better. He hesitated, then gently pressed his mouth to hers. It was neither a social kiss, nor one of passion; it felt to Sophie like an expression of apology, and she schooled herself to face disappointment as he broke away from her. 'What would you like to drink? I've opened a nice bottle of Chablis,' he said, as if trying to atone for the football.

Sophie accepted a glass of wine and settled herself on the sofa, arranging herself in a formal pose with her knees pressed together. She was puzzled; she hadn't envisaged the evening beginning like this. But Matt immediately joined her there, hugging an arm around her so she could snuggle against him. His skin gave off a groomed, masculine scent, and his face was so smooth that she wondered whether he'd shaved for a second time in the day. The screen on the wall opposite was blank, and Sophie had an uneasy impression of sitting in the cinema, waiting for the entertainment to begin. Was she expected to provide it in the meantime?

'Kick off isn't until eight – I won't subject you to the warm-up.'

Matt stroked a strand of her hair and tucked it behind her ear. His face was reflective, and she thought that he was preparing to deliver a speech of regret. 'You know, when I first saw you in France, I thought that Liz had lost her marbles,' he said, smiling and nostalgic. 'You were so beautiful, and it was obvious that Sean and I would have the hots for you. I used to watch you playing with my daughters and my heart would beat faster, because there was a sweet, endearing innocence in the way you went about things.'

Sophie liked him saying that – the words implied a connection which was much more than mere physical desire. Matt emptied his glass and tilted her chin towards him. 'I was worried about you last night. Not because you were upset in the pub, but because I'd never understood that you felt anything much for me, although looking back, I can see the tug of attraction between us started early on. You were right when you accused me of playing away. Liz isn't the easiest partner and women have always come on to me. There have been times when it's been impossible to resist temptation, and I'm just a man for God's sake. But I was gobsmacked to find that *you* might want to sleep with me.'

Sophie stared into his eyes. She had learned to welcome that warm blue regard, but she was still unable to decide what lay behind it. She hoped that Matt was to be trusted, although it seemed to be her impulses which were shaping events now.

'What do you want to do?' she asked him. It would be better to know the worst, and she wouldn't expose herself too far until she understood his intentions. Matt smiled, and he took a deep breath, like someone about to make a difficult confession.

'Don't you know that I want to make love to you, Sophie? What guy wouldn't? I've imagined you in my arms, and I don't mind admitting that I was gutted when you told me you'd slept with Sean,' he said. 'But I care about you too, and we need to know where we stand. You've got under my skin, but I'm not going to abandon my children. I've seen how the break-up of a marriage can affect kids, and I couldn't put Poppy and Boo through that. Would you be satisfied with being my mistress? I can't help feeling you deserve more.'

The word 'mistress' sounded sinful and inflammatory in Sophie's ears. It conjured up dramatic illustrations of penitent women from a Victorian penny dreadful, and she fought down a prickle of warning. She didn't want to put herself in that box; she certainly didn't see herself in that light. Surely attitudes were different and more flexible these days!

Matt continued his argument. 'I can only be in Cambridge during the week: have you considered what that means? What would you do with yourself at weekends? How would you keep this secret from your friends? And you have a whole town full of eligible young men here.'

He looked away, biting his lip as though fearful that he had talked himself out of her arms and her affections, but Sophie was pleased by his unexpected candour. She didn't want to harm Poppy and Boo, although she was scornfully dismissive about Liz's feelings.

'Oh, Matt… I don't want to hurt the children either. But I'm bored with tedious, entitled undergraduates and men who are only up for a quick shag. I want to be with someone adult for a change, even if it means living with the downsides you've talked about.'

Her voice trembled as she thought of George. She'd accepted the limitations on their time together, but she hadn't reckoned on having to do something similar with another love. For a moment, she wondered whether she owed it to herself to override her desire for Matt.

He frowned, and she felt that he was being swayed by her own indecision.

'It's taking a bloody big risk,' he said. 'The physical side is just one part of it, but what happens if one of us falls in love as well as lust?'

'I don't know. The result would be a broken heart, I suppose. Is it possible to stop short of that situation? But Matt …'

A smile crept over Sophie's face, because she loved to look at him. He was so handsome; so beguiling in a wonderfully mature way. She adored the tingle which electrified her body when he gazed at her with desire in his eyes; she longed to run her fingers through the hair curling at the back of his neck and to trace the enticing crease in his cheek when he laughed, and it wasn't a difficult decision to follow her heart. 'Things have gone so far with me that it's a risk I'm prepared to take,' she whispered. 'Are you up for taking it too?'

Matt fastened his mouth upon hers, and for the first time, he kissed her with the hunger of an acknowledged passion. It was the kiss she'd been imagining ever since she left France. The action seemed to put a seal on the words they'd just spoken, as if it was a solemn expression of commitment. He ran his hands over her breasts, murmuring soft words of desire.

Sophie felt her body melting into a lazy, languorous state of pleasure. At length, Matt pulled her into the bedroom, and Sophie had stopped questioning what was right long before he finished undressing her.

Afterwards, Sophie felt she'd undergone an almost mystical experience. The lovers she had known in the past were erased from her memory; even George didn't seem to exist for her anymore. Making love with Matt was more satisfying than anything she'd imagined, and she was astounded by the depths of their intimacy. He propped himself on an elbow and scrutinised her tenderly, and with just a hint of self-satisfaction.

'I don't suppose you realise that I've missed kick-off. I'll forgive you just this once, but you mustn't let it happen again.'

She drew his head down and traced the endearing lines of his profile with a finger which he proceeded to nibble very gently. 'I understand why Sean was in such a state about you,' he murmured, and her eyes grew dark with distress.

'Don't, Matt. This is about you and me now.'

'He's my stepson. I can't write him out of my life.'

'This isn't anything like the time I spent with Sean. I'd rather we didn't talk about him.'

Sophie didn't want difficult memories spoiling her happiness. Matt rolled over and sat up.

'Okay, Sophie. You know now that I'd choose you over football – don't underestimate the compliment – but I think one of us had better be dressed when the food arrives.'

She would gladly have foregone her supper and spent the evening in bed with him, but after a short time of reflection when she lay in a happy stupor, reliving his embraces, the sound of the doorbell prompted her to pull her clothes on and join Matt in the kitchen. He kissed the side of her head with rough affection.

'Chelsea are up two-nil already. I think you'll bring us luck.'

'Who are they playing?'

Sophie couldn't conceal the complete lack of interest in her tone, and Matt's face crinkled in amusement.

'I note that you aren't a footie fan. They're at home to Southampton. Does your dad not follow the game?' he asked, laying out plates and uncovering savoury and steaming containers, and she shook her head.

'No. Sport isn't really his thing, although he does play golf. I suppose there's an awful lot we have to learn about each other, Matt,' she said, her eyes wide with sudden apprehension.

'There is. Don't worry; I'm looking forward to every minute of it,' he replied, and that thought was pleasant to hold on to. After they had eaten, he asked her whether she would be able to spend the night with him. 'But only if it doesn't get you into trouble. I don't know whether some hoary matron stalks your corridors with a lantern to check on the students every night,' he mused, and she laughed at the idea.

'No. Everything's very relaxed these days, but I might text a friend to ask her not to wake me for breakfast like she usually does,' she said. 'I'd adore to spend the night, Matt. I don't want to spend a second apart from you now.'

She opened her eyes just after six the next morning to find that Matt had already risen and was dressed in gym kit. He sat on the bed beside her and squeezed her hand.

'Are you leaving me already?' she yawned, and he smiled.

163

'I'm a gym rat most mornings. Anyway, I can't believe you want more. Wasn't last night enough for you?' he asked, almost with reproof.

'I'm a greedy girl.'

Sophie sat up and stretched, conscious that she made a seductive picture with her dark hair tumbling over her breasts, and Matt gave a groan.

'You musn't tempt me.'

He reached out to caress her, but his tone was adamant. 'Listen, Sophie, I'll try to get back on Monday. You understand that we can't risk any contact when I'm at home, don't you? You can't text or call me, and even in Cambridge, we'll have to be very careful about what we do and where we go,' he said, tapping a little tattoo upon the back of her hand to get the message across.

'Yes, I know all that. But you'll let me know about Monday?' she asked, wondering how she would get through the looming weekend without him. She'd have to accept her solitude; it was part of the deal she'd signed up to now.

'Of course. And if I can't manage Monday, I'll definitely be back the day after.'

Matt ruffled her hair and rose to his feet. 'There's cereal and toast if you want something before you go,' he said. 'Help yourself to whatever you want. When you leave, just slam the door behind you; same for downstairs.' He sent a last, reluctant, rueful smile towards her. 'And, Sophie – please don't leave anything behind. We can't be too careful.'

Sophie watched him stride to the door, smothering her disappointment that he had to leave so soon and with his last words sounding an ominous note in her ears. The morning sun shone a harsher, clearer light on their situation, exposing dusty little crevices of difficulty which hadn't been apparent the night before. Her sense of elation after the events of the night was tempered by a nagging suspicion that she might come to regret the step she'd taken.

She remembered what she'd told herself in France – nice girls didn't get themselves involved in other people's marriages. Things had seemed so much simpler back then, but the time she had spent with Matt in Cambridge had only made her more open to his irresistible temptation. Now she had achieved what she thought she wanted and sleeping with Matt had been an intimate, unforgettable experience, but her life was about to enter an unlooked-for phase of complications. She received an early lesson in double-dealing when she met up with Hannah for lunch.

'Sophie! Did you have a good evening with Mr Liz Lenister? Where did he take you for dinner?' Hannah asked, sounding faintly satirical. Sophie was caught out for an instant; she hadn't thought it necessary to prepare a detailed cover story, and her hands trembled as she reached for the water jug.

'Er... we ate at his hotel,' she said, after a brief pause, where she tried to recall the names of suitable establishments.

'Where was he staying?'

Why couldn't Hannah leave the topic alone? Sophie dredged up a name from a recess in her memory; one that she hoped her friends wouldn't be familiar with, to discourage further questions.

'The White House.'

Unfortunately, this response only prolonged Hannah's interest.

'Oh, I've often wondered what that place was like. Is it nice inside? What did you have to eat?' she asked.

Surely her friends had never taken such a detailed interest in her social life before! Sophie mumbled something about steak and sticky toffee pudding and hoped that would satisfy Hannah's curiosity. Luckily, they were joined by other friends and attention switched away from Sophie's evening, but it was a salutary moment. If she wanted to keep seeing Matt, she would need cunning at her fingertips to deflect the truth and be ready with counter-histories. It dawned on her that she would never be able to let her guard down in this new situation.

Now she was conscious of what lay ahead, Sophie plumped for a course of intense effort regarding her college social life; which she used as a smokescreen to hide her involvement with a married man. She was a willing guest at a party to celebrate a twenty-first birthday at the weekend, although she felt ashamed of the false pretences she was forced to adopt. It wasn't a nice feeling to know that she was deliberately deceiving her friends, and all because of a relationship which she would have been quick to condemn in the past. She accepted every invitation to grace the dance floor, although she was swift to find an excuse to walk away when the mood turned smoochy. Sunday was easier for her: she spent it in another pampering session in case Matt managed to return to Cambridge the next day. He was the brightest star in her universe now.

Chapter Nineteen

Matt didn't return on Monday, and Sophie felt horribly let down. She was consumed with frustration because she had no control over his circumstances, and she didn't want their relationship to judder along in fits and starts, like an old jalopy which could never be relied upon. It made an uncomfortable picture, and she couldn't maintain the high spirits of the weekend.

'What's up, Soph? You were so perky at the party. Who's ghosted you? I swear you'll wear your phone out if you peek at it one more time.'

Hannah was puzzled by her friend's descent into gloom. Sophie pushed the phone into her bag; conscious of revealing her feelings. The pressure of deception was beginning to get to her, and she decided it was time to admit to a heavily abridged version of the truth.

'I have met a guy I like; in fact, I like him a lot. Turns out he's only in Cambridge once in a blue moon, so it makes life difficult. Don't go on at me about him, please, because it doesn't help,' she said.

'He isn't studying here?'

Hannah sounded surprised, obviously wondering where Sophie had run across this mystery man.

'No. I'll tell you all about him one day, but for now, I don't need people to know about it.'

'Okay, no sweat. But Sophie – are you sure you're up for this? It sounds like a lot of hassle to me. I hope he's worth it.'

'Mm, I think he is. I *hope* he is.'

However, Tuesday morning was bathed in radiance because Matt called her immediately after breakfast.

'Sophie? I'm sorry about yesterday; things got complicated here. My train gets in just after lunch today. Can you come to the flat early evening? I'm usually back from the Science Park just after six,' he said, and Sophie was conscious of a lunatic grin spreading from ear to ear.

'Yes, that's fine. Matt – I can't wait to see you; I've really missed you,' she said, quivery with excitement. As she rang off, she was conscious of violating the rules of cool relationship behaviour, but she didn't care. It was easy to persuade herself that her liaison with Matt was something which transcended the ordinary conventions.

Sophie arrived at the flat at about six-fifteen, thinking that Matt would be back from work, but there was no answer to her ring on the bell. She glanced up and down the street, but the only person to be seen was the hurrying figure of a woman, lugging a heavy shopping bag. To Sophie's surprise, she stopped at Matt's outer door, and the two exchanged a wary smile.

'I don't suppose you're looking for me.'

The woman spoke in a flat statement, with an Aussie twang in her voice, and Sophie shook her head.

'I'm expecting to meet Matthew Braybrooke. He must have been delayed,' she said cautiously, thinking that Matt might not want this third party to be aware of their connection, but the woman merely gave a little shrug.

'Suppose so. I'd ask you in, but of course, I don't know you from Eve.'

Sophie was about to say that she didn't mind waiting in the street, but a taxi rounded the corner and pulled up beside them, disgorging Matt and a small suitcase. He got out, his face tense with caution, but the woman smiled broadly at him.

'Hi there, Matt. How's it going? This young lady was wondering where you'd got to.'

Sophie was conscious of curiosity in the woman's voice and waited to see how Matt would respond – she'd take her cue from him. He returned the woman's smile and she promptly flushed with an awkwardness which Sophie found surprising.

'Hullo, Judy. This is Sophie; she's an old family friend. Sorry to keep you waiting.'

This last remark was addressed to Sophie in formal tones, and she muttered that she didn't mind. 'Let me carry your shopping,' Matt added, and he picked up the bag as Judy unlocked the door, following her up the stairs, while Sophie trailed behind. It was a squash for all three on the small landing.

'Thanks, Matt,' said Judy, as he put her bag down. 'How long will you be around this week? We could go for a drink one night if you're free.'

Sophie prickled with annoyance. She didn't want this woman muscling in on her territory. Matt gave Judy one of his super-smiles.

'Sure. I'll let you know when I've got my diary sorted. You take care now.'

He inserted the key in his lock, ushering Sophie in before him. She could feel Judy staring after them, her eyes keen to uncover the nature of their acquaintance, and it was a relief when Matt closed the door. Sophie opened her mouth to speak, but Matt put his hand across her lips. 'Wait a sec.,' he whispered.

They stood frozen for half a minute until Judy's door closed with a bang, and Matt took his hand away, replacing it with his mouth. Sophie received the kiss with gratitude; she'd been longing for this moment. After a minute or so, he drew away, stroking her cheek and smiling.

'She's your neighbour?' Sophie asked softly, and he nodded.

'Yeah. Nice enough. I understand she teaches at one of the schools here.'

'I can see she likes you.'

Matt turned away with a quick shrug of his shoulders.

'Could be. Don't worry; she's no competition. Why eat lumpfish roe when you can have caviar?' he said, and Sophie's forehead furrowed as she tried to work out what he meant.

'I *think* that's a compliment.'

Matt laughed at her puzzled face as he opened the fridge to pluck out a can of beer.

'Do you want a drink? I'm expecting a Waitrose delivery at six-thirty, and after that we can think about supper. You're about to find out that I'm a great chef.'

All this was mundane, but Sophie loved the every-dayness of it, feeling that it bound her more closely to Matt than any number of upmarket meals in restaurants could do. And when the groceries arrived, he prepared a meal of lamb chops and vegetables which was more than acceptable.

'I should have got you to cook when we were in France,' Sophie remarked, intrigued by his slapdash expertise, but he shook his head.

'Liz doesn't like to see me in the kitchen, but I enjoy fending for myself when I have to. You must tell me what you like to eat, so I can order the stuff in. We can still go out for meals, obviously, but I don't think it's wise to do that every night. Just in case…'

169

He didn't finish the sentence, but Sophie understood what he meant. Her contribution to the evening was to wash the pans while Matt relaxed in front of the football – Chelsea weren't playing today, but she accepted that she'd have to get used to competition of the sporting variety. It was preferable to the presence of female poachers, anyway.

She had her reward in bed with him later. Matt made love to her with satisfying and enthusiastic ardour, and she wondered whether it was permissible for a woman to tell a man that he was the most amazing lover she had known. Maybe her reactions already told him that. Matt was threading her hair through his fingers as they lay entwined, and the lazy smile on his lips indicated that he'd enjoyed the sex as much as she had.

'That was sweet. Your body is beyond gorgeous and we have a real connection, Sophie,' he murmured. 'I don't know how things will work out, but for now, they can't get much better.'

Sophie woke in the night and remembered those words. She felt a rush of tenderness for the sleeping man by her side. He'd helped her when she was in trouble, and he had always been upfront with her about their situation and its limitations. Things could be better – there could be no wife in the picture, for a start – but she felt no regrets, only the happy anticipation of many more satisfying nights to come.

In the weeks which followed, Sophie discovered that life as a mistress wasn't unbridled passion and glamour. She and Matt had their own special routine when he was in Cambridge, but she was aware that life was more difficult for her than for him, despite Matt's family commitments. She could rarely hope for any contact between them during his absences, and certain topics of conversation were strictly off the menu.

Sophie had looked forward to hearing about Poppy and Boo, who still held a warm place in her heart, but Matt shut down her attempts to ask about them until she abandoned the effort. It seemed that anything to do with his family life was out of bounds. The subject of Sean was also a grey area. Now that she was at a distance from the upsetting days of Sean's infatuation, Sophie felt inclined to pity the boy. She was genuinely anxious to hear that he was recovering from his obsession with her, but Matt was tight-lipped if she asked about

Sean's state of mind. She suspected this was due to guilt on Matt's part because he was now in possession of what Sean had wanted, but it was impossible for her to voice this thought.

They spent more time together in the flat than anywhere else, because it provided a safe cocoon from the outside world. On occasion, Matt would take her out for a meal, but they almost always went to pubs on the fringes of the city; places where Matt felt they would be safe from the prying eyes of colleagues or people who might recognise him. The cinema also provided a warm, dark haven for a winter evening. However, once she had accepted the conditions imposed by Matt, Sophie didn't regret her decision. She continued to be a social animal at weekends, but this was prompted by a desire to lose herself so she could tolerate Matt's absence. Matt didn't seem bothered if she mentioned that she'd been out clubbing or at a party, merely remarking that he trusted her to be careful.

'I hope you use a condom when you're not with me.'

This comment and its implications almost stunned her.

'I don't sleep with anyone else, Matt! I just go to be part of the crowd. Why would I want to have sex with other people when I have you?' she said, almost tearing up. He uttered an uncertain laugh, but his guarded expression forced her to confront the fact that he still made love to his wife. She told herself that he probably had to; it was a necessary part of their deception, but it was painful to accept, all the same.

But she knew that she was dear to him. One day, she happened to mention that her laptop was playing up, and a few days later, a new, upmarket model arrived at the college for her. When she next saw Matt, she felt obliged to chide him for the purchase, but he delighted in being able to surprise her and her protests were smothered. However, as the term drew to its close, depression began to settle upon Sophie as she recognised that the holiday period would result in several weeks where they were unable to meet.

'Oh, Matt. I know you have to go away, but I shall miss you so much,' she murmured, anticipating that life would be grey and dull in England while he was enjoying himself with his family in the States. He kissed her very gently.

'It's a bummer. But we knew all this at the start. Tell you what – as a special treat before the end of term, I'll take you to the *Petit*

Prince. I promised to do that in France, and I don't see why we shouldn't risk going there now. I don't suppose we'll meet anyone I know,' he said, and Sophie laughed.

'You don't have to do that, Matt. You know that I'm happy just to be with you here.'

'But I want to. Leave it with me, Sophie, and I'll text you to confirm if I can get a table next week. I expect you to get dolled up for me, because I want to see the same reaction on people's faces as there was in that place in Dinan.'

Sophie's skin felt tingly with pleasure as she recalled that occasion; the first time they'd ever been alone together. She could hardly remember why she'd objected to him holding her hand after the lunch. It had been the reaction of a silly girl, and she felt that she had travelled miles from that state of naivety to become a woman of the world, even if it was a world where deceit and careful planning held sway.

When Matt confirmed the booking, she trawled the boutiques for a new dress and visited a hairdresser on the afternoon of the date to have her hair arranged in a stylish updo. It pleased her to take pains for him, but she was almost frightened by her transformation from student to glamour puss, because she seemed to have acquired a new personality in the process. This version of Sophie was an elegant, assured woman who knew her own mind, and the diffident girl was buried underneath the polished surface. She arranged to meet him in the restaurant, and timed her entrance to be a little late, hoping to make an appearance worthy of a diva.

Matt was already seated at a table when she entered the restaurant, and the sight of him, smiling and elegant in a dark suit, made her heart flutter as it always did. The head waiter whisked her coat away and Matt stood up to brush cheeks with her in a demure greeting.

'You look amazing,' he said quietly, feasting his eyes on her, and her face grew pink with pleasure. 'I hardly recognised my Princess Isabelle with her hair like that,' he added, and she gave a happy sigh.

'You did tell me to be smart,' she reminded him, and he laughed.

'I still have a soft spot for that little flowery dress, but you look fantastic in red, and you seem to have caused quite a stir in case you hadn't noticed. There are lots of envious eyes on you, and I like that.'

Sophie looked around at the other diners. The restaurant was dimly lit; the Christmas décor was subtle and low key compared to the tinsel-fest of most Cambridge eating places, and the room hummed with an atmosphere of moneyed sophistication which she found extremely seductive. She was surprised to be handed a menu without prices.

'Is everything terribly expensive, Matt?' she whispered, anxious to curb unnecessary extravagance. He winked at her, looking like a man who holds all the aces.

'Yes. I told you this place was special. But don't let it worry you. As I seem to remember saying in Dinan, my wife is a tycoon, so money doesn't matter.'

Sophie's smile dimmed to a grimace at the unwelcome reminder of Liz. She stared over Matt's shoulder, and noticed an older woman quizzing her with a gimlet eye which seemed to intuit the existence of illicit goings-on, and she hastily turned back to the menu. Matt didn't notice her unease; he ordered the meal with smiling insouciance and his habitual disregard for cost.

The food was presented with creative flair and everything tasted delicious, but Sophie was surprised to find herself wishing they were sitting in the steak pub or one of their other casual haunts. She found it difficult to relax in these formal surroundings, conscious that she was playing a part rather than being her ordinary self, although Matt chatted away with his usual confidence. The waiter had just presented her with an elaborate deconstructed pudding when a woman walking past their table stopped and regarded her with an air of curiosity.

'Sophie? It is Sophie isn't it? I didn't recognise you at first with your hair up.'

It was Jennifer Bradbury. Sophie's cheeks reddened to a strawberry brightness, and she clamped her lips together to inhibit a gasp of surprise. Jennifer hovered, smiling at Matt in a way which suggested an introduction was needed and Sophie forced herself to act naturally, although her scarlet face was proving to be an annoying hindrance.

'Oh, Jennifer... do you know Matthew Braybrooke, Liz's husband? He works in Cambridge during the week, and ...'

Matt rose to his feet and directed his most effervescent beam at Sophie's tutor.

'But Liz has often talked to me about you, Jennifer. How very nice to meet you. And, of course, you know that Sophie was with us in France during the summer.'

Jennifer seemed to be fascinated by the intensity of Matt's gaze. She nodded her head and returned his smile.

'I am the person who recommended Sophie, so I am pleased to see you are still friends. Do give Liz my best regards when you are back in London. I follow her career with great interest, and she is a wonderful example for my students. How nice for Sophie that you have kept in touch,' she added, and Sophie hoped her grin carried conviction rather than desperation.

'The family have been so kind to me,' she faltered. The tension in Matt's face was making her wary. She sensed that he was displeased by the incident, and she couldn't wait for Jennifer to move away. After exchanging a few more pleasantries, Jennifer returned to her table and Matt resumed his seat. Sophie was disconcerted by the grim expression in his eyes.

'Jesus. That's all I needed,' he muttered, and she only just stopped herself from reaching across the table to take his hand.

'What do you mean, Matt? I don't see why Jennifer would suspect anything,' she said, and he shook his head at her.

'For Christ's sake, stop blushing! I've never seen such an exhibition of guilt. You might as well have told her straight out that we're fucking,' he hissed, and his voice was savage. Sophie lowered her head to contemplate her pudding, wondering how she would manage to choke down the confection. It was the first time she'd seen Matt lose his cool, and she didn't know what to do.

Then the maitre d' was hovering over them, aware that something was amiss.

'Is everything satisfactory, Monsieur, Madame?' he murmured silkily, and Matt jolted himself back to his social persona.

'Everything's fine, thanks.'

He grabbed his spoon and began to excavate his pudding. 'Eat up, and let's get out of here,' he said, his shoulders stiff with exasperation. 'Let's hope your Jennifer can keep her mouth shut.'

'But couldn't you tell Liz a version of the truth if she ever asks you about it? You could say you'd met me in the street...'

Sophie's voice dribbled away as Matt raked her with a furious blue glare.

'And brought you here, as if it was a trip to McDonalds? With you tarted up like you are? Liz may be many things, but she's not stupid.'

He ate with rapid concentration, and Sophie began to tackle her own plate. She felt sick with worry now, so each mouthful was an effort and she was forced to leave half the pudding uneaten. Matt remained tight-lipped, merely asking for the bill and frowning over his wallet. When he had paid, he seemed to relax a little. He pulled out his phone, and she realised that he was calling a cab. 'You'd better go straight back to college. I think I ought to be seen to say goodbye to you here,' he said, and Sophie caught her breath in disappointment.

'But – you're going back to London tomorrow, and I won't see you again until after Christmas.'

Her voice tailed off in a teary way, and she saw his jaw grow rigid again.

'That's unfortunate, but I don't think I can risk taking you back to the flat with me now. Listen, Sophie – just chill out and enjoy your Christmas holiday. I expect we'll pick things up when I get back in the New Year. And for fuck's sake, don't start blubbing here. Things are bad enough as they are.'

They stood up to leave, and Sophie saw old gimlet-eye send her a glance of disapprobation which roused her to fury and incidentally restored her self-possession. She returned the woman's scowl with a look of hauteur as she allowed Matt to usher her to the entrance. When he bade her goodbye, she accepted his brief farewell embrace, although her face felt frozen with disappointment. She swept out to the taxi like a queen, and it wasn't until she was motoring through the gaudy Christmas streets on the way back to college that she began to take stock of the situation. She didn't feel like crying now; she was furious that Matt had crumpled at the first sign of trouble.

Chapter Twenty

Sophie slammed the door of her room behind her and leaned against it, breathless with frustration after the dramatic and unsatisfactory end to the evening. Okay, she had been embarrassed when Jennifer accosted them, but she would have had a similar reaction on an innocent date – students weren't expected to socialise with their tutors outside college; it felt awkward. She was afraid that Matt's explosive fit of sulks had only made them more conspicuous, and she had no idea how matters stood now.

She slumped at her desk, scrolling through her mail on autopilot until she had to visit the loo. The mirror in the bathroom still reflected the grown-up person she had been earlier in the evening, but now the image was a mockery, because that life had crumbled to pieces. Sophie returned to her room and tore the pins from her hair until it fell around her face in straggling curls, swearing she'd never wear it up again.

Her phone rang. The caller was Matt, and she was tempted for a second to let it ring out. She wasn't feeling well-disposed towards him, but as usual, her heart overruled her head.

'Sophie? Did you get back okay? I'm sorry the evening fell apart like that.'

Matt's voice was contrite, but this only fanned the flames of her anger.

'I don't know what to say to you, Matt, but I think you over-reacted massively. Why shouldn't we have dinner together? I hope Jennifer didn't notice you kicking me out of the place, because she'll certainly be asking questions if she did.'

She thought his silence held a measure of astonishment because she'd challenged him.

'I didn't kick you out,' he said sulkily, after a long pause. 'But I thought it was best if we didn't hang around. If you hadn't acted so embarrassed, it would have been fine.'

'She took me by surprise. But the way you behaved afterwards made me more surprised. Didn't you understand you were drawing attention to us by getting stroppy in the way you did?'

Sophie suspected that Matt wouldn't take criticism well. For a moment, she thought that he had ended the call, but an exasperated sigh showed that he was still listening.

'Whatever.'

He huffed like a sulky teenager. 'The timing wasn't great. Do you want to come over now? As you reminded me, it'll be January when we get together, otherwise.'

Sophie was tempted, but he had given her such a jolt that she wanted distance to reflect on the evening. It wasn't just his temper and unkindness; this was the first time she'd been forced to confront the unpalatable truth about her relationship with Matt. Their playing at houses together in his flat was a world removed from reality, and the liaison suddenly seemed tainted and tacky. Matt had shown weakness which diminished her regard for him, and she hovered on the edges of indecision.

'I don't know, Matt. It's late. Maybe we need to have a break from each other for a while,' she said.

Sophie's voice wobbled, because she feared the break could become a permanent separation. This time, his silence was more prolonged and edged with hostility.

'Okay, if that's how you feel.'

He was curt. Was he disappointed with her response? 'Happy Christmas, Sophie, and I hope that Santa brings you everything that you want.'

He rang off before she could reply, and she sat with her head bowed, weeping over the phone. Why had she rejected his invitation? She was in love with Matt, and now, she might never see him again. But she clung to the tattered remnants of pride which prevented her from rushing through the night to ring his doorbell. She had to sleep on the problem, even though it would be a tearful and restless sleep, but next morning, she was unhappily convinced that she'd been too hasty in rejecting his request. There was nothing she could do about it. He was about to leave for London and his holiday and there was no opportunity for her to see him again.

It took all Sophie's nerve and acting skills to present an untroubled front to her friends in the remaining days of term. She took to wearing heavy make-up to disguise the ravages left by unhappy nights, and she was grateful for the festive high spirits which distracted others from

177

remarking upon her low mood. The day before she went home for the Christmas holiday, a small box was delivered to the lodge, addressed to her. When she opened it in her room, she found an elegant pair of diamond earrings nestling on black velvet. There was no card with the box, which was supplied by an exclusive Cambridge jeweller, but it had to have come from Matt.

Was this gift a token of farewell or a plea for forgiveness? Sophie couldn't bring herself to try the earrings on. If they spelled goodbye, it would be months before she could contemplate wearing them, although their beauty helped to soothe a tiny portion of her fractured heart. She took them out to gaze upon their fiery sparkle several times every day, trying to find comfort in the fact that Matt had thought enough of her to make such a special gift.

Sophie was forced to continue her role-play throughout the holidays, curling up on the settee in Guildford to watch weepy movies and romcoms so she didn't have to dwell upon her loneliness, and it was hard to evince much interest in her home surroundings. She knew that life would be much easier for Matt during their separation, and she couldn't help resenting this. He would be able to lose himself in company with his daughters; in all the pursuits of a winter holiday and the excitement of being away from England, and he would have little time to brood on events in Cambridge. That didn't seem fair, and Sophie's heart hardened. She returned to college shortly before term began, and this time, she received a lecture from her father as they drove north.

'I hope you'll shake yourself out of this gloom when you are back with your friends,' Mr Elliot said, obviously unable to repress his anxiety. 'You've been a worry to me and your mother all Christmas. You know we don't like to interfere in your affairs, Sophie, but if this continual moping is about some young man, I can only say that he isn't worth it. Do yourself a favour, darling, and move on to someone else.'

'Oh, Dad, I'm sorry. I know I've been a misery. There was someone last term... but it didn't work out. I don't know why I can't seem to find a decent boyfriend.'

Sophie had refused to cry over Matt in recent days. There were times now when she was ashamed of her bold plunge into an illicit affair, and she was teaching herself to be relieved that Jennifer

Bradbury had inadvertently brought the downsides of her liaison into such sharp focus. 'I ought to concentrate on my work, anyway,' she added dully; the prospect didn't inspire her.

'Yes, you ought. And I'd like to think that you were making plans for what you'll do when you finish your degree. I'm not sure another holiday job like last year's will drop into your lap.'

'My God, I hope not,' she murmured, but so softly that her father couldn't hear. She was aware that he kissed her goodbye with worry etched on his face, and the guilt that this engendered prompted her into New Year resolutions to find a new man – or swear off men altogether for a while – and take some tentative steps towards her future career.

Sophie spent her first evening with Sarah and Hannah in a pub full of chattering students, and she cast an appraising eye over the young men sprawled at neighbouring tables. It was a shame that they resembled yapping puppies when compared to Matt, and their boisterous humour grated on her sensibilities, but she tried to persuade herself that it would be possible, even desirable, to lower her expectations in future.

Next day, she was returning to college before lunch when a voice hailed her from across the road. She turned in surprise to see a familiar figure leaning against a lamp post; tall and tailored with an impeccable haircut and arresting blue eyes. All her resolutions tumbled into the gutter as he dodged between cars to reach her side, but she was determined not to succumb without a struggle.

'*Sophie…*'

Matt hesitated, looking surprised at the sight of her solemn face. 'Thank God I've run you to earth. Someone nicked my mobile when we were in the States and I lost your number, so I've not been able to call. But you don't know how much I've longed to see you,' he said, with disarming sincerity. 'Please tell me that you've forgiven me for what happened before Christmas.'

She couldn't find words – she didn't know how to respond to him. He took her silence as assent, and Sophie found her face pressed to his coat; his eager arms igniting memories back to red-hot life. He ignored the other students weaving around them and when he kissed her, gently, lovingly, she was afraid that the game was up.

'Oh, Matt!'

179

Sophie's voice was muffled against him. 'Do you want to go on with this?' she asked. 'I've thought so hard all holiday about what we should do, and I don't know whether I can go back to where we were. I'm beginning to feel we were wrong to get so involved.'

Matt obviously hadn't expected this reaction, and he stepped back as though she'd slapped him.

'Can we go to your room? This isn't a conversation to be had in the street,' he said, and he sounded winded. Sophie thought rapidly.

'Okay. I suppose that makes sense. Aren't you worried that Jennifer Bradbury might see us?' she added, unable to resist a dig at him, and he narrowed his eyes in frustration.

'Look, I said I was sorry. Cut me some slack,' he murmured, and she was silenced by remorse. She led the way to her room, but when they were inside, he made no attempt to embrace her again. He strode to the window and stood looking out on the quad below. 'You live in a different world here, don't you?' he said, and she thought she read something like apprehension in his face. 'Sophie, if you want me to walk away, then you'd better say so now. My feelings for you haven't changed – being apart has made me realise that I want you more than ever. But it's even more important that you don't get hurt by our affair, so I have to leave the decision to you.'

Sophie didn't want that responsibility. It was easy to resolve to end things if Matt wasn't standing before her, but when she was confronted with his person, her willpower drained away like a leaky battery. Just looking at him reduced her to wobbling indecision. She wanted to curl up in the flat with him, to be consumed by passionate lovemaking in a comfortable bed – she'd even settle for watching football if only they could return to the intense and private world they'd shared before the break.

He was watching her warily, waiting for her response, and she gave a shuddery sigh.

'That scene with Jennifer really opened my eyes,' she said. 'We kid ourselves that we're in control; that no-one's going to end up hurt and that it's okay for us to be together. But I'm worried that it's wrong to push your other life aside as though it doesn't matter. It must matter to you, and I almost wish that you'd decided over Christmas that the risks we're running are too big. Do you ever think that we're – well, we're being rather *cheap*? I don't know how else to put it…'

180

He screwed up his face as if in pain, and she took an involuntary step towards him, unwilling to see him suffer.

'What's cheap is pursuing something when your heart isn't in it one hundred per cent,' he said slowly, and Sophie wondered whether he meant his marriage to Liz. 'But that's a lesson I've learned, and I've accepted the consequences. And there are compensations along the way, so I won't complain.'

Matt reached out and stroked her cheek, and the yearning in his eyes seemed to find its way into the depths of her heart. 'I don't want us to finish, Sophie, not yet. I can't predict how we'll feel when the time comes for you to leave Cambridge, but I hope to God that you want to go on seeing me now. Weren't we good together until that night at the restaurant?'

It wasn't remotely the same situation, but Sophie was reminded of Sean's emotional and physical coercion on her last night in France. He had dismantled her defences more easily than she cared to remember, and she felt that Matt was doing something similar; as though he was practised in persuasion. When she didn't reply, Matt tried again.

'You told me that you were brave enough to go for what you want,' he said, and her cheeks tingled. She knew she wasn't brave; she was mixed-up and vacillating, but her hesitation spurred him to action. He pulled her towards him, and she could not resist the pressure of his lips which left her body limp with remembered delight.

'Shouldn't you be at work?' she muttered when she could breathe again, and he smiled, pulling gently on one of her earlobes.

'Yes. But there are other places I'd rather be.'

She stood unresisting as he began to unbutton her coat, and he reached inside her jumper to unhook her bra.

'Ouch! Matt, your hands are like ice.'

The chill of his fingers made her flinch, but he laughed as he began to shed his own garments. There wasn't much room in her single divan, but there was enough for him to do what he wanted, and soon, she began to long for it too. The weeks of separation seemed to spool back as he made love to her, and she felt complete again, as though they'd never been apart.

Afterwards, he levered himself from the bed and reached for his clothes.

'I really do have to go now, my darling. But will you come to the flat this evening? We can go out if you like, anywhere, you choose what you'd like to do,' he said.

Sophie sat up, pushing back her hair and stretching like an indolent cat.

'No, let's eat at the flat. I don't want to risk another confrontation like the *Petit Prince,*' she said.

'Are you sure? Mind you, there is a big match on tonight...'

Sophie chucked a pillow at Matt across the room, but she couldn't be angry with him now. As he was putting on his coat, she remembered the earrings.

'Matt... was it you who sent me some beautiful earrings at Christmas? There was nothing to say who they were from in the box – it was a mystery,' she exclaimed, and he smirked.

'We wanted to surprise you,' he said, and she furrowed her brow.

'We?' she queried.

'Me and Sean.'

'*Sean was involved?*'

Sophie was jolted by the information. She didn't want the gift to have come from Sean; she didn't want him touching any part of her life, especially her secret life with his stepfather.

'When I got home after our little tiff before Christmas, Sean was back from school. We had another long talk about his feelings for you and what had happened after France. He's contrite, and he wanted to do something to let you know he was sorry, so I arranged a little Christmas present from us both,' Matt said, looking preeningly pleased with himself. 'Do you like them?'

Sophie hoped he didn't realise that she was pasting on a smile of gratitude.

'Yes, they are amazing. That was very kind of you. I do hope that Sean's okay now, and that he enjoyed your time in Aspen,' she said, feeling obliged to cover up her earlier outburst.

'We had a great holiday, and he's in much better shape. I'm pleased you like the earrings. You can wear them for me one day.'

He paused at the door, not noticing her sudden abstraction. 'Till tonight, beautiful. I really must get you a key cut now, but I'll expect you at the flat at the usual time.'

He blew her a kiss and she heard his footsteps die away. Eventually, she got up and retrieved the box with the earrings from its hiding place in a drawer under her lingerie. She opened the lid. The gems still sparkled merrily in the sunlight, but she felt, illogically, that their lustre was dimmed by the association with Sean, and she shut the urge to wear them back up in the box.

Now that she and Matt were reconciled, Sophie enjoyed some weeks of unalloyed happiness. Matt often stayed in Cambridge for the working week, so she saw him more frequently than before. Weekends still had to be filled, but it was easier to find excuses to concentrate on work as her final exams inched closer.

One day, she was eating in hall with Hannah when she received an unpleasant reminder that her life wasn't following the usual student pattern.

'I saw you in a pub the other night when I was out with Martin.'

Why did Hannah make that sound like an accusation? The girl put her mouth close to Sophie's ear. 'You were with your *sugar daddy*,' she hissed, and Sophie jumped as the punch landed in the pit of her stomach.

'My what?' she countered, in a feeble attempt to recover herself.

'You heard. Isn't that what he is? He's older than you, and I don't suppose you were picking up the bill for those juicy steaks. And he was wearing a *wedding ring!* Honestly, Sophie, I'm quite surprised at you.'

Sophie stared across the room; every muscle taut with tension and feeling that she was poised to flee. Things sounded cheap and horrible when analysed so clinically, and she wasn't sure how to defend herself. Was a defence even possible?

'It isn't like that,' she faltered, but she couldn't meet Hannah's caustic gaze.

'What is it like, then, *sugar baby*? I hope you're getting stuff out of him, although I have to say he's fit for an older guy. Is he good in bed?' her friend demanded.

Sophie flinched under the pressure of the accusations.

'I don't want stuff. I'm not a sugar baby. I just want Matt – I love him.'

It was the first time she'd voiced this truth to anyone, including Matt. Hannah didn't seem to be impressed, and she hadn't nearly finished with her friend.

'More fool you, then. Do you think he's going to leave his wife? I hope you aren't such a sucker that you believe in fairy tales.'

Memories of Princess Isabelle flashed across Sophie's mind, and she suddenly saw the kitchen in France in vivid detail. She also saw Liz's face; mocking, censorious.

'No. I know he won't leave his wife. He's always been upfront about that.'

Although the conversation was painful, she felt strangely relieved that another person was aware of her tricky situation. Sophie blew out a huge breath, and Hannah groaned.

'Well, what the fuck are you doing with him, then? Did he pay for your laptop last term, and your amazing coat? My ma would call that the wages of sin.'

Sophie shrugged, annoyed by her condemnation now. Hannah continued her attack. 'Is this guy really worth it, Sophie? Why are you wasting time on an affair that can't go anywhere? I imagine you have to pussyfoot around so wifey doesn't get wind of what's going on; that can't be easy. You live in a city full of students. Surely you can find someone who doesn't come with strings attached?'

Hannah was only saying what Sophie already knew. Two girls slid into the seats next to them, and Sophie made faces at her mate to leave off. She was relieved that she'd finished her meal and rose to her feet, hoping to gather some semblance of dignity.

'You couldn't understand. I know it's not ideal, but it's what we both want,' she said. 'Don't go on at me, Hannah, because I need my friends.'

'Be fucking careful, then. Do your parents know about him?'

'No. I didn't think anyone knew. Please zip your mouth about this.'

Hannah's face was dour, but she squeezed her friend's arm as they left the dining hall. Sophie's secret was out at last, but she hoped that it would go no further.

Chapter Twenty-one

During the early weeks of the year Sophie was very happy. She caught herself indulging in dangerous fantasies where she forged a long-term future with her lover, but she didn't want to deprive Poppy and Boo of their father, so Liz had to be removed from the scene somehow.

Sophie was too squeamish to consign Liz to an unpleasant end *(CEO raped and murdered in City break-in!)*, so she used her imagination to dispose of her quickly in a plane crash or natural accident. Electrocution from a faulty charger would do, she decided; that would be quick and relatively painless. Sometimes it seemed easiest for Liz to walk away with a new man, declaring that her relationship with Matt had run its course. Sophie was waiting in the wings, ready to gather the reins of the household into younger, prettier hands. She looked forward to becoming a stepmother to Poppy and Boo, and to giving Matt the son she knew he'd always wanted, although Abbie and Sean posed more of a problem. She couldn't quite decide how to dispose of them, and she feared that Sean wouldn't be wholly happy about the turn of events...

In real life, Matt was unfailingly cheerful and affectionate towards her, and there were times when Sophie felt that it wouldn't take much to prise him away from his family. She began to enquire about research opportunities which would enable her to stay in Cambridge when she had taken her degree and allowed herself to dream that she might end up overturning Hannah's gloomy predictions and make a life with her lover. But in moments where reality forced its way into her thoughts, she was shocked to realise that she felt so little guilt about her involvement with a man who was already spoken for. She was unhappily conscious of Liz's prior claim on mornings when she lay in bed watching Matt dress for the office. He always pulled the same little grimace as he did up the top button of his shirt and straightened his tie and it struck Sophie as an intensely private and personal moment which ought to belong to a wife. She would look away, reminding herself that she only had Matt on loan and smothering an ache of regret.

However, at the beginning of March, she became conscious of a tiny shift in Matt's focus, almost as though he was beginning to shed one skin for another. His business had reached a critical point where a major expansion was underway, and this meant that he was increasingly unavailable because of meetings or visiting suppliers in other parts of the country. Sophie accepted this without complaint, although faint lines of strain on Matt's face made her worry that he was stretching himself between too many competing parties.

In the second week of March he rang with a catalogue of excuses. He couldn't see her until Thursday evening, and she walked to the flat that night barely controlling her impatience to be with him again. Judy, his Australian neighbour, was letting herself out as Sophie approached the door to the street. She eyed Sophie in a calculating way and crinkled her eyes in a sugary smile.

'Oh, it's you. I didn't realise you were still on the scene.'

Sophie frowned, wondering what the woman meant.

'Matt's been busy this week', she said, with a little shrug. She didn't have to explain herself and she made it plain that she wasn't interested in conversation, but Judy's next words caused her to snap to breathless attention.

'Is that what he told you? I've noticed he's had a little blonde visitor who looks as though she'd keep him busy. Good old Matt; he's a player after my own heart.'

Judy strolled away before Sophie could regain her self-possession and ask her what she meant. Had Matt had brought another woman to the flat? It couldn't be Liz, who was away in Zurich, and who wasn't fair-haired... surely Matt wouldn't be seeing anyone else?

A little voice sang a needling chant in her ear. *'He cheated on his wife; why wouldn't he cheat on you?'*

Sophie let herself in to the flat. Matt wasn't home. As soon as she was inside, she threw her things on the sofa and began a minute examination of the bedroom and bathroom, hating herself but desperate to understand whether Judy was right. She wasn't sure what she was looking for and couldn't find any incriminating evidence, but she knew that Matt was careful to keep the rooms free of anything suspicious in case Liz turned up at short notice, unlikely though that might be.

The main door slammed, and Matt's voice called out. Sophie scurried from the bathroom, hoping her flushed face wouldn't cause him to suspect there was anything amiss.

'There you are! Come over here and let me kiss you, stranger.'

He held out his arms, and she glided into them like a sleepwalker. His kiss was warm and easy, and there was nothing in his eyes to suggest that he'd been doubly unfaithful. Sophie wasn't sure how to face him, because the shock of Judy's words was still reverberating inside her head. 'I'm sorry it's been so long, darling. Work is hell, but I think I'm winning,' he said, squeezing her buttock.

'Good.'

Sophie turned her cheek against his shoulder, embarrassed on his behalf and unwilling to meet his smile. The need to know the truth swelled inside her, making her choky and hesitant and Matt evidently twigged that something wasn't right.

'You okay, Sophie?'

He pulled back to examine her and she turned troubled eyes upon him.

'It was just something Judy said. I met her in the street, and she implied that you've been entertaining another woman here this week. I didn't know how to react.'

As soon as she spoke, Sophie realised that this direct approach was a mistake because it came across with an incendiary punch. Matt seemed to freeze before he responded with a sardonic little laugh. He took her face in his hands so she couldn't escape from his penetrating gaze.

'Judy is an interfering bitch. Yes, another woman has been here, but she's a colleague. We've had to put in extra hours to fix a tricky issue, and office politics meant that it was something best done externally. Why else would I bring another woman here, when I have you?'

Sophie shook her head as if to say she didn't know. Matt's expression was bland and innocent, and she tried to convince herself that he was telling the truth. 'Judy's never forgiven me for rejecting some pretty blatant advances on her part when I first moved here,' he added, and this seemed to make sense. She was about to apologise and say that it didn't matter but he dropped his arms and wandered away. The television clicked on. 'You don't mind if I catch up with the golf, do you?' he asked, but she wasn't sure whether the studied carelessness of his voice was hiding something less trivial.

The evening wore away with golf, supper and sofa smooches, but Sophie no longer felt entirely at her ease in Matt's company. Judy's words had lit a fuse which was smouldering slowly inside her, and she was worried that she wouldn't be able to handle an explosion if it came. It gave her a hollow feeling inside to think that Matt might be hiding something so devastating from her. Had he tired of her so quickly?

Matt was away all the last week of March, and Sophie found it hard to keep her frustration at bay. Her parents were enjoying themselves on a Caribbean cruise and they had paid for her to stay on in college after the official end of term, rather than return to an empty house. She'd been pleased about this at first, but now it seemed a waste of time and money if Matt wasn't going to be around. He happened to mention when he called her one day that he'd been invited to a networking brunch on the Science Park on Saturday morning, and she suggested meeting up afterwards. He wasn't very responsive, and she had to press him more than she liked.

'I suppose I could drum up some excuse and tell Liz that I'll be back early Sunday,' he said, sighing slightly as though she was asking an outrageous favour.

'That would be good. I've hardly seen you recently.'

'Mm. You know the score, Sophie. It isn't always possible for me to be available for you.'

It was difficult for her to comprehend the sense of indifference in his attitude. Sophie's fingers grew white as she clutched at her phone.

'You haven't found it a problem until now,' she muttered, but he didn't respond.

'I'll see you on Saturday then. Come around after lunch, but I'll want to watch the rugby,' he said, and rang off before she could voice any further objections. Sophie was left to brood on his growing detachment – things seemed utterly out of kilter. She recalled his question at the beginning of their affair – *'what happens if one of us falls in love?'* It was beginning to dawn on her that he had managed to avoid that trap although she had plunged into it with open eyes, but she couldn't believe that he could be travelling in the other direction.They had been so close, and she comforted herself with the notion that he might be finding their complex arrangements difficult at a time when he had so many outside pressures to contend with.

Saturday morning seemed to stretch out without end. Eventually, lunchtime arrived and then Sophie made her way, excited but apprehensive, to the flat. Matt was fussing around with paperwork as she slipped off her coat and walked across to hug him.

'How was your morning?' she asked, reaching up to embrace him, and he nodded as if to say the event had been satisfactory. She rubbed herself against him and ran a finger down his chest until she felt him relax.

'You look pretty,' he said, almost with reluctance, accepting a kiss, and then another. But his face was sober, and he scowled at his watch as though he felt under pressure.

'Just time for a quickie before the rugby. I don't think I can stay the night.'

Sophie was chilled by this brusque welcome, which was unlike anything she'd received from him in the past.

'Are you sure you even want me to be here?' she demanded, snappy with surprise, and he shrugged.

'Don't be silly. But I don't think you understand how difficult this is for me,' he said, stalking into the bedroom. Sophie lingered in the doorway, aggrieved and feeling that this was the least romantic scene she'd ever had the misfortune to be in.

'Difficult to make love?'

She was being deliberately obtuse.

'Now you're being a smartarse. No; I mean the whole effort of keeping up this dual life. You have no idea how many times I have to stop and check that I'm not giving myself away. It gets bloody wearing.'

Matt was pulling his clothes off in a petulant fashion, like a resentful child who has been sent to bed too early. Sophie tried to find her orientation in this new, uncertain universe.

'I'm sorry you feel like that. Of course, you must go back to London today if you're having problems,' she said gently, and he looked at her with something like an apology in his eyes.

'Sorry, Soph. I'm fucking frazzled at present, but I shouldn't take it out on you. Come here and make me feel better.'

189

Sophie tried to lose herself in the warmth of his body, but for the first time, she felt as though they were on different pages of their story. She had never felt less satisfied with his lovemaking although Matt's grunts of release had an animal earthiness which indicated that he'd enjoyed himself, and she wasn't surprised when he rolled away afterwards without petting her, saying that the rugby was about to start.

Sophie sat on the edge of the bed, watching a sudden rainstorm shroud the street in gloom. It was a wild, stormy day, and there were reports of flooding in the east of the country. She couldn't even feel cosy in her nest of bedding; nothing seemed to warm her today after Matt's frigid welcome. Eventually, she rose and dressed, and went to make herself a cup of tea. Matt was stretched on the sofa, beer in hand, and he appeared to be in a happier temper. At half-time, he went to check train times to London on his laptop and was then struck by a different thought.

'Have I shown you my new company website?' he asked, as if he felt that he ought to make more of an effort to be amenable after his earlier grumps.

'No. I'd like to see it, Matt.'

She stood at his shoulder as he located the site and began to scroll down the page. The design was eye-catching and had evidently been worked up by a professional. Matt's mobile rang, and he picked it up and walked towards the bedroom.

'Hi Liz. I was about to let you know I can make it back tonight after all,' he said, and closed the door behind him.

Sophie wasn't bothered by this call. She didn't even feel very interested because she had stopped viewing Liz as competition long ago, and she continued to scroll through the website, eventually clicking on the page which featured the company personnel. There were more of them than she'd realised – Matt's picture showed his film-star features to advantage – and it was by chance that the cursor hesitated over some of the more recent employees. One was a young lady in her twenties, described as a company researcher. She had blonde hair curling past her shoulders and was extremely pretty in a chocolate-boxy way.

Sophie stared at the woman's face, wondering…

Matt's call didn't last long. He strode back into the room, and Sophie closed the website, reading something wrong in his demeanour.

'What is it, Matt?'

She wondered whether one of the girls was ill, but before he could answer her, there was a rap at his door. They stared at one another, wide-eyed in a moment of suspense.

'Must be Judy. No-one else could get in from below,' said Matt, moving across to open the door.

But it wasn't Judy who confronted him. It was Sean.

Chapter Twenty-two

No-one spoke for the first few electrifying seconds, but Sean was dripping like a seal from the storm outside, and after sending one appalled glance towards Sophie, Matt squared his shoulders and pulled his stepson into the room.

'Jeez, Sean! Your mother just called. She's worried sick; she says you've had a fight,' he said, his voice sharp with anger, but Sean couldn't drag his gaze away from Sophie.

'What's *she* doing here?' the boy demanded, and Sophie shrank back, catching her breath in fright and apprehension. Matt ignored the question.

'How did you get in?' he continued, and Sean uttered a barking laugh, although his eyes were fixed on Sophie as though he feared she was a mirage which might disappear at any moment.

'Some Aussie type I met on her way out. Why, what does it matter? What are you two hiding?'

Sophie's legs turned to wool and she groped her way to the sofa. The rugby match had recommenced, and she stared with concentration at the grappling figures, wishing she was far away and part of the crowd; any crowd. Sean shucked off his wet anorak and threw it over a chair. 'I'm busting for a pee. Where's the bog?' he demanded, and Matt nodded towards the bedroom door.

'Through there,' he said tightly, and it wasn't until she heard the click of the bathroom lock that Sophie remembered the tumbled sheets of the unmade bed and her bag lying open upon a bedside table.

'Matt – he'll see everything,' she mumbled, but it was too late.

'Leave this to me, okay, Sophie?'

Matt's attempt at confidence didn't comfort her. He went to a cupboard and poured himself a large whisky, tossing it back and raking his hair with one hand, looking like a man on the verge of going under. Sean reappeared in a fury of slammed doors and Sophie wilted under his accusing gaze. She looked to Matt to come up with an explanation which might defuse the situation.

'You're banging her! You total arsehole, Matt! What about Mum? What about me?'

192

Sean wheeled round on Sophie, and she cringed from the contempt which disfigured his face. 'And you're a bitch, a mega slag. I can't think why the fuck I ever wanted you. Just wait until I tell Mum what's been going on – you'll wish you'd never come across my family.'

'I've wished that for a long time.'

Sophie's own anger began to kindle, and her cheeks grew hot. Why didn't Matt come to her defence? He seemed to have shrunk in the face of his stepson's tirade.

'Sit down, Sean. There's no need to make a scene,' Matt said, but Sean wasn't buying it.

'It's Mum I'm sorriest for, and Pops and Boo. I really rated you, Matt, but you're just as big a shit as my father.'

Matt flinched as though Sean had punched him, and the room seemed to reverberate with anger. He tried to take Sean's arm, but the boy shook him away and a deafening burst of thunder made them all jump, although it seemed to Sophie to be appropriate in the circumstances.

'My God, the sky's falling now,' Matt muttered. If this was an attempt to lower the tension, it wasn't successful. Sean looked with envy at the whisky in his stepfather's hand.

'I need a drink,' he stated, and Matt seemed glad of the excuse to move to the fridge. He pulled out a can of beer and handed it to the boy.

'Sophie? Do you want one?' he asked, and she shook her head.

'I think it might be best if I go,' she whispered, getting to her feet, but Sean wheeled round on her with a menacing gesture.

'Oh no, you don't. I want to hear all about this thing with Matt; like how long the two of you've been shagging. How Little Miss Perfect squared things with her conscience so she could fuck up a marriage, fresh from putting me through hell. Should be interesting,' he sneered.

Sophie drew a deep breath and summoned her courage.

'I don't have to explain myself to you, Sean,' she retorted, sounding braver than she felt. 'And I didn't put you through hell, you managed that for yourself. But I can tell you Matt isn't going to leave your mother if that makes you feel better.'

Sophie hoped that this admission might defuse Sean's anger, but his brow remained as black as the tempest outside. He looked as though he would choke on Sophie's words as he turned to his stepfather for confirmation.

'Is that true?' he demanded, and Matt nodded.

'I told Sophie from the beginning that my marriage wasn't up for negotiation. She's always known the score.'

Sean glowered at Sophie as if this made her even more of a slut in his estimation.

'So, why go after Matt? I don't understand you, Sophie. You seemed like such a nice, ordinary girl. And you're such a babe; I don't believe you can't pull guys your own age,' he said, his voice trembling, and Sophie wondered how much of the truth he could deal with. Matt was watching her with anxiety puckering his face, and she was conscious of the traps she could tumble into if she put honesty over expedience. But did it even matter now? She realised with a sad clarity that whatever had happened during the past months, her affair with Matt was over. Regret and pain lay in wait for her, but somehow, she felt that was fitting and that she deserved it.

'Matt was sweet to me in France, and it was thanks to him that you stopped harassing me last autumn,' she said, thinking that Sean needed reminding of his own shortcomings. 'Didn't you ever stop to think about how your threats made me feel? I was grateful to him for getting you off my back, and that feeling grew into something deeper. I wish he wasn't married, but I've never tried to pressurise him into getting a divorce.'

Sean slugged down his beer, scowling between the two as he weighed up what she'd told him. The storm howled with a ferocious voice, and Matt walked to the window to watch the torrents of rain scything down the glass.

'I hate this weather. It gives me the shudders,' he murmured, before wheeling round on his stepson, as if trying to regain the initiative. 'Sean; I don't know what you and your mother were fighting about but I must let her know that you're in Cambridge. You took a big risk coming here; I could easily have been away. What do you want me to say to her?'

Sean shrugged as he downed the beer.

'Tell her you've been rubbing bits with her holiday help. Then stand back and wait for the bomb to go off.' He forced an unpleasant laugh. 'Or you can tell her that I felt like a change of scene. Say I've

194

come up here to be with the girl of my dreams – only she's turned into a frigging nightmare. Fuck it, Matt, I don't care what line you spin her, but I'm not going back to London without you. I need to be sure that you and Sophie are kaput. And the three of us have got a lot more talking to do.'

Matt picked up his phone and retreated to the bedroom again, leaving Sophie alone with Sean. Her senses were straining because she didn't trust him. She was frightened of him and her instinct urged her to flight. She moved towards the pegs by the door where her red coat was hanging and tweaked it down, but Sean sprang across the room and pulled her away. His fingers were rough, and she gave a little squeak of pain. 'You're not going anywhere,' Sean hissed in her ear. 'Didn't you hear what I said? I want to understand everything that you've done with Matt, so I can make sure it's the last time the bastard cheats on Mum.'

'Good luck with that.'

Sophie voiced defiance, but she recognised she was effectively a prisoner. They stood face to furious face, and she tried to find the boy from France in his sharp cheekbones and dishevelled hair, but this Sean was older and utterly formidable; honed by disappointment and disillusionment. She couldn't expect sympathy or understanding from him. He reached out to touch her face and she squirmed away.

'Do you know how many days, how many weeks I've wasted in wanting you? I thought my life was over before we went away at Christmas.'

Sean's voice cracked with hurt, and it was hard for Sophie to feel that he was suffering all over again as a result of the latest revelations. He laid his pain at her door, but that wasn't entirely fair. She didn't know whether to reach out and touch him – that might easily be misinterpreted – or turn a cold back on his accusations. If only Matt would reappear, she could attempt to make her escape from the scene, but Sean caught her wrist in a fierce grip. 'I can't fucking believe that you've been sleeping with my stepfather,' he exclaimed. 'What do your mates think of you? What about your parents? Are they cool with the fact that you're shagging another woman's husband? You really had me fooled in France.'

195

'Drop it, Sean. I've already said I don't owe you any explanation. But I promise I won't see Matt again after today, because it's clear that things can't go on as they were. Can I go now?'

'No. I'm not nearly finished with you.'

He released her wrist as Matt emerged from the bedroom. Matt's face showed the strain of harassment from all sides, and Sophie almost felt sorry for him. *Almost*, but she was prevented from taking his part by the fermenting suspicion that his eye had been wandering during recent weeks. The man was an opportunist and at last, like mist dissipating from a mirror, it was clear to Sophie that his only genuine emotions were invested in his children. At least that was something in his favour, but it was painful for her to understand that her initial scepticism about his character had been correct. She had allowed her instincts to be overcome by a combination of flattery and lust, and her sense of obligation after the Sean debacle had finished the job.

'I've told your mother that you'll spend the night here with me, Sean,' Matt said. 'I don't understand what you were fighting about, but it sounds as though you could do with a break from one another.'

Sophie seized on Matt's words, scenting the opportunity for freedom.

'Matt, I've told Sean that we won't be seeing one another again. There's nothing more I can do here. I'd like to go now,' she said, but both men took a step towards her.

'You can't go out in this storm, Sophie. It'll be impossible to find a cab and you'd drown in the attempt. Anyway, I'm not sure that I want you to go just yet. Don't you think we owe it to Sean to try and explain how things came about?' Matt asked, and Sophie's skin crawled with frustration.

'I don't think I owe Sean anything. We're adults, Matt and we make our own decisions.' Her voice faltered and grew raspy despite her efforts to remain in control; tears were imminent as she accepted the devastating conclusions of the afternoon. 'In some ways, I'm relieved the decision to split has been taken out of our hands. Poppy and Boo won't get hurt, and I daresay you will soon be back on your usual terms with Liz.'

Sean fizzed like an exploding bottle at the note of contempt in Sophie's voice.

'Don't take a pop at my mother. At least she's always straight with people. And Matt: you needn't think for one second that I'm going to forget this.'

His face was furrowed with disgust. 'What really bugs me is the fact that you might've told me to lay off Sophie last year so you could muscle in there yourself. You are a bloody plausible bastard when you want to be.'

Matt looked across at Sophie with his eyebrows raised and honesty forced her to come to his aid.

'No, Sean, it wasn't like that. To be fair to Matt, I think I made most of the running at first, because I was flattered by his attention. He was much more fanciable and exciting than the cringey undergraduates I was used to.'

'I wasn't a cringey undergraduate,' Sean said in a snide voice, and Matt jumped upon him.

'No – but she didn't want you, mate. You blew it with the stalking set-up and your threats to let on about what happened between the two of you in France. You don't know how nearly you got yourself into deep shit there and you still owe me for stepping in. Are you pissed off now because of your mother or because I've had what you wanted?'

Sophie felt Matt had taken leave of his senses, because that question risked inflaming the passions in the room to a searing heat. Sean stepped back and she saw that he was going to take a swing at his stepfather, but Matt was too quick for him. He caught the boy's arm in mid-blow, and before a scuffle could develop, she threw herself between them, pulling at their arms until they broke apart.

'Stop with this macho stuff, you pair of prats. *I'm* getting mad now. You're both acting as if I'm some sort of passive *thing*; as if I don't have any feelings about what's happened. I'm sorry, but I'm not the only one at fault. And we can't alter the past, but we can make sure that no-one else gets hurt.'

It was a desperate bid to calm the pair down. 'I don't think it's possible for us to part as friends, but we need to agree a way forward.' Her voice was plaintive as she tried to make them see sense. 'I won't see either of you again, and if you both keep schtum, Liz need never know about me and Matt. Sean, you still don't understand that we've

never been together in any real sense, and I owe you nothing. Matt…
you need to think with your head and not your dick in future.'

'What? Sod that. I seem to remember you told me you wanted to
sleep with me before I had any idea that was on the cards.'

'I don't recall that you needed much persuading.'

But Sophie realised that sparring wasn't going to help the situation.
'Look; there's only one way to get through this, and that's by everyone
keeping their cool,' she said, adding a prayer that both men would take
this sentiment on board.

The storm seemed to be abating. Matt went to the cupboard, looked
with a glum grimace at the empty whisky bottle and opened some wine
instead, and Sophie was glad to accept a glass. Sean's face was pallid
with exhaustion, and his slumped shoulders reminded her of the scene
in the café all those months ago.

She leaned back on the sofa with her eyes closed. It was difficult
to disentangle her feelings after the shocks of the afternoon, but she
felt as though she was stifling under a blanket of sorrow and shame
because she'd been so wilfully blind to Matt's shortcomings, although
there was a dawning of relief beneath the sadness. Suddenly, cringey
undergraduates and callow young men seemed attractive in their
simplicity and lack of baggage. Sighing, she booted the last of her
impractical daydreams out of the window where a faint glimmer of
sulky sunshine was beginning to light up the rainwashed street.

Matt sat beside her at a respectful distance; his eyes fixed on the
last minutes of the rugby, although Sophie didn't think he was taking
much in. When Sean left the room to visit the bathroom again, Matt
reached across to caress her hand.

'Sophie, I'm so sorry. This is a fucking nightmare. Maybe we'd
better take a break for a few weeks, but when Sean goes back to school
—'

'No, Matt.'

Sophie cut him off, prising his fingers away from her own. Why
couldn't he see that there was no way back? 'I've come to my senses.
We need to finish things now. It's not as though you've been panting
to see me recently, anyhow.'

She felt better after getting that dig in. 'And you have to
concentrate on convincing Sean that we're done if you're going to stay
with Liz.'

198

Matt's eyes were dull, and he swallowed hard, but he didn't try to dissuade her.

'What a fucking mess,' he commented. Sean returned from the bathroom, his gaze taut with suspicion, and Sophie decided it was time to make another attempt to leave. But neither Matt nor Sean would agree to her going, and she couldn't decide if this was because they needed her to keep the peace or because they wanted to inflict further punishment upon her. At length, Matt suggested that they should make an early supper somewhere, and both he and Sean insisted that Sophie came with them.

'I'd rather not,' she murmured, but in the end, it seemed easier to agree. The flat was beginning to seem like a prison from which she was desperate to escape, and she felt confident that her oppressors couldn't do anything to hurt her in a public place. Sean said that he wanted to go somewhere anonymous and 'studenty' and Matt looked to Sophie for guidance, but all she could remember was the riverside pub where she'd been with Charles so many months ago. She hadn't enjoyed her first visit there, and it didn't look as though she would enjoy the second one, either.

The pub wasn't very busy when they arrived. As it was the Easter vacation, most undergraduates were away, and the fierce weather didn't provide any inducement for people to leave the comfort of their homes. The city was waterlogged and dreary. The river Cam was in spate, and its murky waters overflowed the riverbanks in muddy and menacing swirls.

Sophie was seated in some discomfort opposite her tormentors, who seemed to have called a temporary truce and dredged up a renewal of family feeling after the explosive afternoon. It was possible that this was encouraged by the effect of alcohol, because Matt had opened another bottle of wine before they left the flat. She allowed herself to drift far away from the beery atmosphere and muted lighting of her surroundings, turning her mind to the problem of what to do with herself before her parents returned from their cruise. The thought of staying on in college wasn't appealing now, because the days would be shadowed with sadness after the messy end to her relationship with Matt. What she longed for more than anything was to lie on her bed and lose herself in a good cry, before unburdening herself to her best

199

mates. But Sarah and Hannah had returned home for the holidays, so their absolution would have to wait for a week or two.

Matt confronted her with yet another glass of wine, although she'd asked for a soft drink.

'Let's drown our sorrows,' he remarked, and she shrugged. Sean had been messaging on his phone since they entered the pub, and now he tasted his pint as if he was testing it for poison.

'Christ, this is heavy, Matt. Do you really like this stuff?'

'I do. You're going to have to develop a taste for real ale, Sean, otherwise people will think you're a wuss.'

'I guess I am a wuss.'

Sean sipped the frothy brew again with his nose wrinkled. 'I s'pose it's not so bad,' he conceded, and his stepfather laughed. Sophie was surprised at the resumption of their ostensibly amicable relations, wondering how they could pick up their normal banter so soon after the drama of the afternoon.

'It's strong, so don't let it fool you. I haven't been able to convince Sophie to take to it,' Matt added, flashing his devastating grin at her, but she didn't feel like smiling back at him. He no longer deserved her approbation. She had a dismal sense that he had been exposed as insubstantial and now she was seeing him as an outline instead of a whole person. A faint feeling of nostalgia for Charles and his family seat in Somerset floated into her mind as she toyed with her drink. That date had been the precursor to the memorable days of her first encounters with Matt. How simple everything seemed back then, and how faulty her vision had been…

The sense of anti-climax didn't last long. When the food arrived, Sean seemed to gear himself up for further drama. He began to grill Sophie about her weeks with Matt, and this time, he inferred that she was more at fault than his stepfather. Matt made several futile attempts to shut him up, but he was evidently relieved to spot someone he knew at the bar.

'Look, I must just have a word with that chap. Try to put a lid on things, Sean,' he said, getting up and walking away with a stride lightened by escape. Sophie pushed the remains of her lasagne aside and looked round for her bag.

'I don't know why you're putting all the blame for this on me, Sean, but if you hadn't given me such a fright last October, I wouldn't have grown so dependent on Matt, and things might have turned out differently. Sod it; you can think what you like. As I'm not going to see either of you again, it hardly matters.'

'It matters to me. I don't think I'll be able to trust anyone for the rest of my life, and I'll never, ever forgive you for that.'

The charge was unanswerable. Sophie and Sean glowered at one another across the table, and despite their enmity, she realised that she could still appreciate the impact of his brooding good looks. It wasn't the same as in France, though. Maybe Sean was justified in condemning her, but Sophie felt that his gaze hinted at something beyond the norm, something obsessive and menacing, and she was very relieved she was about to get away from him.

Matt strolled back to the table, hands in pockets. He still had the careless swagger of a man who was treated well by life, and Sophie thought it wouldn't take long for him to recover his usual poise. No doubt he could anticipate some difficult conversations ahead with his stepson and possibly his wife, but Sophie was sure he would bob back up through rough waters with the buoyancy of a cork. Matt was too shallow a craft to sink, and she didn't think he would waste time mourning her departure from his life. He was probably plotting new moves already, although he'd need to act with caution for some time.

Sophie stood aside while Matt paid the bill, wondering how to take her leave with appropriate dignity. She felt wrung out by events, and the cold evening air brought shivers as they walked outside. The rain had cleared, and a pale moon slipped shyly between clouds, as if it was unwilling to shed its light on the racing waters of the Cam. Sean wandered towards the riverbank and motioned to Sophie to follow him.

'I can't believe it's ever nice enough to go boating here,' he commented, and Sophie shook her head.

'Believe me, it's a very different place in the summer,' she replied, thinking with longing for easy days of punts and prosecco and laughter ringing across the water.

'What's that building over there?' Sean asked, pointing, and Sophie squinted past his shoulder. It was difficult to see where he meant in the dark. He stepped back in order to give her a better view, and she heard Matt's tread behind them at the same time.

'Be careful there. The path's helluva slippy,' Matt said, and Sean laughed.

'So it is.'

Sophie turned, and at the same moment, she felt a sharp shove in the small of her back. It caught her off-balance. She flailed desperately but her feet slipped from under her, and she only had the presence of mind to jettison her handbag before the dark waters of the river welcomed her into their icy embrace.

Chapter Twenty-three

The river was a black and freezing whirlpool. Sophie sank under for some seconds before she surfaced, spluttering, trying to strike out for the bank, but it was a futile effort. She was paralysed by the shocking cold of the water and her coat caught around her legs, hindering her movements and weighing her down. She thought she glimpsed two figures struggling on the bank where she had fallen, but the rapid current instantly carried her downstream and out of their reach. Then it became increasingly difficult to keep her head above the water: she took in one mouthful too many and began to choke. The realisation that she was drowning brought a sensation of hideous panic, followed by a strange, numb curiosity as to whether her life would flash before her as she succumbed to the river.

But Sophie was not destined to die in the chill depths of the Cam. A rowing crew were walking back to their college along the opposite bank after a gym session, and they saw the struggling figure in the water. Two strong young men plunged in to grab hold of her flailing body, and Sophie clung to her rescuers with a renewed will to survive. One of them supported her head, and somehow, the three struggled against the floodwaters to the bank, where eager hands were waiting to drag them up through the rushes and on to the rain-soaked grass. Then the cold seemed to eat its way into Sophie's bones, and a sheet of blackness slowly unrolled itself over her.

When she came to, she was lying on her back in the mud. Her sodden coat had been stripped away and someone had covered her with an anorak, but her body shook as if she was gripped by an ague. Far-away sirens were battling for supremacy, and she heard the rumble and mutter of deep, angry-sounding voices.

A curly-haired young man bent over her; his face screwed up in concern.

'Hello there; you're back with us! How are you feeling? You don't know how lucky you are. If we hadn't been around, you'd have been a goner.'

It was difficult for Sophie to focus, and although she tried to speak, slurry sounds seemed to be all that escaped from her mouth. Another earnest young face swam into her field of vision.

'She's in shock, Tony. The poor thing must be frozen stiff. What's taking the fucking ambulance so long?'

The next face had a halo of dripping auburn hair, but the grin it wore was warming.

'Do me a favour, darling – next time you fancy a swim, wait until the weather's better. I nearly froze my nuts off pulling you out tonight.'

'Give over, Mike. She must've had an accident.'

Sophie turned her head to spit out something vile and sedimenty.

'It wasn't an accident. I was pushed…' she gasped, but no-one seemed to be listening.

'Stand back, boys. That's the paramedics coming now.'

Then there was a babble of voices issuing commands, and Sophie surrendered herself to the capable hands of the ambulance crew. As she was lifted gently on to a trolley the police arrived, and she glimpsed Matt, ghostly-pale and panting for breath in the background. It occurred to her that he would have had to run through the streets and cross by the next bridge to join them on this bank of the river.

'I've got her bag here. Her name's Sophie Elliot, and she's a student.' Matt was gasping between sentences. 'I'm afraid we'd had a few drinks and she caught her foot on a tree root on the riverbank, and next thing we knew…'

His lies filled her with fury, and she tried to climb off the trolley to protest, but the paramedic took hold of her shoulders.

'Keep still, love. We need to get you out of these wet things as soon as we're in the warm.'

Sophie waved goodbye to her dignity in the back of the ambulance as they cut off her outer clothes and wrapped her in special blankets to restore her body heat.

'What about the lads?' one of the crew members asked, and his colleague laughed.

'They seemed fine. They say they weren't in the water very long, and their college is at hand, so they're off to get into hot baths. I've told them where to ring if they have any concerns. This young lady's a different matter.'

204

He directed a cheery smile at Sophie, who was still shivering and coughing painfully.

'I'm going to be sick' she spluttered, and he quickly handed her a bowl. She vomited and felt better, although she continued to cough like a fifty-a-day trooper. The paramedic looked less chippy as he observed her distress.

'Is it hard to breathe, love? It looks like you've taken some water into your lungs. They'll want to keep you in for a day or two if that's the case. I need to take some blood now. Lie still, and you'll just feel a sharp scratch…'

Sophie was dimly aware she was being blue-lighted to Addenbrooke's Hospital on the outskirts of the city. Despite the cocooning blankets, she could not control the shuddering of her limbs and her head felt as though it was bursting. When they reached the Emergency Department, she was just conscious enough to blurt out her thanks to the paramedics before she was whisked off to a cubicle for assessment. The numbing realisation of her narrow escape from death was beginning to overwhelm her. She submitted to all the procedures with tightly closed eyes, feeling as if all the familiar elements of her world had been shaken out of place. However, she was conscious enough to beg the staff not to inform her parents of the accident.

'They're away on a cruise, and I know they'd jump ship to get back here if they heard I was in hospital. I don't want them worried. It's not as though I'm going to die,' she stuttered, and a busy young medic nodded at her with understanding in his eyes.

'We should let someone know you're here. Was anyone else with you when you fell?'

'Yes. Friends; I heard one of them talking to the police as I was being taken to the ambulance. But I've been staying in college, so I'd be grateful if you contact someone there, otherwise they'll think I've gone awol.'

'Try not to worry now. You're hypothermic and we'll need to keep you warm and put you on a drip for a while to deal with that. Any questions?'

'Yes, lots, but not medical ones…'

Sophie lay on the bed, testing every part of her body to see if it still worked. Her coughing was irritating and persistent, but the worst thing for her was the sour smell of mud and water which clung to her limbs. Something felt scratchy against her scalp, and she fished a piece of twig out of her matted hair. 'I bet I look appalling,' she thought, and then she realised how crazy she was to worry about her appearance after the experience she'd just survived. At the same time, she welcomed the concern because it signified a return to something like normal life.

A nurse appeared with a drink for her and nothing had ever tasted so good. Sophie was hooked up to a drip, and then stress and exhaustion and shock overwhelmed her, and she drifted off into a thankfully dreamless sleep.

Some hours later, she opened her eyes to see a calm, bright sunrise outside the windows, then realised she was in a small private room instead of a busy ward. Did that mean the staff were worried about her? Before she could process this concerning train of thought, a nurse rustled in and began to move a bed-tray towards her patient.

'Somebody loves you,' she said in bright tones of hospital cheerfulness, and Sophie frowned, not understanding what she meant. 'This room,' the nurse explained, helping Sophie to sit up against the pillows. 'You have to pay for privacy, and someone's coughed up on your behalf. I expect it was your mum and dad. D'you think they'll be coming to see you today?'

'I doubt it. They're on holiday in the Caribbean, and anyway, I don't want them told about this until they get home.'

Sophie struggled to make herself decent. The hospital gown had bunched itself around her waist as she slept like an ill-fitting skirt, and a nauseating smell of dampness and decay wafted from her body. 'God, I need a wash. Can I have a shower or a bath or something? I feel fine now, honestly.'

But she was racked by a fit of coughing which was noted with concern.

'I'll check with the doctor. You do look a bit of a raggedy-ann, but you need to have some breakfast first. Do you want toast or some cereal?' the nurse asked.

'Toast, please. When can I go home?'

'That might not be for a day or two. They seem to think you've had river water in your lungs and that can lead to pneumonia if it isn't treated. Best to be safe, eh?'

Sophie digested this information, disappointed to think her incarceration might last longer than she'd anticipated.

'Well, when are the police coming to see me? I'm well enough to speak to them now,' she asked, anxious to let her version of events be made public.

'The police?'

The woman's voice soared with surprise. 'You haven't committed a crime, dearie. No-one's suggesting you tried to kill yourself.'

'No; but someone tried to kill me. I didn't fall into the Cam. Somebody pushed me in.'

There was a short pause, and then the nurse's eyes flicked sideways as though she didn't really want to pursue this train of thought.

'Let's concentrate on getting you better, shall we?'

Her saccharine tone frosted over the conversation. 'Your notes show you had a fair old concentration of alcohol in your bloodstream when you were admitted. Maybe you've got yourself in a muddle.'

Sophie seethed with frustration, but she was sensible enough to realise it was pointless to continue to press her case at this juncture. She ate her toast, relishing the ambrosial taste of butter and marmalade, and obtained help to manage the drip in the shower, although washing her hair in liquid hospital soap wasn't much fun. Luckily her bag had found its way to her, and it contained the small travelling toothbrush and paste she always took when visiting Matt, so she could begin to vanquish the lingering taste of the river for good.

Sophie was still obliged to wear a hospital gown, and she wondered who she could ask to visit her college room to fetch her normal night clothes. The effort of showering left her trembly with exhaustion and she reached languidly into her bag for her phone, but it wasn't there. Damn! Its absence made her feel as though she was missing a limb. Had she dropped it when she fell? She didn't think the phone had been in her coat pocket, but it might easily be at the bottom of the river now.

Her door opened again to admit a doctor on his rounds. He was older than the one she'd seen in the emergency department and years of working in the NHS seemed to have diminished his bedside manner to unsmiling robotics. He perused her records with a frowning face as he stood by the bedside, and Sophie found his tetchiness was catching.

'Well, young lady, it looks as though you've been very lucky. It isn't the right time of year for taking a dip.'

Was this meant to be a joke? Sophie scowled back at him.

'You could say I was very unlucky. I'm having difficulty in getting people to believe it, but someone pushed me into the Cam.'

'I understand you were with friends at the time. What had you done to make them want to dispose of you?' he asked, as if humouring a difficult case, and Sophie's irritation swelled inside her.

'Look, this isn't a joke! I was lucky not to die last night. Why won't anyone take me seriously?'

She was interrupted by another bout of coughing, and lay back on the pillows, feeling grim again. The doctor ignored her question and indicated that he wanted to listen to her chest.

'Your temperature is raised, and your lung function tests show some abnormalities,' he informed her when he had finished. 'I'm writing you up for antibiotics and we'll need to keep you for a little longer, but I don't anticipate that you will suffer any long-term damage as a result of your immersion. Don't worry about anything else – you'll have plenty of time to twit your friends when they come to see you.'

Sophie made no reply. She wasn't anticipating a visit from Matt or Sean, and she didn't trust them to be truthful with her anyway. Why couldn't she remember things more clearly? It was true that they'd all had too much to drink, but she could still feel the hard sensation of the hand upon her back. Which of them had dealt the decisive push? Both men had been standing behind her at the time, but only one of them had decided she'd be better out of the way. It was horrible to contemplate the callous impulse behind the action.

She lay back and the urge to doze again became too strong for her to resist. But by lunchtime she was feeling brighter and she managed to eat most of a plate of stew and potatoes, thinking that her lasagne in the pub seemed like a meal in another lifetime. She mourned the loss of her phone, feeling cut-off from the world and bored, and she wondered whether she might expect visitors in the afternoon. It was unlikely that Sean would appear, and she had no desire to see him in any case, but it was possible that Matt would have the decency to enquire after her progress. She had some difficult questions to ask him if he came. However, she almost went into shock for a second time when Liz Lenister strolled into the room on the stroke of two o'clock.

Liz was encumbered by a large M and S carrier amongst some smaller bags, and the taut smile on her face suggested that she was now poised to take control of the situation. Her hair and make-up were immaculate, and her trouser suit beautifully cut, and Sophie noted that the nurse directing her in wore a look of gratified respect at the presence of such an obviously up-market person.

'Sophie... I was so very sorry to hear about your *accident.*'

Liz glided to the bedside, her gaze sweeping over Sophie's recumbent form with its habitual analytic scrutiny. 'I hear you've been very lucky, although they tell me you'll have to stay in hospital for a day or two. I'm glad we were able to get you a room to yourself.'

Liz was paying for her room! Sophie was cynical enough to question whether this was down to kindness or a desire to keep her away from other patients, where her allegations about the incident might arouse excessive interest. She decided to go for the jugular.

'I don't know who told you it was an accident, Liz. My memory of what happened is very different.'

The nurse had disappeared. Liz stood at the bedside, her face a study in consideration, although she ignored the implications of Sophie's last statement.

'Matthew tells me that your parents are away, so I've taken the liberty of getting you a few things I thought you might need.'

She opened the carrier to reveal nighties, a dressing gown, slippers and a pack of knickers. 'I've put in a few toiletries as well. I expect you'll feel more human once you're back in proper clothing,' Liz continued, and now her voice was as creamy as butter.

Sophie couldn't restrain a grudging admiration for the way Liz was handling matters. During the past months she had built up the figure of Liz in her mind as a witchy, selfish manipulator, but she recognised that wasn't an accurate portrait. She also knew that she would be better prepared for the conversation ahead if she was more suitably dressed – there was something infantile, almost demeaning about the skimpy gown which would keep rucking up around her thighs.

'How kind of you, Liz. You must let me know how much you've spent so my father can reimburse you.'

Liz looked away as though Sophie had suggested something faintly obscene.

'That won't be necessary. I hope I've made the right choices', she said.

'I'm sure you have. D'you mind if I slip into the bathroom to change? I'm sick of fighting to keep myself decent in this flappy hospital stuff.'

Liz indicated that she was happy to wait. Sophie summoned a nurse to disconnect her drip for a minute while she closeted herself to put on a nightie and dressing gown. The garments fitted perfectly, and she diverted herself by wondering whether Matt had volunteered any information as to her size – if anyone was familiar with her body, he was. When she left the bathroom, she discovered that Liz had taken possession of the single armchair, leaving Sophie to wheel her drip into position and climb back on the bed.

Sophie wasn't frightened of Liz, but she was apprehensive about the fencing match which awaited her. She had forgotten what a dynamic package her old employer presented, and it seemed scarcely credible that she'd been sassy enough to get herself involved with this woman's husband. How much did Liz know? Had Matt confessed the full extent of his betrayal, or was Sean cited as the reason for the three being together in the pub by the river? Sophie clamped her lips together, acutely aware of the need for caution. She wouldn't give anything away; she'd wait for Liz to state her position first.

Liz was still very smiley, in a way which Sophie didn't recognise from France.

'That's better. Now you look like Sophie again,' Liz said, but there was a forced enthusiasm in her voice which Sophie easily detected. She returned the bonhomie with a blank and suspicious face and Liz immediately changed tack, adopting a tone of disdainful reproach instead.

'I suppose there's little point in beating about the bush. I had a panicked call from Matthew asking for my help last night, and now I know everything that you've done with my son and my husband, Sophie. It amazes me that I didn't realise last summer that you were such an unscrupulous little madam. And you look as though butter wouldn't melt – let me congratulate you on an outstandingly deceptive façade.'

Liz made this statement sound like a business analysis. She waited to gauge Sophie's reaction before continuing, but Sophie wasn't ready to speak. 'You've absolutely abused the trust I placed in you. My poor Sean... if he screws up his A levels after what you've put him through this year, I shall hold you responsible', she said. 'And as for Matt, I'm extremely displeased with him on two counts. Firstly, for keeping the real reason for Sean's breakdown before Christmas from me. And secondly, for being so easily swayed by a pretty face.

'But I'm aware that it takes two to tango. I'd like to understand your motives for pursuing Matthew, Sophie. Did you think he would be a useful source of revenue which you could tap? Did you want to get at me because we'd parted on cool terms in the summer? Or was it something else? I do hope you won't be tempted to hold anything back now. It's very important that we understand one another.'

Sophie lay back on her pillows, trying to formulate her response. She hadn't imagined that Liz would be quite so direct, so quickly, but in some ways, this made things easier. She fought down a cough, drew a deep breath and prepared to put her side of things with equal candour.

'Let's start with Sean, Liz. I can't deny that we became very friendly on holiday, but I had no intention of sleeping with him. What happened on the last night in France was much closer to sexual assault by him than seduction on my part.'

Sophie's voice wavered because she could hardly bear to recall the scene; the trigger for so many unhappy hours afterwards. 'I decided not to make a fuss at the time, but he grew into a real nightmare. I don't know how much Matt has told you, but by October, Sean was harassing and threatening me to the extent where I was totally freaked out.'

A film of frost seemed to settle upon Liz as Sophie continued her tale. 'It was quite by chance that Matt called on me in Cambridge, and when I told him what was going on, he offered to deal with Sean and get him to back off. Can you imagine how grateful I was to Matt after that?'

Sophie paused to let her version of events sink in. Liz was looking disdainful and far from impressed by this bald account of her son's obsession and her husband's desire to assist a maiden in distress. 'Matt took me out for dinner a couple of times. I owed him because of his help with Sean, and the bottom line was I fancied him like crazy, so I thought I'd take a leaf out of your book.'

'I have no idea what you mean by that.'

Liz would have frowned had the botox in her forehead allowed her to; as it was, she compressed her lips into a cold expression of discontent which Sophie recalled very vividly. She ploughed on: the most difficult confession was still to come.

'I know it was wrong of me to sleep with Matt, but I remembered you saying that you always go after what you want. I wanted Matt because he was handsome, and kind and his company was special to me. And I never expected that he would leave you, because he's always made it clear to me that wasn't an option. I suppose you could say that we had an understanding. Does that make things more acceptable?'

Her voice wound down as she observed the growing incredulity in Liz's eyes. Sophie felt that Liz was surprised by her immediate admission of guilt regarding Matt – she'd probably expected her to faff about with tears and excuses. The silence felt heavy with suppressed emotion before Liz finally answered the question.

'No, I don't think it does. You know, Sophie, I'm not entirely stupid. I'm older than my husband, and I'm aware he's indulged in the occasional fling. It never means much. Men are so easily distracted by sex.'

For a moment, Sophie had the oddest sensation that they were discussing someone else's lives. Liz continued her cool dissection of events. 'From his point of view, I can see it was handy to keep a girl at his beck and call when he was away from home. You fitted the bill very nicely, but I'm surprised that you were content with so little in return. Did it never occur to you to examine his motives?' she asked, and Sophie had to think hard about this before she replied. She didn't like the implications of what Liz was saying. Had Matt been using her all along?

'I think that it was good for Matt to have something in his life which didn't owe anything to you, or your influence. It must be emasculating to be faced with your dominance every day, Liz. He copes pretty well, but I'm not surprised if he feels the need to assert himself every so often,' she said boldly. But Liz began to smile as if she'd heard all this before and could hardly believe it was worth repeating.

'My dear Sophie… don't get carried away by the image of a man suffering as a result of a successful wife. Where do you think Matthew would be if I hadn't married him? He knows how much he owes to me, and to be fair to myself, I don't preach at him or look for constant acknowledgement. But I do expect a certain loyalty in return, and he's broached that by conducting this petty little affair with you. He'll need to be satisfied with working out of the Lenister Legrand building for the future. I'm not having him spending more time in Cambridge than is necessary now.'

Sophie didn't think Matt would be pleased with having his wings clipped, but it wasn't worth goading Liz further to say so.

'You must do whatever you feel is right for you, I suppose,' she said slowly. 'As far as I'm concerned, he's a free man. But there's one thing we haven't talked about; one thing we can't ignore. I didn't have an accident last night. Someone – and it can only have been Sean or Matt – pushed me into the river, and you can be sure that I intend to find out which of them tried to kill me; even if I have to make it a matter for the police.'

Chapter Twenty-four

Liz's face gave nothing away, but Sophie noticed that her hands were tightly clenched in her lap and her prominent diamond ring looked almost artificial, like a bauble from a cracker, under the unforgiving glare of the hospital lights. How would she react to the allegation that a member of her family had committed a serious criminal act? Sophie could feel blood pulse in her ears as she waited for a response, but when Liz did open her mouth, it was to speak with her usual calm control.

'Let's consider this impartially, Sophie. You had a lot to drink last night; more than enough to cloud your judgement and impair your capabilities. That's a matter of record, so there's no point in denying it. And don't forget that the people who were with you when you fell maintain that it was an accident – and I'm told that there are no other witnesses.'

This was a blow, but Sophie had been expecting it. 'If you persist with your accusation, it's most unlikely that a prosecution will make it to court, because the police won't find any hard evidence to back up your story,' Liz said smoothly. 'There's no CCTV covering that part of the car park and riverbank; I've checked. Any competent defence lawyer could make mincemeat of your narrative, and in doing so, your relationships with Matthew and Sean will be given a public airing.'

Liz paused, giving Sophie ample time to consider this scenario. 'Think of everyone being exposed to the sordid details of your little affairs,' she continued, her voice soft and lulling, almost as if she was reciting a bedtime story. 'And what possible motive could Sean or Matt have for wanting you out of the way? But people might be persuaded that you've cooked up a story to revenge yourself on Matt because he'd ended your liaison, or on Sean because you were tired of his devotion. How would you like to see yourself spread across the front pages of the red-tops? Not much fun for your parents, I imagine, and hardly likely to impress future employers. I can see your prospects being smashed past any hope of recovery.'

Sophie was mute in the face of this analysis; finding it difficult to breathe as she was forced to visualise this unappealing scene. She hadn't thought further than the immediate impact of the incident, but Liz's interpretation of events had an unpleasant ring of certainty.

Liz seemed gratified to see Sophie's face of stunned surprise. 'Of course, should you decide *not* to proceed down that path, the outcome might be more positive for you,' Liz said, watching Sophie carefully as she spoke. 'Matthew and Sean ought to have intervened to stop you cavorting on the riverbank in a state of inebriation – they were very careless, and it's possible we might think it appropriate to express regret for their inattention. For example…'

She transferred her gaze to the window as if trying to give an impression of spontaneity, although it was obvious to Sophie that the terms had been worked out in advance. 'We could pay off your student loan. And I could recommend you for suitable graduate jobs in the City if that was something you wanted to pursue, although I don't want you working at Lenister Legrand. I hope you'll think about this very carefully, Sophie, before making any public accusations. It might be too late for you to go back after that.'

Liz was examining her with minute attention, and Sophie felt that her feline smile concealed real cruelty. Taking absolute control of a situation was what Liz did best, and it was obvious she was enjoying every minute, even if she was fighting for her family. 'Well? Cat got your tongue?' Liz enquired with a throaty snigger, and Sophie roused herself to return fire, although she realised her ammunition was limited in comparison.

'How do you feel, Liz, knowing that either your husband or your son is a potential murderer?' she retorted. 'That would make me unbelievably uncomfortable. I'd always be watching my back, not knowing what might happen next. Sorry, Liz, but I don't envy your position.'

'That assumes I believe your version of events. And I'm not sure I do, Sophie. Your integrity is already damaged beyond repair.'

The squeaking wheels of a tea trolley came as a welcome diversion as Sophie tried to get her head around what Liz was saying. It was infuriating for her to understand that Liz was playing with a stronger hand, and Sophie began to be afraid that she would always hold the aces, but the fact that Liz was offering to make a deal indicated that she wasn't entirely confident of her position.

The healthcare assistant doling out the tea was curious and chatty, and for a few minutes, the drama had to give way to slapstick as jovial opinions were offered on the desirability of wild swimming in March. Sophie foresaw that she was destined to have this conversation on repeat, which was a tedious prospect. But at least the episode gave her a chance to reflect on her response to Liz. When the assistant left the room, the two women eyed one another like a pair of stalking cats.

'You're offering a kind of reverse blackmail,' Sophie said slowly, warming her hands around her cup. 'If I tell the truth, you'll go for me, but you seem to think it's possible to buy me off.'

Liz's smile was veneered with graciousness, but a tiny tic in one cheek revealed underlying tension. She sipped at her tea and suppressed a sigh.

'No-one has suggested buying you off,' she said, with freezing hauteur. 'I've simply outlined two different scenarios. What happens next is down to you, but I think you'll be sensible enough to make the right choice. It could affect your whole life.'

She put down her cup and got to her feet. 'I don't want to tire you. Is there anything else you need? I'm returning to London with the boys this evening, but I can arrange for something to be sent in if need be.'

'Well, I'd like my phone – it wasn't in my bag. I wondered whether someone might have picked it up without knowing who it belonged to. Perhaps Matt has it safe somewhere.'

Sophie suspected that Matt had trousered it, in order to prevent her from contacting friends and blabbing about her ordeal. Liz, however, looked blank.

'Could you have dropped it when you fell? I can ask at the pub, of course, but I think it's unlikely to be there. I'll order you a new one – what make would you like?'

Sophie was unwilling to accept any more favours, but eventually she was persuaded to give Liz the details of her preferred choice. She hated being confined to the room without being able to contact anyone. 'It should be here tomorrow afternoon,' Liz said, tapping at her screen. 'I doubt you'll be discharged by then, but you can always arrange to collect it later if you've been liberated.'

As she gathered her things to leave, a rare look of hesitation crossed her face. 'I hope you'll be sensible about this, Sophie. If I had my way, we'd write you out of our lives with indelible ink. Please use your head

216

when making your decision, and not your heart – that seems to have led you down some blind alleys in recent months.'

This remark was delivered with the thrust of an assegai, and it struck home. Sophie knew that she had a lot of thinking ahead of her, but there was one other matter she wanted to pursue.

'I'd like to see Matt again, just to clear up a few details,' she murmured, knowing that she stood a good chance of establishing the truth from his reactions, but Liz shook her head, looking almost amused at the request.

'I'm afraid that's not going to happen. And don't think that you can flutter your eyelashes and hope that he'll do your bidding at any time in the future – he's aware that your company is poison now. Please let me know as soon as possible what you intend to do. A text will suffice, when your new phone comes.'

She scrawled something on a page of a diary and handed it to Sophie. 'This is my personal mobile number; don't pass it on to anyone else,' she said, before giving her a long, hard, look. Sophie felt that Liz was memorising her features, albeit unwillingly, before she filed her away for good in some dusty, rarely opened cabinet. 'Remember, Sophie – head, not heart. I hope you feel better soon. Goodbye.'

The rest of the day passed miserably. Sophie received no other visitors, and the hospital staff, although friendly, went about their tasks with emotional detachment, which left her feeling abandoned. She realised that this approach was essential for the people who worked there, but she longed for her parents and friends; for anyone who held her in genuine regard. During the evening a note was delivered to her and she tore it open, hoping to discover words of concern and affection from Matt, but the missive was from Jennifer Bradbury.

'My dear Sophie,

We are all shocked to hear of your terrible accident. Thank goodness for the brave young men who saved you, and what a blessing that Liz and her husband are helping you in loco parentis. Liz tells me that she has visited you and has dealt with your immediate needs, and you must be relieved to have such a kind friend to rely on. The city wunderkind certainly has an unsuspected affectionate heart!

217

I'm so sorry I can't visit you myself, because I'm committed to a conference schedule in college, but I look forward to seeing you when you are back here with us – hopefully, that won't be long now. We're all rooting for you.

With love,

Jennifer.'

It was with difficulty that Sophie stopped herself from screwing up the paper and depositing it in the wastebin. Affectionate heart! She doubted that Liz even possessed a normal human organ. Her anger flickered into a persistent flame, and she determined that she would make her version of events public as soon as she was released.

However, as she lay awake in the cold small hours, coughing, uncomfortable and restless, her feelings wavered, and Liz's warnings began to establish themselves with greater effect. She remembered reading about the ordeals of rape victims in court, where barristers tore apart their private lives with heartless skill. The same thing could happen to her, and it was a horrible prospect. Would the police simply dismiss her story as the ravings of a spurned, drunken woman seeking revenge? Daylight began to filter through her curtains, and she was no nearer reaching a conclusion.

Whatever her mental state, she was feeling in better physical shape. Her chest seemed clearer, and she began to nurture a hope that her release from hospital wouldn't be delayed much longer. During the morning, she was motivated to apply a little make-up from the kit in her handbag and tease out a few remaining tangles in her hair. The mirror in the bathroom was becoming her friend again, and she didn't think it was vain to hope that her ordeal had not affected her looks – they seemed to be the only thing left to her now.

She was dozing after lunch when the door opened to admit a stranger; a burly young man in a hoodie and chinos, and with a distinctive auburn head. He didn't look like a medic, and he approached the bedside with an air of sheepish anticipation as she struggled to rouse herself to a sitting position.

'Hullo, Sophie. I hope you don't think it's out of order for me to come here.'

His voice was deep and pleasant, and she gazed at him, feeling as though she knew him from somewhere. Then the scene on the riverbank flashed through her mind in a jumble of surreal pictures like a slideshow on speed.

'Oh my God – you're one of the men who pulled me out of the river! It's all coming back to me. I hope…'

She broke off, remembering the complaint he'd uttered at the time and her cheeks flamed, but he seemed amused by her discomfiture.

'Don't worry, my bits are all working fine. It was a near thing, though. The Cam's bloody freezing at this time of year,' he said, with feeling.

'It's really nice of you to come to see me. I don't think I'll ever be able to thank you enough; you and all your friends. You were so brave!'

Sophie was more fragile than she realised, and tears spilled from her lashes as she tried to smile at her rescuer. The man frowned, looking distraught now.

'Oh shit, please don't cry. We weren't in any real danger and I'm glad we could help. Everything turned out fine, but I'm sorry to see they haven't let you out yet. Are you going to be okay?'

He moved nearer the bed, and she was heartened to see that his brown eyes were warm and seemed to hold genuine concern for her well-being. On an impulse, she stretched out her hand and he didn't hesitate to take it between his own. His palms were rough and calloused from rowing, but there was something strong and reassuring about his grasp.

'It's just so nice to see a friendly face. Yes, I'm mending fast, but my parents and girlfriends are all away and I've felt rather abandoned here,' she said. 'Sorry for the waterworks.'

He held her hand for a moment longer before releasing it and drawing a chair to the bedside.

'Please don't apologise. You must feel like crap. But I thought you were with friends when you fell in. Don't tell me they've not been to see you?' he asked, puzzled, and she glanced away, unable to repress a little shudder.

'It's a long story,' she muttered.

'Well, I'm in no hurry, if you'd like an audience.'

Sophie scrutinised the young man as he lowered himself into the chair beside her. He didn't have Sean's Italian sultriness or Matt's mature charm, but there was a bright honesty in his features which was cheering. He looked like a person who could be trusted and depended upon in a jam, and that was something she badly needed. But if she confided in him, she would have to reveal herself in all her imperfections, and it was galling to feel she risked losing his good opinion before their acquaintance had really begun. The boy furrowed his forehead as if asking a question of her, and she tried to smile.

'I'm afraid I don't come out of this tale very well,' she said slowly, trying to decide if she could risk the truth. He shrugged broad shoulders, but she thought he drew back a little.

'I suspect we've all got skeletons – or at least, a pile of bones – in our cupboards,' he replied. 'Look, I don't want to force you into anything uncomfortable, but it would probably do you good to talk. And I haven't introduced myself properly. I'm Michael Lefroy; Mike to my friends, and I'm reading Law. I know who you are, because your name was in the local paper this morning!'

'I'm very pleased to meet you, Mike. Sorry I didn't say hi on the riverbank, but I wasn't really up to formalities at the time.'

He smiled, but she sensed that he wouldn't attempt further familiarities until he understood more of her history. It was a hard call, but she tossed a mental coin and decided to give him a fair approximation of the truth. He would have no preconceptions, and maybe an outsider's opinion would help her come to the right conclusions, although she needed to be convinced that he was able to keep his counsel.

'Well, it all started almost a year ago… but Mike, before I go on, will you give me your word that you won't speak about this to anyone? That's really important.'

She held his eyes with her own, emphasising the request. 'I need a friend to help me decide what I ought to do, but I also need that person to be extremely discreet,' she said, overtaken by a little sigh.

He seemed to banish a flicker of unease almost as it arose and reached out to pat her hand.

'You can trust me, Sophie. Nothing you tell me will go further, unless you want it to.'

Sophie gathered her courage and began her account. She dealt quickly with her meeting with Liz and her journey to France and brought a smile to Mike's face when she described relations with the family, especially Abigail, but it was hard to admit what had happened during her last night with Sean. She noticed her companion's breathing grow quiet when she recounted Sean's determined assault, and his knuckles showed white as he clenched his fists.

'What a prick! The only thing he deserved was a kick in the goolies,' Mike exclaimed, and Sophie grimaced as she relived her struggles.

'I can't understand now why I didn't make an almighty fuss at the time. But it happened so quickly, I hardly knew what to think, and I'd been very fond of Sean before then. I had no idea he'd behave like that and then turn paranoid afterwards.'

It was easier for her to describe the events which followed, and Mike swore in amazement at Sean's obsessive actions, especially when he heard about the threat which had been issued in the café.

'Why didn't you go to your parents or friends and ask for their help?' he asked slowly, and Sophie tried to make him understand.

'I didn't want to get either of us into more trouble, daft though that sounds. I kept remembering the friendship we'd had before he got so possessive,' she said, dreading the thought of what was coming next. There was no way she could soften the impact of her decision to begin an affair with a married man. 'But quite by chance, his stepfather Matt called on me the same day, and I ended up confessing the whole miserable story. He was horrified to hear how Sean was harrassing me. After that, Matt took control and was able to turn Sean off like a tap, and I can't tell you how grateful I was as a result.'

Sophie remembered her first night with Matt with a torturing intensity of emotion. She knew by now that he didn't deserve her time nor her affection, but the memory of their relationship haunted her, although she hoped it would be replaced by something more natural and lasting one day. As she stuttered out the admission of her growing dependency on Matt, she was too ashamed to admit that she had been the driving force behind the affair in its early stages. She felt a smidgeon of guilt as she painted Matt as a practised seducer, but she didn't want Mike Lefroy to regard her as a completely lost cause.

'I know it was wrong, but I couldn't resist him. Matt's such a looker, and I think he felt I made a pleasant change from the dominance of his wife,' she continued, hoping this explanation would suffice. By this time, Mike was striding round the room looking almost punch-drunk after her confessions, and Sophie wondered whether he

221

would abandon her to flounder in the wake of his disapproval, but he merely balled one fist into an opposing palm and took his seat again. When it came, his reaction was a surprise.

'Poor Sophie! I'm dead sorry for you. No matter how things came about, I feel that these bastards were willing to sacrifice you and your feelings in order to get what they wanted,' he exclaimed, and she bit her lip, recognising the truth of the statement. Okay, her own behaviour wasn't faultless, but ultimately, both Matt and Sean had used her without compunction to satisfy their own desires. That was the way their family did things. And Liz had never cared two straws about her welfare. She was an expendable commodity; easily thrown aside, and it wasn't pleasant to face up to this knowledge. 'So how did you end up in the river?' Mike demanded. 'Please don't tell me those arses had something to do with it.'

It took a moment or two for Sophie to bring herself back to the present. She shut her eyes, unwilling to recall the stormy night and the treacherous waters of the Cam.

'I'd had the most horrendous day. I hadn't seen Matt for some time, but when I went to his flat after lunch it was clear to me that he wanted out of our relationship. He was fobbing me off with excuses about how difficult things were for him, but I suspect he's developed an interest elsewhere,' she said. 'And out of the blue, Sean turned up and found us there together. It didn't take him long to twig what had been going on with me and Matt, and all hell broke loose.

'I don't know if you remember, but there was a terrific storm during the afternoon, and we were trapped in the flat. We had a few drinks – maybe more than a few; I think we all needed something to help us deal with the drama. I told Sean that I wouldn't be seeing Matt again and he calmed down a bit, and when Matt suggested getting something to eat, they insisted I went with them.'

Sophie's voice wavered for a moment, and she pulled herself together. 'It was a horrible meal. When we were leaving the pub, Sean walked across to the river. He was asking me questions about something, some building, and I couldn't see where he meant, so I went and stood by him. I remember Matt coming up and saying the path was slippery, then I felt a hand shoving my back and I lost my balance and fell into the water. You know the rest.'

The sound of cheerful voices in the corridor seemed unnatural in the bleak silence which followed the conclusion of Sophie's story. Mike Lefroy shifted uneasily in his chair, and his face suddenly looked sober and much older. Sophie had the impression that none of it seemed real to him, although she hadn't deviated from the truth.

'Are you saying that it wasn't an accident, Sophie? There was nothing to suggest that in the paper,' he said, his eyes wide with apprehension.

'But no-one's heard my side of things. I've tried to speak to the staff here, but they keep fobbing me off and saying I'd had too much to drink to be sure of what happened. And now, there's an extra complication.'

She told him briefly of Liz's visit and the attempt to buy her silence, and he jumped to his feet and began to pace the room again.

'This must be impossible for you, Sophie. Are you going to call the woman's bluff? How the hell are you meant to decide between two such difficult options?' he asked, rubbing a hand through his bright hair until it almost stood on end.

Sophie leaned back against her pillows, exhausted by the emotional effort of recounting the horror story. She wasn't sure whether sharing her problems had helped or hindered; the next minutes would show whether she'd been right to expose her dilemma to a stranger.

'You're studying law. Do you think the police would take on a case of attempted murder where the only evidence is word against word?' she asked, and Mike stopped pacing and returned to the bedside.

'I'm no expert, but I think Liz Lenister is right. If you hadn't had so much to drink it might be a different matter, but it would be all too easy to demolish your story. There doesn't seem to be a motive, and how would the police know who to charge, unless they decided it was joint enterprise? Matt and Sean might argue that what you felt was an attempt to stop you from falling, after you'd slipped by accident. It's a mess, and it might be easiest for you to grit your teeth and just make sure you steer clear of anyone from that family in future. You didn't suffer any lasting physical damage, although I guess your emotions must be all over the place. And you shouldn't dismiss the opportunity to come out of uni debt-free,' he added, although she sensed that he wasn't totally convinced about what he was saying.

The room seemed to throb with nervous energy. Sophie twirled a lock of hair round her fingers and watched him as he paced uneasily from bed to window and back again. She almost wished that she hadn't involved him, but it was too late for her to go back.

Chapter Twenty-five

Mike Lefroy glanced at his watch, and Sophie realised that visiting hours were coming to an end. She needed to retrieve the situation and relieve this young man from further responsibility. His face was sober, and she thought that he probably regretted his altruistic intentions now.

'Look, Mike, I'm sorry to have vented,' she said. 'It's been kind of you to listen to me, but can you just forget everything? I needed to talk it through so I could get my head round things, but it wasn't fair to dump on you and force you to get involved.'

She tried to sound more chippy than she felt. 'I think I know what I want to do, so you've been a great help.'

Internally, she was beating herself up for exposing so much of her life to this unknown young man. Whatever had she been expecting? He had no magic wand to make things better for her. She waited for him to seize the opportunity to escape from her presence, and she was astonished when he resumed his seat by her bed instead.

'Which one of the two do you think shoved you in the river?' he asked, and she felt happier because he'd chosen to stay longer, and his question seemed to indicate that he believed her.

'I'd put my money on Sean.'

Sophie pulled a little face of dismay as she spoke, because she still found it unbelievable to accept that Sean might have wanted to harm her. 'He told me in the pub that he'd never forgive me for destroying his trust in people, and the hassle he caused after France demonstrates how flaky he can be when he's thwarted. And Sean was plastered at the time; maybe he thought he'd just give me a fright rather than finish me off. I can't see why Matt would want me out of the way, because I didn't represent any real threat to him by then.'

'They must be a pretty pair,' Mike said, wincing.

'Well, they're both great looking in different ways, so you're right about that. But it's been a hard lesson discovering that beauty is only skin deep. I think I'll be very leery around super-hot men in future.'

'At least that's good news for boys like me.'

225

Sophie was surprised to see the trace of a blush on Mike's cheeks, and he pulled at his sleeves with a self-conscious gesture which was endearing. Was it possible that he fancied her? That was something new to think about. They locked eyes with uncertain curiosity, exploring the possibility that a friendship might be emerging from the aftermath of Sophie's river plunge, but he soon wrenched his gaze away and scanned his watch again.

'I have to get back for training soon. Don't worry that I'll spill the beans to anyone, Sophie. You have my word for that. But I'd appreciate you letting me know your decision when you make it.'

He pulled out his mobile, finger poised over the screen. 'What's your number, so we can keep in touch?' he asked, and Sophie had to explain that she had no phone at present.

'I'll make a note of your number though, if you don't mind,' she said. 'But Mike, I think I've already come to a decision – and I'm not going to speak to the police. I won't even say that I'm blaming anyone else for what happened.'

As she spoke, she felt a weight dropping away from her. Mike drew in a sharp breath as if he was relieved by her words, and she noticed that his eyes shone with the same warmth as when he'd entered the room.

'I think that's the lesser of two evils. It sucks to think that whoever pushed you will get away with it, but I'd hate to see you getting skewered in court,' he said, and it was good to know he understood.

'And I shall tell Liz to keep her hand in her pocket.' Sophie spoke with slow emphasis. 'She needs to know that some people operate with integrity and aren't influenced by money or power – and this way, I feel that I retain control over things for the future. That's very important to me.'

It was unfortunate that a nurse chose that moment to barge in to check her patient's blood pressure and temperature, but Sophie was cheered by the blooming grin on Mike Lefroy's face. They had to endure some arch banter on the presumption they were boyfriend and girlfriend, and Mike gave a gallant impression of a respectful suitor which Sophie knew would be relayed back to the rest of the staff. She could anticipate an evening of being teased about her visitor, but it was an unthreatening, normal feeling which she almost looked forward to. When the checks had been done and they were left alone, Mike reached for her fingers once more, and this time, he kept them between his own muscular hands.

'I'm so relieved you've decided to go down that road,' he said quietly. 'I can't help feeling that if you accepted what amounts to a bribe, you'd always be indebted to Liz, and that would be an awful burden to carry. You know, Sophie, I don't go in for symbolic stuff, but maybe you ought to regard your dunking as a kind of baptism into the next phase of your life, so you can put that family and everything to do with them behind you and move on.'

Sophie grinned at the suggestion, although she could see he had a point. 'I'm sort of serious. I hope you don't want to see either of those jerks again; like they're right out of the picture,' Mike continued, squeezing her hand so tightly that it was hard for her not to yelp.

'They are. I wouldn't trust either of them within ten feet of me now. And I didn't mean to laugh at you, Mike. You don't know how much I've appreciated you being here.'

Her eyes grew shiny with tears again, although she tried to blink them away. 'Please tell the other guys that I'm so grateful for what they did. Maybe I can buy you all a drink when they let me out of here. And I'll definitely come to cheer you on when you're racing.'

'I'll keep you to that,' he said. He returned her hand after giving it a last, gentle pressure. 'I'm glad I came today, Sophie. You know, I wanted to see whether you were as pretty when you're dry as you are when you're soaking wet and covered in mud.'

His cheeks were crimson now, and Sophie smiled sweetly at his embarrassment.

'I won't ask if I am. I don't feel at the top of my game right now.'

'Trust me, you look pretty good.'

Mike lingered at the bedside, obviously reluctant to leave her. 'Listen, if you want some help to get back to college, call me and I'll come and pick you up,' he said, and his eyes brightened at the prospect. 'I've borrowed my mum's wheels for a week or two, so it's no problem for me. With luck, your new phone will be here by tomorrow, and you won't feel so isolated.'

'I do hope so. How did people manage in the days before mobile phones?'

Mike was bold enough to lean over the bed and brush her cheek with his own as he said goodbye. His face was wind-chapped, but his skin had a healthy tang of outdoors and exercise which displaced the clinical hospital atmosphere for a few welcome seconds.

'Can I come again if they don't let you out soon? I'd like to keep an eye on your progress,' he asked, and she nodded assent. The room seemed smaller and duller when he'd gone, but Sophie hugged the memory of his visit to her like a comforting pillow. There was something about Mike Lefroy which made her feel safe, and that was a feeling which had been missing from her life for too long.

She was settling down to sleep that evening when a nurse put her head round the door.

'Sophie? Do you feel up to taking a call? There's someone on the line who's very persistent about speaking to you and won't take no for an answer. They've already rung the desk three times, and it's going to be less of a bother for everyone if you deal with it.'

'Yes, of course. Maybe someone's told my parents about what happened and they're trying to call from the ship.'

She took the handset with trembling fingers, hoping to hear dear, familiar tones, but instead, a smoke-hardened voice almost caused her to drop the phone.

'Sophie? This is Anna; Anna de Vos. Remember me?'

'Anna... yes, how could I forget? I'm so surprised to hear from you.'

'Ah, but you're news now, my dear. One of my gremlins was alerted to your accident in the local rag and I understand that you were with Liz Lenister's hubby and son when you went for your little swim. Such a coincidence! My sensitive journalist's nose has been twitching very hard ever since. I'd love to visit you and hear your version of what happened.'

If anything could have hardened Sophie's resolution to drop her accusation towards Matt and Sean, this was it. No matter how she felt about Liz and co., she had no time for Anna and her gutter-press instincts, and she risked attracting all the unwelcome publicity Liz had described if she involved the journalist in further investigations.

'I'm afraid there's nothing to tell. It was an accident, and luckily, I haven't suffered any real problems. I expect to be going home tomorrow,' she lied with a fluent tongue. Anna snorted down the line.

'Is that so? My contact seems to think there's rather more to the story than what's been reported. And I gather you would have drowned if some rugger-buggers hadn't been on hand – very lucky, that was.'

'They were rowers,' Sophie muttered, but Anna didn't seem to hear. She cleared her throat. 'Sorry, Anna, but there isn't a story here. My memory of what happened is pretty hazy, but you could always contact Matthew Braybrooke and his stepson and see what they have to say.'

She could feel Anna breathing fire.

'For Chrissake, Sophie! People don't just fall in rivers; there must be something else going on. Why are you so reluctant to speak to me about it?'

'I'm afraid I *was* rather drunk.'

It cost Sophie an effort to use this as an excuse: she screwed up her face as she spoke almost feeling as if she was in pain. But the thought of Anna spearheading a tabloid-type charge against Matt and Sean seemed indecent to her, even though one of them was a Judas. Anna huffed her displeasure.

'I don't understand. Whatever Liz Lenister's paying you, I can match it; maybe do a lot better. Come on, Sophie, I can help you here. People in your position don't often have a chance to make money like this – just think, you could wipe your student loan.'

Sophie groaned to herself. Here was another financial opportunity, but she was even less inclined to take advantage of it than the first one, despite the freedom it offered.

'I'm very sorry, Anna, but all this is speculation and I can't help you. Goodbye.'

She ended the call before temptation could swirl out of the handset and mount an attack on her remaining principles. When the nurse returned, Sophie asked her not to accept any more calls on her behalf unless they were from her parents.

'It's very upsetting to be hounded by the press,' she explained, and there was much headshaking and tutting about London journalists and their lack of ethical standards.

The events of the afternoon and evening had left Sophie so tired that she slept well that night. Next morning, her intravenous antibiotics were discontinued, and she anticipated her release from the ward; pacing the little room with impatient feet. And her new mobile phone arrived, enabling her to spend a happy hour playing with its functions

229

and entering a few numbers she knew by heart, as well as those belonging to Liz and Mike Lefroy. She messaged Hannah and Sarah and they called back quickly, horrified to hear of her escape from a watery grave, but she was careful not to speak of the event as anything but a regrettable accident. She had made her decision and had to ensure that the truth remained hidden now.

She also contacted Mike to ask whether he was able to collect her that afternoon, and he agreed at once, sounding as though he'd been hoping she would ask.

'I'm afraid I'll still be in a nightie and dressing gown – I haven't any other clothes here,' she warned him, and a gurgle of deep, masculine laughter emerged from the phone.

'Let me see what I can do.'

And when he arrived, he produced a tracksuit top and bottoms which, surprisingly, didn't dwarf her entirely. 'These belong to David, our cox,' Mike explained. 'He's pint-sized, and I thought they'd do until you get back to your own things. I hope you don't think it's cheeky of me…'

Sophie laughed as she went to the bathroom to put the garments on. They weren't the kind of thing she was accustomed to wearing, but even teamed with slippers, they made her feel more confident about walking back into the outside world. She still had the large carrier that Liz had brought, so she packed her other clothes in that and was soon ready to go.

'What happened to the things you were wearing on the night?' asked Mike, and she shrugged.

'I suppose the coat may still be on the riverbank. Your mates got it off me when I was lying there,' she replied, pushing the painful memory away. 'My top and trousers had to be cut away by the ambulance crew, but I did get to keep my bra and knickers, and I've tried to wash the river out of them in the basin here. I'm tempted to chuck them away, because they'll always be a horrible reminder of what happened.'

As she said her thanks to the staff, she had to endure a few more minutes of banter about her lack of aquatic skills, and Mike assured everyone that he would do his best to prevent a repetition of her dip in the Cam. When it was realised that he was one of those responsible for her rescue, the corridor resounded with praise. The appearance of a consultant dispersed the jocularity, but it was a pleasant way for her to leave.

Mike's mum's 'wheels' turned out to be a smart little town car, and Sophie enjoyed the drive back to college. The bad weather had been replaced with the balmy kind of day which occasionally surfaces in early spring, and the city looked as though it was wide awake after its winter sleep as green shoots and daffodils thrust their way through the earth. Sophie looked at it all with fresh eyes, grateful for the fact that she was still around to see it. Mike pressed her to join him for dinner, but she asked for a raincheck.

'Could we do it another day? I want to spend about three hours in the bath, and after that, I might begin to feel I'm myself again,' she explained, and he was too much of a gentleman to argue. As it was, she was accorded a celebrity welcome by the porters and saw that some weeks of embarrassment lay ahead. Mike carried her bags up to her room for her and hovered awkwardly in the doorway.

'You will let me know if I can do anything?' he asked, his cheerful face showing concern, and she nodded.

'I'm sure I'll be okay by tomorrow. You're a darling, Mike, and I promise that we'll have dinner as soon as I feel up to it.'

Sophie kissed his cheek, and he took the hint. She watched him stride down the corridor feeling happy that she'd found a good friend, but when she was luxuriating in warm water, that feeling vanished and she was overcome with sadness, crying with huge, gut-wrenching, animal sobs. She was crying because she was only just beginning to understand how close she'd been to death, and because her relationship with Matt had been swept away in the flood of events. Sophie couldn't turn her feelings off because he no longer wanted her. She'd never experienced real heartbreak before, and the pain was suffocating. If only she'd known how dangerous a game she'd been playing! The emotional and physical investment had been so easy to make, but it was difficult to see that investment drain away without return.

Someone rattled the bathroom door handle, indicating that she'd hogged the facilities for too long, and she dragged herself out of the bath and back to her room. Her shoulders heaved every so often as she dried her hair, but for the moment, she'd cried enough. The college was full of temporary residents attending courses, and she was pleased

231

that there were no familiar faces in the dining hall. She didn't want to speak about her situation to anyone except those who were close to her.

She still had to send Liz a text to confirm her decision not to pursue Matt or Sean, and she decided to do that as soon as dinner was over, because it would be very easy to change her mind if she allowed sorrow to get the better of her. When she returned to her room, she picked up her new phone and messaged Liz, saying she was prepared to drop her allegation.

'But I don't want your money. This way, I can go forward on my terms,' she wrote, wondering whether Liz would understand, although she didn't much care either way. Sophie also told her briefly of her call from Anna de Vos, and when she pressed 'send' she thought that would be the last contact she had with the financier. She was surprised when a reply winged back promptly.

'I note what you say. Thank you for your decision.'

Liz didn't go in for histrionics. *'Matthew arranged for your coat to be cleaned, but I'm afraid it has shrunk beyond repair. I hope that you will accept a John Lewis gift voucher to buy a replacement. It's already on its way to you.'*

Sophie regretted the loss of her lovely red coat, but at the same time, she was pleased to hear of its demise. She was no longer that person; the elegant incarnation of Princess Isabelle, but she had yet to discover who she would be in future.

Chapter Twenty-six

Sophie's 'accident' was a nine day's wonder which she was heartily sick of by the time her parents swooped to carry her back to Guildford before the summer term began. Mr and Mrs Elliot cosseted their daughter after her unpleasant experience and attributed the odd fits of weeping which overcame her to delayed shock. This was fortunate, because Sophie could never admit that she was mourning the end of her relationship with Matt. Mike Lefroy rang her often enough for her mother to hint coyly at a blossoming romance, but Sophie had to tell her that she was premature in her speculation.

When Sophie finally returned to college, the support of her girlfriends and Mike's attentive presence helped her to settle back in without further trauma. Their final exams were rattling down the track, and she was glad of the distraction they provided. She fell into a routine of hard work interspersed with seeing Mike, although she was in no rush to climb into bed with him. The heedless girl who'd given an easy nod to adultery had disappeared in the aftermath of her plunge; replaced by someone who tried to look at all sides of a situation before making a physical or emotional commitment.

A sense of anti-climax descended when the exams were over. She had the excitement of attending a college ball as Mike's partner and their relationship began to gather momentum, and then she turned her thoughts to the summer vac and her future. Jennifer Bradbury invited her for sherry, and Sophie trod the stone steps to Jennifer's study brushing aside a prickle of unease and crossing her fingers that her tutor had no further job offers lined up for her.

Jennifer was bursting with chat about Liz and her family, and Sophie assumed an expression of polite interest as her tutor extolled Liz's generosity towards the college.

'What a shame that they don't need your assistance this summer,' Jennifer continued, her face losing a little of its enthusiasm. 'But I believe Liz's usual au pair is accompanying them to Florida.'

'Ellie? I'm glad. I believe all the family rate her, and she evidently gets on well with them.' *And Matt and Sean aren't tempted to hustle her into bed*, Sophie thought, with a stab at cynicism.

'And what are your plans now, Sophie?'

'I'm applying to some international consultancy firms who offer trainee positions to modern languages graduates. The work sounds interesting, so I thought I'd have a shot at it.'

It was Mike who had persuaded her to consider this path. He was following his father into the law by undertaking a pupillage at a set of London chambers, and he encouraged Sophie to pursue city-based jobs so they could continue to see one another. She hadn't needed much persuading, because she was coming to rely more and more on his steady affection and commonsense which made a welcome contrast to her experiences with Sean and his stepfather.

'Well, I wish you every success. Please don't hesitate to ask me for a reference when you need one. I've no doubt that Liz would give you a glowing one as well.'

'Britain swelters' screamed the tabloids as the last week of term arrived and summer put in an unexpectedly strong appearance. Sophie was meeting Mike for a drink late one afternoon, and in the process of packing up her wardrobe, she came across the floral sundress she'd bought in France. She decided to wear it, hoping to dispel pitiful memories by creating new ones.

They sat under an umbrella in a busy pub garden and steamed gently in the heat.

'You look stunning in that frock,' Mike told her, his eyes crinkled in admiration, and she smiled at him, feeling as though his approval was helping to lay a certain ghost to rest. They chatted idly, relaxing in the idyllic weather, and then suddenly, Sophie's attention was caught by a familiar echo of laughter from a table at the other side of the garden.

Matt was seated there in company with two men and a woman. It looked as though they were business colleagues, but the woman, a blonde with obvious hair extensions and a tightly swathed dress, touched Matt's arm and demanded his attention in a manner which spelled possession to Sophie's analytic gaze.

Sophie couldn't turn her head away. She felt as though an invisible electric wire stretched between herself and her former lover, and every smile he bestowed upon his companion seemed to send a powerful shock through her body as she watched. Discomfited, she tried to concentrate on what Mike was saying, but her eyes would keep straying to the table where Matt held court.

'You okay, Sophie? You've gone very pale,' Mike observed, and she tried to shrug herself back to reality.

'I'm fine. The heat's knocked me out rather.'

She downed her wine in several swigs, hoping to cover up her distraction, and Mike regarded her empty glass with surprise.

'You were thirsty! Shall I get you another?'

'It's my round.'

She stumbled to her feet, but Mike pulled her down again.

'Have you seen the crowd at the bar? One advantage of bulking up with rowing is that pushing to the front of a queue is child's play. You stay there and continue to adorn the place.'

She forced a smile as he departed, before turning her attention back to Matt and his party. They were standing now; one of the men looked at his watch and she heard the words 'meeting' and 'conference call' amongst the chat. As Matt turned to leave, his gaze fell on Sophie across the garden, and he grew very still. Surprise, confusion and guilt chased themselves across his face as Sophie returned his stare with an expression of stone. Then he appeared to collect himself. He turned and spoke briefly to the blonde and began to walk towards Sophie's table. When he reached her, he was wearing a look of hang-dog apology.

'Sophie... how are you? You're looking very well.'

She hesitated before replying. Matt fidgeted in an embarrassed manner with a cuff button, and she thought of all the questions she wanted to ask him before realising that it was too late to go down that path.

'I'm okay,' she said ungraciously. She refused to help him out, and he ducked his head as if searching for a way to avoid her contempt.

'Er... I suppose you've finished your exams. How did they go?'

'I won't know until I get the results.'

The blonde was peering over at them, her face registering the beginnings of concern. Matt appeared to be trapped in the awkwardness of the meeting. He adjusted his watch strap in a gesture Sophie knew well, and she stared at the fine golden hairs on his wrist. Her mouth filled with saliva. She wanted to sink her teeth into him; to leave a mark on his flesh and hear him groan. It was agonising to think of him with the blonde, wrapped round her in bed and enjoying the same intimate moments with her that they had shared. He gave himself a little shake.

'You're wearing that dress...' he murmured, and now his eyes were misty and seemed to speak of regret. Sophie pulled herself together and ignored the invitation to revive past intimacy.

'I see that Liz still lets you out to visit Cambridge sometimes,' she said, with acerbity, and he shrugged. 'I was amazed that you didn't have the decency to visit me in hospital,' she continued, and now his blue eyes grew defensive.

'You know how it was. Liz told me you hadn't come to any real harm. It seemed best to draw a line under things, considering all the circumstances,' he muttered.

'So, was it you or Sean who tried to murder me?' she asked in sweetly conversational tones, and he flinched.

'Please don't think that. I swear it was an accident. You know I'd never want to hurt you, Sophie.'

'It must have been Sean, then. Thanks for confirming my suspicions.'

Sophie hardly knew whether to feel relieved or saddened by the implication of his words. 'Don't worry; it's too late now to rake things up, but you can tell Sean that I hope I never set eyes on him again. And if I were you, I'd book him in for more therapy before he ends up a total psychopath. Don't you understand that he's damaged goods?'

Sophie uttered the last sentence in tones of cold disdain, and it was satisfying to view the shock on Matt's face – he stepped back as though she'd punched him on the jaw. She saw Mike emerge from the bar with his pint and her wine. 'I don't think my boyfriend wants to meet you. You'd better get back to your friend. Does Liz know about this one?' she asked.

'Sophie...' Matt's voice was a mere whisper of regret. 'I really did care for you,' he sighed, and then he turned and threaded his way through the tables to where the predatory blonde stood scowling. Sophie was relieved to see that Mike didn't appear to recognise the man he'd last seen on the riverbank on a stormy March evening.

Seeing Matt so unexpectedly had given Sophie a nasty jolt. She tried to file their exchange of words away, but Matt's last sentiment left her with a cloying sense of waste and sadness. Mike dropped a kiss on her head as he placed their drinks on the table, and she wondered whether to tell him what had happened but decided against it. She was finally learning caution, and some things were best left in the past.

Mike began to enthuse about their future in London, and she had to remind him that she had yet to secure a job offer, although he brushed this aside as an unimportant detail.

'Are you sure you won't consider shacking up with me, Sophie? My aunt has a nice little flat just off Haverstock Hill she'd let us have at a special rent,' he said, and she was tempted, but only for a moment. She stretched out a hand to caress his fingers.

'Darling Mike, that's amazing of you, but it's too soon. We've only been an item for a few weeks. You know that I adore you, and I'm totally in your debt for all sorts of things, but I don't want to rush our relationship. I've burned my fingers doing that in the past. And I promised Hannah ages ago that we'd find somewhere together. I can't go back on that just yet.'

'Oh, Sophie… and I'm supposed to be the sensible one.'

Mike grimaced at the thought of what lay ahead. 'You're determined to make me spend more time with Ol and his smelly feet then,' he continued, referring to his best mate, and she laughed.

'When they get too stinky, you can come to me for the night.'

'That had better be a promise.'

Then it was time to pack up four years of her life and move back to the parental nest, although this was a temporary roosting. Sophie found her attention pulled in all sorts of different ways. She obtained some casual bar work which gave her the flexibility to attend career interviews, and armed with a good degree and references, she was successful in landing a job with a consultancy firm.

She managed to take a short holiday with her parents before flying out to spend a week with Mike and his parents at their villa in Portugal but juggling all her commitments was taxing. She had to delegate finding a flat to Hannah, although she spent her leisure time at the computer, viewing prospective tenancies online while Hannah did the leg work. Both girls' parents were helping with the rent until their daughters began to climb the career tree.

At last, Hannah called her to say she'd found a suitable berth in Battersea.

'I've just been to see it with the agent, and it's fabulous. Two good bedrooms, and there's even a little garden as it's ground floor.' Enthusiasm spilled from her voice. 'And while I was there, the agent was clinching the let of the upstairs flat – that's on two floors and it's bigger than we need. Some students are taking it. They must have rich mummies and daddies, because it ain't cheap.'

'Oh God. I hope they won't have endless noisy parties, then.'

'Come on, Auntie Sophie, please don't turn into a grown-up just yet.'

Hannah's chortle almost deafened her. 'I met them when I was looking at our flat. They seem an okay bunch of kids, although they're still in the pretend stage.'

'The what?'

'Pretending to be students. You know what first-years are like – wet behind the ears, statement T shirts, hair a bit too consciously gelled-up, and the stubble needs a lot of work. But one of them is scrumptious. He and I got chatting outside and we had a great craic.

'He was very interested to hear where I'd been at college. I told him about you, too. I think that knowing we'd be neighbours helped to make up his mind to take the flat and then he persuaded his mates. You'll like him, but bags I get first go.'

The two girls took up their tenancy in mid-September. They had the whole house to themselves for a week before the students moved in, but one day, Sophie returned from the office to hear thumps and raucous laughter from above as the boys unpacked their belongings.

She sighed, hoping that their enthusiasm would simmer down after a while, and then Hannah burst into the room, having called to see how their neighbours were settling in.

'Come up and meet everyone, Soph.'

'I'm just back from work. Can't I change first?'

'It'll only take a minute. I've suggested we might share a takeaway later.'

Sophie couldn't understand Hannah's determination to return to an undergraduate existence, but she dutifully followed her friend up the stairs. She was introduced to Al and Max, who were polite, self-conscious and slightly spotty, and looked round for the third boy; the one whose looks Hannah had enthused about.

Then she saw him, silhouetted against the window. He was slim and dark, with chiselled cheekbones and a lazy mouth, and his blue eyes seemed to hold her suspended in time. Sophie wondered briefly why Hannah hadn't noticed the chilling calculation in his smile.

She felt as though she was living the painting *'The scream'*.

'Hello, Sophie. This is a nice surprise,' he said.

L - #0154 - 271119 - C0 - 210/148/13 - PB - DID2690885